T0006340

"This page-turner is tightly written with a moody sense of place in the small coastal community, but it is the numerous twists that will keep readers thoroughly absorbed. A satisfyingly creepy psychological thriller."

—*Kirkus Reviews*

# PRAISE FOR *IN THE DARK*

"White (*The Dark Bones*) employs kaleidoscopic perspectives in this tense modern adaptation of Agatha Christie's *And Then There Were None*. White's structural sleight of hand as she shifts between narrators and timelines keeps the suspense high . . . Christie fans will find this taut, clever thriller to be a worthy homage to the original."

—*Publishers Weekly*

"White excels at the chilling romantic thriller."

—The Amazon Book Review

"*In the Dark* is a brilliantly constructed Swiss watch of a thriller, containing both a chilling locked-room mystery reminiscent of Agatha Christie and *The Girl with the Dragon Tattoo* and a detective story that would make Harry Bosch proud. Do yourself a favor and find some uninterrupted reading time, because you won't want to put this book down."

—Jason Pinter, bestselling author of the Henry Parker series

# PRAISE FOR LORETH ANNE WHITE

"A masterfully written, gritty, suspenseful thriller with a tough, resourceful protagonist that hooked me and kept me guessing until the very end. Think C. J. Box and Craig Johnson. Loreth Anne White's *The Dark Bones* is that good."

—Robert Dugoni, *New York Times* bestselling author of *The Eighth Sister*

"Secrets, lies, and betrayal converge in this heart-pounding thriller that features a love story as fascinating as the mystery itself."

—Iris Johansen, *New York Times* bestselling author of *Smokescreen*

"A riveting, atmospheric suspense novel about the cost of betrayal and the power of redemption, *The Dark Bones* grips the reader from the first page to the pulse-pounding conclusion."

—Kylie Brant, Amazon Charts bestselling author of *Pretty Girls Dancing*

"Loreth Anne White has set the gold standard for the genre."

—Debra Webb, *USA Today* bestselling author

"Loreth Anne White has a talent for setting and mood. *The Dark Bones* hooked me from the start. A chilling and emotional read."

—T.R. Ragan, author of *Her Last Day*

"A must-read, *A Dark Lure* is gritty, dark romantic suspense at its best. A damaged yet resilient heroine, a deeply conflicted cop, and a truly terrifying villain collide in a stunning conclusion that will leave you breathless."

—Melinda Leigh, *Wall Street Journal* and Amazon Charts bestselling author

# THE
# MAID'S
# DIARY

## OTHER MONTLAKE TITLES BY LORETH ANNE WHITE

*The Patient's Secret*
*Beneath Devil's Bridge*
*In the Deep*
*In the Dark*
*The Dark Bones*
*In the Barren Ground*
*In the Waning Light*
*A Dark Lure*
*The Slow Burn of Silence*

## Angie Pallorino Novels

*The Drowned Girls*
*The Lullaby Girl*
*The Girl in the Moss*

# LORETH ANNE
# WHITE

# THE
# MAID'S
# DIARY

*A NOVEL*

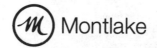 Montlake

Text copyright © 2023 by Cheakamus House Publishing
All rights reserved.

Published by Montlake, Seattle

www.apub.com

Amazon, the Amazon logo, and Montlake are trademarks of Amazon.com, Inc., or its affiliates.

ISBN-13: 9781542034456 (paperback)
ISBN-13: 9781542034463 (digital)

Cover design by Caroline Teagle Johnson
Cover images: © Lyuba Burakova, © Koen Van Damme / Stocksy United;
© timandtim, © Elva Etienne, © Martin Barraud,
© IPGGutenbergUKLtd / Getty Images

Printed in the United States of America

*For Marlin and Syd:*
*Thank you for putting up with me and*
*Hudson during a tumultuous wildfire summer.*
*Love you both.*

# HOW IT ENDS

Slowly, she slides between sleep and consciousness. A shard of cognition slices through her—no, not sleep. Not in her bed. Not safe. Panic stirs. Where is she? She tries to swallow, but her mouth is dry. There's an unfamiliar taste at the back of her throat. A sharper jolt of awareness cracks through her. Blood—it's the taste of blood. Her breathing quickens. She tries to move her head but can't. A rough, wet fabric covers her face. She's trapped, arms strapped tightly to her sides. She becomes aware of pain. Overwhelming pain. In her shoulders. Ribs. Belly. Between her thighs. The pain pounds inside her skull. Adrenaline surges into her veins and her eyes flare open. But she can't see. Panic licks through her brain. She opens her mouth to scream, but it comes out muffled.

What is this? Where am I?

Focus, focus. Panic kills. You have to think. Try to remember.

But her brain is foggy. She strains for a thread of clarity, struggles to focus on sensations. Cold—her feet are very cold. She wiggles her toes. She feels air. Bare feet? No, just the one. She's got a shoe on the other. She's injured. Badly, she thinks. A thick memory seeps into her sluggish brain—fighting people off, being held down. Violently attacked—she has a sense of that, of being overwhelmed, rendered powerless. Then wounded. Now she's wrapped in something and she's in motion. Bumping. She can feel vibrations. Is that the noise of an engine? A car? Yes, she's in a vehicle of some sort. She becomes aware of voices. In the front seat. She's lying on the back seat. The voices . . . they sound urgent—arguing. Underlying the voices is soft music. A car radio. She's definitely in a car . . . they're taking her somewhere.

She hears words. "Dump . . . her fault . . . asked for it. Can't blame—"

She slides into the blackness again. This time it's complete.

# THE SILENT WITNESSES

*October 31, 2019. Thursday.*

It's 11:57 p.m. Halloween night. Dark. A dense fog creeps along the water, and a steady drizzle falls as a silver Mercedes-Maybach with two occupants turns onto a muddy track that leads into an abandoned grain-storage site. Rain glints as the headlights pan over the bases of the old silos. The sedan crosses a railway track and bounces along a potholed road that parallels the edge of the ocean inlet. The Mercedes comes to a stop in deep shadows beneath a bridge that arcs over the inlet, linking the North Shore to the city of Vancouver. The headlights go out. Everything is now black except the glow of the fog-shrouded city across the water.

The occupants feel safe here, hidden, cocooned in the buttery leather and warmth of the luxury sedan. Overhead the bridge traffic is a soft roar, punctuated by rhythmic clunks as vehicles traverse the metal joints.

The man and woman don't waste time marveling at how the incoming tide swirls like ink past the old silo dockyard. Their lust has reached fever pitch. It started this morning—this little game of theirs—over a breakfast meeting, her stockinged calf pressing against his pant leg beneath a table as they calmly discussed legal strategy with city officials. Desire blossomed through subsequent high-level discussions around a lawsuit, followed by lunch. It peaked with a stolen kiss behind the door in the men's washroom. Both knew it would end like this—frenzied sex in her car parked in some louche location. It's the anticipation the couple is addicted to. The danger. The risk. They are both married to other people. He's a member of the provincial legislative assembly. She is a top city lawyer. They both have children.

They always pick a place like this. Something industrial. Dank. Deserted. Tagged with graffiti, littered with urban detritus. Sordid yet delicious in a disreputable way. It's their quirk—fornicating against backdrops of squalor. Juxtaposing their glamour and brains and wealth and privilege against these gritty urban canvases—it piques their desire. Makes them feel powerful. It layers their affair with a noir-film graininess that feeds their carnal pleasure.

She kicks off her Saint Laurent pumps while yanking at his red tie, fumbling with his zipper. He pops open the pearly buttons on her silk blouse, bunching up her skirt, ripping her expensive pantyhose in his hunger. She scrambles over the console, straddles him. As she sinks down onto him, he closes his eyes and moans with pleasure. But she suddenly goes still. She sees two sets of headlights appearing in the mist. The beams punch twin tunnels into the fog—one vehicle behind the other. The cars turn in front of the abandoned silos and head toward the rail tracks.

"Someone's coming," she whispers.

He doesn't seem to register. Eyes still closed, he groans and tilts up his pelvis, trying to guide her hips into motion against his groin. But she clamps her hand over his, holding him still. Her heart thumps. "It's two cars," she says. "Coming this way."

He opens his eyes, turns his head, then sits sharply upright. He scrubs a hole with the back of his fist in the steamed-up window. They peer through it in silence as the headlights cross the tracks and approach, paralleling the water.

"Shit," he says quietly. "This is private land. It's cordoned off for construction. No one should be here. Especially at this hour."

"Maybe it's kids out for some Halloween nonsense, or a drug deal," she whispers.

The cars come closer. The lead vehicle is smaller than the one following it, but the fog, rain, and darkness make it difficult to discern the cars' exact colors or models. And both vehicles are also backlit—silhouetted by the eerie glow emanating from the hidden city across the water. The smaller vehicle could be yellow, or cream, the woman thinks. A hatchback. The larger car is a sedan. Maybe dark gray or blue. The two sets of headlights briefly pan the inky water as the vehicles follow a bend in the track. Seawater shimmers in the light like beaten metal.

"They're coming right at us," the woman says.

"There's nowhere to go, no alternate exit," he says. "We're sitting ducks."

The cars come even closer.

"What in the hell?" The woman quickly relocates to the driver's seat and struggles to tug up her torn pantyhose and pull on her pumps. He yanks up his zipper.

"Wait, wait—they're stopping," he says.

The couple go still. In hidden silence they watch as the driver's-side door of the hatchback swings open and a tall figure climbs out. They see a logo on the side of the door. Another figure exits the larger sedan. Shorter. Stouter. Both drivers are dressed in black gear that shines in the rain. One wears a hat. The other a hood. The drivers leave the headlights on and the engines of both cars running. Exhaust fumes puff white clouds into the darkness.

Mist thickens and swirls around the two drivers as they open the rear door of the sedan. They struggle to tug something large and heavy out of the back seat. It appears to be a big roll of carpet. It drops to the ground with obvious weight.

"What're they doing?" the woman asks.

"They've got something rolled up in that rug," the man says. "Something heavy."

Neither wants to admit what they think it might be.

The two drivers heft and drag their cargo toward the water. At the edge of the abandoned dock, using feet and hands, they push and roll it over the edge. The object disappears. A second later it comes back into sight—a flash of white swirling toward the bridge in the tidal current. It spins in the water, then begins to sink. A moment later it's gone.

The woman swallows.

The interior of the Mercedes turns ice cold.

The man can't breathe.

Both are terrified by what they've witnessed. The chill of it crawls deep into their bones. The tall driver hurries back to the hatchback. He leans into the driver's side and fiddles with something beneath the steering wheel. The two drivers watch as the hatchback moves toward the water, as if of its own volition.

"Oh my God, they've jammed down the accelerator! We need to get out of here." The woman reaches for the ignition.

"Stop." The man clamps his hand over her forearm. "Do not move a single muscle until they're gone. They could kill us for what we've just seen."

They stare in mounting horror as the hatchback seems to hesitate, then tilts over the edge of the dock. As it plunges over, it catches refracted light from the bridge traffic. It's a yellow car, the woman thinks. A Subaru Crosstrek like the one she and her husband bought their son for his eighteenth birthday. The logo on the door seems familiar. She's seen it before but can't think where. The water closes over the car, leaving a luminous froth of foam that travels with the current toward the bridge. It disappears. There's nothing left—no indication that anything went off the dock. Just black water muscling with the tide.

The two drivers hasten to the waiting sedan. The tall one climbs into the driver's side, the shorter one into the passenger side. The doors slam shut. The sedan lurches at speed along the muddy track. Brake lights flare, and it crosses the tracks, then turns and trundles across the deserted silo yard. It vanishes into fog.

Neither of the Mercedes's occupants speaks. Tension hangs thick between them. They should call 911.

Both know they won't.

Neither will breathe a word of this to a single solitary soul, because if anyone learns they were here, together, at this abandoned place beneath the bridge in the dark and very early hours of what is now Friday morning, they will lose everything.

# THE MAID'S DIARY

Just start, my therapist said. Put words down, even if it's stream of consciousness, even if it's only to record something very ordinary you did in your day. If you find it difficult, try noting something that worries you. Just one thing. Or pick a thing that makes you happy. Or enraged. Or something that terrifies you. Write things you'll never let anyone read. Then for every insight, ask yourself why. Why do you think this? What are the stakes of losing that illusion? Ask why, write why, until you want to scream. Until you cannot stare at the words any longer, or until you drop through a trapdoor into something new. Then step away. Be physical. Walk, run, hike, swim, dance. Keep doing that until you're ready to return to the page. The key is just to start. Keep it simple. And I promise you, it will begin to flow.

*So here I am, Dear Diary—my Dear Therapist-by-proxy—just putting it down. Starting simple. My name is Kit. Kit Darling. I'm thirty-four. Single. Vegan. Love animals. Feed birds.*

*I'm a maid.*

*My passion is amateur theater.*

*My superpower is being invisible.*

*Yes, you read that right. I have been bestowed with the gift of invisibility. I move through people's houses unseen—a ghost—quietly dusting off the daily debris of their lives, restoring order to their outwardly "perfect" little microcosms. I wash and tidy and fold and sift through the privacy of elitist enclaves, touching, sniffing, envying, and at times trying on belongings. And here's a thing I've learned: Perfection is deception. An illusion. It's a carefully curated but false narrative. The golden family you think you know from the luxury home down the street—they're not who you believe they are. They have faults, secrets. Sometimes dark and terrible ones. Oddly, as a house cleaner, a processor of garbage and dirt, I am entrusted with the secrets inside these houses. Perhaps it's because I'm seen as irrelevant. Benign. Not worthy of deeper consideration. Just the hired help.*

*So I go about my dusting and vacuuming, and I snoop.*

*That's the other thing: I have a snooping problem.*

*I mean, we all get a dopamine-adrenaline kick when we glimpse something that wasn't meant for us to see, right? Don't pretend you're above it. We scroll through social media, hunting for the train wrecks happening in real time, and we cannot look away. We click on those links that promise to reveal a Hollywood star in a compromising bikini shot, or without makeup, or being a bad mommy in Starbucks. In the supermarket checkout line, we reach for the tabloid that screams with promises of insider tidbits about a British prince's affair. I just take it up a level. It keeps my days exciting.*

*When I arrive at a job, I already have my snooping strategy in place. I set a timer, and I do my cleaning fast enough that I always have a spare chunk of time to go through a dresser, a closet, a box in an attic, or a certain room.*

*And I follow the little clues. I find secrets that the occupants of a house try desperately to hide even from one another:*

*the wife from her husband, the father from his daughter, a son from his mother. I see the little blue pills. A syringe. Breath mints and cigarette butts hidden in a cracked pot in a garden shed. A teen's tequila bottle stashed at the back of an under-wear drawer. A husband's porn links saved in his computer. A wife's carefully hidden note from a not-so-long-ago lover, or a letter from a parole board. A pregnancy test secreted among trash that has been set aside for me to take out.*

*I see these people.*

*I know the occupants of these houses.*

*But they don't see me.*

*They don't know me.*

*Should I bump into one of them on a nearby sidewalk, or in the aisles of a grocery store, they won't recognize the invisible girl in their lives. The anonymous girl. I don't really care—I don't want to be "seen." Not by them.*

*My therapist has some theories on my desire to remain invisible. After I told her I was a ghost in people's homes, she asked if I'd always been a ghost. I wasn't sure how to answer, so I just clammed up. Her question has been worrying me, though. After a few more back-to-back abortive therapy ses-sions of us getting nowhere on the invisibility issue, my shrink suggested journaling.*

*She believes that opening up to private, nonthreatening blank pages might be a way for me to mine deeper into the unconscious parts of my psyche that are hiding things from my conscious (and even subconscious) self. She made it clear I should not feel compelled in any way to share my writing with her. But I can if I want to.*

*"It's only when you look at something long enough, Kit," she said, "and in the right way, that the real image starts to*

*appear. But first you need something to look at. You need words on a page. Even if those words seem banal or tedious or incongruent, or shameful, or even embarrassing, it's from this field of text that your true story will arise. And don't self-edit,"* she warned. *"Because until the full image is revealed to you, you won't know what part of the story is real, true, and what part you should leave out." She said the process is similar to those ambiguous, trick-the-eye reversible images—you know that classic drawing of the young woman? When you stare at it in a certain way, the image of the young woman suddenly flips into an old crone. And then you can't unsee it. It's a matter of shifting your perspective.*

*Honestly, I doubt any miracle is going to magically rise from the Jungian basement of my soul and spill onto these journal pages, but here we are, Dear Diary . . . I'm a maid. I like to snoop. I'm probably snooping too much. Okay, I admit—it's an addiction. I can't stop. It's getting worse. I'm taking increasing risks. Truth is, it's this addiction that made me seek therapy. It's my "presenting problem"—that's what my shrink calls it.*

*"Aren't you afraid that one day you'll poke too deep and see something you cannot unsee?" my best friend, Boon, asked me not long ago. "Because if you do, Kit, if you see a shocking secret that someone desperately wants to keep hidden, you could be in trouble. People—rich people—will do anything to protect themselves and their families, you know," he said. "Even kill."*

*That chilled me.*

*Boon said I needed to be more careful. "They have power. Power that you can't access."*

*He said I was crossing lines, that my habit was becoming reckless, that I was even inviting discovery. I needed to tone it down, watch my back.*

*I thought he was being dramatic. Because that's Boon. And he was messing with my fun.*

*I told him if people truly wanted to hide something so badly, they wouldn't invite a maid into their house.*

*Now I'm not so sure . . .*

# THE WOMAN
# IN THE WINDOW

*October 31, 2019. Thursday.*

Beulah Brown sits in her wheelchair at the long corner window in her upstairs room. The pallid morning sun peeks through a break in the clouds and shines upon her face. The puddle of light holds zero warmth, but it's sun nevertheless. Which is nothing to sneeze at in this gloomy rain forest climate of the Pacific Northwest. Especially during the autumn monsoons. And Beulah doesn't know how many more times she will see the sun. She does know she'll never see another fall. A tartan rug covers her lap. A plate of lemon cream biscuits rests on the small table at her side, and she holds a china cup of milky tea. She's impressed that she can still hold her cup so steadily. Cancer might be strangling away her life, but she does have fairly steady hands for her age. Her illness has not taken that.

Beulah favors this corner window in the mornings because, yes, it captures the morning sun when it does deign to shine. From this window she can also see both the "Glass House" that belongs to her neighbors and the inlet with the graceful green arc of Lions Gate Bridge linking the North Shore to Stanley Park and the city of Vancouver. Traffic is already thick on the bridge. People hustling and bustling to work on this Thursday morning, oblivious to the fact that in the blink of an eye they, too, will be sitting in a chair, waiting to die. Unless something violent and sudden snatches them away first.

Perhaps it might be worth the pain to have a terrible deadly accident, or to be violently murdered, if it meant going quickly. She ponders this as she sips her tea. It's lukewarm, made by her morning carer and left in a flask by Beulah's bed. Or is it a caregiver? Nouns these days are such a challenge. Her palliative nurse—the chatty Kathy—told Beulah that a "caregiver" might dislike the person to whom they are giving care, while a "carer" cares about the person, period.

Beulah carefully dips a lemon cream into her milky tea, her thoughts turning to Horton, her son, who occupies the downstairs area of her home now. He moved into her house allegedly to care for her. Beulah knows he's just after the house. It's a highly valuable piece of luxury waterfront property now. Horton is a caregiver, not a carer. Sometimes she wonders if he's trying to hasten her demise. Horton is Beulah's big regret in life. She bites into the soggy biscuit and wonders what her boy will do with all the family china when she's gone.

While chewing, she allows her gaze to drift across the Burrard Inlet toward the skulking tankers awaiting entry to the port, but a flash of color catches her eye. She turns her head to watch a little yellow Subaru Crosstrek with a familiar blue logo pulling into the driveway of the Glass House next door. Instantly she brightens. It's the maid. Beulah checks her watch. On time. Thursday morning. Like clockwork. Dependable help is so hard to get these days.

Beulah sets her cup down and reaches for her birding binoculars and trains her scopes on the neighbor's house. It's a modern architectural monstrosity—all windows with some metal and concrete. She can't detect movement inside yet. The owners must be sleeping late.

The comings and goings of Beulah's neighbors, the people who stroll their dogs along the seawall in front of her house, or those who sail boats in the bay—they're her entertainment, her daily reality show.

She recently began logging people's movements just to prove to herself that what she remembers did in fact occur. Horton keeps insisting that her memory is going. He claims she fabricates things and her imagination runs wild and is fueled by far too much streaming of dark Nordic crime and British detective shows. *Vera* is Beulah's favorite series. She likes *Shetland*, too. Mostly just to watch Jimmy Perez. And *Wallander*. She loves dear, sad Wallander.

With her gnarled and liver-spotted hands, she struggles to adjust the focus on her binoculars. The scopes are new—she's still getting the hang of them. She zeroes in on the nimble blonde woman with space buns who climbs out of the driver's door of the little yellow car.

*Well, hello, pet.*

Beulah channels Vera's voice. Empowered with her new binoculars, she can now also observe with Vera's shrewd detective eye, carefully cataloging details.

The maid is in her uniform—a bubblegum-pink golf shirt, practical navy-blue drawstring pants, and sensible white athletic shoes with an orange stripe on each side. She wears a black choker around her neck, and her blonde hair is in the updo: two untidy buns perched like little teddy bear ears atop either side of her head.

The maid opens her trunk, removes her vacuum cleaner. A Dyson. The maid glances up at Beulah's window, smiles, and waves.

Beulah's mouth curves slowly. She returns the wave with as much gusto as she can muster. For a brief moment they see each other—the old lady and the maid—then the maid gives a nod and goes about her job, getting the remainder of her cleaning supplies out of her car and ferrying them into the Glass House.

"Morning, Beulah!"

Beulah winces as the perky palliative nurse from the hospital bounces into her living area, lugging her bag of medical paraphernalia.

"How are we today, Beulah? How did we sleep?" the nurse asks as she disappears behind Beulah's chair and out of her line of sight.

"I slept alone," Beulah mumbles, struggling to turn her wheelchair around so she can face the nurse. The woman is dressed in cycling gear, for heaven's sakes. The nurse sets her bike helmet and bag down on Beulah's hospital bed and begins to unpack the equipment needed to take measure of Beulah's old heart and blood oxygen levels.

"I beg your pardon?" the nurse says.

"I said there is no *we*. It's just me. Alone. I sleep alone."

The nurse laughs and traps the tip of Beulah's finger in a clamp. She checks her stopwatch as she takes her readings. "Are you using the oxygen compressor when you sleep?"

"No," Beulah says.

"You should. It will help increase the levels in your blood. You'll have more energy. How's the pain?"

The rest of Thursday dissolves into the sameness of all those days that have come before. A dull routine of meds, another carer visiting to bathe her and to make lunch and set her up with a flask of afternoon tea. More meds. Yet another palliative nurse checks in. More medicine. Then a deep, dead-to-the-world, opioid-induced slumber, followed by a carer who preps her dinner. A heavier dose of meds for the night. But despite the meds, Beulah remains uncomfortable and propped up in her hospital bed so she can breathe.

At some point in the darkness, she fades into a groggy slumber. When Beulah wakes again, it's with a sharp start. She's drenched in sweat. Her room is dark. It's raining outside. She lies there, listening to the rain and the oxygen compressor huffing and sighing as she tries to orient herself.

She heard a scream.

She's sure she heard a terrible scream.

A woman's scream. It's what woke her. She's certain of it. Beulah's heart begins to beat very fast. The red glow on her clock radio reads 11:21 p.m. She listens for a while longer, wondering if she imagined the scream. Horton will say she did. A few moments later Beulah hears the bang of the wooden garden gate next door. Then a car door slams. She struggles to sit upright and tugs the cannula from her nose. Breathing heavily, groaning in pain, she gropes for her wheelchair and draws it closer to her hospital bed. She presses the bed's buttons and manages to lower it. She transfers herself into the chair. Beulah is fueled with adrenaline, determined to get to the window, to see. Sweating, she rolls herself to the corner window. She peers down into the neighbors' yard. The motion sensor light in the driveway has flared on. It takes a moment for her eyes to adjust, for Beulah's brain to register.

What she sees is wrong. All of it. Very, very wrong. Something *terrible* is happening.

Beulah quickly rolls herself back to the bed. Dizzy now, she fumbles to find her mobile phone on the bedside table.

With shaking hands she dials 911.

# MAL

*November 1, 2019. Friday.*

Detective Mallory Van Alst halts her unmarked vehicle at the road barrier. She powers down her window and shows her ID to the uniformed officer.

"Sergeant Van Alst, good morning," the officer says as she writes Mal's name on a clipboard. "Good luck in there—it's a bloody one." The officer moves the sawhorse barrier aside, and Mal drives into a lane of exclusive oceanfront mansions. West Vancouver PD cruisers with flashing bar lights are parked in front of a house constructed mostly of glass. Uniformed officers chat near the vehicles. At the end of the lane, onlookers gather, hair and coats ruffling in the cold breeze. Mal parks behind a forensic ident van. She kills her engine and studies the property.

It's one of those ultramodern, "architecturally designed" affairs—all windows, some concrete and metal. It rises like an angular, shimmering phoenix from the ruins of what was probably once a characterful home—something unique but not quite old enough to claim protective heritage status. A bronze plaque on the driveway pillar says NORTHVIEW. The driveway is cordoned off with yellow crime scene tape that flutters in the wind. Crime scene techs in white boiler suits and booties traverse a delineated path between the ident van and the house. Behind the property the Burrard Inlet sparkles.

Benoit Salumu, Mal's partner, is already waiting for her near the entrance. He stands stone still. Benoit has a way of doing that, being utterly motionless. At almost seven feet tall and carved as if from hard, black wood that has been burnished to a sheen, Benoit resembles a statue guarding the place. In fact the whole scene looks surreal. Especially against the backdrop of the rare and windy bluebird morning.

Mal quickly swallows the dregs of her coffee, unbuckles her seat belt, and reaches for her crossbody bag on the passenger seat. It contains spare gloves, booties, a digital camera, a small water bottle, and other backup basics she might need at a scene. She exits her vehicle and draws in a deep breath, focusing her mind. Compartmentalizing. Finding her zone. After thirty years on the beat, she finds it harder to center herself these days. A human can take only so much depravity and senseless loss of life.

"Morning," she calls out as she approaches Benoit. "You beat me to it. The baby let you sleep last night, then?"

Benoit gives a half grin. "You'll be the first to hear when that happens. Sadie did night duty, bless her heart. Can't wait for some old-time peace."

"Take it from an old pro, my friend," Mal says as she slides booties over her shoes. "Your peace is over. They will become teenagers. Then adults. Brace yourself. What've we got here?"

"Signs of a violent struggle. Plenty of blood. No body."

She crooks up a brow. "Photographers done their thing?"

"Yeah. Still some techs busy inside. I've got statements from the first responders. They're on standby down the street if we need more." His voice is deep, resonant, rhythmic. He speaks with an accent. French and Swahili are Benoit's first languages. Congo French, not Canadian French. When Benoit speaks French, it's the sound of the Belgian colony that once occupied his native Democratic Republic of Congo.

"Who made the 911 call?" Mal asks.

"Neighbor in that house." Benoit points to a traditional structure next door with brick walls covered in ivy turning shades of red and orange. "Beulah Brown. Eighty-nine. She called it in shortly before midnight. She's in palliative care. Occupies the top floor. Spends most of her days—and nights, it seems—watching the neighbors. She's also made five 911 calls in the last six months, which turned out to be nothing."

Mal frowns. "Unreliable witness?"

"Guess we'll find out. Take a look at this." Benoit points to the polished concrete floor in front of the door. A bouquet of wilting flowers— white orchids, lilies, chrysanthemums, baby's breath—lies in a puddle of water on the concrete. Nestled between the blooms is a small white envelope. Beside the flowers is a crushed pie box with a clear window on the top. It contains a smashed berry pie. Dark-purple juice oozes from under the box. On the box is a logo in the shape of the mathematical sign of pi, and words beneath it say Pi Bistro.

"This was a red flag for the first responders," Benoit says. "And the front door was ajar when they arrived. All the downstairs lights were on, and the glass sliding door at the rear of the house was wide open as well."

Mal raises her gaze slowly and studies the wood-trimmed glass front door. "No obvious sign of forced entry. And no one was home?"

"Negative. Just signs of a struggle and the blood spatter."

"Do we know who owns the place?"

He checks his notebook, flips a page. "Vanessa and Haruto North— guess that explains the name, Northview. There are two vehicles still parked in the garage. A red Lexus convertible and a silver Tesla Roadster. Both are registered to the Norths. The couple hasn't been located. No response to the phone numbers on record, either."

Mal crouches down and examines the wilting floral arrangement and smashed pie. She takes her own photos, then with a gloved hand she carefully removes the little wet envelope from beneath a white Japanese anemone and a sprig of baby's breath. She opens the envelope and extracts a white card. A message handwritten in dark ink bleeds into the damp paper. It reads:

*Good luck before autonomy dies, friend. It's been a ride.*

*Thanks for the support.*

*Daisy*

*X*

The card is embossed with a logo that reads Bea's Blooms.

Mal comes to her feet. She has a really bad feeling. She tries to imagine someone—a Daisy?—standing here in the doorway, holding a bouquet of white flowers and a pie, in full view of whoever comes to open the glass door. Then something happens—the pie and bouquet are dropped. Why? Shock? Fear? Threat? Medical incident?

Mal runs her gloved fingers down the inside of the doorjamb. Definitely no signs of forced entry. She enters the home. Her bad gut feeling sharpens instantly.

# DAISY

*October 17, 2019. Thursday.*
*Two weeks before the murder.*

"No—move it farther to the left, closer to the windows. Yes, like that. But angle it more to face the view," Daisy Wentworth Rittenberg instructs two muscled men in turbans as they manipulate a leather sofa to her specifications. She's staging a luxury penthouse for an open house, but the rental furniture has arrived late. It's already 5:43 p.m., and she's hungry and tired. She presses her hand to her aching lower back in an effort to support the weight of her pregnant belly.

Daisy is almost thirty-four weeks into her first pregnancy. She's due December 1, but it feels a lifetime away, and the extra pounds she's carrying that are *not* baby weight are making her irritable. Her dress is too tight—it pulls across both her belly and her butt. Her ankles are swollen. Her face is puffy. Her feet hurt. Her usually bouncy hair is limp. Her normally enviable complexion is blotchy, and she has a fat zit bang in the middle of her chin.

Daisy tries to shake her discontent and focus on her job. The penthouse boasts a glorious ocean view, and she's aiming to leverage it with the furniture layout. The property has just been listed by Wentworth Holdings for a cool $6.7 million. Wentworth Holdings was founded by Daisy's mother, Annabelle Wentworth, before Daisy was born. Her mom is still hands-on. Of course, Annabelle Wentworth doesn't *need* to work. She does it because she enjoys it. And because she cannot relinquish control. Daisy's mom has a reputation as the crème de la crème of Realtors who cater to very-high-end buyers and sellers of luxury properties in the greater Vancouver area. Annabelle launched Wentworth Holdings when she was only twenty-seven. With Wentworth family money, of course—marrying Labden Wentworth certainly came with perks. Daisy's dad, Labden, had by then already founded TerraWest Corp., which develops and manages ski resort holdings across North America, in Japan, and increasingly in parts of Europe. Daisy's husband, Jon, an Olympic downhill ski racer who won two gold medals at the Salt Lake City Winter Olympics in '02, now works for TerraWest.

Daisy has never done home staging before. Her background is in interior design. She ran a small bespoke company in Silver Aspens, Colorado, but since she and Jon moved back to their home city in July, Daisy has been helping her mom.

"Is this good?" The mover with a massive mustache interrupts Daisy's thoughts. She's so distracted these days. Can't keep her mind on one thing. Stupid pregnancy hormones.

"Perfect. Thanks, guys. We just need the coffee table brought up, and then we can call it a wrap."

The two men exit the penthouse to take the elevator down to their delivery truck twenty-six stories below. Daisy checks her watch. She'll never last to dinner. The little human growing inside her belly has seized control of her body and mind in ways Daisy did not anticipate. Like a little virus. She's just the host. And the little virus is morphing Daisy into a miserable creature who is not the Daisy she knows. She shakes herself. She shouldn't think like this. She *wants* this baby. It will change things for her and Jon. This baby is the whole reason they moved home. That, along with a promise from her father that Jon would get a big promotion. Their marriage *needs* this baby. And being near her mom and dad when the baby comes is something Daisy feels *she* needs. It will help put all the nasty business in Silver Aspens behind them. Perhaps she'll pick up a pizza on the way home. Or Chinese—

"Well, hello, Daisy."

Daisy jumps and her pulse quickens. She spins around as a tall black-haired woman breezes into the apartment on impossibly high heels. The penthouse owner. The woman tosses her car keys onto the marble kitchen island.

Daisy tries to calm herself. But the words—*Well, hello, Daisy*—reverberate inside her skull. They're the exact phrasing of the weird, disappearing text messages she's been receiving since she and Jon arrived back in Vancouver.

Well, hello, Daisy.

Welcome home, Daisy.

It's been a while, Daisy.

I know who you are, Daisy.

They appear via her WhatsApp app, then vanish twenty-four hours later. All from unfamiliar numbers. She blocks them, but they just arrive again via another number.

The condo owner absently plucks three grapes from a bowl that Daisy has very carefully positioned on the kitchen island. She saunters into the center of the living area and plops one of the fat grapes into her mouth. Chewing, she turns in a slow circle, critiquing the furniture layout and the paintings Daisy has hung. The woman's hair is pixie short. Her face is all elegant angles. Luminous white skin; big, flashing dark eyes. And she's runway-model thin. Basically a coatrack. Daisy feels herself bristle.

The woman plops another fat green grape into her mouth, carefully avoiding her red lipstick. "Sorry I'm late. My meeting ran over time, and I—" She stops suddenly. Her eyes flare to an art piece above the fireplace. She spins back to face Daisy. "Are you confident this is the right look for—"

"Designing for a show home is not the same as designing for living," Daisy snaps.

The woman's brow crooks up at Daisy's tone.

Daisy fights to temper her irritation and her dislike for the coathanger woman. This is her mom's client. Reputation is everything in this business. The Wentworth name is on the line.

She inhales deeply, slowly, and says, "Our goal here is to subtly emphasize the openness of your gorgeous space, to draw one's eye to the artistic angles of the architecture. We want to be inviting, yet also remain neutral enough so as not to overshadow that magnificent view. We want prospective buyers—no matter their tastes—to be able to step in here and immediately have their eyes go out to the view. We want them to be able to imagine themselves inhabiting this space."

The penthouse owner plops the third grape into her mouth. "Well, I trust Annabelle. She's well recommended and gets results. So . . ." She trails off, chewing as her gaze flits over Daisy's tight dress and the comfortable walking sneakers Daisy picked up at the mall on her way over here. Daisy detests her mass-produced white sneakers with the orange stripes, but she was running late, and her other shoes were killing her back and swollen feet. She needed an emergency replacement.

"I'm over eight months pregnant," she says in her defense, then immediately hates herself. Why did she even say that? What an idiot. As if she needs to explain her body and her comfortable shoes to this . . . this coatrack snob.

"Oh." The woman turns her back on Daisy and faces the view.

Heat flares into Daisy's cheeks. She expected a perfunctory *Congratulations* at the least. She goes to the grape bowl on the island

25

and turns over the bunch of grapes to hide the ugly stalks that the woman exposed.

*I don't have to work. I could buy your fucking penthouse twice over myself with my trust fund.*

Instead, Daisy says, "Do you have kids?"

A deep, dark laugh.

Daisy turns. "Of course you don't. Silly question."

"What do you mean?"

"Anyone can see from this penthouse that no child comes near this place."

The woman's eyes narrow slightly. "My husband and I made a conscious choice when we married—a commitment—to not have babies. We don't want to bring children into this world."

"So it's not your first marriage?"

The woman blinks. "Excuse me?"

"He's had a vasectomy, hasn't he? Your husband. Snip snip. I'm guessing he's already got his kids. Grown up. From a first marriage?"

The woman's mouth opens.

*Bingo.*

Daisy manages to say sweetly, "Such a male privilege, isn't it? Meanwhile, you and I have to worry about those ticking biological clocks. And if your husband trades up again, it'll be too late for you." She reaches for her purse. "Well, it was *so* nice to help make your place look salable. Some places just need that extra help, you know? Oh, when the delivery guys come up with the coffee table, show them where you want it. I'm running late myself." She waddles to the door on her swollen feet. Her heart thumps as she exits the condo and makes her way to the elevator. But inside she grins with glee. Daisy Wentworth Rittenberg has just refound some of her mojo. The young, popular "It girl" that Daisy once was at school is *still* buried somewhere deep beneath the puffiness and pregnancy hormones. The attractive, wealthy, blonde teen who could cut anyone to the quick with a scathing comment has not totally vanished. Deep inside Daisy is *still* the schoolgirl who snagged famous gold medal downhill ski racer and sex icon Jon Rittenberg when everyone else was throwing themselves at him.

A little shaky and a lot exhilarated, Daisy enters the elevator and triumphantly jabs the button. She forgot just how damn good it feels to stand her ground, stick in the knife . . . and twist.

Outside the high-rise the October air is cool and welcome. When Daisy reaches her BMW parked down the street, she sees a white envelope tucked under the windshield. She reaches for the envelope, opens it, and extracts a simple card.

I SEE YOU @JUSTDAISYDAILY.
I KNOW WHO YOU ARE.
TICKTOCK GOES THE CLOCK.

# DAISY

Daisy drives home with her wheel in a death grip. Her throat is tight, blood pressure going up.

*Not good. Not good for the baby. Calm down, Daisy. Breathe. Focus.*

The note left on her windshield lies on the passenger seat.

Whoever is doing this is circling in. Becoming brazen. Now there's a ticking clock—a time bomb. A warning something is going to explode.

It's clear that the sender is familiar with her Instagram handle, @JustDaisyDaily. Which means they know a *lot* about her life—that she is pregnant with a baby boy, that she and Jon have recently moved back to Vancouver from Colorado, that Jon is up for a top job at a brand-new mountain resort being developed north of world-famous Whistler. They also know which car she drives.

She feeds onto the Burrard Bridge, racking her brain—did she post on social media about the condo staging? No. She's sure she didn't. So how did the note sender know where to find her car? Was she followed? Daisy needs to quit that job anyway. She hates it. Her mom will understand. Jon will be relieved. He doesn't want her to work. He says it's beneath her and that she should stay home and just focus on being pregnant. She's going to be a stay-home mom, anyway, once the baby comes.

The interior of her car is hot. The traffic on the bridge is stop-start. She glimpses the North Shore Mountains across the inlet, and her mind slams back to the days she and Jon were in school. They both grew up on the North Shore, on the flanks of those densely forested mountains across the water. They both learned to ski on Grouse. They met in high school, started dating in grade eleven. They had the best parties . . . Unease creeps deeper into Daisy. They also did some wild things as kids.

No one told her at the time how unbelievably stupid those things would seem when she became an adult. Or how memories of them could sneak up out of the blue—like now—and make her think, *No, that could not have happened. I was never a part of that.* She tightens her vise grip on the wheel. Returning "home" is really rattling her.

*We were just stupid kids who drank too much. Teens make terrible decisions all the time. Peer pressure. Herd mentality. Collective stupidity. Mix in equal amounts, and something dark, disturbing, primal takes over.*

Daisy is so preoccupied that by the time she arrives home, she barely recalls having stopped to pick up a pizza. She unlocks the front door, balancing the hot pizza box and her purse. She enters the hallway and disarms the security system. The interior of her house is spotless and smells fresh. From the entryway Daisy can see straight through the living room to their lush green garden out back. Instantly she decompresses. She kicks off her ugly runners and carries the pizza into the kitchen. She opens the box, lifts out a cheesy wedge, takes a massive bite, then another, and groans with pleasure. While chewing, she rips off her too-tight dress and goes upstairs to find sweatpants and an oversize T-shirt.

Once changed, Daisy returns barefoot to the kitchen. She puts on the kettle for some tea and finishes the pizza in great big gulps like a ravenous She Beast. While she chews and hungrily swallows, she thinks this is all the little parasite's doing—the one growing inside her belly, consuming her from the inside out. Controlling her urges.

Again Daisy shakes the macabre thought. She has no idea where these images are coming from. She's really not herself at the moment. As she pours boiling water over her teabag, she notices the note Jon left for her on the counter. It rests beside a printout of their latest ultrasound scan. She picks up the note.

*Remember! Dinner with Henry at the pub—6:30 p.m.*

Jon has taken to leaving Daisy notes because he says she's so forgetful these days. Henry Clay—the longest-serving member on the TerraWest board of directors—has invited Jon to discuss a work-related issue over an early meal tonight. Daisy wonders if it has something to do with her father's abrupt retirement. Her dad suffered a health scare two weeks ago. A minor heart attack. The doctors suggested lifestyle changes, so Labden shocked everyone by announcing his immediate departure from TerraWest, saying he wanted to enjoy what remained of his years.

As Daisy sets down the note and removes her teabag from the cup, a sudden movement outside snares her attention. She tenses and stares at the bushes at the bottom of their landscaped garden. A breeze has risen and the fall-color leaves are stirring. No one is there. But she's almost certain she saw someone in black moving behind the trees that screen their property from the lane that runs behind their fence. Daisy leaves her tea and slowly goes up to the sliding glass doors. With a hand on her belly, she peers carefully into the garden. Several crows erupt into flight and scatter up into the darkening autumn sky. A crow? Did she see a wretched crow and think it was a person behind the trees? Even so, she can't shake the feeling of being *watched*.

*Followed.*

Daisy drops the shade. She places a call to Jon. She knows he'll be busy with Henry, but she needs to hear his voice. Anyone's voice.

The phone rings, then kicks into voice mail. A bolt of irritation slices through her. She calls again. No answer again. It must be noisy in the pub, she thinks. Maybe Jon can't hear his phone ringing. Still needing human connection, she texts her friend Vanessa.

**Are you up for lunch tomorrow? Pi Bistro?**

Tomorrow is maid service day. Daisy always leaves the house when the help comes. She can't handle watching someone clean up under her feet—like she should feel guilty or something when she is paying a top wage and actually providing someone with a job. She prefers to just return home to a sparkling-clean house and believe the house fairies have been there. That's what her mom always called the cleaning service when Daisy was little. House fairies.

Her phone pings with a response from Vanessa.

**Great idea! What time?**

Daisy types:

**Is noon too early? (I'm hungry all the time these days!)**

Vanessa's reply pops through.

**No kidding. Haruto and I have an appointment around noon. How about later—2 pm?**

Daisy smiles. Two p.m. is rather long to wait for lunch. She'll have a snack earlier, though. She enjoys her time with Vanessa, whose baby is due a week after Daisy's. It feels good to share with someone who actually relates. And Vanessa doesn't judge. Daisy cannot handle people who tell her she can never complain because she's "privileged" and she should be thankful for all the things she has in life. Everything is relative—can't people understand that? Vanessa is not one of those people. She and Haruto live in one of those designer houses across the water—a stunning, shimmering glass structure with an infinity pool to die for. Vanessa attends the Yoga Mom's prenatal classes near Daisy's house because Haruto does some work nearby—that class is where Vanessa and Daisy met. Daisy types:

See you then!

Feeling a little more centered, she carries her chamomile tea upstairs, runs a bath, and climbs into the bubbles with a book.

An hour later Daisy is in bed with her novel, reading between dozing on and off. When she checks the clock again, it's 10:26 p.m. She sits upright. Jon is not home. He should be back by now.

She reaches for her phone, calls her husband. It goes to voice mail again.

Daisy lies back on her pillow, thinking, *What if he drank too much and got in an accident? What if he's in the hospital somewhere?*

She waits thirty minutes, then calls again. It flips to voice mail. Daisy begins to wonder if Jon has gone somewhere after the pub. A club or something. This makes her even more anxious.

When she calls yet again, Jon picks up. Relief surges through Daisy.

"Hey, hon," she says carefully. "Is everything okay? I was worried about you."

"I'm fine." She hears noise. Music. A woman's voice in the background. Jon says, "Let me take this somewhere quieter. Hang on a sec—" Daisy hears the woman's voice again. Then the phone goes muffled, as though Jon is holding it against his body.

"Jon? Are you there?"

When he comes back on, he clears his throat. "Sorry, love. I should've called. Just as Henry left the pub, some of the guys from work came in. They're all talking about the new development. One of the environmental assessors is with them. I figured I should connect with him, build some contacts. He's still here. Could be a late one. You okay with that? I can come home now if—"

"No. No—I—it's fine." Emotion wells up inside her. She feels lonely, sidelined. "How'd it go with Henry?"

A beat of silence. "Fine. It went fine."

"What did he want?"

"He had—ah, some interesting info. We can talk tomorrow, okay?"

Daisy's earlier unease deepens. She feels a sense of something looming. *Ticktock goes the clock.* She glances at the shuttered blinds. The shadows of the trees move behind them. The wind is increasing. A storm coming.

"You okay, Daize?"

"Yeah. I—I'm good." She was about to tell Jon about the note on her windshield but decides to hold off. "I'll see you later."

"Get some rest, love. I won't be too long. Don't wait up."

She says goodbye, but as she's about to kill the call, she hears that female voice in the background again. This time Daisy catches a few words: *Jon . . . early. Thank . . . lovely evening.*

She drops back onto her pillow, clutching her phone upon her belly. She stares at the ceiling and tells herself it's a busy pub. It's located downstairs in a popular hotel next to the building where Jon works. The voice could've belonged to anyone. A server, even.

Daisy imagines a waitress leaning over Jon's table, smiling at him, her cleavage in line with his gaze. No, she tells herself. It was probably just some woman walking by in the hotel lobby, calling out to someone. She cannot let this happen again—the mounting suspicion. The paranoia. Seeing things in shadows and bushes. Just because she and Jon were victims of an obsessed stalker in Colorado, that does *not* mean it will happen again here.

*Will it?*

What if the woman in Colorado didn't get the message and followed them all the way to Vancouver?

*It's going to be fine. It was taken care of. She's no longer a problem.*

But as Daisy drifts off into that lucid, elastic time between sleep and being fully awake, she hears the woman's voice in her dream again, but her mind fills in missing words.

*Jon . . . I need to be up early. Thank you for a lovely evening.*

# MAL

*November 1, 2019. Friday.*

Natural light floods into the Glass House from all directions, and Mal blinks against the stark brightness of the interior. The downstairs area is open plan. White marble floors, white walls, white furniture, mirrors, and a few slashes of angry, abstract art.

"Were the window shades found open like that?" she asks, watching as a tech dusts an upturned glass coffee table for prints. More crime scene techs traverse up and down the stairs. There's an eerie stillness inside the house despite the movement and chatter. A pressing solemnness, emptiness.

Benoit says, "There are no shades to draw down on those sea-facing windows."

She glances at him. "You're kidding? These people live in a glass box with no option to shut the world out? That's kind of—"

"Exhibitionist. Yeah. Fishbowl-like."

"I was going to say *vulnerable*," she says softly.

Benoit tilts his chin toward the glass doors that lead out to an infinity pool. "Human blood streaks, drag marks, lead out through those sliders. The marks track along the pool deck to a yard gate that opens onto the driveway. Main event appears to be upstairs in the bedroom. Want to start there?"

"Down here," Mal says. "We'll work up to the main show." She likes to approach a crime scene from the perimeter, moving inward in concentric circles. It keeps her mind open, stops her from leaping to conclusions. Once she's made an overall assessment, she'll go back for detail, often revisiting a scene several times. She crosses the polished marble floor, carefully avoiding the markers left by the forensic ident techs. Benoit follows in her tracks, minimizing potential to contaminate the scene.

The white sofa is spattered with blood. So is the white floor. A broken wineglass, a martini glass, and a tumbler lie in puddles of liquid on the floor beside the upturned coffee table. Stuffed olives and a cocktail onion have rolled toward the door. A television remote rests among the broken glass and spilled booze. Mal can smell the alcohol—the sourness of wine, whisky. An ashtray on an end table holds an artsy-looking weed pipe made of green glass.

"You know what they say about people in glass houses?" Benoit says.

"They shouldn't throw stones?"

"They shouldn't get stoned."

Mal rolls her eyes and bends down to study the blood on the sofa. She takes a photo. "Consistent with expired spatter," she says. "And down there on the floor, that trail and line of heavy drops—"

"Could be arterial."

She nods. "And more on the wall over there."

Benoit walks toward the spattered wall. "Signs of a struggle—maybe it starts there." He points to the sofa. "Three glasses, three people sitting having drinks. They begin to argue, fight. One gets up. Is followed. The victim is slammed against the wall here. Victim could have been standing at this point. Possible impact spatter there at average head height." He points.

Mal comes up behind him. "Maybe hit with an object? Blunt force trauma could have created that patterning there."

Benoit nods. "Or cut—stabbed. Victim then slides down the wall. Maybe crawls away in that direction." He points. "The victim is bleeding close to the floor there. Victim tries to use the sofa armrest to pull back up into a standing position. Is hit again. Aspirates blood there? Victim crawls away."

"Then what?" Mal asks. "Where did our victim go? Where's the body?"

Benoit drops to his haunches. "Look at this straight line of blood. It appears something was in place here that stopped the spatter."

"A rug," she says quietly. "There was a rug here. Under the coffee table."

"Might explain the drag marks," Benoit says. "Victim could have been dragged out on the rug."

As Mal shoots more photos, she notices a glint of gold between the sofa cushions. She takes another photo, moves the cushion aside, and with her gloved hand, lifts up a gold pendant. She whistles. "Big-ass diamond set in a gold teardrop," she says. "Chain is broken." She calls a tech over to bag the pendant, then walks slowly toward the open sliding door, studying the floor.

She steps out onto the pool deck. The surface of the infinity pool is riffled with wind. Behind the pool the Burrard Inlet sparkles. An ident tech is busy taking samples on the deck. The tech glances up.

"More blood trace out here," the tech says. "Something was dragged out of the living room, along the deck, around the side of the house, then out the yard gate into the driveway. The yard gate was found open. The blood trace ends where it appears a car was parked."

"As though something was put into a vehicle," Mal says.

"That would be consistent with our observations so far."

A movement next door catches Mal's eye. She glances up at the neighboring house. There's an old woman in the upstairs window, watching. A tartan throw covers her lap. The woman gives a small wave. Mal hesitates, then raises her own hand in a slight salute, feeling odd while she does it. Waving at witnesses is not a habit she's accustomed to. Quietly she says to Benoit, "That must be her—the one who called it in. Would freak me out to have an old woman watching me from above like that. She must be able to see right over the pool and partway into that living room."

Benoit follows Mal's gaze. "We can get a statement from her next."

They reenter the house and move to the bar counter. On the counter are a martini shaker, an ice bucket with melted ice, a silver bottle of Belvedere vodka, a bottle of Balvenie Caribbean cask fourteen-year-old whisky, a bowl of stuffed olives, and a board of assorted cheeses going dry.

Mal studies a framed photo on the wall behind the bar. It's the only photo downstairs. It shows a man and woman, likely in their midthirties. The female is a fair-skinned and rather stunning brunette. Long wavy hair. Slender. She wears a silky cream jumpsuit and ridiculously high-heeled sandals. She poses with the panache of a *Vogue* model beside a man who is slightly shorter than her because of her heels. The male has his arm around her waist in a proprietary way. He appears of Asian cultural descent. They stand in front of a turquoise pool. Clearly confident and comfortable together. They look rich—if rich has a look. In the background are palm trees, cascades of orchids, a colonial-looking building with white columns and rattan furniture on a black-and-white-tiled veranda.

"Haruto and Vanessa North?" she suggests as she shoots her own photo of the framed image. "Taken some place in Asia would be my guess from the vegetation and that rattan furniture on the deck?"

Benoit moves into the kitchen. Mal follows. It's massive, all stainless steel and gleaming white. Spotless. No signs of recent cooking at all. Benoit opens the Sub-Zero refrigerator.

"Nothing inside the fridge apart from a bottle of rosé," he says, opening and closing doors. "Nothing in the dishwasher, either. It's like this home was staged for a photo shoot. Oh, wait, take a look at this."

He points to a knife block. "One is missing." He meets Mal's gaze. "One of the big carving knives."

Tension winds tighter as they climb the staircase, stepping to the side of tags marking droplets of blood on the steps. Blood is smeared down the handrail.

A tech comes down the stairs, nods in greeting. The upstairs area is carpeted. Bloody footprints track along the plush cream carpeting, coming from the bedroom. They enter the main bedroom. Mal stalls. For a moment she can't breathe.

She's no stranger to violent homicide scenes, but this one is shocking. An abstract painting—almost beautiful—done in blood spatter across the pristine white decor of the room. The red blood streaks and drops arc across the walls, the ceiling, the mirror, the lampshades, the carpet. And in the center of the king-size bed, in the middle of rumpled, silky-white sheets, is an area almost black with saturated blood.

A chill creeps over her skin. She swallows, steps forward. "Wow," she says quietly.

The two crime scene techs collecting blood trace from a jade statue on the floor beside the bed both glance up. "Right?" they say, almost in unison.

"And no sign of a body?" she asks.

"Not yet," says the female tech. "But I'm pretty damn sure whoever lost this much blood did not walk away from this."

"The statue look to be a weapon?" Benoit asks.

"Possible," the tech says. "We've got traces of matted hair and blood on the corner of the statue. Fine blonde hairs. Dark at the roots. We also found longer dark strands in the sheets. There's something on the other side of the bed you might find interesting."

Mal and Benoit go around to the far side of the king bed. A lone sneaker lies on its side—a white shoe with a decorative orange swoosh on the side. A worn, bloodied sock hangs out of it.

Mal frowns. "Just this one sneaker?" she asks. "Any sign of the other one?"

"So far nothing," the tech says.

Mal drops to her haunches, captures a photo, then studies the shoe. "A practical, midrange women's sneaker. Designed for comfort." She picks it up, peers inside. "Size seven."

Benoit says, "You'd expect to find a super-high-end exercise shoe in a place like this, not a middle-of-the-road sneaker like that."

Mal chews the side of her cheek. "It definitely looks like the odd thing out here. Could've been yanked off the victim's foot, the sock coming off with the shoe, perhaps when she was dragged. We'll get DNA off that sock, see if it matches the rest of this blood." She regards the king-size bed. The rumpled linen. Another framed photograph of the couple stands on the dresser. They're in formal wear, dressed for some kind of gala occasion. Very handsome. Very smooth. She thinks of the drinks glasses downstairs. The pie and flowers outside. No body. House owners gone. Luxury vehicles still in the garage. She gets to her feet and goes to the walk-in closet. She opens the doors, flicks on the lights. The closet is as large as Mal's husband's home office. She and Benoit enter. Female clothing lines the right side of the closet, male apparel on the left. Everything is impeccably pressed, neatly hung, evenly spaced. The wall at the rear has been given over to shoes. Racks of them. Luxury designer brands for both sexes. She picks up a stiletto, turns it over.

"Size eight and a half," she says quietly.

Benoit checks another. Then another. "All the female shoes are either a women's eight and a half or nine," he says. "The male shoes are a men's ten."

"The woman in the photo downstairs—she looks tall," Mal says. "She'd easily be a nine. The man with her, easily a men's ten."

"Yet the bloody sneaker by the bed is a women's seven," notes Benoit.

"That sneaker definitely does not fit this picture," Mal says quietly, scanning the obviously outrageously expensive designer contents of the closet.

"If the sneaker does not belong to Mrs. North of the photo, maybe it's our victim's," Benoit says.

"So where is she?" Mal meets Benoit's gaze. "Where is her body? Where are the owners?"

"And who in the hell is 'Daisy'?" he adds.

A yell comes from downstairs. "Sergeant, we've found the knife!"

# THE MAID'S DIARY

While my snooping addiction might be my "presenting" problem, the *reasons* behind my addiction are what my therapist seeks to uncover. Through journaling, I've realized two key events have recently triggered me, thus exacerbating my addiction and taking my behavior into risky—dangerous—territory. In fact, these two triggers coalesced in one day, which amplified them both tenfold. It's funny how we can't see these things ourselves sometimes, even when they're screaming in our face.

*I'll tell you about this day now. I'm just going to write it down, Dear Diary, as the day played out, blow by blow, in real time:*

*Boon and I get up very early on this morning to go to Lighthouse Park before work.*

*The day has dawned bleak, cold. Rain falls in a gentle veil as we trudge along a shadowed trail of black mud and gnarled roots. Huge dripping conifers tower around us, and fog sifts like specters between the ancient trunks. It creates a sense of brooding, as though the trees are sentient, watching over us. Sheltering us, protecting us. Provided we stay on the trail.*

*In a small pack on my back, I carry a cylindrical biode-gradable bamboo urn that contains my mother's ashes. They're surprisingly heavy, a human's ashes.*

*My mother died twelve months ago today. The whole process leading up to her death has messed me up, and it's not done messing yet. My mother's voice curls through my mind as I seek for the right place to scatter what remains of her.*

*"You had such promise, Katarina. You were top of your class in mathematics, in chemistry, physics. You won the English essay contest. You were on the honor roll. You could have been anything you wanted, but now you are a maid, cleaning up after other people."*

*"You also cleaned houses, Mom. I take after you."*

*"Your father and I, we immigrated, Katarina, so you wouldn't grow up like us. We did it for you. We struggled for you. I cleaned houses and hotel rooms for you. All for you. Everything. And look at what you have done to us."*

*Then my mother got sick.*

*Really sick.*

*I tried to help. I tried to stop it from getting worse. I drove her to all her doctor appointments and scans and blood tests. We spent whole days at the cancer center for chemo. Nothing stopped it.*

*She went into hospice. She died. All within eight months from diagnosis. I didn't think it would be such a shock, or that I would actually miss her moaning and chastising so much. Maybe she's scolding my father in heaven right now, wagging her rough, chapped cleaner's hands at him. I can almost hear her voice in that Ukrainian accent that never left her: "Oh, Pavlo, just look at our daughter we have left behind on this earth. She is in her thirties, Pavlo, and still she cleans other people's houses—"*

*"How about here?" Boon asks, interrupting my mother inside my head.*

*I turn to see where he's pointing. Rain drips from the bill of my cap. It drips from the sad, heavy branches of the deep-green forest. It feels as though it drips from my heart.*

*"Bit of a steep drop," I say, peering cautiously over the edge of the cliff as I hold on to Boon's sleeve. "Those rocks along the ledge down there look slippery. I don't want to go over the cliff and into the water with her ashes. 'Cause that would really make her day."*

*He laughs. Boon has this really strange, distinctive laugh. Once you hear it, you'll recognize it anywhere. It reminds me of a whooping crane when he gets wound up. Or nervous. I don't often see Boon nervous, but when he is, he laughs and cranks up into the high whooping sound. It always makes me smile, although I know others find it intensely annoying.*

*"You talk like she's still watching you," he says.*

*"She's always watching me. She's inside my head."*

*"See?" Boon says. "It's you—you are the problem. Not her. It's never been about her. She's just the internalized voice of your own conscience, and you have named your conscience, your inner judge, 'Mom.'"*

*"Oh, don't you start, too, Boon." I'm getting enough of this stuff from my therapist. I start to walk away, but stop and abruptly spin around to face him. I lean forward and lock my gaze onto his. He takes a slight step back in surprise. I narrow my eyes and glower into his. I make my expression—my whole body posture—intense, aggressive. His smile fades. He takes another small step backward, closer to the slick rock edge.*

*"What are you doing, Kit?"*

*"Is she inside you now, Boon?" I point at his nose. "Is that you in there, Mom?" I step closer to him. "Have you possessed Boon—are you inhabiting Boon's body, Mamma?"*

*"Cut that out."*

*"Ha—you're spooked!" I slap my thigh.*

*"I am not. And you need to grow up."*

*"Now you sound like my dad."*

*"And when did you last hear your dad speak? He died like ten years ago, didn't he? You always told me it was just you and your mom after that."*

*I shrug and start back along the twisting trail above the water. Far below, the waves make little suck-and-slap noises. Boon follows in the wet mud behind me, his steps making a slurpy sound. My boot dislodges small stones. They clatter down the rock face. He's right, though. I did hear my dad again. Coming right out of the past. Taking me back to when I was sixteen. "You need to grow up and take some responsibility, Katarina. Always lies. Lies, lies, lies. You are disgusting, Katarina. You whore. You have disgraced this family. Do you know that? You have shamed our entire family—"*

*I walk faster. A more purposeful stride.*

*I hear my mother countering him. "Leave Katarina alone."*

*The balloon of grief in my chest suddenly explodes. Tears surge to my eyes, and I feel like this thing is going to consume me. Lives gone. Opportunities gone. I failed them. I've failed me. And I am thankful for the rain—the insidious coastal mist of a rain that hides the salty wetness on my face.*

*I stumble slightly on an exposed root. Catching myself, I glance up. And I see it—a wooden bench bolted into a smooth slab of rock that looks out over the gunmetal sea.*

*"This," I say, turning to Boon, "this is the spot."*

*"Someone has already memorialized this place, Kit. Look, there's a plaque on the bench—it's someone else's grieving place. They paid for this bench."*

"Oh, don't be ridiculous. It's donated in the name of this other dead person. Besides, it would be fitting, wouldn't it? Me and my mom, the parasite recyclers of other rich people's garbage, using some other rich person's memorial. Secondhand clothes—secondhand benches." I face him. "It's not like they own this rock, or the park. It's a public park. For everyone's enjoyment. They just funded it."

"It's a joke, Kit. Jeez—what's going on with—" But he swallows his words. He knows what's going on. I'm having trouble dealing with this. That's what's going on.

"Sorry," I say. "Let's just get this over with."

"Okay. Fine."

I shrug the backpack off my shoulders and fish out the urn. Then freeze. I can't do it.

So Boon and I sit for a while on the bench. In the soft rain and fog. Me holding tightly on to the biodegradable bamboo cylinder in my lap, suddenly unable to let my mother go.

All these years, thinking I would be fine without her wrongful judgment. Now—

I run my hand over the bamboo. It's so smooth. The funeral director told me I could bury the urn after scattering the cremains, maybe even plant a tree on top of it, and it would decompose.

The fog presses in. The forest drips more heavily. We can hear the distant sound of the city, the far-off wail of a siren.

Boon says softly, kindly, because Boon has always been kind to me, "We should do it, Kit. I need to get to work. So do you." His set-designing job in "Hollywood North" awaits. He's working on the second season of a TV series about a coroner. And my new clients' home awaits—I'm wearing my Holly's Help uniform beneath my coat. Still, I'm unable to move. I'm welded to the bench with the cylinder of Mom's *ashes between my hands. Tears begin to stream down my face. My shoulders heave.*

*Her ashes have sat on my mantel for an entire year because I couldn't bring myself to do this. As though I wanted her there on the mantel continually pointing her accusing finger at me. "See, Katarina, you clean up the mess of other people's lives, yet you can't keep clean your own. Now you can't even dispose of your dear mother's ashes, the mother who gave up everything in native Ukraine for you so you could have a better life. You never could finish things off properly. You even dropped out of school after we saved all the money for your university education. Too much drinking. Too much partying. Bad crowd."*

*Boon puts his arm around me. He says nothing. He's just there for me. There are all kinds of love, and the love I have for Boon is just one kind. He's my best friend. I will do anything for him and he will do the same for me. It's a bond stronger than blood.*

*"You know what her last words to me were?" I say quietly.*

*Boon makes a moue beneath his dripping rain cap. "Let me guess." And he commences a perfect imitation of my mother's Ukrainian-accented voice. "You could have amounted to something, Katarina."*

*I laugh-choke. "No. No—it went like this—" I take a moment to collect my own theater voice, then in a precise echo of our "conversation" in the hospice room, I say:*

*"I need to get out of here, Katarina. Help me get out of this bed. At once."*

*"Mom, you're weak. You're going to fall. I'll call the nurse for—"*

*"No, no! Dear God, I have to leave this place."*

*"Stop, Mom. Let me help you lie back."*

*"Leave me alone! Let go of me! Mother of God! Hail Mary, dear Jesus, 911, help me somebody! Help get Katarina off me. Let me go. I will kick you, Katarina. I will kick you so hard, I will donkey kick you!"*

*Boon stares at me. Then a slow smile curves his lips. "Donkey kick?"*

*I give a snort of laughter, wipe my nose with the back of my hand, nod.*

*"What's a donkey kick? I thought it was a yoga move."*

*"Probably the hardest kick my mother could imagine. Kicking backward, you know, like a horse."*

*"Maybe someone on the farm she grew up on was kicked by a donkey."*

*"I have no idea. It was partly the medication, partly the natural dying process. There are stages, you know? Like there are specific stages in pregnancy, there are identifiable, predictable stages in the process of leaving this world."*

*"Guess that's why there are doulas at each end—both entry and exit can be pretty violent and traumatic. And scary."*

*"Yeah."*

*Boon sits silent awhile. "I guess donkeys kick pretty hard."*

*"I guess. She was injected with meds and died a few hours later." I suddenly feel a need to kick these ashes free. "Let's do this."*

*I stand up, release the bamboo pin on the lid of the urn, twist the top, and empty her ashes into the wind. My mom's cremains blow up and out and sideways and down—she literally explodes from the urn. Against the gray fog, the explosive cloud of her ashes appears silvery and white. She booms up into the air like a little atomic cloud, blows back over us, scatters down into the sea, up into the branches and sky. She goes everywhere. And I laugh and laugh and laugh, feeling her delight. Her wild freedom. Recycled. Back into the universe.*

*I inhale deeply, feeling her go. But I feel lost, too. Adrift suddenly on this ocean of life.*

*And that was that.*

*We hike back to our cars. The pack on my back is light with the empty urn.*

*When we reach the parking lot, there is a bright-blue Tesla Roadster parked at the opposite end of the parking lot, about as distant as it can possibly get from the cheap ordinariness of Boon's ancient brown Honda and my yellow Subaru Crosstrek.*

*"Stop—wait," I say to Boon.*

*He catches the gleam in my eyes and grins broadly. Our little game is afoot. Our private joke against the world of money and false narratives, because things are never what they seem.*

*Without speaking, we move in unison toward the blue Tesla. We go into improv mode, falling naturally into our poses as we lean against the Roadster. Boon drapes his arm around my shoulders. I look adoringly up into his face as I hold out my phone and click. You can do so much with body posture, facial expressions. You can exude confidence, appear as though you own this world. It's our mockery of those who think they do, and who exploit others.*

*We adjust our poses, click again. I blow him a kiss—he throws back his head and laughs.*

*We shoot one more.*

*Boon gets into his old Honda and drives off to his movie set in Burnaby (which is posing for Boston). I climb into my Subaru with my mops and Dyson in the back and the Holly's Help logo on the doors. As the engine warms and mist clears from my windshield, I select one of the photos. I open my @foxandcrow Instagram account (tricksters both, the fox and crow—and I have a fondness for corvids). I upload the image. I type the hashtags #meandmyhoney #earlymorninghikesbeforebreakfast #lovelife #westcoastliving #teslalove #planningnexttrip. I post the image.*

*I engage my gears and drive to my new job.*

*Little do I know as I enter the stream of traffic on the highway that, after this moment, everything will change.*

*I told you, Dear Diary—two events. Same day. Coalescing. Letting go of my mom's ashes. And . . . the new clients in a house called Rose Cottage.*

# JON

*October 17, 2019. Thursday.*
*Two weeks before the murder.*

Jon Rittenberg is in the Hunter and Hound with Henry. It's a men's kind of pub. Heavy wood paneling, dark leather upholstery, low lighting, antique-green shades. It's here that silver-haired TerraWest board member Henry J. Clay has invited Jon for drinks and an early dinner. Which by Henry's definition means top-shelf whisky and Wagyu beef.

Henry hunkers like a toad in the booth opposite Jon, aggressively carving his steak with a wooden-handled knife. The old man's meat is so rare it's almost blue. Henry lifts a chunk to his mouth but pauses his fork midair. He nods at Jon's untouched meat. "Not hungry, son?"

Jon regards the blood leaking into the potato mash on Henry's plate. He's lost his appetite. He's still struggling to digest what Henry has just told him.

"Go on, it's the best meat around." Henry reaches for his glass of fourteen-year-old Balvenie and washes his meat down.

"So there are definitely *two* of us in the running? Are you *sure*?" Jon asks. Because it doesn't make sense.

Henry laughs, takes another swig of Balvenie, and motions to the pretty young server in a low-cut top to bring another round. He dabs the corners of his mouth with his linen napkin and says, "Look, if

Labden hadn't gone and retired so suddenly, your promotion would be in the bag. You know that."

"But?"

"But things have changed, Jonno. Labden no longer holds the cards. He's handed the reins to fresher blood. I'm the only old fart still hanging in there."

A cauldron of acid begins to bubble in Jon's gut.

*This was supposed to be mine. Labden guaranteed me the COO position for the new resort when it comes online. I've put my heart and sweat into this company for years. TerraWest has traded on my name, my Olympic fame, my gold medals, for God's sake. I'm married to the founder's daughter.*

"And frankly, son, even Labden could see it was time to switch things up. Perception is everything, Jonno. TerraWest needs to be seen as making changes that keep us in pace with sentiment around the world."

"Who is he? My competition?"

"Have you considered it might be a she, not a he?"

"*Is* it a she?"

Henry laughs again. "It's a he." His eyes narrow. "You met him. At the presentation last week. Fresh off the plane from Zermatt. The new guy in the office."

"Ahmed Waheed? The guy from North *Africa*?" Jon is stunned. His mind reels back to meeting the new arrival last week. "What in the hell does Waheed know about running a ski resort?"

"A lot. He might have been born in Africa, but as a kid, he moved all over Europe with his family. His father was a diplomat. Waheed learned to ski in Italy. Speaks five languages, including Arabic. Graduated from Grenoble Ecole de Management, which, as you know, is renowned for teaching innovation in management. He's worked his way up the ski industry chain—hands on—from Kitzbühel, Val d'Isère, to Chamonix. He's also an ace snowboarder."

*"Snowboarder?"* Fuck. "Is that why he was brought into the head office? He's already been pegged for my job? Did this happen on Labden's watch, because the timing . . . It did, didn't it? My own father-in-law, who promised me this job, who lured me and Daisy back out here—he brought in someone else."

Henry sits back and swirls his drink. Coppery light dances in the liquid.

"It's goddamn deception, not perception," Jon snaps as he grabs his glass. He throws back his entire shot of whisky, wincing as it burns down his throat. "It's about political correctness. Give the brown boy the top job because he's brown. We all know it. It has nothing to do with experience and suitability for the position."

The waitress arrives with fresh drinks and a fresh smile. Fresh, dewy complexion. She reaches across the table for the empties, and Jon catches the soapy scent on her skin. He notices a tiny tattoo on the inside of her wrist. And briefly he feels incredibly old. Not old like Henry, but washed up and angry about the cards he's been dealt. The instant the waitress leaves, Jon reaches for his new drink. As he tilts back his head to take a swig, he becomes aware of a woman at the far end of the bar. Watching him.

She's a brunette. Pale skin. Long, thick, wavy hair. Her eyes meet his across the pub. Electricity crackles over his skin. She holds his gaze, and for a brief moment, they're connected by an intangible current across the busy establishment. The live music fades into a blur, and so does Henry. She's beautiful. She's interested in him. It's like old times. When he was an Olympic ski god. A golden stud. She breaks the connection and turns her head away. Jon is dropped back into reality. But his heart beats faster now. He feels a lingering zing. Then he realizes Henry is watching him.

Jon clears his throat, sips his drink, and meets Henry's eyes. And all Jon wants in this moment is to bust out of the confines of his own skin, to release this pent-up fire he tries so hard to hold inside. He craves the exhilaration, the explosion out of the start gates at the top of a mountain, the roar of the wind past his face, the clanging of cowbells as he plunges down the course. He wants that old feeling of standing on the podium, his fists held high. Number one. Golden Boy. *BergBomber.* The crowd chanting, *JonJon JonJon JonJon JonJon.* Girls clamoring to get close to him in the clubs at night. He's in a prison. Trapped. In an increasingly dull marriage. Living in a place called "Rose Cottage." A baby on the way. The shattering responsibility of somehow becoming a father. How is he supposed to do that? His own dad never figured it out. His dad busted free of his marriage shackles and abandoned Jon with his mom. Sure, his dad sent money from Europe, where he was shacking up with one young model after another, but it cost his mother. Dearly. She sought solace in the bottle, which tumbled her into a complex set of affairs that killed her in the end. *My dad killed my mom.* The only time his father called was when Jon did something amazing, like winning Olympic gold. That's when his dad wanted to say to the world, *Look, that's my boy.*

"Look—" Henry is saying. "I know you felt this was your due right now—"

"It's why we moved back," Jon says quietly as he raises his hand to call for yet another whisky. "It's why Daisy and I relocated from Colorado. It's why I slaved all those years for TerraWest at the resort in Japan. It was all in preparation for this next step."

"Times are a-changing, Jonno."

Jon sits back as the server brings more drinks and takes his plate of barely touched food. What will Daisy say? What will everyone think? It's a public humiliation. Jon has practically ordered new business cards already. He'd never have returned to this city if not for Labden's promise. Now Jon feels things closing in. Henry's eyes are boring into him. Jon refocuses and notices a wicked little glint in those eyes—mischievous and dark.

"You're . . . looking at me like it's not a done deal, Henry."

"Nothing is ever a done deal, Jon."

Jon moistens his lips. He sees the brunette watching him again. She glances quickly away, her hair falling across her profile. He feels a dissonance. The end of something. Or a beginning?

"You mean I still have a shot? Realistically?"

Henry leans forward. His tone changes. "I tell you what, lad. Never let people decide what you can and cannot have. You might not be as old as I am, but I know you, Jon. I know you well." He lets that sink in. Jon wonders if Henry is referring to a particular dark incident in his past.

"Guys like us," Henry says, "whether we want to or not, we belong in the same club, and we are under assault. Us middle-aged and older men, because we were born white, and born male. And born at a time when we were told to grow up and be a man. To 'man up.' It's an impossible situation. We need to stick together in the face of this rampant affirmative action that lauds skin color over experience." He raises his glass and points it at Jon. "You need to *take* what's yours, boy. Fight for what you want." A pause. His eyes laser deeper into Jon's, into his soul.

"Why did you even invite me here to tell me this?"

"To give you a heads-up. You'd have been blindsided." He leans closer. Jon can smell his meaty, boozy breath. "*I* wanted you for that job, Jon. But I was voted down. So now I want to give you this small window of opportunity to strategize. You used to know how to fight, *JonJon*. You used to fight dirty. You never took shit when people tried to cut you off at the knees. What did you do when they said you wouldn't make the gold? You showed them. You brought home not one medal, but *two*. Or has *BergBomber* lost his edge?"

Tension straps across Jon's chest.

Henry leans back. "Everyone has a crack. A weakness." His gaze holds Jon's. "Everyone, Jon, *everyone* has a past. Everyone has made a mistake. Everyone has a secret. A vulnerability." He pauses. "Especially young men like Ahmed Waheed." He slides a small white card across the table. "Find his."

Jon picks up the card. It displays a simple logo. PRESTON PRIVATE INVESTIGATIONS. His mobile rings on the table. It's Daisy. Jon lets it go to voice mail. How is he going to tell Daisy that her father has let them both down? He feels tricked. Baited and switched. He stares at the card.

"What's this?"

"Someone who specializes in such things. Ex-cop. Knows what he's doing. When you call, ask for Jake. Tell him Henry Clay sent you."

Henry gets up and leaves.

Jon stares at the card. The woman at the bar watches. He feels as though he's sitting on a bomb counting down, waiting to explode.

# THE MAID'S DIARY

After releasing my mom's ashes, I follow GPS directions to Rose Cottage, my new clients' house. On the passenger seat beside me is the empty urn. Ash still sticks around the rim. Bits of my mom. Somehow I've still managed to keep part of her despite my best efforts.

*Rose Cottage is in Point Grey, a high-end community west of the city, near the university, with nice beaches. The neighborhood houses many of the "one percenters" I clean for.*

*As I drive over the Burrard Bridge and glimpse the North Shore Mountains across the water, I think about the Glass House on the opposite shore. It's one of my long-standing jobs. The house belongs to Vanessa and Haruto North, and I can imagine old Beulah Brown, their neighbor, sitting in her upstairs window with her new binoculars trained on the happenings across the inlet. Maybe she's even watching the traffic as I drive over the bridge.*

*As I take the off-ramp and get closer to Rose Cottage, anticipation grows. My spirits lift. I love getting new clients. It's like a first date—you just don't know what to expect but hope to be pleasantly surprised. A new house is a new package. A fresh mystery. Full of clues that might lead to hidden secrets. What will this house tell me about the occupants? For how long will these new clients entertain and intrigue me? How vested will I become in solving their mysteries? Will they have social media accounts I can follow? Might they even be worth stalking in person? I wonder if a detective feels similarly when approaching a new crime scene.*

*I pull into the driveway and study the house. Rose Cottage is no cottage. Perhaps it was once, but now it's a completely redesigned and renovated structure. West Coast modern. Solar panels on the roof. Lots of glass and unfinished wood that is supposed to scream "I care about the environment." There's a sign stuck in the freshly laid sod on the front lawn that reads* Passive Designs Solar Heating. *My first question is: Did the occupants of "Rose Cottage" leave the sign to prove a point? Is this who they are? Wealthy with a guilt-driven narrative that screams: I care. About climate! The environment! Racism! The underclass!*

*I check the Rose Cottage worksheet on my phone. Holly has indicated the clients want service twice per week. Mondays and Fridays. A deeper clean on Mondays, after the weekend. A more superficial one on Fridays.*

*No one appears to be home. I exit my car and ring the front doorbell to be certain. (I once walked in on clients having sex. I never want to repeat the experience.)*

*Once I'm certain the place is empty, I follow the instructions on my phone to retrieve a front-door key from a lockbox. I open the door, go directly to the security panel on the wall, and punch in the listed code to disarm the security system.*

*I stand for a moment in the hallway, breathing it in. All clean lines, modern, mostly white interior with bold splashes of color and touches of rustic. From the entryway there is a view through to a lush garden. Excitement crackles through my blood. Yes, I know, I know—it's the addictive dopamine, adrenaline, serotonin—a delicious hormonal and biochemical cocktail mainlining into my veins. A salve to my whomp of grief this morning. And I grab hold of it. I allow the protection it gives me from my deeper feelings.*

*I go fetch my Dyson and other cleaning supplies from my car, change my shoes, hang up my rain jacket, and pull my cobbler apron over my head. Then I start my walk-through. (As always I remain cognizant of the potential for nanny/maid or pet cams that would require adjustments to my snooping behavior.)*

*Kitchen first.*

*It's white and black. Wine fridge. High-end espresso machine. Breakfast dishes have been left in the sink—eggy with bits of toast. Dirty coffee mugs. A half-eaten grapefruit. On the edge of the kitchen island is a piece of paper. I gravitate toward it. It's a printout of an ultrasound scan alongside a reminder note for some appointment. Something cold washes over my skin. I pick up the scan and feel a punch deep in my belly. I glance up, shocked. Although I'm not sure why. The fact that the occupants of Rose Cottage are a pregnant couple as well as wealthy enough to hire a cleaning service twice a week should not surprise me. Yet something about it burrows into my chest.*

*I regard the scan more closely. My mood shifts down another gear. I set the scan down and walk into the living room area. My eyes are drawn by the maintained garden beyond the big sliding doors. At the rear of the garden is a bushy hedge and trees. The property appears to back onto a laneway. I turn and catch sight of the two massive paintings on either side of the fireplace. And I freeze.*

*Stone cold.*

*Can't move.*

*Can't think.*

*A high-pitched shriek begins in my brain. It rises in a crescendo—like a desert sandstorm blasting against the windows of my mind, banshees screaming and scratching to get in. My feet are rooted to the wooden floorboards. My pulse begins to race. I'm going to faint. A panic attack. My body is reacting before my mind can catch up.*

*My therapist told me—when she was discussing trauma—that the body keeps the score even when the mind can't. Sometimes a person has no reasonable narrative for a traumatic event, so the conscious mind blocks it completely, trying to act as though nothing unusual occurred. But the body remembers. She explained it like this: A woman has a terrible car accident, and she saw people die horribly. The woman tries not to think about it. She tries to "get on" with life. And she does. She thinks she is fine. Months or years go by, and then she drives past the exact spot where the bloody accident occurred. And a chemical trigger is pulled. All the survival fight-or-flight hormones swamp into her body. Her neural memory is once more alive. And because the woman never developed a narrative to cope with the event, she short-circuits.*

*My body is short-circuiting, reacting to the paintings. They dominate the room. Maybe seven feet tall by four feet wide each. They depict a warrior of a ski racer in a helmet and goggles, his muscled body clad in Lycra, thighs like pistons. He's bombing down a mountain. And it feels as though he is coming down at me. In one painting his body is at a wild angle as he barely clears a slalom gate. In the other painting he's skidding to a stop in a spray of snow, one bent ski pole held high in victory.*

*I try to swallow. Try to breathe.*

*It's him.*

*I tell myself it doesn't mean I'm in his house. It doesn't mean the ultrasound baby is his. Rose Cottage could belong to anyone. Someone could have bought those paintings at an auction. The Rose Cottage couple could be ski fans.*

*I glance around in a sweat. There are several framed photographs on a bookshelf. I lurch toward them. A wedding. An engagement photo. Photos of a happy couple in settings with pyramids and lions and elephants and oceans and jungles and mountains. One after another. The same couple through the years of their life together.*

*It is him.*

*Jon Rittenberg.*

*With his wife, Daisy.*

*He's here. Back. In my city—this is my place now. He left. Long ago.*

*Yet here I am. I'm inside his house. I've been hired to clean his mess.*

*A bolt strikes me. I whirl around to face the kitchen. The scan on the counter—Jon Rittenberg has a baby on the way.*

*My hands fist at my sides, nails cutting into my palms. My vision blurs. I'm shaking. All this time. All the new life that I have worked so hard to build over the past years—new friends, a measure of peace. Happiness finally. And suddenly I'm back as though nothing at all has happened in between.*

*My stomach heaves, catching me by surprise. I run for the downstairs bathroom. I retch into the toilet bowl. I sink down to the cool tiles, and holding on to the bowl, I throw up again.*

*First my mom's ashes. Then this.*

*Two things.*

*Triggers pulled.*

*I've dropped through that trapdoor, Dear Diary. And everything has changed. I am inside Jon Rittenberg's house . . . and I have a key.*

# MAL

*November 1, 2019. Friday.*

Mal and Benoit knock on the front door of Beulah Brown's house.

The knife missing from the block in the Northview kitchen was found at the bottom of the infinity pool. It's being sent to the lab along with the other trace evidence. Mal has also tasked local uniforms with a canvass of the neighborhood. She hopes to find additional witnesses. Her team at the station is working to locate homeowners Vanessa and Haruto North. They'll gather for a briefing later this afternoon, when they have a better idea what they're dealing with.

Benoit knocks again, louder. Ivy grows thick around the door. The entryway is dark and gloomy compared to the starkness of the glass structure next door.

A man with a pale, round face opens the door. "Yeah?" He holds on to the knob, unsmiling.

"I'm Sergeant Mallory Van Alst, and this is my partner, Corporal Benoit Salumu." They show their IDs. "We're investigating the incident that a Beulah Brown from this address called in. We'd like to have a word with her."

"My mother? She dials 911 at least once a month since she's been on opioid medication. She's got end-stage cancer. She imagines all sorts of things. Noises in our house. She sees stalkers in the garden, lights in the bushes at night, boaters spying at us from the water. The local cops send officers, and I have to wake up and explain to them that nothing's going on. They take a look anyway, because they never trust the guy who answers the door and says everything's fine, right? But same result each time—nothing apart from a stray cat or raccoon in the garbage, or an old bum collecting cans from the recycling bins." He doesn't move his position at the door. He holds it against his body so Mal can't see inside.

She keeps her features neutral. "And your name, sir?"

"Horton. Horton Brown. This is my house. Well, it's my mother's, but I live here."

"Can we come in? I understand from dispatch that Mrs. Brown is confined upstairs."

He exhales heavily and steps back, allowing them entry. Mal exchanges a quick glance with Benoit. He gives a small nod and says, "Mr. Brown, I have some questions for you, too. Shall we talk down here in the living room while Sergeant Van Alst goes up to chat with your mother?"

He grunts and leads Benoit into a living room furnished with overstuffed chairs upholstered in a cabbage rose print. Crocheted doilies hanging over the backs. Clearly Horton's mother's furniture. A dirty-looking Maltese follows Horton, nails clicking on the wooden floor.

Mallory climbs the steps, wondering how often Beulah Brown manages to get downstairs, if at all.

She reaches a landing with a small window that looks out toward the sea. A door stands ajar.

"Mrs. Brown?" Mal knocks on the open door. "This is Sergeant Mallory Van Alst. I've come to talk to you about the 911 call you made."

"Come in." The voice is thin.

Mallory enters a large room. It's equipped with a hospital bed, an oxygen compressor, a wheelchair, a comfortable-looking sofa, and reading chairs. A bathroom leads off the room, and a small kitchenette has been installed along the rear wall. The front windows face the sea. The corner window has a clear view of the house and driveway next door. French doors lead onto a small balcony. At least she can get out, thinks Mal.

Beulah Brown sits dwarfed in a wingback facing the ocean. Her legs are swollen and propped up on an ottoman. A crocheted throw covers her lap. A flask, a teacup, cookies, and a pair of binoculars rest on the small round table at her side.

"I didn't think anyone would come," the old woman says.

Mal detects a faint British accent.

"They all think I'm a nutter, you know? Come closer. Take a seat. Would you like some tea? You'll need to fetch yourself a cup from the kitchen cupboard first, but I have some extra in my flask. It's still hot."

"I'm fine, thanks."

"Sit, then, sit. Please. It's so nice to have the company."

Mal seats herself on an overstuffed chair. "Nice view," she says. She can see her boiler-suited techs busy by the pool, and she can see into the part of the living room where the coffee table is upturned. Movements are also visible in the upstairs windows. Police tape flutters across the driveway.

"Yes, it's a marvelous view. Horton bought me binoculars two weeks ago so I can see to the other side of the Burrard. I can sometimes see the sailors on the tankers in the bay. They come from all around the world, you know. Today is a twelve-tanker day. Just look at them all waiting to go into the harbor."

Mal looks. The water sparkles. "You also have a good view of the house next door and the driveway, too."

Beulah pulls a wry mouth, but her rheumy eyes light up. "I'm too old and too far gone to pretend I don't turn my scopes on the neighbors." She leans forward and lowers her thin voice in a conspiratorial way. "Between you and me, that is. And the binoculars make it so much nicer. My spectacles were failing me as it was."

Mal smiles. "Do you get downstairs much?"

Beulah's features change. She glances away. Then quietly she says, "Horton . . . he means well. He did buy me the binoculars."

Mal opens her notebook. She clicks her pen. "You reported hearing screams early this morning, Mrs. Brown. Can you tell me in your own words what you saw and heard?"

"Beulah. Please call me Beulah. Something woke me at 11:21 p.m. I lay there awhile and I'm sure I heard it again. A woman's scream."

Mal makes a note in her pad. "You seem very certain of the time."

"Well, yes. I keep a log now."

Mal glances up. "A log?"

"Like a journal. A recording of everything I see. Out in the garden. On the water. Next door. Along the little seawall path in front of my property. Sometimes a yacht docks in the bay, and I watch the people on board having their sundowners, and I write it all down—what time they anchored and sailed off. Which stand-up paddleboarders go past, and when. I started a few weeks ago because Horton kept telling me I was misremembering and mis-seeing things. He said I was forgetting my medication and that I needed to take more pills. I began to worry he might be right. Or that I might be taking the wrong pills, because the days just started blurring one into the next. So now I write down which pills I take, and when. And I write the names of all my carers and nurses. I also record how often I go to the loo." She chuckles. "Otherwise they make me try again. Getting old and sick is not for the meek, I tell you." She hesitates, coughs. "It's such hard work sometimes I wonder if it's worth fighting to stay alive."

Mal feels a clutch in her chest. "I'm sorry to hear that, Beulah."

"Calling 911 does offer some respite, though."

Mal wonders again how reliable this witness will prove to be. "About what you saw—"

"Pass me those reading spectacles," Beulah says abruptly as she reaches for her notebook.

Mal hands the glasses to her, and Beulah perches them on her nose. She opens her book, runs a gnarled finger down the text on the page. "I'll start from when I believe it began yesterday. At six fourteen p.m., Thursday, October 31—that's Halloween. We never used to celebrate Halloween when I was a girl. We—"

"Go on. What happened at six fourteen p.m.?"

"The Glass House got visitors—that's what everyone in the neighborhood calls Northview: the Glass House."

"What visitors?"

"A couple in a dark-gray Audi. It pulled into the driveway at six fourteen p.m. At six fifteen p.m. the couple exited the Audi. The male was tall, well built, sandy-brown hair. The female was a brunette. Long wavy hair."

"Very precise—sounds like a police report, Beulah."

"Oh, I love detective and mystery stories, Sergeant. Watch them on all the streaming channels. I mean, what else am I to do? The British ones mostly. And I always used to read mysteries as a little girl in Yorkshire." A wistful look deepens the old woman's wrinkles. "One time I thought I might try to write my own. About a lady detective. One should follow one's heart, you know, because before you realize it, your time on this earth is done and you're at death's door."

Mal gently steers her back, a sense of urgency tightening. The first forty-eight hours of a homicide investigation are critical. Success could hinge on this old woman's statement. But Mal can also see that rushing this old witness might backfire and have the opposite effect.

"Can you tell me anything else about this couple, Beulah?"

She consults her notes. "Well, the man was maybe forty years old. The woman a bit younger. She was very pregnant."

Mal's gaze narrows sharply. "Pregnant?"

"Yes, like Vanessa North is."

"Vanessa North—the homeowner—is also pregnant?"

"She's certainly showing now. I saw Vanessa last Friday. It was the first time I saw that brunette as well. The two of them had a late lunch by the pool. It was very clear they're both pregnant."

Mal's pulse quickens. She thinks of all the blood, the signs of violence. Urgency bites harder. "Beulah, this couple who visited yesterday, were they carrying anything?"

Beulah consults her log. "Flowers. Mostly white. And something like a cake box. It looked like they were arriving as dinner guests."

Mal makes another note. "What happened next?"

"I don't know. My carer came, then it was dinner and bathing time, and I was put into bed, and I . . . I must have passed out with the medication. But I woke all hot and bothered in the dark. It was raining, and I realized a scream woke me. I managed to get into my chair and roll to the window. And that's when I saw."

"Saw what, Beulah?"

"All the lights were on next door—it was a great glowing box of glass. Even the pool light was on. Kind of a haunting, glowing green. The living room doors were wide open in spite of the rain, and the coffee table was upturned. Then I saw them, the couple, dressed in black rain gear, and they were tugging something heavy rolled up in that white carpet from the living room. Tugging it alongside the pool toward the yard gate. I know it was the carpet because when I looked with my binoculars this morning, it was gone. They dragged the carpet through the gate into the driveway. The motion sensor went on. It lit the rain up. It was also very foggy out."

"Go on, Beulah. What happened next?"

"Well, they struggled quite a bit. That carpet looked heavy, and she was awkward because of her pregnant belly, but they got it into the back seat of the car. The Audi, not the other one."

Frustration nips at Mal. "What *other* car?"

"The little yellow one. The maid's Subaru with the Holly's Help sign on the doors. The maid arrived earlier that morning. But her Subaru was still parked in the driveway when the couple arrived in the Audi. I assumed the maid was helping with catering, or waiting to clean up after dinner."

"Could you tell if it was the woman from the Audi dragging the rug, or if it was Vanessa North, the homeowner?"

Beulah frowns. "I'm not sure which one. I wasn't wearing my spectacles, and her head was covered by the hood of a voluminous raincoat. But I assumed it was the brunette, because she got into the Audi."

"And the maid didn't appear again?"

"No. After the carpet was put into the Audi, both cars sped away. Didn't even pause at the stop sign at the end of the lane. You can see the sign from my corner window. The tires squealed, and they just sped right off into the darkness and fog. I was worried they would hit some trick-or-treaters, but I guess all the kids were in bed by that hour."

"Did you see any movement in the house after that?"

"No. But I was also busy trying to call 911, and my phone was over there by my bed."

"Can you describe the maid?"

"Late twenties or maybe thirty. About the same age as my cousin's granddaughter. She's dead, my cousin. She died last month."

"I'm sorry for your loss, Beulah. What was the maid wearing? What color is her hair?"

"Blonde. She's pretty. I've seen her face through my binoculars. She always waves when she sees me. Sweet girl. She wears the Holly's Help uniform—blue drawstring pants with a pink shirt. She wears her hair up in two little buns, like cat's ears. Jaunty-looking. And she always wears a choker." Beulah frowns. "Maybe it's the hairstyle that makes me think she is younger, but she is perky like young people are. Peppy walk." She reaches for her teacup. Her hands shake. She seems tired as she takes a slow sip of tea that must surely be cold by now. Her eyes water.

A little more gently, Mal asks, "Did you happen to see what shoes the maid was wearing yesterday?"

"Oh yes. White running shoes with an orange streak on each side." Beulah takes another wobbly sip of tea, then carefully sets the cup into its saucer. "Horton has spoken to the maid before. I saw them talking over the garden fence once. I asked if he knew her name." She pauses. A strange look enters her eyes. "He says it's Kit."

# THE MAID'S DIARY

I splash cold water over my face in the little bathroom downstairs in Rose Cottage and stare at my eyes in the mirror. They judge me. And I argue with myself—all the sides of myself. All my internal voices that have been rudely shocked into life and are clamoring to be heard one over another, louder, louder:

> *"Quit this client while you still can. Call Holly right now, tell her."*
>
> *"But imagine what you could find in here. All the dark secrets the Rittenbergs might hide. You have the key, girl. You know how to disarm the security system. Rose Cottage is your freaking OYSTER, girl. It will keep you occupied for months."*
>
> *"Are you fucking serious? This is bad news, Kit. You need to step away. STAT."*
>
> *"This will destroy you. This will push you way over the line of no return. This is you in destructive mode, Kit. This is next level."*
>
> *"Oh, come on, it'll be fun! When did you last clean a celebrity athlete's home?"*
>
> *"What would your therapist say? She'd say you need help. This is not normal."*
>
> *"Who cares about normal? What in the hell is normal anyway? Normal is overrated."*

*I listen to all the voices, and I hear a certain tone begin-*
*ning to dominate the cautious, scaredy-cat Kit. The bold,*
*brash Kit is winning. I pat my face dry, stand erect, shoulders*
*squared, and I take in a deep and steadying breath. I reach*
*into my apron pocket for my tube of hot-pink lipstick. I always*
*keep a bright lipstick in my pocket. It's my armor. I lean*
*forward into my reflection and carefully reapply the bright*
*splash of fun and aggressively feminine color. I smack my lips*
*together. There. I study my work. I approve of the look—sort*
*of cute, playful, but a weaponized femininity. I'm sure my*
*therapist has big thoughts about this. I smooth wisps of hair*
*back from my face, pop a stick of cinnamon gum into my*
*mouth, and begin to chew. Chewing always helps channel my*
*adrenaline, hones my focus.*

*I check my watch—barely enough time for a quick walk-*
*through before I must start cleaning in earnest. I set the timer*
*on my watch.*

*Studiously avoiding the brash paintings of "BergBomber"*
*in the living room, I hurry upstairs. There are four spacious*
*bedrooms and an office. The first two bedrooms—queen*
*beds. Appear to be guest rooms, unused. The office—Jon*
*Rittenberg's. A man cave. Framed black-and-white photos of*
*craggy mountains. Bookshelves with nonfiction works penned*
*by the "survivors" of extreme pursuits. Conquerors of peaks,*
*oceans, and jungles. Plenty of self-help books—how to be bet-*
*ter, bigger, stronger, how to make people listen to you. Low-*
*carb and "keto" diet books—"build more muscle," "maintain*
*a strong physique." A Peloton with a large monitor and spin*
*shoes hanging on the back. Yoga mat. Weights. It all screams*
*of an aging Olympian going soft around the middle, losing his*
*edge, and worrying about it. This fills me with a sadistic spurt*
*of pleasure. I touch the glass desk with its iMac and a massive*

*curved monitor. I get the sense Daisy and Jon Rittenberg have not been in this house long. It all feels very newly moved into.*

*I start to exit the office but stop as one of the mountain photos snags my attention. I recognize the crags. It's one of the peaks that looms over the village I grew up in. A small, world-class ski community two hours north of the city to which my parents immigrated because the resort municipality offered my father a job. My dad was a sanitation engineer. He worked at the wastewater treatment plant that treated the town's sewage. A darkness clouds my mind. I start to hear the taunting, sing-songy voices of the kids at my school: "Katarina Poop-ovich's father works at the poo plant. Hey, Turd-ovich, what's your dog's name—Stinky?" I hear the roar of mocking laughter. The old pain and anxiety crunch through my chest. Suddenly I feel fat and pimply again. My eyes flood with tears. My mom would hug me when I came home from school crying. She would stroke my hair and tell me I was beautiful, and God I miss her so much.*

*I hurriedly exit the room and slam the door shut, locking the laughing, jeering rich-bitch kids inside. Those kids whose houses my mother cleaned, whose beds she made, whose clothes she put away.*

*I move to the main bedroom. It's done in soft shades of gray. Big windows that allow a beautiful slant of light. There's a walk-in closet and en suite bathroom. With one eye on my ticking timer, I enter, absorbing the atmosphere of the room. I stare at the king-size bed. Slowly I walk up to a bedside table with a box of tissues and a book.*

*I pick up the book. It's the story behind the making of a reality show about rich housewives. This must be Daisy's side. My gaze goes to Jon's side. This is where they make love, and babies.*

*A hardness coalesces in my core.*

*I imagine my therapist's voice: "Why, Kit? Why do you feel these things? Why are you doing this? Write why, why, why until you fall through the trapdoor into something new."*

*I don't need to ask. I know why.*

*I'm already through the trapdoor. All I see are dark warrens burrowing farther down into shadows, deeper into crypts filled with fun house mirrors that bounce back my reflection in a thousand kaleidoscopic ways. In one mirror I see fat, sad teenage Katarina Poop-ovich. I'd managed to forget about her for a while. She's back now quite clearly.*

*I see the Katarina who got good grades. A noise begins in my head as Katarina drops out of high school and blurs into smoke. Then I see Kit the maid, who has great friends and a contented life, cleaning homes because there's no pressure to perform and she can be invisible. I see Kit on a stage under bright lights with her amateur theater group, acting countless parts, wearing masks, being characters other than herself and completely at ease with that. I see her on the streets in the summer doing improv, engaging audiences with interactive theater art, blowing balloons for kids . . . and there are glimpses of other Kits and Kats . . . I can't see those properly. They slip from mirror to misshapen mirror, sliding deeper into the tunnel shadows—darting, watching, whispering at the edges of my consciousness.*

*I shake myself, clearing all the Kit-Kats from my head before entering the bathroom. Quickly, I open and close the cabinets, scanning cosmetics and medicines. I see anxiety meds. Uppers. Downers. There's quite a bit here for me to come back to. My timer sounds. My pulse quickens. I must start cleaning.*

*I hasten to the last room, open the door, and freeze.*

*It's the baby's room.*

*I enter cautiously, run my hand along the edge of the waiting crib. There is a little stuffy bear inside. A strange emotion fills me. Above the crib hangs a musical mobile of pastel circus elephants and unicorns. I turn the music on. The elephants and unicorns begin to twirl to a tinkling lullaby that makes me think of little cottages in dark woods and lost girls in red riding hoods seeking grandmas and finding wolves. While the eerie music plays and the elephants and unicorns dance, I go to the dresser and smooth my palm over the changing table. This room sucks my energy. It suffocates my breathing.*

*I'll come back another time.*

*Dear Diary, if I read this entry to my therapist, I know she'll ask if I want—or wanted—kids. Maybe I'll tell her I was pregnant once. And that I can't have them now. That my uterus was damaged the first time round followed by an infection. Maybe I'll explain how that happened. I might even tell her it's why my fledgling marriage crashed before it could even take off. Or . . . maybe I won't.*

*I go downstairs and carefully examine the ultrasound scan once more.*

*Maybe if I clean this house fast enough today, I'll have just enough time to run back upstairs and pose for a selfie in front of the dancing elephants and unicorns while holding this scan in front of my tummy.*

*#surprise       #babyontheway       #wearesothrilled #meandmyhoney*

*I'll post it on my #foxandcrow account. My secret joke. Laughing in the face of all the other false narratives out there.*

*This gives me a jolt of pure pleasure. I start the vacuum cleaner.*

# JON

*October 17, 2019. Thursday.*
*Two weeks before the murder.*

Jon sits in the booth at the Hunter and Hound, staring at the business card Henry left.

He's shaken. He feels a climbing rope has been cut, a belay partner has deceived him. He's falling, falling, the noise in the wind rushing past his ears. He hears the chant *JonJon JonJon JonJon* as he spirals down.

*Has BergBomber lost his edge—*

"Sir?"

He jumps, and his gaze shoots up to the server who interrupted him.

"I didn't mean to startle you," she says, placing a fresh whisky and a coaster in front of him. "It's from the woman at the bar."

Jon glances across the room. The sultry brunette is still there. She raises her martini glass, smiles.

Confused, then immediately flattered, Jon lifts the gifted drink in reciprocity. He hesitates, then makes a motion with his hand and mouths the words: *Would you like to join me?*

She shakes her head. Smiles warmly, then turns her back to him.

Curiosity piqued, Jon sips, watching her. Then he gets up, weaves his way through the growing throngs of patrons to the bar counter.

He's forced to sandwich himself between the occupied barstool on his left and the brunette herself on his right, which brings him up close. Very close. She smells good. Music goes louder—the live act has come onstage, an Irish fiddling duo.

"Thank you," he says.

Her lips curve. Deep-red lipstick. Big green eyes. She's as attractive up close as from afar.

"You didn't need to come over," she says.

"Felt rude not to."

"I'm sorry—the drink wasn't a solicitation. Perhaps it was a miscalculation on my part."

She has a slight accent. Very faint. He's not sure what it is. German? Maybe a touch of Dutch, or even French. Intrigue deepens, and something in his body that is instinctive and primal begins to stir.

"So why then?" he asks. "I looked like I needed a boost?"

"Do you?"

He huffs. "Maybe. Probably. Yeah."

She gives a self-deprecating laugh. "I felt bad for staring. You looked so insanely familiar that I was trying to place you, and you caught me," she says. "I was utterly convinced I knew you. You know that sensation? When you run into a TV star who's been on the screen inside your home so often that they seem like a friend, and you're hit with this bolt of instant familiarity? You *know* them, but you don't. Then it struck me. You're downhill ski champ Jon Rittenberg." She grins, raises her martini glass. "Here's to the BergBomber. I was a ski groupie once, a million years ago. I was in Salt Lake City for the '02 games. I was a spectator in the crowd when you won that first gold. My God, it was electric, just being part of that. I also saw your earlier accident at the Alpine Cup. It was devastating. We all thought you'd never walk again, let alone ski *and* come back to win two gold medals. So forgive me for staring." She takes a sip from her glass. He watches her lips. "The drink was just my way of saying thanks. For the spectacular skiing and giving us something to root for."

Jon is galvanized. He feels like he did when he was in his late teens and early twenties and on the ski circuit. This woman *sees* the hero in him. She *knows* him, is proud to have reveled in a part of his athletic life. She is *thankful*. This woman has plugged Jon directly into a magnetic current, and he feels that vestigial part of himself rising. It's intoxicating. He's *alive* again.

She angles her head, holds his gaze, and he has to lean closer to hear her speak as the music from the band goes louder. "To tell you the truth, Jon," she says, "I'd forgotten all about the BergBomber, until I saw you in that booth. Here's to glory days."

He pulls a wry mouth, his body so close now their arms are touching. "Sounds like a sad old Springsteen song."

"Yet here we are."

"You a skier yourself?"

His phone vibrates in his pocket. Daisy again. Jon can't face talking to Daisy right now. He'd have to confront the falsity of all the reasons they moved here. He feels anger at her, too. And something a little more sinister needles into him—could she have known? Daisy is very close to her parents, her mother especially. Why would they *not* have told their daughter that this move back home might come to naught? Unless . . . maybe he's been set up. Maybe the Wentworths wanted Daisy home before they cut him loose. His heart begins to pound.

"I am."

"What?" Jon asks.

"A skier. You asked if I was a skier."

"Right, yes. Are you local? I detect an accent."

"I'm originally from Belgium. I live in Switzerland now. I come and go for business here."

"What sort of business?"

She falls silent. Her eyes appraise him.

"Apologies. I . . . I don't even know your name, and here I am asking what business you're in."

"It's okay. I'm Mia. I'm a banker."

Impressed, Jon holds his hand out. "Pleased to meet you, Mia-the-banker."

She laughs and places her hand in his. It's slender, and her skin is soft and smooth and cool. Her nails are deep red. They match her lips. He notices no ring on her ring finger. And she has noticed him noticing. She withdraws her hand.

"Does Mia have a last name?"

She hesitates again. And Jon quickly dials it back.

"No worries," he says. "We can leave it there." But now he really wants to know. He wants to know everything about Mia the sultry banker who has awakened the beast in him that had begun to shrivel with time and complacency and the mundane.

"I should go." She finishes her drink and begins to slide off her barstool.

"Do you—ah—would you like to join me for one more? In the booth—it's so noisy here, so close to the band."

She checks her watch and Jon's heart sinks a little.

"I—okay. Just a quick one. I have an early start tomorrow."

Instantly buzzy again, Jon hurriedly orders two more drinks. They relocate to the booth. Mia is easy to be with. She flatters him in all the right places. She talks about ski racing and the ski industry with knowledge. He feels a kinship as well as sexual arousal.

She says her last name is Reiter. Mia Reiter.

He tells her he's still with TerraWest.

"It's a good fit for a skier, the ski resort business." She laughs. He laughs, too, leans closer.

"Was that a business colleague you were with earlier?" she asks.

"Henry? Yeah, one of the old toads. He goes way back with Labden Wentworth."

"Your meeting looked intense."

He gives a shrug. "He wanted to give me a heads-up about some job competition."

"Serious competition?"

"It's nothing I can't take care of."

She regards him intensely, then says, "Labden Wentworth's resort business has grown into an international powerhouse with global impact. Their latest quarterly report shows summer visits are booming. In some TerraWest resorts they're now outpacing winter visits."

"Thanks to the mountain biking."

Her gaze locks with his. "Industry magazines also tell me you're married to his daughter."

Daisy's face floats into Jon's mind. He's instantly reminded of the joy he felt while holding her hand and watching their baby boy moving on the ultrasound monitor. What in the hell is he doing here? He glances at his watch, his heart beating faster.

Mia notices him checking the time, and her features change. "Of course, I—you know, I really didn't mean to monopolize you like this. I should go. I need to call it a night." She reaches for her purse and begins to slide out of the booth.

"Thank you for the chat, Mia," he says. "I needed that."

She stills. "Needed what exactly?"

Jon's phone vibrates again.

Mia exits the booth.

His phone continues to vibrate. Tension coils in his chest. Before he can reconsider, he blurts, "Wait. Don't leave just yet. I need to take this. Give me a moment?"

She hesitates, then reseats herself. He connects the call.

"Hey, hon," Daisy says immediately. "Is everything okay? I was worried about you."

He holds up two fingers to Mia, mouths, *Two minutes.* "I'm fine. Let me take this somewhere quieter. Hang on a sec."

Jon scoots out of the booth. Pressing his phone against his shirt, he hurriedly weaves through the crowd, making for the quieter lobby area outside the pub. He puts the phone back to his ear.

"Sorry, love. I should've called. Just as Henry left the pub, some of the guys from work came in. They're all talking about the new development. One of the environmental assessors is with them. I figured I should connect with him, build some contacts. He's still here. Could be a late one. You okay with that? I can come home now if—"

"No. No—I—it's fine. How'd it go with Henry?"

Jon says it went fine. Daisy presses and he says he will explain at home. He tells her not to wait up. But before he can kill the call, Mia enters the lobby.

"Jon, I really do need to be up early," Mia says quietly. "Thank you for everything. It was a lovely evening." She walks past him, out the hotel doors, and into the autumn night.

Jon ends his call, pockets his phone, and rushes to the doors. "Mia!" he calls after her.

She stops on the sidewalk, turns. Streetlight glints on her hair. She looks at him expectantly.

Suddenly he feels awkward. He slides his hands into his pant pockets.

"I—good night," he says. "Thanks."

They stand there for a moment. Facing each other. Man and woman. A chemistry crackling between them. They're on a knife's edge—either they act on their desire, turn it into something. Or walk away. Jon does not act.

Mia comes quickly forward. She puts her mouth near his ear and whispers, "Bye, JonJon Rittenberg. I'm pleased to have met you. Finally. In the flesh. After all these years." She gives him a feather of a kiss on the cheek, turns, and walks away.

"Fuck," he mumbles under his breath as he stands in the cool night, watching her go—the seductive sway of her hips. Those high, sexy heels.

The swish of her long hair on her back. He's hard with lust. He's sweating, breathing heavily. She disappears around the corner of a building, and is gone.

He swallows, slowly becoming conscious of the city sounds. Of reality. And he says a silent thanks to whatever gods rule the universe, because he's just been saved from making a terrible mistake. He turns and reenters the pub. He did the right thing, holding back. This knowledge gives him a little burst of self-satisfaction. But as he returns to his table to collect the bill, he sees a napkin with a smudge of deep-red lipstick. It's a Schrödinger's-type conundrum, he thinks. He simultaneously wants and does not want to see Mia Reiter again.

Jon considers folding the napkin and sliding it into his pocket. But he leaves it and goes up to the bar to settle his tab.

"The lady paid already," the bartender says as Jon fishes in his wallet for his credit card.

He glances up from his wallet. "I was going to settle for the earlier steak meals and whiskies as well," he says.

"Like I said, she settled it."

"The *whole* thing—the two steak meals and drinks?"

"Whole thing."

He starts to leave, stops. "Did she pay by credit card—leave an address or anything?"

"Nice try, buddy. She paid cash."

# THE PHOTOGRAPHER

Jon Rittenberg appears to have no idea he's being watched from a vehicle across the street as he converses with the brunette outside the hotel entrance.

The watcher in the car raises his camera and aims his telephoto lens out the open window. He adjusts focus to ensure that he's capturing the name of the hotel above the entrance as well as Rittenberg and the woman.

*Click. Click. Click.*

The brunette steps forward and kisses Rittenberg on the cheek. The photographer clicks again.

The brunette turns and starts down the sidewalk, moving with the flair and sophisticated ease so often displayed by women on the streets of Milan. Or Paris. The photographer smiles as he watches Rittenberg watching her go.

Instead of following the brunette, Rittenberg reenters the hotel lobby.

The watcher clicks again, capturing Rittenberg's entrance.

The photographer lowers his camera, wondering if things might have ended very differently tonight if Rittenberg had gone after the brunette. She appeared to be leaving him an opening. He didn't take it.

# MAL

It's late afternoon when Mal and Benoit gather with the rest of their major crimes unit. Seated around a boardroom table in the incident room with them are two other investigators, Arnav Patel and Jack Duff; admin officer Lula Griffith; and Gavin Oliver, an affiant who deals with search warrant applications and case documentation. While her core team is small, Mal has at her disposal the forensic ident unit, uniformed officers from various PDs, analysts, and tech support. She can ramp up or down at a moment's notice.

As the lead investigator Mal sits at the head of the table with a laptop in front of her, a monitor behind her. The room is overly warm, and someone has brought pizza. The scent of pepperoni, garlic, and melting cheese is cloying. Mal is keen to get out of here and back into the field.

"Okay, we don't have conclusive evidence that we're dealing with a homicide, but we're working on the assumption we are. So let's move fast here." She hits a key on her computer. An image of the Glass House fills the screen behind her.

"So far we have signs of a violent struggle and a serious blood-letting event at a luxury West Vancouver waterfront home known as

Northview, or the Glass House. The incident was called in by neighbor Beulah Brown—a senior in her late eighties—who claims she was woken by a woman's scream at 11:21 p.m. last night. Brown takes opioids and other meds for palliative reasons. We must take into consideration that her testimony may not be entirely reliable, although she does log events as they occur in her day, specifically to aid her memory."

Mal hits another key. An image of the driveway and neighboring house fills the screen.

"Brown's corner window is on the second floor of her home up here." Mal points. "She's able to look down on this driveway here. She says a cleaner from Holly's Help arrived yesterday morning and parked a yellow Subaru Crosstrek there." She points with her pen. "The Subaru has the Holly's Help logo on both front doors." She pulls up an example of the logo.

"The maid's car was still parked in the driveway when a dark-gray Audi sedan pulled in behind it at six fourteen p.m., according to Brown's log. A male and a female—late thirties to early forties—exited the Audi. Brown reports that the female was heavily pregnant, a brunette. Long wavy hair. The male was tall, well built, sandy-brown hair. The female was carrying a bunch of white flowers and what looked like a cake box."

Mal brings up an image of the wilting flowers lying on the concrete in front of the door next to the smashed and oozing pie box. "The flowers and pie appear to have been dropped here, outside the front door. This bouquet contained a card from someone called 'Daisy.'" Mal hits a key. An image fills the screen. "This was written inside the card."

*Good luck before autonomy dies, friend. It's been a ride.*

*Thanks for the support.*

## Daisy

## X

"The card is embossed at the bottom with a logo—Bea's Blooms, a florist in Point Grey. The pie comes from the Pi Bistro, also in Point Grey."

Arnav says, "So, this 'Daisy' picks up the flowers and a berry pie in Point Grey, then drives with the male in the Audi to the Glass House. They arrive just after six p.m. Maybe for dinner? The pie is dessert? Maybe this couple lives in the Point Grey area."

"Benoit and I will visit the florist and bistro after this briefing," Mal says as she moves her mouse and clicks open more files. Images of the front door and the bloodied living room flare to life on the screen.

"No signs of forced entry," she says. "No victim found at the scene. No one home. Front and back doors were left wide open in spite of cold and rainy weather. All the lights on, shades open, and the home CCTV system was disabled, so there's no record of the events." She consults her notes. "Owners of the house are Haruto and Vanessa North. Neither of the Norths have been located, although two vehicles registered to the Norths are both still parked in the garage."

Mal describes to her team what she and Benoit found in the interior. As she talks, she brings corresponding images up onto the screen, including the drag marks, blood spatter, upturned furniture, bloodied statue found in the bedroom, the bloody sneaker and sock located near the bed, the carving knife from the bottom of the infinity pool, the diamond pendant found on the sofa.

The next image Mal displays is of a blonde woman in her early thirties.

"Benoit, want to take it from here?"

Benoit leans forward. His is a commanding presence, and the energy in the room shifts toward him. "Brown claims she saw a couple in rain gear dragging what could have been the rolled-up rug missing from that living room. The couple put the rug into the Audi, on the rear seat. One person got into the Audi, the other into the Holly's Help Subaru. Both vehicles left the Glass House at speed." He points at the image of the blonde woman.

"This is Kit Darling," he says. "The maid Beulah Brown saw arriving that morning. The photo was provided by Darling's employer, Holly McGuire, owner-operator of the cleaning service Holly's Help."

Everyone in the room falls still as they study the image.

Darling is attractive in an unconventional way. A mischievous look in her eyes, a slight smile on her lips—as though she finds something secretly amusing. She wears bright-pink lipstick, big false lashes. Her fine blonde hair is done up in untidy space buns. Around her throat is a black velvet choker.

Benoit says, "McGuire told our officers Darling is a valued, trusted, and longtime employee. She's worked for the cleaning service for eight years. She's been doing a basic twice-weekly cleaning at the Glass House for just over six months. McGuire confirmed Darling drives a yellow Subaru Crosstrek with the Holly's Help logos on the side doors. According to McGuire, Darling did not check in at the end of her shifts yesterday, and did not show up for a company Halloween gathering yesterday evening." Benoit studies the image of Kit Darling for a moment.

"Darling's listed emergency contact is her closest friend, Boon-mee Saelim. McGuire says she phoned Saelim, and he had not heard from Darling, either. She's not answering her phone, either. Saelim went to her apartment. She's not there. Neither is her Subaru. Saelim has already tried filing a missing person report."

"Not looking good for Kit Darling," Jack says.

"Or the others," Lula says. "We've still not located Vanessa and Haruto North, or the mystery couple with the Audi, and so far we have two pregnant women unaccounted for." She pauses. "We have unborn babies in possible jeopardy."

Mal says, "Arnav, can you start on socials? Anything we can find on Kit Darling, her friends, comments, any indication of her recent movements, or her plans leading up to last night."

The investigator nods. "On it."

Mal turns to Jack. "How are we doing with other witnesses and CCTV? Did any cams pick up the Audi and Subaru in the vicinity as they sped from the scene?"

Jack says, "The door-to-door yielded one additional witness, who was on the corner of the lane, walking his dog around midnight. He saw two vehicles matching the description of the Audi and Subaru. As per Beulah Brown's statement, he says the vehicles did not stop at the stop sign. He heard tires squeal as both vehicles turned east onto Marine Drive. We've got techs combing through Marine Drive cam footage, plus footage from the bridge cams. If the vehicles headed east on Marine, there are a few options—either they turned off Marine and went into a residential area, and are now lying low somewhere on the North Shore. Or they headed all the way east toward Deep Cove area, or they crossed one of the two bridges over the Burrard into the city."

Benoit says, "Take a close look at the Lions Gate Bridge cams. If this Audi comes from Point Grey, there's a chance it might have headed back that way."

"Or not," says Jack. "Maybe they went to dump their rug somewhere first."

"Okay," Mal says. "Let's get moving with what we've got. We need to locate those vehicles. We need IDs on our mystery couple. We need to find the Norths. And we need everything and anything on the missing maid, Kit Darling. We've got a lot of mileage to put in today still.

We'll reconvene here at six a.m. sharp tomorrow. Hopefully forensics will have some preliminary results, and we'll know more about what we're dealing with."

She meets the gaze of each of her team members. "Given the blood loss and type of spatter, our victim is either critically injured or we're looking for a body. Lula, can you get someone to check hospital ERs?" Mal assigns other tasks, checks her watch. "Let's go. Clock is ticking."

# THE MAID'S DIARY

Holly called me right after my Rose Cottage shift yesterday. It was a sign. A window of opportunity to beg out of the Rittenberg contract before I got sucked in too deep. But I froze. I couldn't make myself ask. So I said nothing as she inquired whether I could squeeze in some extra shifts over these next few days for another maid who'd called in sick. I agreed. It would keep me busy and stop me from googling Jon and Daisy Rittenberg. Stop me from scanning for their accounts on social media. Buy me time to still back out. Because the smart Kit would. The wise Kit knows no good can possibly come of poking about in the Rittenberg house.

*Today was thus super busy with back-to-back work. I'm home now. Exhausted. And I must leave for the theater in an hour—our nonprofit troupe has been staging a production of The Three Lives of Mary. I play the role of Mary. We have two more nights in our eight-week run. Tomorrow is final curtain call. After that, Mary goes dark. So I will be quick with my journaling before I leave.*

*Now you know, Dear Diary, about my snooping issues. But who doesn't have issues, right? If my therapist insists on calling mine an addiction, then I'm a "high functioning" addict, because I hide it well. Outwardly the rest of my life is pretty fun, to be honest. My hobby—my passion—is amateur theater. Improv, immersive acting, pop-up performances "in the wild," puppetry, mime—I enjoy it all. I also love dressing up to attend drag shows with Boon. It's the pageantry, the costumes, the imagined narrative, that I love. I can be anyone while still being Anonymous Girl, the invisible cleaner who rifles through your drawers. The ghost in your house.*

*Boon and I have a tight group of friends. We're all part of the same amateur theater troupe. We act together, socialize together, and meet regularly to play Dungeons & Dragons. D&D is also about role-playing. So there you go—I see what you're doing again, Dear Diary. You're showing me that even my happy social life, the "normal" part of me, hides behind roles, masks, theatrical characters. It's me being the ghost. It's me journaling on these pages because my therapist wants to know why I need so badly to remain the ghost.*

*But what I really want to tell you, Dear Diary, is I am proud of myself. I have managed so far to not google the Rittenbergs. I have not trawled social media in search of their accounts. And I can still tell Holly I need to back out.*

*I am still in control.*

*I check my watch.*

*I need to leave. Mary is waiting. The play is about a young woman who gets to make a pivotal life choice three times over. Each time she chooses differently. Each choice spins her life into a vastly different direction. In one life Mary chooses to keep a baby from an unwanted pregnancy, and she marries the father. In another she kicks the man to the curb, terminates the pregnancy, and becomes a powerful businesswoman. In another she's a freewheeling, single-mom bohemian. Each life comes with its own unique battles and triumphs.*

*Before I go, I quickly check my @foxandcrow Instagram account. I pull up my most recent post. A "reel" of me standing in the baby's room at Rose Cottage, holding Daisy and Jon's ultrasound scan in front of my tummy. I'm smiling. The elephants and unicorns dance in a circle behind me. The tinny music sounds like background for some horror show. I've added a filter that makes it look both innocent and darkly spooky. #babyontheway #lifechoices #whichlifedidshechoose*

*Already 207 hearts. People love my post. The comment section is filled with congratulations and smiley faces and more hearts. I have no idea who these people are who have decided to follow some arbitrary false narrative in the name of @foxandcrow, but they are happy for me.*

*Usually this makes me happy, too.*

*But today it leaves me oddly hollow.*

*I've created in myself a longing.*

*Sometimes life direction is not a choice. It's imposed on us. Against our will.*

*But what if, years later, we get an opportunity to redress that? Like Mary. We choose a different path.*

# DAISY

*October 18, 2019. Friday.*
*Thirteen days before the murder.*

Daisy holds her smartphone up high, angles her head, smiles, and clicks. Shifting her position, she clicks again. She's searching for a perfect image for her daily @JustDaisyDaily Instagram selfie. For the next shot she tries to capture in the background the people fishing along the Stanley Park seawall. They sit with buckets at their sides, dangling lines into rocky pools. As she clicks, Daisy considers potential hashtags:

> #SeaWalkFishermen   #StanleyParkMorning   #Sunny-
> Break #PregnantMomsNeedExercise

She likes to capitalize the first letter of each word in her tags. Uppercasing helps visually impaired screen readers, as well as Instagrammers who struggle to identify patterns and relationships between words. Someone with dyslexia, perhaps, or some other cognitive disability. Or so she's been told. Her goal with her social media account is to demonstrate that she's warm and inclusive. Culturally aware. Her narrative—the story Daisy so very carefully curates—has to land just right.

No, #SeaWalkFishermen doesn't work because there's a female fishing, too, with a child at her side. #FishersFolk? That doesn't sit well with Daisy, either. The people fishing all appear to be of Asian cultural descent. #Folk might infer that she sees them as an inferior grouping. She decides on:

#Fishers #RareSunnyDayInPacificNorthwest #GladToBe-BackInMulticulturalVancouver #PregnantMumsNeedExercise #BidingTimeTillBistroLunch

Daisy shoots a few more selfies capturing her tummy. She also takes a shot of the shimmering skyscrapers that rise high above Coal Harbour, where seaplanes come and go. Jon works on the top floor of one of those glass towers, sitting at his desk like a golden god in sunlight, surveying the ocean, mountains, and ski slopes across the Burrard. Daisy is tempted to use hashtags that declare:

#JonsOffice #Penthouse #TerraWest #SkiLife #Married-ToAnOlympian #DoubleGoldMan

But she'd never do that. Jon abhors her Instagram habit. He says it invites trouble. He particularly dislikes the fact that Daisy is becoming something of an influencer and that she's being sent items from top companies catering to pregnant moms. Last week she received the cutest musical crib mobile with dancing unicorns and elephants. The week before a package arrived at Rose Cottage with the sexiest yoga leggings designed to accommodate growing bellies.

Jon thought the leggings were amazing until she told him she was going to pose in them for Instagram. He said "gifts" in exchange for publicity are demeaning. He said they were beneath her.

*We don't need handouts, Daisy. It makes us look needy. It makes it look like I am a failure and can't take care of my own wife. It makes us look poor, for God's sake.*

Daisy lowers her camera, her gaze still fixed on the shining office tower where her husband works. His voice curls through her mind.

*The only reason you even have a following of so many thousands is because you're my wife. You openly exploited that association in the early days of your social media account. And you know it's dangerous, Daisy. It's not like we haven't had nutjobs stalking us before. Anyone can use geolocation to pinpoint exactly where you are and when you're there. If you post a photo of yourself in a restaurant as you sit down, by the time your order shows up, so can your stalker.*

Daisy shakes the memory, but Jon's chastising tone lingers like a cold, tight thing in her chest. Her thoughts turn to last night, when Jon came home reeking of alcohol.

He climbed quietly into bed in the dark, obviously thinking she was asleep. But she wasn't. She'd been lying there for hours fretting over whether she dreamed the female voice on Jon's phone. It didn't help that she was already worried Jon might be finding her newly chunky body unsexy. He hasn't tried to make love to her in a while. Daisy replays, blow by blow, her interaction with Jon this morning as he came down for breakfast.

*"So what did Henry want to talk to you about?"* she asks as she pours a fresh coffee for him.

*There's a tightness in his face, a guardedness in his eyes. Worry trickles through Daisy.*

*"Jon?"*

*He inhales, rubs his brow. He's hungover, she thinks. Surely that's all it is.*

*"Jon, please. Talk to me. Why did Henry invite you to dinner?"*

"*Something came up at the last board meeting. Henry wanted to discuss it with me in confidence. He felt I should have a heads-up.*" He accepts the mug of coffee from her, sips, and when he speaks again, his words are quick. "*He said I'm not a shoo-in for the new COO position.*"

"*What?*"

"*There's a competitor.*"

"*I don't understand. What do you mean 'competitor'?*"

Jon sets down his mug. He begins to straighten his tie. Tension rolls off him in waves.

"*Jon! Talk to me.*"

"*Did you already know this, Daisy?*"

"*Know what? What on earth are you talking about?*"

"*That TerraWest has hired someone new, and he's already been brought into the HQ office, and they're pegging him as the new COO for the Claquoosh Resort. Did your father or mother not mention it?*"

"*Of course not. I wouldn't keep something like that from you.*"

"*Wouldn't you? I mean, maybe it was all part of the plan, Daisy—you and your parents tricking me into moving back home. Just like you stopped taking those birth control pills.*"

"*How dare you—*"

"*Forget it. I'm sorry. I didn't mean that.*"

Hot tears fill her eyes. "*What did you mean, then? You think I tricked you into getting pregnant? And then tricked you into moving home? Why would I do that? You said this is what you wanted. A baby, a family. A fresh start. After that . . . that nightmare in Colorado.*"

He sinks onto the counter stool. His shoulders slump. He rubs his face hard. "*Forgive me. It was a shock last night. I'm sorry. I—I'm still trying to process, Daize.*" He glances up, meets her eyes. "*I think it's a done deal. I think this other guy is getting the position.*"

Daisy stares at her husband. Her world spins. "*Who is this person?*"

"*Ahmed Waheed. Some guy much younger. Less experience.*"

"*Why would TerraWest do this? What's wrong with you as the—*"

"What's wrong *with me? I'll tell you what's wrong, Daisy. This Waheed guy is brown and I'm white—I'm a white guy nearing middle age and times have changed and everyone needs the optics of diversity. I peaked at the wrong fucking time. I fucking missed my slot. I've been usurped by this . . . this new wave of political correctness.*"

"Jon, that's not—"

"Isn't it? I won two goddamn gold medals for this country. Skiing runs through my veins. I was born right here—" He jabs his fingers hard on the countertop. "Right on the flanks of these North Shore Mountains, in this very city where TerraWest was born. I was iconic. My name carried weight in this industry. It was monetized. My face and body could sell anything from beer and aftershave to toothpaste, time-shares, and lifestyles. The company—your family company—traded off my fame, off me. They've cashed in, and now they reckon I'm washed up because I'm not brown and don't speak five fucking languages.*"

"Don't swear in this house, and don't you dare bring my family into this. My father had a heart attack and he was forced to retire. This is not his decision. I bet it was decided after he retired and stepped away.*"

"You know what that would mean, then? That your dad—and maybe Henry—are the only ones at TerraWest who wanted me in that COO job? Is that what you're saying? That everyone just leaped to cut me loose the instant Labden walked out that door?*"

"Have you considered that maybe this Waheed guy is a better fit?*"

"Are you serious? Did you just say that?*"

"Jonnie—"

"Don't 'Jonnie' me."

"I'm just saying, five languages? He sounds impressive, and given TerraWest's renewed push into the global market, it could be that—*"

"That they need a Muslim? He's a bloody Muslim, and now they think they can check off a box.*"

Anger tightens her throat. "Well, is he Muslim?*"

"Probably."

*"See? You're jumping to conclusions. You know nothing about this guy, do you?"*

*"And you do? Christ, Daisy. I thought at least I'd have your support. I—I need to go."* He shoves himself off the stool and moves toward the entryway.

*"Please don't walk out on me like this."*

*"I'm late."* He reaches into the hall closet for his jacket.

*"What about breakfast? I went to some trouble. Please sit, eat something."*

He shoots a glance at her pretty spread of eggs, toast, marmalade, juice, and ruby red grapefruit on the table. She even cut fresh flowers from the garden. Colors of fall. Oranges and yellows with sprigs of green foliage.

*"That's for Instagram, not me,"* he snaps as he punches his arms into his jacket sleeves.

*"That's not fair."*

*"Oh, tell me you haven't already shot and posted photos of that breakfast on social media."* He grabs his briefcase.

Daisy is shaking inside. Filled with anger, fear, and a fierce drive to calm her husband down, placate him, fix this. Make all the nastiness go away.

*"Right,"* he says curtly. *"It's already on Instagram."* He reaches for the front-door handle.

*"Do you want me to speak to Dad?"* she calls after him as he steps out the door. *"Do you want me to call him? See if he can sort this out?"*

Her husband mutters something under his breath and bangs the door shut behind him. Daisy stares at the door. She hears Jon's Audi starting up in the driveway.

Tears slide down her cheeks.

◆　◆　◆

Sun glints off the glass tower, and Daisy is suddenly sparked back to the present. She realizes her eyes are filled with tears again. She swipes them quickly away and checks her watch. Relief floods her. It's almost time to meet Vanessa at their favorite little bistro in Point Grey. Daisy begins walking back to her car. She drove to the park for some exercise by the sea, and to get out of the house while the maid came. She often meets with Vanessa on maid day.

As she crosses a lawn, she tells herself Jon didn't mean to wound her. He spoke from his own place of hurt. A place of damaged pride, defensiveness. A visceral concern over their now-uncertain future. She knows her husband well. Too well. She's intimately acquainted with the dark, angry corners of his warrior psyche. They're the same attributes that helped him win at a competitive and dangerous sport against fierce and dedicated athletes from around the world. One didn't come without the other. And right now Jon doesn't have a physical outlet. She will speak to her father. Surely he'll be able to do something. She won't tell Jon. It'll just humiliate him further. A wife needs to keep some secrets from her husband.

As she beeps the lock on her little BMW, a more sinister thought snakes into her mind.

Could Jon have been overplaying his anger this morning to distract her from the fact he'd been with a woman last night?

Again, Daisy shoves the twisted thought from her mind. She climbs into her car, pulls the seat belt across her round tummy, and starts the engine. But before pulling out, she quickly scrolls through the fresh batch of selfies on her photo roll.

She selects one and uploads it. She types in her hashtags and smiles to herself as she notices how she captured the sunlight sparking off the diamond pendant that hangs just below the hollow of her throat. A gift from Jon to celebrate their pregnancy. She sets her phone on the passenger seat and engages the gears.

*We're going to be fine, Little Baby Bean. We all are. This is just a blip. Challenges make life worthwhile. The only consistent thing is change.*

As she is about to reverse out of her parking space, her phone pings. And again. And again. Responses to her Instagram post. Daisy cannot resist taking a quick peek. She craves the dopamine hit. Those little hearts of approval, the validation. She needs it. She grabs her phone, does a fast scroll through the comments:

> OMG how do you look so good?
> What's your secret? Spill, girl!
> Love that jacket!
> Awesome photo.
> Love love love Vancouver.
> A month and a half to go! We're counting down with you.

A contented, connected feeling swells through Daisy's body. Her followers adore her photo. They approve of her life. Of her. She feels less alone. Less overweight. Less unattractive.

> Can't wait to see more preggers pics.

Another comment pops through. It stops Daisy in her tracks.

> You're nothing but the wife of the once-famous, washed-up JonJon Rittenberg.

Then another.
> I SEE you @JustDaisyDaily. I KNOW WHO YOU ARE. Ticktock watch the clock. It's followed by two googly eyes oscillating back and forth, followed by an exploding bomb.

Another pings through.

Hope your baby dies. DIEDIEDIEDIE little Rittenberg
boy.

Her hand covers her mouth. She blinks. Then before she can even think, she deletes the awful comments. She notices a direct message has come through. She's scared to look. Her hands tremble as she opens it.

It's a GIF of a Chucky doll. Chucky clutches a knife. Chucky is covered in scars and blood. Chucky makes repeated stabbing motions with the blade—up down up down up down. The GIF is followed by text.

Chucky knows who Bad Mommy iz.

Chucky knows what Bad Mommy didz.

Die die die die Baby Bean die.

# THE MAID'S DIARY

Last night was curtain call for *The Three Lives of Mary*. I will no longer wear the costumes of Mary, or be her in her different lives. I feel oddly empty. I should've gone out with the others to celebrate, but I asked Boon to tell them I was unwell. I came home alone instead. I know he's worried about me. He has been since we scattered my mom's ashes. He senses something. I haven't told him about the new clients, though. He knows nothing about Rose Cottage. My silence says a lot—ordinarily Boon and I share pretty much everything about our lives. So what does this say, Dear Diary? I already know from my snooping that what people choose to hide from others tells you the most about them.

> *I did try to speak to Holly yesterday when I went into the office to collect my pay. She was busy. I lost my conviction and walked out.*
>
> *Which means I am off to the Rittenbergs' home today. I have missed my window to back out. I am now committed.*
>
> *I wake up extra early, take some scraps out of the fridge to feed Morbid, the one-legged crow who visits me on my balcony, then I plop onto my sofa, peel open a red lollipop, stick it into my mouth, and fire up my iPad.*
>
> *I have two hours before I must be at Rose Cottage.*
>
> *I start with Facebook.*

*I can't find an account for either Jon or Daisy Rittenberg. I open Instagram and search for "Daisy Rittenberg." Guess what? "Daisy" plus "Rittenberg" is apparently a rare combo—try searching it yourself. Only two names pop up. The first is definitely not my Rose Cottage Daisy. The second is. While she has registered her account using her real name, she goes by the handle @JustDaisyDaily.*

*Sucking on my lollipop, I scroll quickly past the more recent posts (I'll return to those later) until I come to a photo taken in Colorado. It shows Jon and Daisy Rittenberg sitting at a rustic picnic table on a massive wooden deck. They're in the alpine, surrounded by snowcapped peaks and blue sky. A sign behind them says "Silver Aspens Ski Resort." They both have deep tans. Both wear sunglasses. Beer bottles beading with droplets stand in front of them. They're dressed in ski gear. I peer very closely at Jon.*

*He resembles a caricature of the athlete he once was. Softened in body, yet his complexion has coarsened. His face seems larger, a little puffy. Lines bracket his mouth. I can't see his eyes behind the shades.*

*I study the caption.*

A day in the mountains with my guy. Spring snow. Fast skiing.
#Perks #SkiIndustryLife #CanadiansInColorado #ColoradoDays #InteriorDesignerLife #BestRunsOfTheSeason

*My emotions slide into some dark, dank place. The world around me fades.*

*I go through post after post. Going backward in time. Beautiful Daisy doing this. Beautiful Daisy doing that. At yoga. Out with the girls. Wine night. Painting night. Book club. Shopping and lunch. New shoes. A trip to Denver. Visiting vineyards. Glorious meals. More vacations in far-flung places across the globe. India, Australia, a safari in Botswana, and a trip down the Nile.*

*A buzz grows loud inside my head. I've always longed to travel. Ever since I was eight, when I saw a show on the Knowledge Network about the Serengeti and all those animals. I wanted to go to Kenya. The Galápagos. The Amazon. Indonesia. I always thought I would. All around the world. Not just to Nicaragua with Boon's film crew when I got a part as an extra.*

*But this dream was before I dropped out of school. My dreams became out of my reach for all sorts of complicated reasons that I prefer to not dwell on.*

*But here—Daisy and Jon, Rose Cottage, their little baby on the way—it's cracking open that heavy old chest with the secret longings that I have buried deep in my soul. I can feel the contents rising, unfurling slowly inside me. Like a visceral ooze seeping up from the bottom of a lake, because with the rising dreams comes a slimy detritus—things I don't want to see. Or feel.*

*I scroll more. Faster, sucking on my lollipop more urgently.*

#ColoradoDays #BabyNews! #NewJobForJon #Going-Home #VancouverHereWeCome #FarewellParties #MovingDay!
#BackHomeInVanouver #NewHouse #RoseCottage #Revis-itingWhistler #SpringSkiing #JonsOldStompingGround

*I learn from Daisy's account she joined a mom's yoga group.*

#PrenatalYogaForMomsInThePark

*I learn she loves #ThePiBistro. She's posted photos of tarts she bought there. Another photo shows Daisy and a pregnant girlfriend lunching at the bistro.*

#DiscoveredGreatNewPlace #FewBlocksAway #DangerousForMyWaistline #HungryAllTheTime

*I feel ill.*

*I stop because I need a breath. I know it's fake. No one's life is that perfect. It's a curated illusion. Smoke and mirrors. Misdirection. Just like my @foxandcrow account. I'm letting this get to me.*

*But here's another thing about reality and perception. Like Mary in my play, when you choose your Story, you're in fact also choosing your life. We are—or we become—what we pretend to be, so we must be very careful who we pretend to be.*

*I check the time. I have a few more minutes before I must get into my uniform.*

*I open a browser and search for "Jon Rittenberg" "Colorado" "Silver Aspens Ski Resort."*

*Articles from the local Colorado newspapers pop up. The older articles mention that Silver Aspens, a TerraWest property, has a new operations manager—gold medalist Jon Rittenberg. There are stories quoting Jon about the state of the industry. A clip where Jon tells a reporter that after his wins at Salt Lake he had a ski run named after him at Whistler, where he used to train and where his team had a lodge. He tells the journalist he considers Whistler his "home" mountain.*

*A black cloud descends over me.*

*I remember the day they named that run.*

*I find more articles. About Jon leaving his post at Silver Aspens to take up an interim position at TerraWest HQ in Vancouver. The article says it is rumored that Jon Rittenberg is being groomed for the chief operating officer position at Claquoosh Resort, a brand-new "property" TerraWest is developing in the mountains north of Whistler.*

*I search more, going deeper. And bam. Another headline jumps out. I go dead still.*

*It's dated almost a year ago.*

Famous ski racer and operations manager of Silver Aspens Ski Resort Jon Rittenberg and his wife, Daisy Rittenberg, are claiming to be victims of an alleged stalker. A female in her 30s has been arrested in connection with the allegations. The woman—a dancer and server at Club Crimson—is also formally accusing Jon Rittenberg of sexual assault after Rittenberg and a group of his friends allegedly spent a night at the club. The dancer claims she is now pregnant with Rittenberg's child. The woman was arrested while hiding in bushes outside the windows of the Rittenbergs' mountainside mansion. She alleges Rittenberg ruined her life, which is why she became obsessed with following him and his wife. The woman claims she intended no physical harm to either Rittenberg or his wife . . .

*My pulse quickens. I scroll faster. According to another article, the dancer's name is Charlotte Waters. Her friends call her Charley. There's a photo. She's blonde. Thin. Sort of worn-looking. Sad eyes. I read further.*

*"It never happened," Rittenberg said.*
*The words blare like a Klaxon through my brain.*

"The woman is a cheap liar," said Tom Gunn, a male friend who was with Rittenberg at Club Crimson on the night in question. "She's an opportunist. Show me the proof that she's pregnant, because I don't believe it. She just wants money. She's crazy in the head."

*I find another article.*

Police confirm charges have been dropped in the alleged Rittenberg stalker case. Lawyers for Jon Rittenberg say Charlotte Waters has also withdrawn her accusations of sexual assault against Jon Rittenberg.

"I am sorry," she said in a written statement provided by her legal counsel. "I erred in judgment. I was never assaulted. I was never pregnant. I deeply regret any harm that I might have caused the Rittenberg family."

Waters is now subject to a restraining order and has agreed to seek therapy. Rittenberg's lawyer says his client will not be pursuing any further recourse.

"We wish her well and we hope she gets the help she needs," Jon Rittenberg said in a written statement. Rittenberg told the *Silver Aspens Times* that he feels sorry for Waters.

"I don't understand what happened in her life that drove her to do this. But I was accused of something that never happened. It can wreck lives."

*My watch timer chimes and I jump. I'm breathing so fast I am dizzy. I blink. I feel as though I'm resurfacing through a wormhole. Hurriedly, I save the links to the articles. And I save the "alleged" stalker's name in my brain.*

*Charlotte "Charley" Waters.*

# DAISY

*October 18, 2019. Friday.*
*Thirteen days before the murder.*

Daisy seats herself at a rustic table in front of the street window at the Pi Bistro. Her leg jiggles. Her hands twitch. Her back is against the wall and she faces the door. She feels more secure with the wall behind her. From here she can watch everyone inside and also see anyone approaching along the sidewalk.

Jon's warning snakes through her brain.

*You* know *it's dangerous . . . Anyone can use geolocation to pinpoint exactly where you are and when you're there. If you post a photo of yourself in a restaurant as you sit down, by the time your order shows up, so can your stalker.*

She should call Jon. She should tell him about the shocking comments on her Instagram post. But she can't. Not now. Not after the Chucky GIF.

> Chucky knows who Bad Mommy iz. Chucky knows
> what Bad Mommy didz.

She cannot let Jon know about Chucky. That was—is—her secret. Her dark secret. Wives on occasion need to do certain things in order to keep their marriages intact, to keep their lives on track.

Besides, if she mentions terrible comments even in a generic context, he'll insist she shut the account down. Daisy can't bear shutting off her Instagram space. What would she have left? She'd have no daily connection, no love, hearts, validation. She needs it all so badly just to keep going. Her life would be so empty. Lonely. Why can't she be more like the old schoolgirl-teen Daisy? What happened to that strong, snarky Daisy? Her mind loops back to the condescending bitch in the $6.7 million condo. Daisy wants that feeling back—that sense of sticking in the knife and twisting just so.

The bistro doorbell jangles, and she jumps. A group of young people enters. Flushed and joyous with bright fall scarves and windblown hair. Their exuberance is unnerving. Like the dead leaves skittering along the sidewalk are unnerving. Where's Vanessa? She checks her watch. Vanessa should be here by now.

Daisy flicks her gaze over the other patrons again. They sit close, talking animatedly, intimately. Some laughing. Drinking their pumpkin spice lattes and eating harvest soups with fragrant fresh bread. One man sits alone with a newspaper. Daisy eyes him. Fear rises in her belly.

*I'm safe here. I did not post that I was coming here to the bistro. Did I?*
She opens her Instagram account again and checks her recent post.

#BidingTimeTillBistroLunch

Panic flicks through Daisy. She did mention it. Anyone following her account would already know she loves the Pi Bistro, which is near Rose Cottage. How could she be so stupid? Hurriedly, she deletes her morning selfie completely.

The bell over the door jingles again. Vanessa breezes in with a rush of cool air from outside. She smiles broadly. Her cheeks are pink.

Relief cuts through Daisy like a knife. As usual Vanessa is perfectly presented. Her long hair has been blown out—brown with honey highlights. Her dress fits, which is more than Daisy can say about her own clothes at the moment—even her special pregnancy clothes. Vanessa wears boots with small heels—no hastily bought discount sneakers for her. Daisy makes a mental note to go shopping for comfortable boots so she can throw the hideous sneakers away.

"Sorry I'm late," Vanessa says as she unwinds her scarf and slides into the chair opposite Daisy. Her hazel eyes are bright, but as Vanessa settles into her chair, her eyes narrow. "Are you okay, Daisy? You look— is everything all right with the baby? Did the scan and doctor's appointment go okay?"

Daisy smooths down her hair, fighting the urge to blurt everything out to her friend. "I'm good." She forces a shaky smile.

But Vanessa's gaze lasers into Daisy's. "Are you sure?"

Daisy nods.

"You ordered yet?"

"I—I was waiting for you first." Daisy secretes her phone under the napkin at her side as she speaks. Vanessa watches Daisy's hand, then her eyes meet Daisy's again.

"I was thinking about trying the butternut soup special," Vanessa says.

"Yes, yeah, that's fine with me. Soup," Daisy says.

Vanessa regards her. "Are you certain you're feeling okay?"

"Fine," she snaps. Then quickly she dials it back. "I'm hungry, I guess." She feigns a laugh. "Or hangry, I should say. My mood dips if I don't eat on schedule."

Vanessa motions for a server. They place their orders and Daisy asks for a glass of water. As soon as the server retreats, Vanessa leans forward, lowers her husky voice, and says, "Okay. Spill. What's the matter? Is it the baby? Because I can see something is going on."

Daisy glances out the window as she clasps her hand around the diamond pendant at her throat. She desperately racks her brain for an excuse for her jittery behavior. Instead, something crumples inside her chest, and she cannot hold it in any longer.

"I feel like I'm losing my mind," she says, meeting her friend's warm gaze. "I'm this crazy roller coaster of emotions. One second I'm sky high, next I'm at the bottom of despair. I feel nervous, scared, even paranoid. And so forgetful—my memory is totally screwed. I can't regulate my own body temperature. I'm craving food all the time. I feel fat. My skin's breaking out. I feel ugly." Emotion blurs her vision. "Look at me. I can't control a damn thing. I'm going to sit here bawling into my harvest soup."

Vanessa covers Daisy's hand with her own. "It's okay. It's *normal*, Daisy."

"Not for you. Christ, look at you. You're—"

"Oh, believe me, I'm having my moments. I even spoke to my ob-gyn about it. She told me that during pregnancy and postpartum periods, a lot of women experience at least some degree of cognitive change. Colloquially it's known as 'pregnancy brain.' My ob-gyn said the most common symptoms are forgetfulness, memory disturbances, poor concentration, increased absentmindedness, difficulty reading and concentrating. Pregnancy can even make you fearful, or paranoid. She gave me some material to read. I can pass it on if you like."

They sit back in their chairs as the server arrives and places the soup bowls and glasses of water in front of them. When the waitress leaves, Vanessa says, "My doc tells me it's the body's way of preparing for motherhood, for nesting, becoming biologically primed to protect your baby at the exclusion of everything else in the world. You become afraid of things that you were not scared of before—to keep yourself and your baby safe." She laughs. "Pregnancy can literally make you a stupid, fearful beeotch."

Daisy smiles halfheartedly and picks up her soup spoon.

"Don't worry so much," Vanessa says, taking a sip of water. "It'll pass—it'll all pass."

"I don't know." Daisy stirs her soup. She glances up. "I think I'm being watched, followed. I'm pretty sure I am."

"What?"

She's done it—she's said the quiet part out loud; now she has no choice but to follow through. She inhales deeply. "Someone has been watching our house from the lane behind our yard. And while we were at yoga the other day, there was this guy in black lurking up on the sidewalk."

"I didn't see him."

"Well, I did, and I'm sure he was watching us—me. And I . . . I've had some weird text messages via my apps—texts from unknown numbers that disappear. And—"

"Disappear?"

She can see the doubt in her friend's face.

"Yeah, you know those self-destruct texts? You can program them to vanish after a set time. And then today, for the first time, I got a bunch of really horrendous—threatening—comments on my Insta post."

"What did they say?"

"They said they wanted my baby to die."

Vanessa goes pale. "Can I see them?"

"I—I deleted them. Right away. Just reflexively killed them all on the spot. And a DM with a horrible GIF."

"So you don't have any way of finding out which account sent them?"

"Not unless the account sends them again. I know, I should have kept them. For proof. If I need to go to the police or something."

"You have *nothing*?"

"No."

"What did the comments say, exactly?"

"That I am nothing but the wife of a washed-up ski racer. Another that said they 'see' me—as though they're watching everything I do."

"You need to go into your settings, Daisy, and disable the comments," Vanessa says. "And make your account private."

Daisy's chest constricts at the idea of cutting off all the love and approval. "It's not just online. Someone stuck a physical note on my windshield that referenced my Instagram account handle—whoever is doing this is in this city. They *knew* I would be staging a condo downtown."

Vanessa stares. "My God," she whispers. "You need to report this, Daisy. You need to go to the police."

Daisy inhales deeply, looks away. At all the faces passing the window. Anonymous faces. Could be any one of those faces. She has more than eight thousand followers now, and whoever posted the comments doesn't even need to be a follower.

"How can I go to the police? Just walk into some station with nothing to show them?"

"You have the note from your car, right?"

I SEE YOU @JUSTDAISYDAILY.
I KNOW WHO YOU ARE . . .

Daisy feels as though she's going to throw up. She doesn't want police asking too many questions about what she might have done to incur this.

"Look," Vanessa says, "there will always be trolls. If you put yourself out there, someone, for whatever reason, is going to have a go. The more followers, the bigger you are, the more someone wants to tear you down, cut you to size. It's just the human way. And the anonymity of social media makes it possible. It's like being behind the wheel in a car. People do things in a car they'd never do up close face-to-face. Social media is road rage on steroids." She scoops up a spoonful of orange soup and delivers it to her mouth. "Have you considered getting rid of the account? Getting off social media altogether, now that you're having a baby? I mean, a lot of people never post about their kids. On principle. To keep them safe."

"It shouldn't have to be like this," she snaps. "There are tons of pro-files out there—mothers-to-be, moms with tots. They discuss pregnancy issues, postpartum stuff, breastfeeding challenges, support groups, baby decor. Gorgeous baby clothes. Family issues. Recipes. Postpartum diet and exercise. Why should motherhood be a threatening, scary, danger-ous thing? I refuse—" She realizes with a shock that giving it up is not on the table. Not at all. Not even for a minute. And she's furious that some asshole out there has forced her into this corner. More quietly, she says, "I refuse to be intimidated. I will *not* run away."

Vanessa's lips curve into a slow smile.

"Seriously, fuck them." Daisy stabs her spoon into her bowl of chunky harvest soup. *Jabbity jabbity jab like Chucky with the knife.*

Vanessa's smile broadens. "There's a girl. You go, Mom."

Daisy nods, heart hammering, still uneasy, but firm now.

"Have you told Jon about these comments?"

"No. He doesn't like me being in cyberspace on principle. He'll just tell me to kill the account."

"Men," says Vanessa.

"Yeah," says Daisy. She eats her soup, feeling better already. She makes small talk with Vanessa. They laugh about one of the other moms at yoga, talk about a favorite boutique, and critique an amazing new restaurant that opened downtown. Daisy begins to feel as though she just imagined the whole thing.

"How about you?" she asks Vanessa. "How come you don't have a social media presence?"

"Oh, I did have," Vanessa says, "but I killed all my profiles about a year ago and went cold turkey."

"Because you were planning a family?"

Vanessa inhales, sets down her spoon, dabs her mouth carefully with her napkin. In a very measured fashion, she says, "I told you that Haruto works in cybersecurity, right? Well, he got a new contract with a company based out of Singapore. It's a secretive government thing, and Haruto was concerned that if someone found his wife's social media profile, it could be used to . . . compromise his work. And it could risk our safety. I don't know. We just decided it was better."

Daisy crooks up her brows, suddenly distracted from her own cyber trolls. "Risk your safety? You mean like . . . kidnapping or something?"

Vanessa shrugs.

"So Haruto is, like, in government intelligence, or counterintelligence—is that what he does?"

"Something like that."

Now Daisy is super interested. "So Haruto wanted you off social media?"

Vanessa's cheeks heat. She looks embarrassed. This only intrigues Daisy further.

"What *exactly* does Haruto do?" she asks.

With a wave of her hand, Vanessa says, "I'm sorry, but it's not something I can really talk about. God, look at my bowl. I've eaten everything. Do you want dessert?"

Daisy returns her attention to her bowl and realizes she needs to pee. Like right now. It's another irritating symptom of her pregnancy. She excuses herself and hurries to the bathroom. When she returns, she sees her phone is no longer hidden beneath the napkin, where she's sure she left it. It's on the other side of the table, facedown.

As she reseats herself, she regards Vanessa, then picks up her phone and slips it into her purse.

"The server took the plates," Vanessa says. "I wasn't sure if you wanted more."

*That's probably what happened—the waitress moved my phone.*

As Daisy is about to suggest ordering a slice of her favorite pie, a man in a coat appears outside the window. He stops right by their table and peers into the window. Vanessa gasps. Daisy's gaze shoots to her friend.

"What is it?"

"Haruto," she whispers. Her cheeks go bright red and she hurriedly digs in her purse, finds her wallet. She slaps a wad of cash on the table. "I didn't realize what the time was. I—I agreed to meet him down the street after our lunch." She pushes back her chair, but before she can get to her feet, the door swings open with a blast of chill air, and a sturdy Asian-looking man steps into the bistro. He glowers at Vanessa.

The man is not that tall, but he's built, and he has a presence that seems to shrink the space around him. It certainly shrivels the gorgeous, streamlined Vanessa, who is suddenly flustered, almost panicky, and definitely no longer streamlined.

The man approaches their table. Vanessa, half-risen to her feet, says, "Haruto. I didn't expect—"

"Have you lost track of the time again?" British accent. Curt voice. Emotionless face.

"I—I was just on my way. This is my friend Daisy Rittenberg, the one I was telling you about from the Yoga Mom's yoga class?"

Haruto gives Daisy a dismissive nod, then takes hold of his wife's arm. It's not a gentle touch. His grasp is firm, and it forces her fully up from her chair.

Shock seizes Daisy's heart.

"Nice to meet you, Daisy," Haruto says. "Vanessa, come. Let's go."

Vanessa shoots Daisy a desperate, embarrassed look. "I'm so sorry, Daisy. I—I really need to go." She gives a light laugh that comes out more of a choke. "That pregnancy brain—I *completely* forgot what time I told Haruto I'd be done."

Her husband ushers her to the door and out into the windy day. The door swings shut. Riveted, Daisy watches them through the window. Haruto steers his wife across the street and down the opposite sidewalk beneath the turning trees. Daisy realizes her mouth is open, and she shuts it.

Vanessa—so self-assured, so poised, cool, and collected—crumbled in that man's presence.

A bitter taste leaches into Daisy's mouth. She doesn't like the feeling of recognition. She glimpsed something of herself in Vanessa in that moment her husband walked in the door. Daisy knows exactly how it feels to be confronted with an angry, coercive, and strong husband.

Maybe that's what happened to snarky teen Daisy, the confident schoolgirl. She's been slowly eroded over time by her own marriage. Daisy thought she was in control of the relationship. But maybe she's not. Maybe she never was. Maybe her increasing isolation from family and friends blinded her to what she was becoming. Perhaps her campaign to convince Jon that a baby and a move home would fix them as a couple was misguided. Or even a subconscious cry for help, safety.

A little warning bell begins to clang in her head.

# DAISY

After paying for her and Vanessa's lunches and saying hello to Ty Binty—the bistro owner—who popped out from the bakery, Daisy shrugs into her coat and walks down the sidewalk to where she has parked her little white BMW. She goes in the opposite direction to the way Vanessa and Haruto went, and the couple weighs heavily on her mind as she walks. She keeps replaying Haruto's arrival, and their departure. The way Haruto manhandled his wife. Her fear. Daisy did not anticipate that her sleek and beautifully pregnant friend might live in a scared and dark shadow. Vanessa might not be sleek and controlled at all. Appearances can be so deceptive.

Daisy decides she's worried for her friend.

Perhaps she should swing by Vanessa's house one of these days. Arrive unannounced. Because not only is Daisy worried, she's also insatiably curious. She reaches her BMW, the autumn wind flicking her hair about her face. Daisy beeps her lock and climbs into her safe, buttery-leather cocoon. As she starts her car, she sees it. A note. On her passenger seat.

WELL, HELLO, DAISY.

It's *inside* her car.

Her heart begins to slam against her rib cage.

It's inside her *locked* car.

Her phone pings. She jumps and grabs it. A WhatsApp text appears. It's from an unfamiliar number. A roaring noise begins in her brain. With trembling hands, she opens the message.

It's another GIF. Chucky with blood on his knife. With the GIF are the words:

Chucky's INSIDE now.

Ticktock

Quicker goes the clock.

# MAL

*November 1, 2019. Friday.*

"You know what they never show on TV?" Benoit asks as he feeds their unmarked vehicle into the stop-start congestion on Lions Gate Bridge.

"I'm sure you're about to tell me." Mal starts to type a text to her husband as she speaks.

"Traffic. Cops in fictional shows go straight from point A to B, score parking right outside the establishment. They never sit for hours in traffic."

Mal laughs and continues typing.

Did you find the lasagna?

She waits for an answer from Peter. Wipers squeak as they smear rain across the windshield. It's coming down hard now, and at 5:00 p.m. it's already full dark. The clear day was short lived, as they tend to be in this part of the world, and at this latitude at this time of year.

"Is everything okay?" Benoit asks as he glances at Mal's phone.

Mal tightens her lips and nods, still waiting for Peter's reply. Perhaps her husband has his headphones on and can't hear his phone. Or he's forgotten to turn on his mobile. Or misplaced it again. Mal turns to look out over the inky waters of the Burrard Inlet. She sees the silhouette of the old grain silos and abandoned dockyard on the shore far below. The area is slated for a new residential development. She notices the cam high up on the bridge struts. That cam is a cop's friend. It's caught people trying to climb over the railings to jump—it's saved more than a few lives.

"Peter's getting worse," she says finally. "He left the stove on again yesterday. Whole day. Lucky he didn't have oil in a pan or something. He's forgetting words, using wrong ones, and then he gets furious with himself and whoever he's trying to talk to, which is usually me." A long pause. "So much anger," she says softly. "It's the embarrassment, the humiliation. For a cerebral man like him, a professor of forensic psychology who's defined by his mind . . ." Her voice fades.

"I'm sorry, Mal."

The emotion that surges into her eyes at Benoit's words surprises her. Mal hasn't really opened up to anyone about her husband's young-onset dementia. Benoit knows of Peter's diagnosis, though. Mal is close to her working partner. It happens with people you trust with your life. Benoit has been candid with her, too, about his struggles in being a young, first-time dad. About the sleepless nights with a newborn. He's told her bits about his horrific childhood in the Congo, when he was kidnapped by rebels at age seven and forced to kill people from his own village as a drugged-up child soldier. If not for a Ghanian-Canadian NGO worker, Benoit might never have been extricated from his situation. The worker brought young Benoit to Quebec for treatment. Without this intervention and a subsequent adoption, Benoit's life probably would have ended violently a long time ago. How he's managed to survive, Mal will never know. That kind of trauma doesn't leave. She suspects a part of Benoit Salumu's psyche still inhabits that dark place of childhood nightmares and always will. Being a cop, fighting for justice now—he says it's what keeps him moving forward. And there is Sadie, his wife, and now their new baby. Sadie is working to complete her law degree long distance while caring for a new baby. Mal is in awe of both of them.

When they finally enter the Point Grey neighborhood and head down Fourth Street, Benoit says in an exaggerated voice, "Oh, look, Detective, a parking space right across the street from Bea's Blooms florist. Just like TV." He chuckles darkly and pulls into the space. Mal smiles in spite of herself.

The bumblebee logo on the florist door is a match to the logo embossed on the card found at the Glass House. Mal and Benoit enter the store. It's humid inside. Warm. It smells like a greenhouse. Ferns hang in pots strung from the beams across the ceiling. A wall of fridges houses a variety of freshly cut blooms in a rainbow of colors. The background music is soft. Classical piano. Peaceful.

Mal whispers to Benoit, "I could live in a place like this."

An arrestingly beautiful woman in her late thirties approaches them. Her brown skin is smooth and flawless. Long locs woven through with a fine silver thread are pulled into a ponytail that hangs down her back. Both her arms are full with silver bracelets. No makeup. She moves like a ballet dancer, with a powerful and fluid grace. The kind of woman Mal can never be. The kind of woman who makes Mal feel like an oversize, blundering Labrador retriever.

They both show her their IDs, and Mal asks if she is the manager.

"I'm the owner, Bea Jemison. What's this about?" The woman's eyes flick from Mal to Benoit. Mal sees the flare of interest as Bea's gaze settles on Benoit. Mal is a veteran interrogator, a shrewd student of human tells. And while the interest she detects in Bea Jemison might be subtle, it's definitely there, so Mal holds back and allows Benoit to take the lead. They'll get more that way.

"Ms. Jemison," Benoit says. "We're hoping you can assist us with a missing person case."

Good call, thinks Mal. Everyone wants to help find the missing. Mention violence or murder and the leery kicks in.

Benoit shows Bea Jemison a photograph on his phone of the card found in the wilting bouquet.

Jemison leans in to take a closer look.

"This card and bouquet were found outside a home on the North Shore. Can you tell us who bought this arrangement? We're presuming it did come from here?"

"Yes, that's ours." She points at the image. "The dendrobium orchids with the baby's breath, Japanese anemone, spider mums, white calla lilies—I put it together myself yesterday. What happened?"

"That's what we're trying to piece together."

"Is she . . . okay? Is the person who bought this the one who's missing?" There's concern in her eyes. "She's pregnant—you do know that she's pregnant?"

A frisson of energy shoots up Mal's spine.

"Is her name Daisy?" Benoit asks.

"I—we can't give out personal information."

"We'll return with a warrant tomorrow, Ms. Jemison," he says, "but we'll lose valuable time. This woman's life and her baby's life could be in danger."

"Oh God, oh—yes, I—her name is Daisy. She comes in often. Ever since she moved into the area in about July, I think."

"Does Daisy have a last name, address, a contact number?"

Jemison regards Benoit, making her own business risk assessment. "Sure, yes. Come this way, to the computer."

She looks it up in her system. "Her name is Daisy Rittenberg. Rose Cottage, number 4357 West Third. It's basically a few blocks away from here toward the water." She gives the cell phone number.

Mal and Benoit thank the florist, and as they exit the store, Mal says, "The Pi Bistro is over there, kitty-corner across the street. Want to check it out before we go to West Third?"

"Might as well—we're here."

They stride down the dark sidewalk. Tires crackle on the wet streets, and rain droplets glisten on the passing cars. As they walk, Mal punches in the mobile number Jemison gave them.

The call flips to voice mail. "Hi, this is Daisy. Leave a message."
She kills the call.

"No answer," she tells Benoit. She phones Lula at the station.

"Corporal Griffith." Lula's tone is crisp.

"Hey, Lu, I need anything and everything you can find on a Daisy Rittenberg of Rose Cottage, 4357 on West Third. Criminal record check, employment history, whatever you can dig up. We're headed to that address now."

"Is this the 'Daisy' in question?"

"Looks that way."

"Gotcha."

Mal pockets her phone as Benoit pushes open the doors to the Pi Bistro. A bell jingles overhead as they enter. It's warm and cozy inside, the air rich with the scents of freshly baked breads. Mal's hunger hits hard even though she wolfed down a wedge of solidifying pizza before leaving the briefing room.

"Looks like your regular wealthy vegan-yoga crowd," Benoit says quietly as they make their way through the rustic tables. At the counter they ask for the manager. A guy in his mid-to-late thirties exits from the open-plan bakery area. He's tanned despite the season, lean, muscled. His sandy hair is sun bleached. Beneath his baker's apron he wears a faded long-sleeve T-shirt printed with an image of a surfboard and the name of a small coastal town in Mexico.

"Ty Binty," he says as he wipes flour off his hands with a cloth. He stuffs the cloth into the front pocket of his apron. "What can I do for you?"

Mal shows her badge and explains they're investigating a missing person case and are hoping to learn the identity of someone who bought a berry pie here yesterday.

He crooks up his brows. "One of my pies was involved in a crime?"

Mal and Benoit say nothing.

"You're *serious*? One of my blueberry-blackberry pies is connected to a police incident? What happened?"

"What makes you think it was a blueberry-blackberry?" Mal asks, thinking of the dark-purple ooze on the concrete outside the front door of the Glass House.

"It's the only berry pie we're making at the moment. They're a special preorder."

"Did a pregnant woman purchase one yesterday?" Mal asks. "Most likely in the late afternoon?"

"You mean Daisy? What happened? Is she okay?" His worry looks genuine.

Mal says, "You also seem pretty certain it was Daisy."

"Look, it was Halloween yesterday. It's October. We're stocked to the hilt with pumpkin pie everything. Daisy called ahead to specifically order our blackberry and blueberry mix. And those are special order because they're made with wild berries and we don't always have supply."

"So you know Daisy?" Benoit asks.

"For sure, yeah. Daisy Rittenberg. She comes in at least once a week, usually for a late lunch or afternoon tea, and most often with her friend, Vanessa, who's also pregnant. Sometimes they're joined by other pregnant moms from the yoga class that's held in the park across the street. In good weather the class is held outdoors on the grass, under the trees," he explains. "When it rains, they go to the studio around the block. Daisy came in late yesterday afternoon to pick up her order. Maybe around five thirty p.m. or so?" He wavers. "Can you tell me if she's okay?"

"We're trying to make contact with her."

"She's married to Jon Rittenberg."

"You say his name like we should recognize it," Mal says.

"Sorry, I guess not everyone is a winter sports enthusiast. Jon is a Canadian Olympian—a downhill skier. He brought home two gold medals from the Winter Olympics at Salt Lake City in '02. Jon—they called him BergBomber—grew up on the North Shore Mountains. He's like a local hero—or was. He attended a secondary school near mine, and us tykes who were a few years younger all wanted to *be* JonJon Rittenberg. He was a girl magnet. Big parties at his house and up at the ski team lodge in Whistler. One or two events got quite out of hand back in the day. Police had to shut them down. Jon married Daisy Wentworth of Wentworth family fame. Her father, Labden Wentworth, founded TerraWest, and their name is, like, huge in the ski and golf resort industry. Daisy told me Jon now works at the TerraWest office downtown. He and Daisy recently moved back to Vancouver from Silver Aspens in Colorado. She wanted to be closer to her parents when she has the baby." He hesitates. "Can you please let me know what's going on?"

"We're not sure yet," Mal says. "Early stages. Just checking off basics. You've been a great help, Mr. Binty—really great. Do you happen to know the last name of this Vanessa, the pregnant friend?"

"Yeah, North. Vanessa North."

# THE MAID'S DIARY

Wind whips leaves from trees as I pull my Subaru into the Rittenbergs' driveway.

*I unload my gear, enter the house, and almost run up the stairs and into the main bathroom. Still thinking of Charley Waters, I open the laundry hamper, breathing fast. Everyone's hamper has a scent—human body odor overlaid with fragrance from individual shampoos, lotions, perfumes, deodorants. The smell of Daisy and Jon fills my nostrils, and a discordant clanging begins in my head as I quickly check pockets for items that should not go up in the washing machine. I hear a snatch of raucous laughter in my head. I go still.*

*A memory surfaces. I hear strands of music over the laughter. They rise as if from a dark vault of memory. Old tunes once popular. Loud voices suddenly thump heavily through my brain. More laughing. It grows into mocking, jeering. Cheering. My hands start to shake. I take in a deep breath, fiddle in my apron pocket, find a stick of cinnamon gum. Extra hot. I stick it in my mouth. The taste burns. It clears my mind, focuses me. I chew, chew, chew as I gather the laundry and take it downstairs to the machine.*

*I load the machine, set it in motion, then hurry into the kitchen. The Rittenbergs have left another eggy mess. The fatty smell of bacon hangs in the air. It's nauseating—I've been a vegan for over ten years now. I rinse dishes and pack the dishwasher, studiously avoiding the powerful paintings of BergBomber on the living room wall. I feel him, though. Like a presence. As if taunting me to look. Look, Kit! Look at me, the golden ski god. Did you not have a poster of me inside your locker, fat little Katarina Poop-ovich?*

*My skin prickles with heat as I grab the big carving knife on the counter and begin to rinse it aggressively. I focus on the blade. The sharp, shining blade. I imagine Jon's or Daisy's hand holding this hilt. Cutting, carving up something. I can't not look any longer, and I glance up.*

*I stare at the paintings next to the fireplace. I feel my fist tense around the hilt of the knife. I feel myself slashing those paintings. I gasp as I realize I've cut myself. Shit.*

*I hurry to the bathroom, find a Band-Aid, and I tape up the cut. I stare at my blood—pink in the basin as I rinse it away. I get darker and darker thoughts. I realize I'm in trouble. I should have left this Rose Cottage Pandora's box alone. Should not have lifted the lid. Should've told Holly I would not clean this house. Too late now. I'm sliding down.*

*I begin to dust and vacuum and tidy. Jon's shoes lie in the entryway. I open the hall closet to put them away. In the closet I see their scarves and jackets hanging neatly. A basket of gloves for the winter. Spare car keys on a row of key hooks. The fobs tell me the Rittenbergs drive an Audi and a BMW. I take mental note, absorb everything. It's all burning into my brain.*

*But it's when I go up to vacuum Jon's office that I strike pay dirt. Without even trying.*

*While vacuuming the carpet in his office, in my frenzied haste, I bump his desk. His computer monitor flickers to life. I stare. My pulse quickens. It's a Mac, and the little beach ball of death is spinning around and around on the monitor. Jon must have tried to shut his computer down or put it into sleep mode, but the system has gotten hung up on a glitch. Perhaps something is stuck in the print queue, or a Bluetooth device is attempting to wake his machine, or it's some misconfigured file.*

*My heart kicks. I seat myself slowly at Jon's desk.*

*His calendar is up on the screen. All his daily appointments are listed. Excitement shimmers. I run my gaze over his upcoming engagements. He's got meetings, a golf game scheduled, a booking to service his Audi, a dentist's appointment—his whole world is in here. It's an Aladdin's cave of treasures.*

*I reach for the mouse and open his file finder. A buzzer sounds. I jump, then realize it's the washing machine. I check my watch. I need to get the laundry into the dryer. I'm running out of time. I need to finish both snooping and cleaning before Daisy Rittenberg comes up the driveway and catches me in the act.*

*But before I attempt to put the computer back into sleep mode, I quickly scan the list of recently modified folders and documents. And I see it.*

*Oh, stupid boy.*

*Inside a folder named* PERSONAL *nests an Excel document named—yes, you guessed right, Dear Diary—it's named* PSSWDS. *Believe it or not, some people have in their computers a file called exactly what it is. They don't expect to have their intimate details violated inside the safe, nurturing cocoons of their own homes. They're naive enough to trust they won't be hacked into. I open the file.*

*Listed in alphabetical order are the keys to Jon's digital life—passwords for everything from his Netflix and Dropbox accounts to his Apple ID, along with the password to this very desktop device.*

*My first thought is: Flash drive! I need to copy all these passwords to a flash drive!*

*But I don't have one.*

*I glance at his printer. Print it?*

*I have a better idea.*

*I open his Safari browser, access my own Gmail account, and I attach a copy of Jon's password files. I mail it to myself, then delete recent browser history. My mouth is dry. I can barely swallow. My skin prickles. I now possess the "Open Sesame" to Aladdin's cave. I can access Jon's desktop and all its contents whenever I want. I can know where Jon Rittenberg will be at any given time, as long as the appointment is listed on his calendar. I can even send texts and place calls via his number.*

*I put the computer in sleep mode.*

*Pulse racing, face flushed, I quickly finish vacuuming the room. I drag my Dyson out of the office, smooth down my apron, give the room one last check. It looks just as it did when I entered.*

*I shut the door quietly.*

# JON

Jon flips the card Henry gave him over and over and over between his fingers as he sits at his desk in the TerraWest tower. His hungover head throbs. His thoughts are not on work. His brain is consumed with Ahmed Waheed, who sits in a glass office diagonally across the corridor from Jon's glass office.

He glances up from the card and regards Ahmed. As he watches, Anna Simm, the TerraWest front desk receptionist, enters Ahmed's office carrying a steaming mug. Ahmed looks up as Anna approaches his desk. Anna's red dress fits her curves so well it seems painted onto her body. She sets the mug in front of Ahmed and smiles as she flirtatiously moves her hair back from her face. Ahmed says something, and Anna tosses back her head and laughs. Really laughs. As though Ahmed has said the funniest thing she's ever heard. Jon has never seen Anna laugh that hard.

A hot dislike oozes into his veins. He flicks the card faster between his fingers. Jon cannot bear losing. If he loses the COO job to that man, it means this whole move back home—this whole baby-family thing—has been for absolutely nothing. Losing it is not even an option. Jon figures Ahmed is in his very early thirties. Maybe even late twenties. Far too young for the responsibilities of running a brand-new world-class four-season mountain resort. It's blatantly obvious this is not about skill and all about optics. Christ, just look at the man—he can't even organize his own hair, let alone a resort. His shiny black locks are wavy and hang almost to his shoulders. Unkempt, in Jon's opinion. Totally unprofessional. Like he just got out of bed after sex or something. And Ahmed has a beard. It gives him a certain smoldering quality that women like Anna clearly find irresistible. He wears glasses, too. They bestow Ahmed with a pseudo aura of intellect. Jon thinks Ahmed looks like an owl in those round glasses. Fucking poseur. Jon has no idea why the young women at work flock around him. Can't they see through the guy?

Jon's mind turns to Mia Reiter—the hot banker babe he allowed to slip through his married fingers last night. He wonders how differently things might have turned out if he'd run after Mia instead of just watching her walk away.

His jaw tightens. Adrenaline pumps softly through his body. His breathing grows deeper, faster. He glances down at the card in his hand.

Preston Private Investigations.

Jon sets the card down on his desk. From his briefcase he extracts his laptop and opens it up. Into a browser he types in the URL displayed on the business card.

The landing page for Preston Private Investigations fills his screen.

A moving banner across the top of the page promises: "Fast Results. Full Range of Services. Discretion."

Jon scrolls down the page.

*Extramarital Affairs, Adultery, Infidelity, Unfaithful Cheating Spouses: These terms cause enormous amounts of stress for those who suspect a spouse's activities. Name it whatever term you want, but statistics show that cheating is more common than most people think. Statistics also show that, unfortunately, once someone seriously suspects infidelity, more often than not, their suspicion is correct.*

Jon glances up and once more studies his rival in his glass office. Ahmed is busy working on his computer again.

*Enormous amounts of stress.*

The website has got that right. That's exactly what Ahmed Waheed is causing Jon. Stress.

*What if I caught him having an affair? Something worse?*

Jon considers what Henry said in the dimly lit pub.

*Someone who specializes in such things. Ex-cop. Knows what he's doing. When you call, ask for Jake.*

Jon wonders what work "Jake" has done for Henry in the past. He watches as Anna-in-the-red-dress struts past his glass wall without so much as a glance inside. Let alone a mug of coffee and a smile.

His jaw tightens.

He spins his chair around so that his back faces the interior glass wall, and using his personal mobile, he punches in the number of Preston Private Investigations.

A woman answers. Jon asks for Jake.

A man with a gruff voice says, "Jake Preston."

Jon clears his throat. "I—ah, this is Jon. Henry Clay recommended you."

"And what can I do for you, Jon?"

Jon shoots a furtive glance over his shoulder, then explains that he's got some competition for something that should rightfully be his. "I need to know what I'm up against."

"You mean you need dirt? Something you can use to eliminate your competition?"

Words defy Jon for a moment. The implication, the reality, of what he's asking is suddenly stark. He bites his lip.

"Look, Jon-without-a-last-name, if we agree to a business relationship, one thing you need to know about me is I don't mince my words. I say things as I see them. Much easier to avoid confusion and misunderstandings that way. And it helps me to operate within the context of the law. For example, if you pretend you're hiring me for one thing but want—"

"Yes," Jon says quickly. "Yes, I want dirt. Intel. Anything I can use to undermine someone who is trying to steal my job."

"Okay," Jake says slowly. "That's one of my specialties. If there is 'kompromat' to be found, I will find it. Can I email you a copy of our contractual arrangement and rates before we go further? Or would you like to do everything in person? It's your preference."

"I prefer in person."

"Good call. This evening? Or afternoon? Where are you generally located, Jon?"

Jon swallows. He's balancing on the tip of a black run. He's leaning over. If he commits any further, he will start a racing ride of no return down to the bottom. He needs to be certain this is what he wants. He also needs to win. And in order to win, Jon is not beyond sabotaging competition. He's not beyond playing foul. He was, after all, a top-level athlete who'd do anything to succeed at his game.

"I work in downtown Vancouver. I live in Point Grey," he says.

"Does the Jericho Beach parking lot work for you?"

"Yes. Yes—that works fine."

"Okay, Jon. What I need from you is the name of the subject you want investigated, plus any other information that might be relevant, or that might give me leads. Address, age, hobbies, gender, sexual proclivities—does this person have a partner, kids, siblings, parents? Who are their friends? Where do they hang out? A gym, a favorite pub, club. Do they drink, do drugs, attend a church—"

"Mosque. If he's religious, I'm sure he goes to a mosque."

A pause. "Okay." Another pause. "If our subject has any ardent political or ideological affiliations, it could help. The more personal information, the better. Say six thirty p.m. at the Jericho lot?"

"That's fine." Jon will access TerraWest's HR computer database. He will compile a file of whatever details he can find in there before he leaves the office. He can rendezvous with Jake on his way home. Jericho Beach is not far from Rose Cottage.

Jake says, "I drive a pale-blue Toyota Camry. Blends in everywhere—incognito is the name of my game." The phone goes dead.

Jon sits, holding his mobile. His pulse races. But a smile begins to curve his mouth. He feels empowered. He's taking action. *Doing* something. He feels the old Jon that Mia awoke last night stirring and swelling in strength. Bolstered by his chat with the PI, Jon attempts a quick internet search for "Mia Reiter."

Several Mia Reiters pop up. But there is no one who looks like *his* Mia Reiter. Just as well. His place is with Daisy and the baby. He remains proud of himself that he stepped away last night. It's imperative he keeps his head screwed on right, because losing Daisy on top of possibly losing this TerraWest promotion—it's not tenable. Daisy and the baby are also his link to Wentworth money. Jon is fully aware that if he fucks around and Labden or Annabelle Wentworth find out—he's toast. They will drag him through the courts and sue him to the cleaners and back. He needs to stay smart, keep low on the radar.

He also did not handle Daisy well this morning. He decides he will buy her some roses at that Bea's Blooms place after meeting Jake. He'll text her and tell her he's bringing takeout for dinner.

By the time Jon drives his Audi out of the underground parking garage and feeds into downtown traffic, it's 6:10 p.m.

A manila folder lies on the passenger seat beside him. It contains private details on Ahmed Waheed.

# THE PHOTOGRAPHER

When Rittenberg's Audi pulls out from the underground parking garage of the TerraWest tower, the photographer waiting in his car across the street pulls out and follows him, staying two cars behind. It's already dark, so he feels confident he won't be detected by Rittenberg. The photographer's camera rests on the passenger seat.

At 6:29 p.m. Jon Rittenberg's Audi turns into a parking lot near Jericho Beach. Rittenberg parks near a low concrete building that houses a concession, showers, and washrooms.

The photographer stops his vehicle below a tree on the residential street that runs past the parking lot. He kills his engine and watches the Audi.

Two minutes later a light-blue Toyota Camry turns into the lot and parks near the Audi. The driver's door swings open. The parking lot lights illuminate a heavyset guy with a belly exiting the Camry. The man's head is shiny bald. He goes straight for the passenger door of the Audi, opens it, climbs in.

The photographer raises his lens, points through the open car window.

*Click click click.*

The Audi door shuts. The photographer waits.

Almost seven minutes later, the bald man exits the Audi. This time he holds a large brown envelope in his hand. The photographer clicks again, making sure he captures both the envelope and the Audi license plate.

The bald man climbs back into the driver's seat of the Toyota Camry.

The photographer clicks. He captures the Camry's plates as it drives off.

The photographer then hesitates. He can wait until Rittenberg leaves the lot, and follow him. Or he could follow the Camry. The photographer slides down into his seat and out of sight as the Camry passes his parked vehicle. He comes upright, starts his engine, puts his car into gear, and follows the Camry down the dimly lit street.

The Camry leads him all the way to a small strip mall in Burnaby. The Camry enters the mall lot and parks in front of a Laundromat. The bald man exits the Camry and makes for a recessed doorway tucked between the Laundromat and a busy Vietnamese restaurant.

The photographer waits. Patrons come and go from the restaurant. There are two people inside the Laundromat. Time is now 7:52 p.m. The photographer notices a light go on in windows upstairs from the Laundromat. He exits his vehicle and goes up to the recessed door into which the bald man disappeared. A plaque at the side of the door names three businesses located upstairs. One is a ballroom dance studio, another is a cobbler, and the third is Preston Private Investigations.

The photographer smiles. So Jon Rittenberg is working with a private investigator.

He returns to his vehicle, opens his phone, and finds the website for Preston Private Investigations.

*Extramarital Affairs, Adultery, Infidelity, Unfaithful Cheating Spouses: These terms cause enormous amounts of stress for those who suspect a spouse's activities . . .*

Does Jon Rittenberg suspect his wife of adultery? Something more sinister?

The photographer waits awhile longer inside his dark vehicle. It begins to rain. No one exits the door. He starts his car and drives home, thinking about Rittenberg.

*People can seem so ordinary on the surface, but scratch the veneer and there's always a secret beneath the gloss.*

# MAL

*November 1, 2019. Friday.*

When Mal and Benoit arrive at Rose Cottage in search of Daisy Rittenberg, they see a dark-gray Audi parked in the driveway. They exchange a quick glance as Benoit pulls in behind it. Their headlights illuminate the Audi plate, but it's so plastered with mud that it's illegible.

As they are about to exit their vehicle, Mal's phone rings. It's Lula.

"Hey, Lu. I'm putting you on speaker. What've you got?"

"Okay, no criminal record on file for either Daisy Rittenberg or her husband, Jon, but photographs that we've found of the couple match Beulah Brown's description of the mystery pair who arrived at the Glass House in the Audi. We're still gathering further information, but something has just come to our attention. The Rittenbergs of Rose Cottage are named as Kit Darling's clients on the list that Holly's Help sent us." Lula pauses, apparently consulting the list. "Darling cleaned Rose Cottage up until October 27. She stopped four days before the incident at the Glass House."

"The Rittenbergs canceled the contract?" Mal asks.

"No. Holly McGuire says it was Darling who asked to be removed from the Rose Cottage roster due to a sudden 'scheduling conflict.' McGuire said the request from Darling was unusual, but she also reiterated that Darling is one of her best employees, and that she's been consistent over the eight years she's worked for the service. McGuire's sense was that something about the Rittenbergs had upset Darling, but Darling declined to offer any additional input when McGuire pressed. McGuire thus ceded to her employee's request—she wanted to keep Darling happy. She sent another cleaner to Rose Cottage starting Monday, October 28."

Mal shoots a glance at Benoit. They now have another link between Kit Darling and Daisy Rittenberg. One cleaned for the other. And both were at the Glass House on Halloween night. Both still unaccounted for.

Mal thanks Lula and ends the call. She and Benoit exit the vehicle with renewed purpose. A foghorn sounds in the darkness. Rain continues to drizzle down. They walk slowly past the Audi.

"Mud on the tires as well as the plates," Benoit says as they make for the house entrance.

Mal knocks on the door.

"Doesn't look like a cottage to me," Benoit says.

A light goes on inside. Mal detects movement through the opaque glass panel down the side of the front door. But no one answers.

Mal hammers her fist on the door as Benoit rings the bell repeatedly. "Hello! Police!" she calls. "Anyone home? Open up, please."

The door finally opens a crack.

A tall, well-built male in his late thirties or early forties peers at them with puffy, red-rimmed eyes. Fresh scratches run down his cheek and neck. He wears pajama pants, a dirty sweatshirt. His feet are bare, his hair disheveled, and a strong scent of alcohol radiates off him. He holds the door close to his body. Mal notices a bandage spotted with fresh blood on his hand. He angles his head as if trying to pull them into focus.

"Mr. Rittenberg?" Mal asks.

"Who are you?"

"I'm Sergeant Mallory Van Alst, and this is my partner, Corporal Benoit Salumu. We'd like to ask you and your wife, Daisy, a few questions."

A panicked look explodes across the man's face. "What about?"

"Is Daisy Rittenberg in? Are you her husband, Jon Rittenberg?"

He tenses as though he's going to bolt, and Mal braces in anticipation. She senses Benoit doing the same, repositioning himself slightly more to her right and rear.

"Yeah, I'm Jon."

"Is your wife home, sir?"

"No."

"Where can we find her?"

"She's gone."

A frisson crackles through Mal. "Gone? Where?"

"I don't the hell know. She just packed her bags and left, and she's not answering her phone."

"Can we come in, Mr. Rittenberg?"

"What for?"

"Just to have a look around, see if your wife is here."

"I told you. She's gone. What's this about?"

"How did you hurt your face and hand, sir?" Benoit asks.

He moves his hand behind his back. "None of your business."

"Do you or your wife know a Vanessa and Haruto North?" Mal asks.

The man pales. A muscle pulses at his jaw. He says nothing. Mal can see him struggling to think clearly through his alcoholic haze.

"Could you answer the question, please, Mr. Rittenberg?" says Benoit.

"What's it to you?"

Mal says, "We're investigating a missing person incident on the North Shore. We have reason to believe you and your wife can assist us in that investigation. Do you mind if we come in?"

His eyes narrow. He pulls the door even closer to his body. He seems to be sobering up, tightening, coiling. Walling off. He swallows and says very slowly, "I'm sorry, officers. I am not my wife's keeper. I don't know her every move, and I don't know where she is right now."

"We understand your wife is heavily pregnant, sir. She and the baby might be in jeopardy. It's important that—"

He begins to shut the door. Mal blocks it with her boot. She's treading toward a fine line she can't cross without a warrant, but her pulse hammers hard, and she fears for the well-being of this man's wife and unborn child. "Is that your Audi in the driveway, sir?"

Rittenberg glowers at her in silence.

"Were you at a house called Northview yesterday evening? In that Audi?" Mal asks.

He doesn't respond.

"We have a witness who places you and your wife at Northview, sir. Also known as the Glass House—home of Vanessa and Haruto North."

He tries to pull his door shut, but Mal's boot is in the way.

She presses. "Who is your house cleaner, Mr. Rittenberg?"

"What in the hell does that have to do with anything?"

"Do you use Holly's Help cleaning services, sir?" Benoit asks.

Rittenberg's eyes flick up to Benoit's. Distaste fills his face. "I have no idea. My wife handles that."

"Do you know Kit Darling, the maid from Holly's Help?" Benoit asks.

Rittenberg swears, his eyes still fixed on Benoit. "What's wrong with you people? I told you—my wife, Daisy, handles the cleaning service, and I doubt even she knows which maid comes on cleaning days. She isn't home when they come. Now get your fucking foot out of my doorway."

Very calmly, Mal says, "Mr. Rittenberg, when you and your wife arrived in your Audi at Northview around six fourteen p.m., with a bouquet of flowers from Bea's Blooms and a blackberry pie ordered from the Pi Bistro, did you see a yellow Subaru Crosstrek with Holly's Help logos parked in the driveway?"

"There was no other car in the driveway."

"So you do confirm you were at the house?"

"Get the hell off my property before I sue your asses off, and if you want anything else from me, get a fucking warrant or speak to my lawyer."

Mal steps back, removing her boot. "We need to know where your wife—"

He slams the door.

They hear a lock click.

She glances up at Benoit. His face is tight, the whites of his eyes stark. She can see he's also thinking about that carving knife found at the bottom of the infinity pool, and the blood spatter all over the white interior of the Glass House, the evidence of a violent struggle. And they're both thinking about the fresh injuries on Jon Rittenberg's face and hand.

"We need to lay eyes on his wife," she says.

"And we need to find that maid," Benoit says.

# JON

From an upstairs window in the baby's dark room, Jon watches the detectives leave his front doorway. His heart gallops. He tries to sober up, to pull himself together. He's panicking. Shaking. Sweating.

*Focus. Focus.*

Keeping one eye on the cops moving down his driveway toward his Audi, Jon tries to call Daisy's mobile. It rings and rings, flips into voice mail.

"Hi, this is Daisy. Leave a message."

"Daisy, pick up for God's sake! *Call me.* Wherever you are. Please. We need to talk."

As he speaks, he watches the two cops circling his Audi with flashlights. They bend down to examine his muddy tires and plate. The female cop wipes the plate and takes a photo with her phone.

The next call Jon makes is to his lawyer.

# THE MAID'S DIARY

Today I'm cleaning a luxury condo unit high above the city in the trendy Yaletown area, where shimmering towers of glass look out in all directions. So many people on top of one another in glass boxes. This unit is used as an Airbnb. Holly has several of these nightly rentals on her books. This time around, it's a superquick job. The recently departed solo guest appears to have done nothing but sleep in the bed and shower and shave. Probably a businessman in town for a day. No signs of wild sex like the last time. Booze bottles everywhere. Evidence of cocaine use. Used condoms. A discarded vibrator. I even found a pair of padded handcuffs under the bed last week.

*I yank back the drapes, letting in the pale sunlight. Across the street is a flashing neon sign above a club called* CABARET LUXE. *It's a new "it" venue. I have no idea how that 24-7 pulsing pink neon sign doesn't annoy the hell out of all these people living in their glass boxes.*

*I make the bed while thinking of my Glass House job yesterday and how I caught Horton Brown spying from behind the hedge into the bedroom window where I was vacuuming. The memory gives me a small shudder. Horton always makes my skin crawl. I shake the memory off, finish cleaning, and* use my bit of spare time to sit at a table by the window and jot down my thoughts.

I have not journaled in a little while. I'm rethinking this whole journaling thing. I also skipped my last therapy appointment. I guess I'm afraid my psychologist will confirm what I already know: I'm on increasingly dangerous ground now. Both mentally and physically. And the very fact I want to quit the diary is probably a warning sign that I'm also getting close to something my unconscious wants to keep hidden.

I spoke to Charlotte "Charley" Waters yesterday.

I found her after calling the nightclub mentioned in the Silver Aspens newspapers—Club Crimson. She still works there. Just like I still work for Holly's. Girls like Charley and me—we tend to stick. We stay where society thinks we belong. The club manager wouldn't give me her number, of course, but said if I called back during one of Charley's shifts, I might get lucky.

After many tries over the past days, I finally got lucky.

So, Dear Diary, this is how it goes:

I get Charlotte Waters on the phone, and I tell her I'm an ex-employee of Jon Rittenberg's and I have reason to believe she can help me.

She's immediately suspicious. This is not surprising.

"I read about you in the newspapers," I say carefully. "Women like us, we need to have each other's backs. Do you know what I mean?"

She's silent for a while. I hear music in the background. I hear voices.

"What did you say your name was?"

I hesitate, clear my throat, and say it: "Katarina Popovich. But everyone calls me Kit. My married name is

*Darling, but I'm divorced now." It's been a long time since I've introduced myself as Katarina Popovich, and it has a strange effect on me. I feel something shift inside—the old Katarina taking up more space, trying to meld herself with the newer, happier "Kit." I worry I'm making a huge mistake in reawakening Katarina. I fear I won't come back from this—that this right here is my point of no return. My hill I will die on. But finding myself inside Jon Rittenberg's house—seeing those big paintings of him coming down the mountain at me—it's fundamentally changed everything. There can be no turning back now. Even if I try. I know this instinctively.*

*"Kit." Charley repeats my name, and I sense the wheels of her brain churning, trying to figure me out. But she hasn't killed the call yet. This is a positive sign. She says, "I don't have a lot of time. I'm on a smoke break. Make it quick."*

*So she's curious. Good, this is all I ask. She can take it or leave it, but I just want her to listen, and to consider my questions. If she balks, maybe she'll still talk at a later date after the idea sits with her awhile.*

*"Look, Charley, all I know is what I read in the papers— are you okay with me calling you Charley?"*

*"Everyone does."*

*"Okay. While reading some online news from a year ago, I came across an article where Jon Rittenberg claimed you were stalking him and his wife. You, on the other hand, accused Jon of sexual assault—of spiking your drink and making you pregnant. You filed your accusation after you were arrested on Jon Rittenberg's property and charged for stalking and harassment. Police later dropped all the charges. You in turn dropped all sexual assault allegations and said you'd fabricated the whole thing. You apparently agreed to get psychological help. What really happened?"*

*"What in the fuck? What the hell do you want? Why are you asking me this? It happened over a year ago. Are you media? Did she put you up to this?"*

*My pulse quickens. "Who's 'she'?"*

*Silence.*

*I'm losing her—she's going to hang up.*

*Quickly, I say, "Look, I believe you, Charley. I believe your story—the original one. The one you retracted. I believe it's the truth and . . ." My voice hitches. I'm suddenly scared. But there really is no about-face now. "I'm not a reporter. I . . . okay, I wasn't exactly truthful, either. I'm not an ex-employee of Jon Rittenberg's. I still work for him. I clean his house. I'm a maid." I hesitate. Charley's still listening. "And I need some help because I—I know he's done this before. I think he's done this many times before. After finding your stories, I know I'm not alone."*

*There is a long silence. "Has he done something to you?"*

*This time it's me who remains quiet.*

*"Are you okay?" she asks.*

*"No," I whisper. "I don't think so. I—I needed to talk to someone. I had a feeling he's done this before. I'm not sure what to do. I'm afraid if I make a complaint, they could drag me through shit like they did to you."*

*"How do I know you are who you say you are? Why should I even begin to trust you?"*

*"You don't have to. But I also couldn't not reach out. I'm sorry. It was a mistake. I—"*

*"Wait." She curses. "Look. I want to believe you. But even if I wanted to talk, I can't. I'm bound by a gag order. I signed a nondisclosure statement. Both parties did."*

*My heart starts to hammer. Sweat prickles. Jackpot—I've hit the freaking jackpot. I knew it!*

*"An NDA? They made you sign an NDA?"*

*"I can't talk about it. I got money and I signed a gag order. That's all I will say."*

*I take in a deep, steadying breath, trying to tamp down my excitement. "Okay," I say softly. "How about I just put something out here. No need to agree, but if I'm wrong, feel free to hang up. Will you do that? Just hear me out?"*

*I can hear someone calling her name.*

*"My break is almost up. I need to go."*

*"Wait! Please. Tell me what happened to your baby. I believe you—that he made you pregnant. Did they make you get rid of it? Was that part of the money deal? Did he pay you to have an abortion, retract your accusation, and they in turn dropped stalking charges? He treated you like shit, Charley, and I bet that he said 'it never happened.' Did I get that right?"*

*She swears viciously on the other end. I hear her clearing her throat, then blowing her nose.*

*"Charley, I understand if you stalked him. I do. I really do. These things make a person crazy. Especially the spiked-drink shit, because you start questioning your own memories even as everyone is questioning you and your motivations. But you don't deserve this. No woman deserves this."*

*Very quietly, she says, "So maybe you are who you say you are, lady, or maybe you're not, but I will tell you this. It wasn't his lawyers. It was her lawyers. It was her."*

*"What do you mean?"*

*She inhales deeply. "She made me sign the NDA. Jon Rittenberg didn't know anything about it. He knows he raped me because he did. But now he just thinks I made the pregnancy part up. Because she cleaned up after him to protect her own reputation and her family's name. She tried to intimidate me into getting rid of it at first. I . . . God, I'm going to get into a shit ton of trouble for saying this if you let it get out, but it wasn't explicitly part of the gag order—her lawyers don't even know this part—"*

"What part?"

*"She first tried to intimidate me, tried to frighten me away. Tried to make me crazy. She harassed me, spooked me, by sending me GIFs of a Chucky doll with a knife and the words: 'It's not all child's play—die baby, die, die, die. I hope your baby dies.'" A pause. "I don't know what you want with the Rittenbergs, Kit, but be careful. You might think Jon Rittenberg is bad, and he is, but he's just your generic entitled male asshole. His wife, though—Daisy Rittenberg—she's dangerous."*

# DAISY

*October 18, 2019. Friday.*
*Thirteen days before the murder.*

Daisy is careful. She's cooking a nice but simple supper of fish that she picked up at the market on her way home from lunch with Vanessa. Jon called earlier to say he would bring takeout, but she told him she was happy to cook. As she melts butter in the pan, her mind churns over the note left *inside* her BMW.

There was no sign of a break-in. And she's certain she beeped the lock open as she approached her car, and that it *was* locked. The only other person who has a set of keys to her BMW is Jon. And Jon would not mess with her head like that. It's out of the question. Isn't it? All Daisy can deduce is perhaps she *was* mistaken—maybe she *did* leave her car unlocked. Even so, the fact someone knew she was parked near the bistro . . . it must've been because she posted the hashtag, #BidingTimeTillBistroLunch. One of the trolls must have seen it before she deleted the post.

What frightens her more is that a troll is physically stalking her.

Daisy jumps as the butter catches and smokes. She whips the pan off the stove and curses. She pours out the burned butter and starts again. As the new pat of butter melts, Daisy resolves to hold off posting on Instagram for a while. And she'll reconfigure her privacy settings.

Maybe the trolls will forget about her. As she squeezes fresh lemon juice into the butter and tastes it, her mind spirals back to the Chucky GIF.

*That's* what's really messing with her head. Chucky.

Only one person in this world would know what Chucky means to Daisy.

But it could be coincidence. Chucky is a common horror meme—a ubiquitous GIF to denote nasty things. It's just her own guilt that's turning a coincidental Chucky into a real monster. It's nothing. *Nothing.* It's going to be fine. And she certainly cannot tell Jon. The best thing is to stay off social media for a while. Like Vanessa.

Her mind goes to Vanessa and Haruto.

It's worrying her—Haruto's angry grip on Vanessa's arm. The fear in her friend's eyes. Daisy pours the lemon-butter sauce into a small serving dish and sets it on the warmer. She reaches for the sharpest knife in the block to fillet the fish. As she slices and peels gray skin away from delicate pink flesh, she decides she will talk to Vanessa about Haruto. She'll broach the topic, delicately, of course, coming at it in a circuitous way.

She starts pulling fine bones out of the glistening flesh, humming to herself.

Perhaps she'll even confess to Vanessa something personal. To break the ice. It will show Vanessa her friend is vulnerable, too, and can be trusted, and it might make it easier for Vanessa to spill on her husband.

Daisy hears Jon's Audi in the driveway. Her heart spasms. The outside security light flares on. Hurriedly, she sets down the sharp blade, wipes her hands, and lights the candles. She puts on a playlist of soft, jazzy music. For an instant she worries she has taken too much care—the last thing she needs is to be accused of creating an Instagram dinner.

Quickly, Daisy plops the fish fillets into the hot pan. The wine is chilling. For him, of course. She's not drinking right now.

Jon enters carrying a pile of mail, his briefcase, and a monstrous bouquet of red roses. Daisy adores roses. It's why she wanted to keep the name Rose Cottage even though the house has been updated and no longer looks remotely like a cottage.

He sets the pile of mail on the counter, kisses her, and presents her with the roses.

"Damn, it smells good in here, love—I'm ravenous." He smiles that charming smile of his, and Daisy's heart lightens. He holds her tummy. "How's our little man doing?"

"Kicking like a football player." She fetches a vase and fills it with water. Jon carries his briefcase upstairs to his office and returns with his sleeves rolled up, his tie off, looking relaxed. It's good to see him like this again. But it's a fragile moment, and Daisy is cautious, even a little suspicious.

She carries the dishes to the table. Jon opens the wine. He makes approving noises as he tastes her cooking. And while they eat, she waits for him to broach the sensitive topic of the promotion. But he doesn't. So she refrains from asking. Jon relaxes visibly with each additional sip of wine.

Finally he says, "I'm sorry I snapped this morning, Daize." He pours another glass. "Henry's news about Ahmed Waheed was just such a shock. I needed to let off some steam. I needed to process. But you're right. Maybe Waheed does look to the board like the perfect prospect right now. However, I have a few weeks to show them I am even better. I just need to position myself so they can see I'm the *only* one for that job." He sips from his glass. His eyes are bright.

Daisy suppresses her surprise at his turnabout. She wonders what shifted while Jon was at work today. The little thread of suspicion snakes deeper into her—he's up to something.

"Are you sure you don't want me to talk to Dad?" she asks. "I know he's no longer on the board, but—"

"No." He wipes his mouth with his napkin and sets it firmly on the table. "There are some fresh faces on the board, and I want their support wholly. I aim to win that COO position fair and square, prove I'm the best man to take the new TerraWest resort forward."

"Even if you don't get it, Jon, it's fine. I mean, we're back home, close to family. We can have the baby here, and you will still have the position in the downtown office. That's not going anywhere. Then once Bean comes, we can think again."

His eyes flicker at her mention of staying in Vancouver if he loses the promotion. Mistake. Jon is not going to take loss well. Not at all. He has one plan only. Win. Just as he did when it came to downhill racing—he wanted the gold. There was no backup plan. No room for concession.

"Well," Jon says, "I'm sure Labden will want to keep his *Princess Daisy* 'home' where he can—"

"Jon," she warns. "Please, no. Please don't go there."

He reaches for the wine bottle, pours another glass, fuller this time. "It's true, though, Daisy, isn't it?" He sets the bottle down, takes a big sip. "Maybe Daddy Wentworth tricked us into coming back."

Her mouth opens. She stares at him. Wind ticks a branch against the window.

"That's absurd," she says quietly.

"Is it, though?" He points his glass at her. "I saw that flash of hesitation in your face. Even *you* can see that it might be possible. Maybe Mommy Wentworth suggested it. Maybe they never had me in mind for COO. Maybe this was the plan all along. Bring you and the grandbaby back, then cut me loose."

"Why on earth would they do that?"

A darkness enters her husband's face. Daisy's pulse begins to race. She knows her dad is manipulative, controlling. But he'd never do that—would he?

"Because they love you, Daize. It's a fact. And the Wentworths get what they want. They own people and they own things. It's what they do. And what if they decided after the Colorado nonsense that I am no longer good for their little girl, their little *princess*? You should never have told them."

"Don't put this on me, Jon. It was in the news. Everyone at Silver Aspens knew about it. Of course Mom and Dad were going to hear about the stalker. At least coming from me, I could control the narrative and soften the blow. Besides, it blew over. Everyone now knows that the woman was mentally unstable and desperate for attention. She set you up, targeted you. She admitted it."

He holds her gaze. Something inside him seems to back down. He smiles, but it looks harsh. "I'm sorry. It's just—Henry made me wonder. And the fact Ahmed Waheed was brought into HQ two weeks ago—it smells like a premeditated and done deal. Doesn't it? But it's fine. And it's better that Labden is gone from the company. I don't want to be seen as winning the job only because I married his daughter." He gets up, kisses her. He holds her face in his hands. "It's going to be fine. You'll see."

She smiles nervously as her pulse kicks up another notch. Jon gathers up the plates and carries them to the kitchen. "So how was your day?" he asks as he packs the plates into the dishwasher. "It was the maid's morning, wasn't it? Where did you end up going? Did you have lunch with Vanessa again?"

"I went for a walk and then met Vanessa at the bistro."

"How is she?"

"Pregnancy suits her better than me."

"That can't be true. You're blooming."

"Ballooning."

He laughs. "You're gorgeous to me."

Daisy hesitates. "I met her husband, Haruto. Briefly. He came into the bistro to fetch her."

"Fetch? You make it sound like a dog coming for his ball."

"Well, that's sort of how it seemed."

He stills. "What do you mean?"

"Sort of . . . I—I'm not sure."

He waits.

"Controlling, I guess. Vanessa is always so enviably poised, but when Haruto appeared outside the bistro window, she just unraveled. Got totally flustered. Couldn't even speak straight. Honestly, Jon, she looked scared. And the way he gripped her arm—the more I think about it, the more I'm concerned for her."

"*The* perfect Vanessa? Afraid of her own husband?"

"Maybe we should have them over for dinner or something. Then you can meet them both and check it out for yourself."

"Maybe we should."

Jon clears the rest of the table, and Daisy reaches for the mail he left on the counter. As she opens bills and junk mail, Jon's mobile pings. Daisy reaches for the last item, a brown manila envelope. But a sudden stillness in Jon makes her glance up. He's studying a text on his screen, his body tense. Daisy sees her husband's features change. For a moment it appears as though he's not even breathing. He suddenly notices her watching, quickly pockets his phone, and moves swiftly to pour the remainder of the wine into his glass.

"What is it?" Daisy asks.

"Nothing."

"Well, who sent 'nothing'?"

"Just a junk text. Spam." He doesn't meet her gaze.

"Jon?"

"What?"

"We don't hide things. We're not that couple. Not anymore."

"Jesus, Daisy. It was spam, okay? Relax."

"Can I see it?"

"What?"

"Can I see the spam?"

"I deleted it."

She regards him steadily, recalling how quickly she deleted her own troll messages without even thinking. Just reflexively. Why can't she just believe him? Why is she mistrusting everything right now? She hears Vanessa's words again:

*Pregnancy can even make you fearful, or paranoid.*

"Sorry," she says. "I didn't mean to pry."

"It's okay."

Daisy realizes she's clutching the letter opener like a dagger in her fist. She carefully resumes opening the manila envelope, but her heart is hammering. An image slices through her brain like a piece of glass—the GIF. In her mind she sees the knife stabbing *up down, up down, up down.* She can almost feel herself holding it, jabbing it into white flesh.

Jon's phone pings again. This time he doesn't check it in front of her. He says he needs to send a work email. He excuses himself and takes his wine up to his office.

Jaw clenched, Daisy slices the plain brown envelope open. An A4-size glossy photo slides out and falls onto the table.

It's an image of a bloody Chucky doll. Knife in fist.

Daisy drops the letter opener with a small gasp.

Beneath the image are the words:

I KNoW WHaT YOU aRE.

I KnOW WhAT YoU DId.

I wilL DEStROY yOU.

DIeDiEdIeDIEBaBYdiE

Daisy can't breathe. Her baby kicks. In slow motion she turns over the envelope to see what's written on the front. She was so absorbed with Jon she never checked.

No name.

No address.

Nothing.

Someone came to their house—right up to their home—and hand-delivered this into their box.

First her car. Now her home.

She shoots her gaze to the stairs, where Jon disappeared.

She's terrified. She should tell him. Report it to the police.

But then they will all know what she did.

# JON

*October 18, 2019. Friday.*
*Thirteen days before the murder.*

Jon sets his wineglass on his desk and locks his office door. A thrill rushes through him. Mia Reiter has found his mobile number. She must have gone to some effort to hunt him down. She *wants* him. This rubs Jon in all the right places.

He seats himself, takes a big sip of wine, and opens the text message, which he did not delete, contrary to what he told Daisy.

Was so great to meet you last night, Jon. Can't stop thinking about you.

Jon swallows, aroused. He brings images of Mia to mind. Those bloodred lips. Those clear green eyes. The way she looked at him as though he were the only person in the universe at that very moment. That smile—how he felt the power of it right inside his chest. The matching red nails. The feel of her slender, cool hand in his. Her seductive accent. The way she carried herself on those high heels—hips sashaying as she walked along the pavement, the city lights glinting on her hair.

This is what it is to feel alive. To thrive. His marriage, this little family growing, this "cottage"—it's stifling something in him.

He opens the second message sent from the same number.

**Would love to meet again. Hope we bump into each other. Soon. Here's to serendipity. Mia. Xoxo**

Jon opens a drawer and takes out his special whisky and a glass. He pours himself a few fingers. He takes a sip. It's better than the wine. He begins to type a reply.

**Let's meet. Same pub? Or we can go somewhere quieter. When are you back in town? JR**

Jon hesitates with his thumb over the SEND button. He thinks of Daisy downstairs in the kitchen. Guilt expands in his chest. Conflict torques through him. A kind of resentment, too—because he can't lose Daisy. If he gives Daisy grounds for divorce, he loses everything.

*But if something "happened" to Daisy?*

Jon curses. It's the wine. The whisky. It's the promise of this woman, Mia Reiter from Switzerland, who skis and is sexy as hell and also a brainy banker. She looks and smells like money, too. Maybe she's even wealthier than Daisy and her trust fund. He closes his eyes, heart thudding. He's got a devil on one shoulder, saying *do it*. An angel on the other who is truly trying to protect him from himself. But then the devil whispers into the secret part of his soul . . . *The world doesn't end at Daisy. What harm will a little fling bring if you keep it quiet? No foul if no one finds out, right? A man like you, Jon, you need an outlet. You need to release some of that pent-up alpha energy.*

Jon hits SEND.

# MAL

With their flashlights, Mal and Benoit pan the exterior of the Audi S6 sedan parked in the Rose Cottage driveway. Rain drips from the bill of Mal's cap. Rivulets run down their jackets. The air is cold. The foghorn sounds mournfully in the Burrard.

"No dents," Benoit says. "But it could have been off-road, given the mud."

Mal shines her beam in through the car windows. She can't see anything unusual inside.

A slash of yellow light upstairs in Rose Cottage catches Mal's eye. She glances up at the second story. A drape falls back into place, cutting the light.

"He's up there. Watching us," Benoit says. "The guy is lying through his teeth, and I don't like those wounds."

"You can smell the fear on him," she says. "Never mind the alcohol."

"We need to get inside that house, and we need to impound and search this Audi," he says.

"Yeah, but we also need something solid in order to secure the warrants." Mal crouches down, wipes mud off the rear plate. She takes a photo of the registration and a few more shots of the Audi exterior and tires.

Once back inside their unmarked vehicle, she sends the images to Lula. Benoit starts the engine, and Mal tries once more to call Daisy Rittenberg. Again, it flips to voice mail.

Mal says, "Ty Binty at the Pi Bistro claims the Rittenbergs moved back to Vancouver to be closer to Daisy's parents. What did he say her father's name was?"

"Wentworth," Benoit says as he backs their unmarked into the residential street. "Labden Wentworth."

"Pull over across the road. I want to wait here until we can get surveillance on Rittenberg. He looks ready to bolt."

While Benoit parks under trees across the road from Rose Cottage, Mal places a call requesting surveillance detail for Rose Cottage. She gives the Rittenberg address, then asks to be put through to Lula again.

"Lu, can you find us a phone number and address for a Labden Wentworth? He's the father of pregnant Daisy Wentworth. She's not at her home, and we have reason to fear for her and her unborn child's well-being."

"On it," says Lu.

Mal hangs up and quickly punches the name "Labden Wentworth" into a search engine. A host of links associated with the name "Labden Wentworth" pop up. Ty Binty was correct—the Wentworth name *is* big.

Mal scans the linked articles. "Says here that Labden Wentworth founded TerraWest Corporation, which is a global developer and operator of luxury mountain resorts. The company also owns ancillary businesses, including a chain that sells outdoor gear. They employ more than fifty-five thousand employees worldwide. Annual revenues around 5.2 billion. Apparently Wentworth's wife, Annabelle, is a big name in her own right, in luxury urban real estate. She owns her own company. They live on the North Shore, up in the British Properties area, but no phone numbers I can see so far."

While they wait for the Rose Cottage surveillance detail to arrive, and for Lula to come up with contact details, Mal quickly texts Peter.

Everything okay?

No response.

Her worry about her husband deepens. This is probably going to be her last case. She's going to need to step away sooner than she'd hoped in order to care for Peter.

Her phone rings. It's Lula with Labden Wentworth's number and address.

"Four four five six Eyrefield Drive, British Properties," Lula says on speaker. As the details come through, a police cruiser approaches slowly down the street. Mal exits their unmarked and hurries through the rain to speak to the officer inside the cruiser. He winds down the window, and she bends in to talk to him.

"If Rittenberg leaves, call it in, and stay on him." She explains the situation, then hurries back to Benoit, waiting in the unmarked. As she buckles in, he pulls out, and they start toward the bridge that will take them over to the North Shore. As they drive, Mal phones Labden's number.

It goes to voice mail.

She calls Peter. When her husband answers, her relief is sharp. She consciously tempers her voice. She must remain calm with him.

"Hey, how're you doing?" she asks.

"Good. You going to be late?" He's forgotten already.

"Yeah, looks that way. Got a new case. You're not checking your texts?"

"Oh. I . . . ah . . ."

"No worries. Did you manage to warm the lasagna?"

Silence.

"You got my note about the lasagna?" Mal curses at her framing of the question. She's been getting advice on how to talk to Peter in ways that don't force him into confronting the fact he can't remember something, because it puts him on the defensive. It doesn't help anyone.

"Yes, I warmed the lasagna, Mallory."

She closes her eyes at his patronizing tone. "Great. Don't wait up, okay?"

"A homicide?"

"Looks that way."

"Who's the victim?"

Mal feels a pang in her chest. She's always discussed her cases with Peter. He was a brilliant professor of forensic psychology before he took early retirement last year due to his mental health issues. They were a team, and she feels her husband, their relationship, who they once were as a unit, seeping away.

"We're not sure yet who the victim is," she says. "But someone has sustained serious injuries—likely life-threatening. If they are still alive, time is not on their side."

"Go get 'em, love."

Emotion burns hot in her eyes. "Yeah. We will. We'll do our best." She says goodbye, kills the call. She feels Benoit's curiosity and his empathy. It's his empathy that makes it worse. Mal does not want pity. To Benoit's credit he lets her be and says nothing. As they negotiate city traffic and feed onto the bridge, it's Mal who finally breaks the silence.

"Is Sadie okay with your late nights?"

He smiles. "It's not like a choice, is it?"

"There are admin jobs in the department, you know."

He chuckles. "That's not me, Mal."

"Yeah, I know."

A pause.

"Besides, it's not like we have a homicide every day, right? On slower days I take the night shifts at home. And I do the baby minding on my days off."

"Sadie still pursuing her degree?"

"Determined as ever. Correspondence right now. Can't stop that woman." He glances at Mal. "She's going to make a damn fine immigration and refugee lawyer. I'm so freaking proud of her."

Mal smiles. "The world is in good hands."

He laughs loudly and darkly. "The world is not within our control, boss."

"Well, at least my team will be left in good hands if you're offered the helm."

"You've got a few months yet," Benoit says.

She gives a rueful smile. "Maybe. Maybe not."

# THE MAID'S DIARY

Dear Diary, I'm sorry I have not visited with you in a while. Not only have I not written, I have also officially quit therapy. My shrink said: "You're regressing, Kit. By shutting me out, the damaged part of you is slinking into hiding again. Finding out what drives you is scary, I know, but it's always most challenging right before we have a major breakthrough. You're almost there, Kit."

*Maybe I am.*

*But I disagree about the hiding. I'm not pulling up the drawbridge. I'm not slinking away. This time I am holding my ground. I'm standing in my power. And where did I find power? From Charley. Then in Daisy's safe.*

*I told you at the beginning of this journal I know where people tend to keep their secrets. I know where to search for them.*

*On this cleaning day at Rose Cottage, I finish the laundry, the dusting, vacuuming, and I wash and pack away the dishes in the kitchen. I set my timer for my snoop session.*

*I decide not to go into Jon's computer today. It's bathroom day. Pills and medical secrets are what I'm after. But the medicine cabinet offers nothing scintillating—cold meds, some uppers, downers, old prescription painkillers, wart remover, pregnancy vitamins, antiseptic spray, Band-Aids, aspirin, that sort of thing. I crouch down, and I open a cabinet below the washbasin on "her" side of the bathroom. There's a drawer inside the cabinet. It's full of female hygiene products. Sanitary pads, packets of tampons, a vaginal lubricant, intimate wipes. I feel the packets of pads and tampons. Women love to hide things in places like this—particularly secrets from their men. Husbands and boyfriends usually don't go poking around in menstrual products. I feel something inside one of the tampon boxes. It's small. Hard. Angular. Not a tampon. I open the box. Tucked into one of the tampon wrappers is a key.*

*My pulse kicks.*

*I extract the key. I know what lock it fits—I'm certain of it. On my last visit to Rose Cottage, at the back of Daisy's underwear drawer, I found a document-size safe with a key lock and a handle. It's pale blue. Many of my clients have lockboxes in varying shapes and sizes. Not only for secrecy, but for fire protection. The color of this safe, the fact it's hidden at the back of Daisy's underwear, that the key is with her tampons—it all screams, Wife wants to keep secret from her husband.*

*Tension whips through me. I check my watch. Barely any snooping time left. I should quit. Now. Do this next time. If Daisy arrives a minute or two early, I'll be toast. But I can't abandon this.*

*I leave the bathroom cabinet door open, rush into the bedroom, yank open the underwear drawer, ferret around in her lingerie, and pull out the box.*

*It's heavy. A solid metal. My excitement is over the top.*

*Mouth dry, I sit on the edge of their king-size bed. I insert the key. It slides in perfectly. I turn it and open the top of the box.*

*Inside are two manila envelopes and a flash drive.*

*I touch the flash drive. I can't take it with me to view what's in it. If she finds it missing and reports it to Holly, I will definitely be fired. I remove one of the manila envelopes, open it.*

*Inside is a multipage legal document. I begin to read. As the meaning of the legalese becomes clear, I grow dizzy, can't breathe. My world narrows and time slides into a dead zone as I struggle to process what I'm seeing. My gaze shoots down to the signatures at the bottom. I go numb. With trembling hands, I open the other envelope.*

*A thudding sounds in my ears, and I try to swallow as I absorb the weight of the text—what it means to me. My timer buzzes. I jerk back. I hear a car in the driveway. Panic licks through my belly.*

*Shit!*

*I rush to the window and peer down into the driveway. I almost faint with relief. It's a UPS van. The driver gets out of his van and comes to the front door with a package.*

*I hurry back to the bed, ignoring the doorbell—the courier will leave the package or come back tomorrow. I spread the documents out on the bed. I take one photo after another with my phone. My hands shake so hard I pray the images will be in focus.*

*I stuff the documents back into the envelopes and return them to the safe. I see the flash drive still lying on the bed. Given what's in these documents, I can't even begin to imagine what the flash drive contains. I pick it up, clutch it tightly in my hand. My brain whirls. Definitely no time to view the contents on Jon's computer. If I do take it, examine it at home, then return it next time, it would be a major risk.*

*I hear Boon's voice.*

*If you see a shocking secret . . . you could be in trouble. People—rich people—will do anything to protect themselves and their families . . . even kill.*

*This is one of those secrets.*

*It will destroy the Rittenbergs and everyone close to them if I tell.*

*And if I don't tell, it will destroy me.*

*I have no choice. Not anymore.*

*I pocket the flash drive and rush back into the bathroom to shut the cabinet. I hurriedly pack and load my cleaning supplies and Dyson into my Subaru. I'm sweating, panicked Daisy or Jon will come up the driveway, terrified Daisy will discover the flash drive missing and come hunting for her maid.*

*I'm also betting on the fact Daisy will not say anything to Jon.*

*Given the contents of those documents, I'm also counting on the fact she won't report me to Holly.*

*Like I said, it's a black secret. And Daisy will fight to keep it buried.*

# MAL

*November 1, 2019. Friday.*

When Mal and Benoit arrive at number 4456, the Wentworth mansion, it is lit up like a mountainside castle in the darkness. Outdoor lights line a paved driveway that curves up toward the house. A small white BMW is parked in front of the four garage doors. Mal and Benoit pull in behind the BMW, exit their vehicle, and make their way up a staircase to the entrance. As Benoit rings the bell, Mal turns to survey the night view over the distant city. The city itself is shrouded in a thick blanket of fog. The lit suspension cables of Lions Gate Bridge peep over the fog like garlands. The tallest buildings in the downtown core also protrude like shining beacons above the clouds. The Wentworth mansion is at a high elevation on the flanks of Hollyburn Mountain. No rain or clouds up here. The air is icy cold, and the night sky is filled with stars, but down in the fog it's raining.

"It looks magical," she whispers.

The door opens.

Mal spins around and finds herself staring at a pregnant brunette. Her heart kicks.

"Daisy Rittenberg?" she asks.

"What do you want?" She glances at Mal, then Benoit. She looks like she's been crying.

*Thank God she's all right. One pregnant woman: safe.*

"I'm Sergeant Mallory Van Alst, and this is Corporal Benoit Salumu. Can we come in? We have some questions about—"

A male's voice booms through the hallway. "What is it, Princess? Who's there?" A man comes into view. Tall. Lean. Tanned. Silver hair. Chiseled jawline and chiseled attitude. Mal recognizes him from the photos she just saw online.

"Mr. Wentworth," Mal says. She reintroduces herself and Benoit. "We're investigating a missing person case, and time is of the essence. We have reason to believe your daughter might have information that can help us. Can we please come in?"

Labden Wentworth hesitates. His gaze shoots to his daughter. "Princess" shakes her head almost imperceptibly.

Wentworth stiffens his shoulders, seemingly growing taller. "What could Daisy possibly contribute—" His features change as a thought appears to strike him. "Does this have to do with Jon?"

Mal feels a quickening in her blood. "Can we come in?"

Reluctantly, Daisy and Labden step back to allow the two detectives into the warmth of the opulent home. Mal and Benoit are led into a cavernous living room. A gas fire flickers. The view from the living room windows over the distant city is even more spectacular. A woman appears—elegant. She moves like a dancer. Hers is as commanding a presence as her husband's, but with a sharp, feminine edge.

"What is this?" the woman asks, her gaze flicking between Mal and Benoit. "Who *are* these people?"

"It's okay, love. It's just the police. They want to ask Daisy about a missing person."

She exchanges a hot look with her husband. Mal and Benoit share a brief look of their own. They're onto something here. Mal can feel it.

Both Mr. and Mrs. Wentworth begin seating themselves on the sofa in the living room.

"We'd like to speak with Daisy alone," Benoit says.

They hesitate. Labden Wentworth regards his daughter. "We're right outside if you need us, Princess." He turns to the detectives. "Daisy is tired. She needs her rest. She's had a bad day, and we're worried about the baby."

"Understood," Mal says.

The Wentworths leave the room and quietly close the glass french doors behind them.

Daisy, puffy eyed and blotchy, lowers herself clumsily into a chair near the fire. She appears both nervous and hostile as well as distressed.

Mal and Benoit sit on the sofa opposite her. Benoit allows Mal to take the lead.

"Mrs. Rittenberg," Mal says, leaning forward, "we're investigating an incident that occurred at a home called Northview. It's also known locally as the Glass House. We understand that you know the owners, Vanessa and Haruto North?" Mal is fishing to see what this woman might offer up first.

Daisy swallows. "What happened—what incident?"

"Have you visited the Norths' house recently?"

Daisy looks trapped. She glances at the doors, and her hand protectively covers her baby tummy. "Do I need a lawyer?"

"Do you?" Mal asks.

Her face turns red.

"Look, Mrs. Rittenberg, you're not in trouble. We're simply trying to gather information at this point. We do know that you purchased a blueberry-blackberry pie from the Pi Bistro in Point Grey yesterday afternoon. You also purchased a bouquet of"—she glances at her notebook, flips to the page—"dendrobium orchids, baby's breath, Japanese anemones, spider mums, and white calla lilies from a florist called Bea's Blooms." She meets Daisy's gaze. "Both the pie and the flowers were left at the Northview property sometime after six fourteen p.m. yesterday. Tucked into the bouquet was a card that came from you." Mal gets up, goes over to Daisy, and shows her a photo of the card on her phone.

*Good luck before autonomy dies, friend. It's been a ride.*

*Thanks for the support.*

*Daisy*

*X*

"Who is this note intended for, Mrs. Rittenberg?"

The woman doesn't blink. Or speak.

Mal reseats herself. "What happened at Northview? Why were you and your husband there? Why did you drop the pie and flowers outside the front door?"

Daisy Rittenberg moistens her lips and says, very slowly, "My husband, Jon, and I were invited to dinner at our friends' place."

"Who are your friends?"

She breaks eye contact, smooths her pants. "Vanessa North—she's a pregnant friend of mine. And her husband, Haruto."

"Are they good friends?"

She hesitates. "I . . . met Vanessa in August at a prenatal yoga class." Her eyes begin to water. "Like I said, she was also pregnant."

"Was? As in past tense? Did something happen?"

"I—no, I mean, she *is* pregnant. I'd only met Haruto once before. Jon had yet to meet either of them. We picked up the flowers and the pie on the way over."

"Can you explain why you dropped the flowers and pie outside the front door?"

Without hesitation she says, "I got a bad cramp. I thought I was going into labor or something. It spooked me. I dropped what I was holding to grab hold of my belly."

Mal inhales slowly. "And how was dinner with your friends?"

"We didn't actually stay. Because of my cramps we went straight home. Jon was worried I might need to see my doctor."

"And how did the Norths seem last night?"

"Fine."

"Have you spoken to them since?"

"No."

"So your friends didn't call to find out how you are after the cramps?"

She says nothing.

"Mrs. Rittenberg, was anyone else apart from Vanessa and Haruto North at the Glass House that evening?"

"I didn't see anyone else."

"Did you see any other car parked outside?"

She pales. Her breathing quickens. She glances again at the french doors.

Mal shifts tack. "Your home—it's named Rose Cottage, right?"

"What does my house have to do with this?"

"Who cleans Rose Cottage, Mrs. Rittenberg?" Mal asks.

"I don't see what relevance th—"

"We can do this at the station, ma'am," Benoit says. "Or you can help us here."

Daisy Rittenberg's mouth flattens. When she speaks again, her voice is tight and thin. "We have a cleaning service. Holly's Help. The service started three days after we moved into the house in July."

"Do you know the name of the specific individual who cleans your home?"

"No." Her answer is quick. Firm. Too quick.

Mal nods slowly. "Did you notice a yellow Subaru with the Holly's Help logo parked outside the Norths' residence when you and your husband arrived in the Audi?"

"No. I told you. I didn't see anyone else, or any other car."

"Are you certain?"

"There was no other vehicle in the driveway." Her gaze darts back toward the doors. The woman is getting flighty, looking increasingly cornered. Mal senses their window for obtaining information from Daisy Rittenberg is closing fast.

"What if I told you that we have a witness who saw both you and your husband pulling into the Northview driveway in a dark-gray Audi S6 sedan at six fourteen p.m.? You parked the Audi right behind a yellow Subaru. And our witness saw your Audi and the yellow Subaru were still in that driveway until just before midnight. After which both the Audi and the Subaru were driven away together. At speed."

"I'd say your witness is lying. Or seeing things. And that we're done here."

Benoit says, "Someone was seriously hurt inside that house, Mrs. Rittenberg, and your cooperation would—"

"*What?*"

"I said, someone was hurt—"

"Who? *Who* was hurt?" Panic brightens her eyes. Red spots form on her cheeks.

"If you could just answer our questions," Mal says.

"Dad!" She pushes to her feet and waddles toward the french doors, her hand pressing on the small of her back. The doors swing open before she reaches them.

Her father steps into the room. He takes one look at his daughter and says, "Okay, officers, you need to leave. Now."

Mal surges to her feet. "Just one more question. Please. A woman's life could depend on it."

Labden Wentworth wavers, then glances at his daughter. Mal uses the moment to reach for her phone. Hurriedly, she pulls up the image of Kit Darling provided by Holly McGuire. She holds her phone toward Daisy.

"Do you recognize this person?"

Daisy leans forward, swallows hard. "No."

"Are you certain? Take a good look."

"Of course I'm certain. Who is she?"

"Your maid. Up until October 27."

Daisy goes sheet white. "What?"

"Her name is Kit Darling. She cleaned Rose Cottage for Holly's Help until October 27, after which you got a new maid."

Daisy keeps her gaze fixed on the photo as though afraid to meet Mal's eyes again. "I'm always out of the house when the maid comes. I've never laid eyes on this person. If Holly sent someone different at the end of October, I don't know that, either. All I know is my house gets cleaned." Her hands start to tremble. "Dad, I—I think I'm going to faint. I need to lie down. Tell these people to get out of here. Now."

As Annabelle Wentworth hurriedly ushers Mal and Benoit toward the front door, Mal hears Daisy Rittenberg's voice going shrill as she says to her father, "I don't know! I have *no* idea what happened at the house. Of course I'm telling you the truth."

# THE MAID'S DIARY

I'm hot and edgy with anxiety as I insert Daisy's flash drive into my laptop. I do it as soon as I am back in my apartment. I'm besieged with a sharp urgency. What I saw—what I now know, the evidence I have in my phone—it makes me dangerous to both Jon and Daisy, which in turn makes them dangerous to me. I need to return this drive ASAP.

*I open the flash drive folder. There is just one file inside. A video. I click on it and hit PLAY.*

*At first the footage is confusing. Bad angles, jerky camera, lots of moving people, grainy, low light. Music, loud voices, laughing. But as the footage unspools on my laptop monitor, I realize with horror what I am seeing.*

*Someone recorded that night.*

*This is the visual proof that underpins the contents of the documents that Daisy hides under lock and key.*

*I watch in mounting dread. Then I hear something in the footage. A laugh. It rises above the music and the voices. A high, whooping laugh. It winds up, higher. I go ice cold. I can't breathe. I hit STOP.*

*I sit back, struggling to catch my breath.*

*I rewind a little, hit PLAY again. There it is. Barely audible at first, buried in the party noise. But then it rises, goes higher. Winds up into the whoop. My eyes burn. My heart races. I rewind, hit PLAY again. Then again. And again. I lean close to my monitor. I can identify many of the faces in the footage from that terrible night, including my own. But I can't see Boon. He never said he was there. But he is. He's here, in this footage—not a doubt in my heart. That's his laugh. I'd know it anywhere in this world. No one has a laugh like Boon's. Surely?*

*I slump back, energy punched out of me. All this time. All these years of friendship, of him caring for me . . . and he knew. He was there. He saw. And he never came forward.*

*He never told the police what he surely must have witnessed, given this footage. Not only that, Boon appears to have found the assault that night laughable.*

*He's told me only that he believed my claims from "back then." But he never confessed to me he was there. Not even close. The betrayal is overwhelming. Especially on the back of those signatures at the bottom of one of the documents in Daisy's safe. I can't seem to even begin to process yet how this changes everything that I thought was true in my life over the past two decades. Talk about dropping through a trapdoor. Talk about ambiguous images. When you suddenly see the old, evil hag in the image of the beautiful young woman, you cannot unsee her.*

*I begin to cry. Great big body-shuddering sobs.*

*Fuck.*

*I've lost a friend. If he ever was one.*

*I put my hands over my eyes. I press my head. The pain is intense. Bam Bam Bam. A mallet that hammers inside my skull.*

*But now I have proof. After eighteen years, I have proof. It's all here. It's been here all this time, all those lost and painful and dead years. Locked in fucking Daisy Rittenberg's safe.*

*What in the hell for? Why does she keep it? Surely she must know what this will do to her husband if it gets out? Maybe that's exactly why she keeps it. To control Jon.*

*Charley's warning slithers into my brain. "I don't know what you want with the Rittenbergs, Kit, but be careful. You might think Jon Rittenberg is bad, and he is, but he's just your generic entitled male asshole. His wife, though—Daisy Rittenberg—she's dangerous."*

*I sit there, staring into nothingness, trying to comprehend, until the night grows black as ink. I sit there while it stays black. I sit until I hear the rain begin. Until I know what I am going to do. Those weeks since I first walked into Rose Cottage, since I first laid eyes on those paintings—they have been leading to this. All the pieces have been slotting together for a purpose.*

*I pick up my phone. I struggle to compose myself, suck in a deep breath, and I call Boon.*

*"Kit?" He sounds sleepy. I woke him. "Are you okay, Kit? Do you know what time it is? What's going on?"*

*"I'm not okay, Boon. I need to see you. I have something I must show you."*

# DAISY

*October 25, 2019. Friday.*
*Six days before the murder.*

Daisy is irritable as she drives to Vanessa's house for a late lunch date. It's Friday—maid's day—so she needs to be out of her house, but she'd prefer to be in bed with her swollen legs up. She's two days shy of thirty-five weeks pregnant, and she feels the world closing in on her in all ways. Her body is uncomfortable. She's deeply rattled by the Chucky that arrived in the envelope last week. And Jon's weird behavior is worrying. Plus she's increasingly paranoid, feeling followed, forgetting and misplacing things. She couldn't find her diamond teardrop pendant this morning. She swears she left it on the bathroom counter. And Jon was yelling at her about where *she* put his damn shoes.

She just wants Baby Bean out now. She wants to feel normal.

But as Daisy turns her BMW into the lane near the water and sees Vanessa North's shining glass house ahead, her spirits lift. Vanessa has invited her for a late lunch, and Daisy has to admit to herself that the autumn weather is glorious. Blue skies, a balmy temperature, leaves everywhere turning bright shades of red and orange and yellow. She tells herself the Bean will be here soon. Meanwhile she'll continue to keep off social media. Jon's job will sort itself out. This phase will pass.

Daisy parks in the Glass House driveway. As she exits her car, a flock of tattered black birds erupts with a clatter from a nearby tree. She startles, then watches them—ragged harpies fluttering up into the blue sky. Crows. Ugly, bloody crows. Creepy scavengers. What does one call a flock of crows again? A murder. She shivers because at the same moment the word *murder* enters her head, she catches sight of the tombstones on the front lawn across the street, and a skeleton dangling by its neck from an upstairs window. *Stupid Halloween.*

"Daisy!" Vanessa steps out of her glass front door, wearing an emerald-green jersey dress that shows off her pregnant tummy. She looks utterly gorgeous.

Daisy and Vanessa hug and exchange air-kisses.

"It's such a gorgeous day," Vanessa says, "I thought we'd eat by the pool. Are you good with that?"

"Absolutely."

Vanessa takes Daisy through the living room and leads her out to a table set for two beside an infinity pool that overlooks the inlet. Daisy is instantly green with envy. Her and Jon's home is on the opposite shore and nowhere near waterfront. Daisy would much rather live on this side, and right on the water. Being on this side of the inlet would also place her closer to her parents. In fact, the more Daisy thinks about it, Rose Cottage does not convey the sort of image she would like to project. The property was a hasty $7.7 million purchase from afar, something they could move into the moment they arrived from Colorado. A stopgap, really. Because the idea is to relocate to the new resort once Jon is offered the COO job. Now Daisy isn't at all certain it's going to happen.

"Take a seat," Vanessa says. "I'm just going to fetch the food."

Daisy sits facing the pool and the ocean, relieved to get off her throbbing feet. Vanessa comes back out, carrying a charcuterie board with an assortment of cheeses, smoked meats, pickles, olives, grapes, sliced vegetables, and nuts. She sets the platter down, hesitates. "I thought—no, never mind."

"'Never mind' what?" asks Daisy.

"I miss my wine *so* badly. I was thinking . . . maybe just a little spritzer." Vanessa pulls a wry mouth. "Or some sparkling rosé. But—"

"Oh, let's do it. Just a little drink. It'll be relaxing." Daisy grabs on to the idea. They're both due in a month or so. Surely it can't harm the babies now?

Vanessa frowns. "Are you sure?"

Daisy smiles. "Of course I'm sure."

Vanessa puts her hand on her chest. "A woman after my heart, thank God. Can you cut that salami while I get the drinks? The knife's over there." She disappears into the glass doors of her beautiful house.

Daisy takes in a deep breath and reaches for the sharp knife on the table. As she carefully slices the sausage, she thinks she really could do with a glass of wine, something to take her tension down a notch. The anxiety and all the resulting cortisol pumping into her body are probably far worse for Baby Bean than a teensy bit of wine in the balmy fall sunshine.

Vanessa comes out of the house with a big smile, two wineglasses, and a frosted bottle of French rosé. She pours the wine, and they sip in the soft sunshine as they pick at the meat and cheeses and fruit. The alcohol blossoms like warmth in Daisy's chest and makes her feel amazing.

"God I miss this," Daisy says as Vanessa tops their glasses up.

"Me too." Vanessa sets the bottle down and takes a healthy sip from her own glass. "It's so unfair. Men get to carry on as normal, going to the pub, drinking, whatever, and we have to be holy saints and abstain."

"And then we get to give birth and breastfeed and deal with leaking boobs and breast pumps."

Vanessa laughs. "Never mind ripped vaginas. I was just saying that to Haruto the other day."

Daisy reaches for some Cambozola cheese that Vanessa has warmed slightly. It's soft and buttery as she smooths it onto a cracker. The knife blade glints in the sun. "It was good to meet Haruto at the bistro," she says cautiously.

"Was it?"

Daisy glances up. "Well, yes," she says, taking a bite of the cracker. "I think it would be great if both of you could meet Jon, too. Maybe we could all have a dinner together."

Vanessa regards her in steady silence for a moment, then she leans forward. "Look, Daisy, I know what you saw. I know what you must've thought. It was written all over your face. But you need to understand—Haruto is a good man. He's just—a little coercive at times. He also has a quick temper, not much patience. But his temperament is also what makes him good at business. His mind is incredibly sharp. He doesn't tolerate fools or people who think too slowly. It's what enables him to bring in the big bucks and afford us places like this." She gestures to her home. "I'm sure you understand."

Daisy is fully aware of what Vanessa is doing. She's holding a mirror up to Daisy's face and asking her to look at herself, her own life, her own man. Her own sets of compromises and values.

"Take Jon, for example," Vanessa says. "Your husband is a champion downhill ski racer, a winner of Olympic medals. His sport is extreme. High stakes. Dangerous. All about power. Money, too. Only certain A-type personalities with privilege can consistently excel—thrive—in a milieu like that. But those A-plus alphas come with other issues, too, right? Can't have it both ways." A pause. "Not so?"

This woman is inside Daisy's head. She reaches for her glass and sips quietly because she's unsure how best to respond.

"How long have you guys been married?" Vanessa asks. "I don't think you ever mentioned it."

Daisy gives a little huff of a laugh. "We married pretty much right after Jon came home with the gold in '02. We were really young.

Probably too young. We'd been dating since high school, though. And my parents loved him. Dad felt Jon was a really good fit all round, with our family ski resort business and all." Another sip of wine—it's going down so well and so fast it's making Daisy heady. "Dad thought Jon had such potential."

"Had?"

Daisy's cheeks flush. She didn't mean for it to come out like that, but she supposes it's true. She clears her throat and deflects. "How about you and Haruto? How'd you guys meet?"

"An airport bar. How cliché is that?" Vanessa reaches for her glass, sips. "We got chatting and learned we were on the same flight back to Vancouver. We hooked up afterward, and it went from there. We married in Singapore, where Haruto was born. His mother is Japanese, and his dad's family has deep roots in the UK."

"So that's where his surname comes from?"

Vanessa nods.

Daisy sips more wine. She's still insatiably curious about Haruto but doesn't want to send Vanessa's defenses back up. When people feel humiliated, shamed, they go into defensive mode. So she aims for another angle.

"I saw the framed photo near the bar when we came through. The one of you and Haruto. It's a stunning shot. So exotic. That waterfall, those rocks, that jungle and orchids in the backdrop, your bare feet, and that beautiful white bohemian skirt with the colorful trim—it looks Mexican. Is that where the photo was taken?"

"Nicaragua." Vanessa smiles. "It was some years back. I found the skirt at a local market."

Silence falls over the pair. The wind picks up a little and the weather turns cooler. Clouds begin to scud across the sky. Vanessa offers nothing more, but now that Daisy has gotten going, she craves additional details, and the wine is making her bold.

"Have you guys been planning a family for long?"

Vanessa laughs, but in a self-deprecating way. "We thought we'd never be able to have kids. And then wham, out of the blue, it happened."

"Is Haruto happy?"

"Of course—why do you ask?"

"No reason." Then, as if struck by some need to tell a truth, or perhaps it's the wine after not having had alcohol for so many months, Daisy says, "Sometimes I wonder if Jon and I—I mean, I *know* we're doing the right thing having a baby, but I do wonder if Jon really wants it."

"Seriously?"

She nods.

"Has he expressed regret?" Vanessa tops up their wine.

Daisy breathes in deeply and exhales. She explains that Jon suddenly has unanticipated competition for the job they thought was guaranteed to him. And it's rocked their plans.

"Part of me wonders if Jon only said yes to getting pregnant because of the whole job-offer deal," Daisy says, reaching for her newly full glass.

"You don't mean that?"

"Well, he knows that *I* believe a baby would be healthy for our marriage, and that becoming a family unit would make me happy. And he knows that if I am happy, my parents are happy, and my dad is the one who offered Jon the promotion, so . . ." Daisy's voice fades. She clears her throat. "So maybe he just went along with it."

Quietly, Vanessa says, "I didn't know your marriage was in trouble."

"I shouldn't have said anything."

"What went wrong?"

Daisy feels a darkness beginning to descend. The wind blows a little harder, and a cloud crosses the sun. "I . . . I think I've had a bit too much wine. I feel a bit odd, to be honest. Sort of woozy."

"I'll get you some water."

Vanessa hurries back into her house and returns with a jug of ice water and clean glasses. She pours Daisy a glass.

Daisy swallows half her water, but it doesn't seem to clear her head. A movement in the upstairs window next door catches her eye. She turns and notices that a woman in a wheelchair is watching them from a corner. Vanessa is sitting with her back to the woman, so she probably can't see her. Daisy feels strange, like things are closing in even tighter. She glances up into the sky. The clouds are thickening. That ragged murder of crows is still circling like little black buzzards.

"Daisy?"

"What?"

"You were telling me you thought a baby would fix your marriage."

Daisy rubs her brow, trying to focus. The cold wind blows even harder, whipping up the edge of the tablecloth, but she feels hot, sweaty. "I—Jon screwed up in Colorado. He did something stupid. I . . . I had to clean up after him both times."

"What do you mean?"

"I—it's nothing. The women—they accused him of stuff. Took it all out of proportion. They were seeking attention. I helped clean it up without his knowledge."

Vanessa's gaze turns intense. It makes Daisy feel scared. She's crossed a line. She shouldn't have said this.

"Are you able to share what happened?" Vanessa asks quietly.

"It's like you said. Those A-type male personalities. He just made a mistake. Boys do what boys do—it's so hard growing up male these days."

"What kind of mistake?"

Daisy swallows, struggling to pull clarity back into her brain, but she feels as though she's sliding deeper into some kind of trap of her own making, and she can't back out now that she's baited her friend's curiosity. She attempts a dismissive wave of her hand and says, "Oh, the first incident was forever ago—he was basically a teenager. The other was in Colorado, and it was definitely a manufactured accusation and not Jon's fault. These two women—for whatever their reasons—they tried to destroy his life."

"What exactly did they accuse him of?"

Daisy is fully cornered. In desperation she glances at the Glass House. She will have to go through the house to get to her car. She must find a way to politely excuse herself. How did she even get started down this road? But part of Daisy knows the answer. She craves an ally, a real friend. She's lonely. It's human nature to share, unburden. But it was a mistake. Her brain is acting strange. She feels so tired. So confused . . . She needs to get home. She needs a nap.

"Daisy?"

She shakes herself, clears her throat. "They accused him of sexual assault."

Vanessa stares at her, shocked.

"Of course he didn't do it, Vanessa. It was all lies. All attention seeking. When you're famous, the higher you go, the harder people try to tear you down. It's human nature. They lied about the pregnancies, too. Totally lied."

Vanessa's face changes. Daisy is terrified now. She's crossed a Rubicon, and this friend of hers is about to become an ex-friend.

"You have to understand, Vanessa, Jon was under a lot of pressure in the lead-up to the Olympics. He was young. He got very drunk at a party, had a one-night stand with a girl who was infatuated with him and also very drunk, and she threw herself at him. And the other guys egged him on and kind of got involved, too."

Vanessa's jaw drops.

Daisy cannot stop now. She has to normalize this. She *must* make Vanessa understand. She *needs* Vanessa to understand, to approve of her, to support her.

"The girl took it out of all proportion. She cried rape—gang rape— and then she started saying she was pregnant with Jon's baby, but thank

God no one would back her up. She went to the cops, and they felt obliged to open an investigation, but even the police couldn't get any corroborating witnesses or find any evidence, because there was none, and so of course there were no charges."

"So he claimed the sex was consensual?"

"It was."

"And with the other guys as well?"

"Whatever happened, they were drunk teens having a bit of fun, including her. Jon screwed up by trying to deny the intercourse at first, because he was embarrassed. I mean, she was so not his type. She was this overweight, unattractive thing with bad skin and a bad reputation, and he was blind drunk. Plus he was going out with me. And then when she said she was pregnant with his baby, that's when he confessed it was consensual, and that there were other guys involved. It could have been one of theirs."

"Was a paternity test done?"

"The girl went away. I never heard anything more about any baby, so it was clearly a lie. That girl's accusations could have cost Jon and half the ski team. It would have meant no gold medals for the country the following Olympics. She could have destroyed Jon's future—"

"And yours."

A bolt of irritation goes through Daisy. "Yes—yes, and mine. Jon and I had plans for the future."

"But, Daisy, what if the girl *was* telling the truth?"

Daisy rubs her face. "Look, even if there was an element of truth, my mother gave the girl's parents a fortune for her college fund provided she retracted everything and stopped making trouble. Her family would *never* have gotten that kind of money, Vanessa, not unless they won some lottery. They scored in the end. Her mother was a maid. She cleaned hotel rooms and houses. Her dad worked at the sewage plant.

If you really think about it, they were lucky Jon never sued *them* for damages; plus they got a ton of money."

"Hush money? *Your* mother paid *her* parents hush money?"

"I need to go home. I'm not myself today. I'm sorry I ever broached this. Can we just let it go, please?"

Vanessa stares at Daisy. Her gaze bores a tunnel right through Daisy's head. She feels ill.

"Did you pay off the woman in Colorado as well?"

Daisy pushes herself up to her feet and wobbles slightly. "Thanks for lunch. I need to get home."

Vanessa stands. She places her hand gently on Daisy's arm. "I'm so sorry you went through all that, Daisy. Men suck. They can really suck."

Tears fill Daisy's eyes. She nods.

"Is there anything I can do?"

"No. I—I'm fine. Honest."

"What if he ever does something like this again?"

"Jon?"

"Yes, Jon. I mean, guys like him—they don't change, Daisy, do they? They just learn. They evolve. Adapt. They figure out how to be more careful and how not to get caught next time around."

She inhales a shaky breath. "If he does, I—I swear, next time I will cut him loose. I'll sue him to high heaven. I'll deny him access to our son. And I *will* win any suit because I—I have insurance. I would use that insurance. A woman always needs insurance when they're married to men like my husband."

Softly, Vanessa says, "Insurance?"

Daisy nods, emboldened by Vanessa's concern, by her own desperate need for Vanessa's continued approval, her love.

"Someone at the ski lodge party recorded parts of the 'incident' on their phone. I got the phone afterward. I copied the footage and made the owner of the phone delete it in front of me. I kept the copy.

It's stored on a flash drive in a safe at my house. I also have copies of the nondisclosure agreements signed by the stripper in Colorado. And I have a copy of the NDA signed by the mother of that girl from Whistler. It all proves Jon did those things. And—" Daisy realizes what she's saying. She shuts her mouth.

Vanessa leans forward and hugs her tightly. "It's going to be okay," Vanessa whispers. "It'll all be fine." And Daisy cries.

# DAISY

Daisy drives home in a state. She probably shouldn't be behind the wheel, because her brain and body feel totally weird. How did Vanessa get it all out of her? How did it even start? Daisy remembers—she slipped by mentioning her fear that maybe Jon didn't really want a baby.

As Daisy turns into the Rose Cottage driveway, she sees a piece of brown paper sticking out of her mailbox. She drives up to the garage door, parks, gets out of her car, and walks back down the driveway to the mailbox. She needs the air. But she stumbles and almost falls, catching herself on the mailbox. It sends a shock through her. Her heart pounds. Her skin is hot despite the chill autumn wind. She holds on to the mailbox, feeling woozy, disconnected from reality. Leaves skitter around her feet.

She should never have drunk that wine. It went straight to her head in a weird way. She tells herself it's probably because of abstaining for so long since she learned she was pregnant.

Daisy reaches for the plain brown envelope sticking out of the mail slot. She freezes. The envelope looks exactly the same as the one Jon brought inside last week. No name. No address. Her pulse races even faster. She glances around the neighborhood. More leaves blow off trees and clatter across the sidewalk. A dog walker stands near the corner, holding a leash attached to a Pomeranian trying to pee. Daisy's old neighbor is on all fours near the sidewalk, deadheading flowers along his fence. A crow caws. She glances up. The bird watches her from the telephone wires. She hates crows.

Daisy moistens her lips and rips the envelope open.

Inside is another A4 piece of glossy photograph paper. Daisy slides it out. Her breath stalls. It's an image of a carving knife next to a tombstone that says:

RIP BABY BEAN. 🏴

At the bottom, printed in block letters, are the words:

🎵 IT'S NOT ALL CHILD'S PLAY—DIE BABY, DIE, DIE, DIE. I HOPE YOUR BABY DIES 🎵

Fear cracks through her. And right on the back of her fear rides a white-hot burst of rage.

There is one person—just one person in this entire world—for whom these words and images would mean anything.

Their stalker from Colorado.

Charley Waters. The stripper.

Daisy's gaze darts around her neighborhood again. Is Charley here? Did she follow them from Colorado? Is she stalking them again?

*She's gaslighting me—she's fucking gaslighting me.*

Daisy waddles hurriedly over to the fence and calls out to her elderly neighbor. "Frank! Hey, hi, Frank?"

The old man looks up, then pushes to his feet and approaches the fence.

"Hello, Daisy. How are you guys doing—is everything okay?" His eyes narrow as he comes closer. "Are you ill?"

She's shaking. Hard. Her face feels beet red. Her skin is on fire. Her eyes burn.

"I'm fine. Totally fine. Did you see anyone come onto my property and put something in my mailbox?"

"I don't think so. I've been out here most of the day, puttering away in the front yard. Are you sure you're okay? Can I fetch you a glass of water or something?"

"No one suspicious came to our mailbox?"

He frowns, regarding her intently. "I can't say that I saw anything strange."

"Are you certain? Nothing unusual at all?"

"Just the maid. The usual one, same as always."

Daisy stares. "The maid," she repeats slowly.

"From Holly's Help. The one who drives that little yellow Subaru with the sign on the doors."

"Thanks, Frank." She turns and walks slowly to her front door, breathing hard.

Once inside, Daisy paces. The maid? Surely there's no way some cleaner from Holly's Help knows what she did in secret to Charley Waters back in Silver Aspens.

Daisy knows she should call the police. Report Charley. Tell them she's here. That a vindictive and dangerous stalker in violation of her restraining order has followed them across the border.

But then Daisy would have to explain why she believes this note came specifically from Charley Waters. There's no way Daisy is going to reveal she terrorized, then pressured and paid, Charley to eliminate Jon's offspring. And that she did it because there was no way in hell she was going to let that piece of trailer-park stripper trash tie Jon to her forever through a child they shared. No freaking way. Women like that just keep coming back for more—more money, more childcare, more attention. For as long as that child was alive, Jon would be chained in some way to its mother.

Daisy paces some more, her hand supporting the small of her back. There's only one thing to do.

She heads up the stairs. She locates her small address book, scans through the contact details, finds Charley's mobile number, and punches it into her phone.

The phone rings. Daisy tenses.

The instant her call picks up, Daisy barks, "Is it you? Are you doing this to me? What in the hell—I will sue your ass to high heaven, Charley Waters."

"Daisy? Daisy Rittenberg? Is that you?"

"You damn well know it is. You were at my house. You're following me again. You followed us all the way into Canada, and you're stalking me. Lurking behind my hedge in the alley, following me. You put that note inside my car. I know it's you who's been posting that crap on my Instagram account. You are dead, Charley Waters. You are so fucking dead. I will destroy you."

"I don't know what you're talking about."

"Only you know about the Chucky doll. Only you."

"Chucky doll?"

"The ones I sent you. The notes I used to threaten you into getting rid of Jon's baby, before you relented and agreed you'd take the money and have the abortion. Before you signed the gag order where you legally agreed to never talk about this or to contact us again. Before you were slapped with a restraining order. I am going to call the police right now—tell them you are harassing and scaring me again."

There is a long silence. Daisy's mouth is as dry as bone dust. She's trapped Charley. She's got her. It's Charley who has done this. She can hear it in her silence. A cocktail of rage and triumph powers into Daisy's chest. It makes her feel big, strong.

"I can't believe you just said all that, Daisy," Charley says quietly on the other end. "You just came out and straight out confessed what you did to me—with the Chucky. You admitted you were harassing and terrorizing me into having an abortion, and then you paid me to have one. How much was it again?"

Daisy lowers her voice, and her words come out tight. "Don't even think about trying to get another half million out of me, Charley Waters. I don't have time left for your crap. I paid you to shut the fuck up. Is it you who's trolling me on Instagram? Did you follow us here? Are you gaslighting me?"

"Oh, wait, I get it. This is about Kit, isn't it?"

Daisy stalls. "Who's Kit?"

"Listen, lady—" Charley suddenly speaks fast, as though she's realized she slipped and is quickly trying to cover up. "You're crazy. Mad in the head. And I want you to know that *you* are in breach of our contract by calling me, and—"

"Oh, please."

"And I'm recording this. Contact me again, Daisy Rittenberg, threaten me again, and I go straight to the media with this audio, because the other half of the deal was that you would leave me alone."

The call goes dead.

Daisy stares at her phone. Her blood pounds.

*Who in the hell is "Kit"?*

# MAL

*November 1, 2019. Friday.*

Mal and Benoit climb the stairs to Kit Darling's apartment. It's 8:43 p.m., and rain clatters loudly on the roof of the stairwell.

Lula and the rest of the team are still working to locate the Norths while Mal and Benoit check the maid's residence for clues of her whereabouts. Mal also wants to obtain something that will provide a DNA sample to compare against blood evidence at the crime scene.

As they reach the second floor of the old building on Vancouver's east side, Benoit says, "Daisy Rittenberg not recognizing that photo of Darling—do you buy it?"

"I'm not buying anything yet," Mal says as they walk along the corridor, checking apartment unit numbers. The hallway is dimly lit, and it smells of curry from an Indian restaurant downstairs.

"And Vanessa North not calling after Daisy and Jon Rittenberg allegedly dropped flowers and pie and left in medical distress?"

"Daisy claims she met pregnant Vanessa at prenatal yoga classes. Ty Binty also said Daisy came into the bistro with her pregnant friend. We can check in with the yoga people tomorrow. Maybe they can shed some light on where Vanessa and Haruto North might be."

As they reach Darling's unit, Benoit freezes. His hand shoots up, stopping Mal. He puts a finger to his lips and points.

There's a light on inside Darling's apartment. The door is slightly ajar. A silhouette moves inside.

Mal and Benoit exchange a hot glance. Benoit motions to Mal, and without a word, they move in unison into positions on either side of the apartment door. They hear a crash inside, followed by a groan.

They withdraw their weapons.

Standing to the side of the door, weapon drawn, Mal reaches forward, knocks. "Hello? Anyone in there? This is the police."

Silence.

"Hello?" Benoit yells. "Police. We're coming in!"

Mal shoves the door. It swings open wide. Benoit pivots into the entryway, giving Mal cover as she follows.

They see a man bending over a table near the window, his back to them.

"Police." Benoit's voice booms through the small apartment. "Step away from that table, sir. Identify yourself."

The man spins around, sees them, gasps. His hands shoot up into the air, and he drops the glass jar he was holding. It crashes to the floor. The glass shatters, and the contents explode across the apartment.

"Stop!" the man yells with his hands in the air. "Please. I—I wasn't doing anything wrong."

"Identify yourself, sir," Benoit demands.

"Excuse me?" The man cocks his head to the side and leans slightly forward, like he can't hear.

"Your name, sir," Benoit booms. "What is your name?"

"S-Samuel Berkowitz. I-I live next door." He's stuttering, shaking in fear.

"What are you doing in this apartment?" Benoit asks. "Why did you not respond?"

"Pardon me. I can't hear."

Louder, Benoit says, "What are you doing in this apartment, sir? Why did you not respond?"

Mal glances at the mess on the floor. It looks like birdseed.

"I don't have my hearing aids in. Do—do you mind if I put in my aids?"

Benoit lowers his weapon. Mal keeps hers trained on the old man in case he pulls a trick.

Sam Berkowitz, with shaking, liver-spotted hands, fumbles in his pocket and extracts his hearing devices. He struggles to insert them into his ears because he's shaking so hard.

"I don't like to wear them all the time," the old man says. His eyes water, tears gathering in creases. "I came to get Morbid's food. He's Kit's one-legged stray crow. I-I have a key to her apartment. Kit has a key to my place, too, just in case either of us needs help with anything. She asked me to feed Morbid if something happened to her. You . . . you shocked me."

"Apologies, sir. I'm Corporal Benoit Salumu." He holsters his weapon.

"And I'm Sergeant Mallory Van Alst." Mal secures her own weapon into the holster under her jacket. She produces her ID. "We're trying to locate Kit Darling."

"Is she officially missing, then?" Sam Berkowitz asks. He looks crumpled.

"Can we help you step away from that broken glass at your feet, sir?" As Benoit steps forward, glass crunches under his heavy work boots. He takes the man's arm and steers him carefully away from shards among the seeds scattered across the floor.

"Can I sit down?" Berkowitz asks. "My heart—such a shock. It's a galloping horse."

Benoit pulls up a chair and helps Sam Berkowitz seat himself. "Are you in need of medical attention, sir? Can I check your pulse? I am first aid certified," Benoit says.

The man pushes up his sleeve and holds out his arm. "I'm sure I'm fine. Just need to catch my breath."

Mal notices a tattoo on the inside of the man's forearm. Benoit sees it, too. He glances at Mal.

Concentration camp, she thinks. Sam Berkowitz is a Holocaust survivor. Her chest tightens. As Benoit checks Berkowitz's pulse, Mal goes into the kitchen to fetch the man a glass of water.

As she runs the tap, she casts her gaze over the kitchen. It's small. Old. A pot of basil on the windowsill. A collection of colorful little teapots. Photos are stuck to the fridge along with postcards from places like Thailand, Iceland, Kenya, the Galápagos, Patagonia, Australia, Cambodia. While the water is running, Mal checks the backs of some of the postcards. No text, no postmarks. These were not sent from anyone. Kit Darling must have acquired them in some other way, and kept them. Mal leans forward and studies a photograph of a group of young people. Kit is among them. There's another photo of Kit Darling alone in front of a waterfall. Laughing, vibrant, tanned, her blonde hair blowing loose, her arm full of bracelets.

Mal fills a glass and takes it to Sam Berkowitz. "Do you know who those people are with Kit Darling in that photo on the fridge, Mr. Berkowitz?"

His eyes mist. "They're her theater-group friends. I don't know all their names—just Boon's. She collected those postcards. All places she'd like to go. Kit dreams of traveling around the world, you know. She always says if she wins a lottery, that's what she'll do. What happened to her? Is she okay?"

"That's what we're trying to find out." Benoit releases the man's wrist. "Your ticker seems to have calmed itself down, sir. Let us know if you feel unwell. Sorry to have spooked you like that."

Mal hands him the glass of water. He drinks it using two hands.

"We understand Kit was absent from her job today," Mal says. "Her employer and her friend have expressed concern. Can you tell us when you last saw her?"

"Day before yesterday. She helped me carry grocery bags up to my apartment. I knew something was wrong. I could tell. She was quiet. Sort of a pensive mood. Then she asked me to feed her wild crow if something happened to her." His eyes fill with moisture again. "I should have done something. I could see she was scared."

"What do you mean if 'something happened to her'?" Mal asks.

Berkowitz says, "I asked her. She said if she died or went missing suddenly, or something strange like that."

Mal glances at Benoit and says, "Did she say why she was scared?"

He shakes his head sadly. "Only . . . well, about a week ago, maybe more, she asked if I'd seen someone in the shadows across from our building the night before. She said he was watching her windows."

"He?" Mal asks.

Berkowitz nods. "And a few days prior she mentioned someone had followed her from the SkyTrain station. A man dressed in black, she said."

"Did she describe this man?" asks Benoit.

"She said he had light-brown hair and was tall, well built. But that's all she saw."

"Did she say anything else?" Mal asks.

"No. But I was worried for her. And then I didn't hear her come home last night. And I didn't see her car parked in its space down in the lot outside, either. And this morning, Morbid was flapping around outside my window. He flew around to my balcony. It was like he was trying to tell me something. All fussed, he was, hopping about on his one leg. I had a few seeds and gave them to him. Then I came around and knocked on Kit's door, and called out. But no one answered. Her friend Boon came by later in the afternoon, looking for her. Then Boon knocked on my door and asked if I'd seen Kit. He looked very concerned. Boon told me Kit wasn't answering her phone. So we used my key to come inside together. We wanted to check she hadn't fallen in the shower and hit her head or something terrible. But no one was here."

Mal scans the apartment as he talks. It's tiny. Cozy. Full of trinkets. Boho decor. Salt rock lamp. Candles. Cushion covers from Asia sewn with little mirrors. Macramé. Lots of plants. Posters from theater productions. Greek theater masks on the wall. Shelves packed with books.

Mal says, "Do you know if Kit has been doing anything differently recently, or seeing anyone out of the ordinary?"

Berkowitz shakes his head. "All I know is that she seemed distracted these past months. Maybe since July. That's when she began keeping a journal. I suppose that's something different? I hadn't ever noticed her doing that before."

"What kind of journal?" Mal asks. "You mean like a diary?"

"She said it was a therapy thing. Her therapist suggested it."

"Kit Darling was seeing a therapist?"

"I honestly don't know any more than this. I just saw her sitting on her balcony one day. She was writing in a book that was bright pink with purple polka dots on the cover. I asked her if she was writing the next great novel. She just laughed and said it was her therapy journal and that it was her therapist's idea."

Benoit says, "And you didn't ask why she was in therapy?"

"Who asks people why they go to see a psychologist? It's not right to ask such things."

"Do you know where she keeps it?" Mal asks.

"Of course not. I expect she carries it with her, to jot things down as they come to her. That's what I would do."

Mal and Benoit finish questioning Sam Berkowitz, and Benoit escorts the old man back to his own apartment while Mal begins to look around, searching for the diary, or anything that could throw light on Kit Darling's recent movements, plus something that can be used for a DNA sample.

In the bathroom Mal finds a hairbrush with fine blonde hairs. The hairs are dark at the roots. She bags the brush, along with a toothbrush.

Since foul play is suspected, the paperwork for this has already been processed by her team.

Benoit returns. While Mal searches through Darling's bedroom, Benoit tackles the living area.

"No laptop, no tablet, no phone here," he calls out.

"Nothing like that here, either," Mal says. "She must have taken those things with her."

Benoit joins Mal in Darling's bedroom. "Maybe they're in her vehicle."

Mal finds a cylindrical container on the floor next to the closet. She picks it up. It feels empty. She opens the top. "It's a cremains urn," she says with surprise. "What is Darling doing with an empty urn on her bedroom floor?"

"Can't quite let a loved one go?" Benoit suggests as he opens the bedroom closet. He bends down, removes a sneaker. He checks inside. His gaze shoots up to Mal.

"Size seven," he says. "Same size as the bloodied sneaker in the Glass House."

# DAISY

The morning after Daisy found the tombstone Chucky note in her letter box, she has Rose Cottage to herself. It's Saturday, and Jon is off playing golf with clients from out of town. After golf he's got some big dinner with them. He told her it could be a late night—the clients are potentially major investors for the new resort, and he needs to woo them. Jon seems very preoccupied. Daisy is certain he's up to something and that it's tied to Ahmed Waheed. At least Jon found his missing shoes this morning. Right where they'd always been—at the back of the closet, next to his golf shoes. She, however, has not found her missing diamond pendant.

Daisy sinks into a chair in the living room and props her feet up on an ottoman. She sips her tea. She's exhausted after a sleepless night tossing and turning, and her feet are even more swollen. All she can think about is the threat left in her mailbox and Charley Waters's words:

*This is about Kit, isn't it?*

And her neighbor's words:

*Just the maid. The usual one, same as always.*

Daisy's mind goes again to her missing diamond pendant. Surely the maid would not have taken that? However, the maid might have seen someone suspicious on their property, or approaching the letter box, or lurking in the back lane behind the bushes.

Daisy has no idea who this maid is who drives a little yellow Subaru. She has always preferred to think of her as an anonymous house fairy. Not some woman with a fully fleshed life. Daisy doesn't even know her name. She makes a decision.

It's maid day again on Monday. Daisy will stay home until the maid arrives on Monday morning. She will ask the maid to her face whether she has witnessed anyone suspicious lurking around Rose Cottage.

And Daisy will ask the maid directly if she has seen her diamond pendant.

Maybe the woman just stashed the diamond somewhere "safe," because Daisy does not want to assume the worst of her servant. Holly's Help came well recommended. The service has incredible reviews online. It's bonded. Reputable. Even Vanessa uses them.

But it's time to meet her maid.

# MAL

It's almost 10:00 p.m. when Mal and Benoit pull up outside Boon-mee Saelim's rented house on the east side of the city.

Saelim answers the door as soon as they knock. He's expecting them because they called ahead. Saelim is slightly taller than average height for a male. Smooth brown skin. Broad forehead. High cheekbones. Intense, black eyes. A nose ring. Silver ear spools. He wears a black T-shirt and jeans. He's a good-looking guy, thinks Mal.

"Call me Boon, please," he says after they have introduced themselves. "Do you mind if we talk outside, in your car or something? I share the house with a bunch of tenants, and it's full of people right now, and—" His voice cracks. His eyes glisten with tears. "It'll be easier to talk away from the noise," he says.

Mal and Benoit take Saelim to their vehicle. He sits in the back while they sit in the front, turned to face him. They keep the inside light on. Rain patters on the roof and squiggles down the windshield. It's cold, so they have the engine running, and the windows are fogging up.

"When did you last see Kit?" Benoit asks him.

He closes his eyes, and Mal immediately senses he's going to lie. She's a veteran interrogator. Or perhaps he's just struggling to hold in his emotion.

"I think it was two days ago."

"You *think*?" Mal says.

His eyes flick to hers.

"Here's the thing, Boon," Mal says. "Sam Berkowitz, Kit's neighbor, says you went around to her apartment looking for her. Sam tells us you were worried. Holly McGuire at Holly's Help also says you expressed concern for your close friend. You've been looking for Kit all day, and you haven't yet determined when you last saw her?"

"Am I a suspect here or something?"

"Are you?"

His eyes narrow. His energy turns hostile. "I didn't see her today. Nor yesterday. I saw her the day before Halloween, so that would have been Wednesday. For our D&D session."

"D&D?" Benoit asks.

"Dungeons and Dragons. It's a game."

"How did Kit seem when you last saw her?" Mal asks.

"Not herself, to be honest. She hasn't been herself since July 15."

"That's very specific," Mal says. "What happened on July 15?"

"It's the anniversary of her mother's death. Kit was pretty messed up by her mom's dying. It was a long and difficult process for her. Afterward, she was unable to scatter the ashes. But when July 15 rolled around again this year, I said I'd go with her. We went to Lighthouse Park and released them. So that was one thing that happened on that specific day. It was on the same day, right after the scattering of her mother's cremains, that she started a new cleaning job. She's been getting progressively weird since then."

"Do you know which new job?" Benoit asks.

"Rose Cottage. The Rittenbergs."

Mal's energy sharpens. "And Kit told you about the Rittenbergs specifically?"

"Yeah. We share a lot about each other's lives. We're real close. We grew up in the same ski town, except she was a few years behind me at school, so I didn't know her back then, but we connected here in the city some years ago when we ran into each other in a coffee shop at a mall."

"And what is it about the Rittenbergs that might have created issues?" Benoit asks.

Boon shuffles in the seat, rubs his knee, clears his throat. "I don't know. She didn't say."

"I thought you shared a lot," Mal says.

"That's why I say that she was off. She got weird. Closed off. Something happened. And I don't know if it happened in that house. Rose Cottage. Or if she was having some unresolved grief issues. When I asked, she refused to talk about it. It put a rift into our relationship, okay? I continued to press her because it upset me. I felt cut out of her life. Which made her even more defensive. More closed. So I have no idea. I even drove past that house to see. When Kit learned I'd done that, she lost it. Totally went apeshit. She said I'd crossed a line, and I was not to mess in her professional life. But it wasn't just her work stuff. Whatever was going on, it had spilled into her private life. She was messed up. And . . ." He exhales heavily. "She seemed frightened these past few weeks. Jumpy. Edgy. Paranoid, even."

"And she didn't say why?" Mal asks.

He rubs his jaw. "No. I suspected it had to do with those clients. I think she saw something. I—" He swears, then rubs his face harder. "Okay, I'm just going to say it, because I'm worried for her. I mean really worried. Kit has a snooping problem. Like an addiction. She jokes about it, but it's serious. Like next-level serious. And I think she's been crossing lines. I told her some time ago she was going to get herself in trouble. She was going to see something that some client wanted to keep hidden. And it could get her in danger."

Mal and Benoit regard Boon in silence. Tension thickens in the car.

Quietly, Mal says, "When you say snooping 'problem'—"

"I mean, digging into closets, trying to open safes, hacking into computers. And—" His eyes glisten with emotion again. "I feel like I'm betraying her. But she also has this Instagram account. Under the name @foxandcrow. Both tricksters—the fox and the crow. It's her joke on the world of false narratives. Her mockery of a social media lifestyle where everyone projects some kind of brand, like they're selling a product. And she pretends she's this rich chick with an ultraglamorous globe-trotting lifestyle. And I join in sometimes. Because it seemed fun. No harm, no foul, right? But lately she's been posting more and more photos of herself *inside* her clients' houses. Wearing their clothes and shit. But mostly inside the Rittenberg house. There's—" He glances away.

"Go on," says Mal. "Please, Boon. This could be important."

He moistens his lips. "There's this one photo with her in front of their unborn baby's crib, and she's holding an ultrasound image in front of her stomach, and her caption makes it seem like *she* is the one having their baby. Maybe they saw it. It would freak the hell out of anyone. Or maybe Kit found something in Rose Cottage. That's what I believe— that she got into something that the Rittenbergs want to keep secret. Like big-deal secret. Like—I . . . I don't even want to say it."

"You mean, something someone would kill to keep secret?" Benoit asks. "Is that what you're trying to say, Boon?"

He drops his head, stares at his hands in his lap. "Yeah, that's what scares me," he says quietly. "Really scares me. She's vulnerable that way. She's messed up that way."

"And you think her disappearance is definitely tied to these clients in particular?" Benoit asks.

He swallows. "I don't know. But it was after she got Rose Cottage that she got weird."

Benoit says, "You mentioned you and Kit grew up in the same town."

He hesitates. "Whistler. I left right after graduation. She dropped out of school and left, too."

"So you're a skier, Boon?" Mal asks.

He gives a snort. "Funny how everyone thinks you're a skier just because you live in a ski town. Do you know what a lift ticket costs, Detective? We never had money to ski. My parents worked at McDonald's. The franchise owner in Whistler found it impossible to hire ski-town locals. And those kids who flock into town each year from all over the world, looking for work, they come for the ski experience. They all fight to get hired by the mountains, or jockey for jobs that will give them free ski passes. They don't come all the way from the UK, or Australia, or from Japan to work at McDonald's. So the owner started a program to import labor from the Philippines and Thailand—the kind of poor people desperate to immigrate to Canada. It was a way in for my parents. That's how I ended up living in an expensive ski town and attending the only school in the valley that was full of rich ski-town kids."

Mal studies him. She hears the bitterness. She guesses school life was tough on this kid.

"How about Kit?" she asks softly. "Is she a skier?"

"Her mom cleaned hotel rooms and houses, and her dad worked at the sanitation plant. Kit never had money. If she got a chance to go skiing or snowboarding, it was because of a handout. What's this got to do with her disappearance?"

Mal holds Boon's gaze. "The clients you mentioned. Jon Rittenberg. He was a top downhill skier. An Olympian. Apparently he grew up on the North Shore, which means he skied plenty at Whistler. The ski team also has a lodge up there."

"So?"

Benoit says, "Did you or Kit maybe know Jon Rittenberg back in the day? When you were kids? It's a small town. Maybe you crossed paths."

Boon says nothing. But his energy has shifted, and there's a new tightness in his body. This guy knows something he's not telling them.

Mal suspects it might tie back to the ski town. Boon-mee Saelim edges a little higher up Mal's persons-of-interest list.

"But you knew of Jon Rittenberg when you were a kid, right?" Mal says.

He moistens his lips. "Yeah. I'd heard of him. They named a ski run after him."

Mal tries a new tack. "Can you tell us where Kit might keep her diary?"

"Diary?"

"Yes. A journal. Pink book with purple polka dots."

"I didn't know she kept a diary."

"Do you know who her therapist is?" Benoit asks.

Boon's gaze shoots to Benoit. "Kit doesn't have a therapist."

"So there are quite a few things she doesn't share with you?" Mal says.

"Look, I would know if Kit had a therapist. I suggested one, way back. And she said not even if hell froze over would she see a shrink."

"Why did you suggest one?" Mal asks.

Boon suddenly looks trapped. "Are you going to sit here asking me irrelevant stuff, or have you actually got a plan to search for Kit? Because she's in danger. I know it. I can feel it in my heart."

"Are you and Kit romantically involved, Boon?" Benoit asks.

"I'm a gay man. I had a boyfriend until recently. We broke up. Kit's like a sister to me. More than a sister."

"Does she have any siblings, any close relatives we can call?"

"She was an only child. Her father died when she was nineteen. And now her mom is gone."

"Is Kit involved romantically with any significant other?" Mal asks.

"No. She was very briefly married once. It soured her on relationships."

Surprise ripples through Mal. She didn't see this one coming. "What happened to her marriage?"

211

"He—Todd Darling—wanted kids. She couldn't have them." He swallows. Mal's instincts detect something. She thinks about the Instagram post Boon just described—Kit holding an ultrasound scan of someone else's baby, posing in their nursery, pretending it was hers.

"Boon," Mal says more gently, "I'm going to show you some photos on a tablet. One of them might be a little disturbing. It's from the crime scene. Are you okay with this?"

He nods but looks terrified.

Mal shows him an image of the bloody shoe. "Do you recognize this sneaker?"

He stares. A great big silent sob shudders through his shoulders. Tears begin to slide down his face. He swipes his hand across his nose, sniffs, and nods. "It's hers. It's Kit's." He lifts his eyes. "What happened? Is this from the Glass House? Oh, God, please let her be okay. Is she hurt?"

"What makes you think it's from the Glass House, Boon?" Mal asks gently.

"I heard on the news that police had descended on the house. People were saying it was a homicide unit. I tried to drive past, but the street was blocked off. Kit works there."

"How about this photo? Do you recognize this?" Mal shows him an image of the diamond pendant.

"No."

"Okay, and who are the people in this image?" Mal shows Boon the photo she shot of the group picture on Kit's fridge.

"That's Kit. That's me there." He points. "That's Azim Shariff, a philosophy professor. Ella Carter there is his partner. And this is Onur Osman, he's an EMT, and this is Vicky-Lee Murtagh. She works for a pathology lab. It's our D&D group. We're all close. We're also all in the same amateur theater group."

"One more question, Boon. Kit's last name—"

"Is her married name. She kept it. She was Katarina Popovich before. She started going by 'Kit' after she dropped out of school and moved to the city."

"And what happened to Todd Darling?" Benoit asks.

"He immigrated to the UK. He married a British woman. They have a toddler and an infant."

"Did Kit express concern about her inability to have children?" Mal asks.

"Yeah. It messed up her marriage. Todd wanted kids, and apparently Kit had not told him about her damaged uterus before they married. It became a big problem between them. Todd said he was cool, that he'd deal with it. But I do think he must have felt betrayed. It was Kit who ended up shutting him out, letting him go. I think she wanted to give him a chance to marry again and have the things he'd dreamed for in his life."

"Why did she not tell her prospective husband she couldn't have kids?" Mal asks.

He shrugs. "I think she was just scared Todd wouldn't want to marry her. I think she was desperate to be loved, wanted."

"And now her ex has babies," Benoit says.

"Yeah."

"Did this upset her?"

"Probably. A little. Maybe a lot."

Mal says, "You have in the past recommended therapy to your friend, Boon. You say she has a snooping addiction. You say she has not been herself, possibly due to unresolved grief. You think she's been messed up by something she saw at Rose Cottage. She runs this questionable social media account, posing in clients' clothes and pretending she is carrying their babies—how emotionally unstable would you say Kit is?"

He inhales deeply. "Kit is just a little eccentric. Unconventional. Theatrical. Sometimes dramatic. But it's a shield. She's soft inside.

Kind." His eyes fill with emotion again, and Mal finds him a tissue. He blows his nose. "It's like she feels that if she hides in plain sight—behind her makeup, costumes, theatrical roles, her pretend Instagram life—then people won't see past it all to the hidden, broken Kit. They won't ask too many questions of her."

"So what is she hiding from that she's afraid of questions?" Benoit asks.

"I-I don't know. I think something bad—really bad—happened when she was at school. And that's why she dropped out and left town."

"And she has not spoken about this to you?" Benoit asks.

He looks away. "No."

Mal feels this is a lie. "Can you come into the station tomorrow, Boon? Make an official statement, give us a DNA sample?"

"DNA? *Me?* What for?"

"Just for elimination purposes."

"I . . . I guess."

When Boon exits the vehicle and walks through the rain back to his front door, Mal says, "He's hiding something."

"For sure he is," Benoit says.

They watch in silence as Boon opens his front door. Yellow light slices into the darkness. Boon steps inside, shuts the door behind him, and the light is extinguished.

# DAISY

Only five more weeks, Daisy thinks as she presses her hands firmly into her lower back. She's upstairs in the baby's room, where she can watch the driveway for the arrival of the maid. She paces in front of the window as she tries to ease the pinched nerve in her hip.

She checks her watch. Jon left very early again this morning. And he'll be home late. He told her not to wait up—he's going out with those prospective investors again. TerraWest is apparently throwing out all the stops to wine, dine, and entertain them. Jon said after dinner tonight they might all go to a club. The clients are from China and want to sample the local nightlife, he told her. Daisy feels edgy about this. She's not sure she can trust Jon. Her interaction with Vanessa has unsettled her deeply.

It was at an "adult entertainment club" that Jon and his clients encountered exotic dancer Charley Waters. And look what happened.

*What if he ever does something like this again? . . . I mean, guys like him—they don't change, Daisy, do they? They just learn. They evolve. Adapt. They figure out how to be more careful, how not to get caught next time around.*

She inhales a shaky breath.

*I will cut him loose. I'll sue him to high heaven. I'll deny him access to our son. And I* will *win any suit because I—I have insurance.*

Daisy winces and stops pacing as her back spasms again. Her mind spirals to the documents and flash drive she keeps in her safe. If Jon ever repeats what happened in Silver Aspens, he's so done.

If Jon hadn't made trouble with a stripper, Daisy would not be vulnerable to the kinds of threats and paranoia and harassment she is experiencing now. She would not be frightened of damn Chucky dolls and trolls on her Instagram account. She would not see shadows dressed in black behind trees or think someone is following her.

Another little voice deep inside Daisy rises to the surface.

*It was you who chose to protect him. You who cleaned up behind him. You who learned from your mother that in order to keep your own reputation and family intact, sometimes a woman needs to take radical action and look the other way. It's you who chose to believe boys will be boys, especially in groups, and you who put your head in the sand. You who still choose to believe there are slutty females out to lure and entice men expressly to gain favors, and that the men are powerless in the face of free sex and those women are to blame.*

Daisy hears a car in the driveway. She hurries back to the window and peers down into her front yard. A Holly's Help car pulls up outside her front door. Daisy steps back slightly behind the drape. She watches discreetly as the maid gets out and starts unpacking a vacuum cleaner and cleaning supplies. From a distance she looks attractive. Blonde with a trim figure. She moves with energy. Daisy feels a stab of resentment. The maid starts lugging her vacuum toward the entrance.

Daisy hastens downstairs. Her coat and purse are already waiting near the front door. She will leave as soon as she has spoken to this maid. She has no intention of remaining home to watch this person cleaning her house.

Through the frosted glass panel that runs the length of the door, Daisy sees the shadow of the maid approaching. She opens the door.

The woman jumps back and gasps in surprise. She was busy at the lockbox.

"Oh, I'm sorry," the maid says. "I thought—" She points to the lockbox that Daisy and Jon installed specifically for the cleaning service. "I was told there was usually no one home and that I should use the key. My apologies. I should have knocked to be sure."

"No worries. I'm about to leave. I just wanted to meet you." She smiles. "My name is Daisy."

The woman looks tense, leery.

*Aha! The maid is up to something.* Daisy can see it, feel it. Her pulse quickens.

The maid's gaze drops to Daisy's belly. Daisy defensively puts her hands over her baby tummy.

"Congratulations," the maid says.

Daisy nods. "And your name is?"

"Oh, sorry. I'm Sofia. Sofia Ramos. Nice to meet you." The maid offers her hand.

Disappointment stabs through Daisy. Her name is not Kit.

As Daisy leans forward to shake her cleaner's hand, she says, "I wanted to ask if you've seen my necklace. It's a diamond pendant. The diamond is set in a gold teardrop shape. I usually leave it on—"

"Oh, I'm not your usual maid. I'm the replacement—the new one."

"What?"

"Your usual maid, Kit, has a conflict in her schedule. Holly assigned me. I'll be servicing Rose Cottage going forward."

Daisy's heart skips a beat. *"Kit?"*

"Yes."

"Kit *who?*"

"I'm not sure what Kit's surname is. I'm pretty new with Holly's Help. I haven't met all the employees yet."

"Oh."

"Is there a problem?"

"No—no, I . . . Kit has done such a great job here at Rose Cottage, I—I might like to send her some flowers. With a personalized note. Do you perhaps have an address or phone number for her?"

Sofia frowns. "I don't. I'm sorry. You could try calling the Holly's Help office?"

"Yes, yes, I will definitely do that."

# DAISY

After being foiled in her attempt to corner the maid named Kit, Daisy repairs to a café downtown. She orders a chai latte and sits at a table near the window. She watches pedestrians huddling in their jackets as they lean into a blustery fall wind, dead leaves being trampled under boots.

She decides to bite the bullet. She reaches for her phone, looks up the Holly's Help website, and calls the office.

"Holly's Help, Sabrina speaking. How may I direct your call?" The voice is high pitched and annoyingly sunny.

"Can I speak to Holly McGuire, please?" Daisy says.

She is put on hold for a few moments.

"Holly here."

Daisy sits upright. "Hi, Holly, I'm Daisy Rittenberg, one of your clients. One of your employees, Kit, has been cleaning our home—Rose Cottage—and I understand she's been replaced. I was wondering what happened?"

"With Kit? Oh, she had a scheduling conflict. We juggled the roster. Is everything okay with your new cleaner?"

"Great so far. I just met her this morning. I was wondering if you could tell me what Kit's last name is?"

There is a moment of silence. Holly says, "Why? Is there a problem?"

"Not at all. Kit has been doing an excellent job. We are sorry to lose her. We want to send her a bouquet of flowers with a personalized note as a thank-you, and I realized I never got her surname."

"Thank you. Kit always has such great feedback. We get so many referrals through her. It's Kit Darling."

Daisy's pulse quickens. She writes "Darling" on her napkin. "Do you have an address for her? So I can have the flowers delivered to her home?"

"You can just send them here to our head office. I'll make sure they get into her hands. Thank you so much."

"Wait, please, it would be so much more special for her to be surprised at home, don't you think?"

"I'm sorry, Mrs. Rittenberg. While it's a lovely idea, it's not policy to give out the personal information of our employees."

Daisy tries again, but Holly refuses to give additional details on her employee. Daisy curses to herself, thanks Holly again, and hangs up.

Immediately she opens a browser on her phone and starts searching for "Kit Darling" online.

She finds a New York–based model named Kit Darling. She finds lots of other Kit Darlings—a veterinarian, a research scientist in the UK, someone named Kit who has completed several ultradistance marathons, a romance novelist from Arizona named Kit Darling, but no one who appears to be a maid in Vancouver.

Daisy returns to the Holly's Help website and opens the "About Us" link, hoping to find photos of the maids. But there is only a photo of Holly McGuire and her happy admin staff.

Daisy absently chews her lip, thinking. Then she remembers Vanessa also uses the Holly's Help service. She phones Vanessa.

"Hey, Daisy," Vanessa says. "I was just thinking about you—I was wondering if you and Jo—"

"You do use the Holly's Help cleaning service, right?"

There is a pause. "Yes. Why?"

Daisy clears her throat. "Do you know who your maid is? Have you personally met her?"

"Of course, yes. What's this about?"

"What's her name?"

"Are you having a problem with the service?"

"No, I was just wondering if we might have the same maid."

"You mean Kit?"

Heat flushes into Daisy's chest. "Yes—yes, I think that must be the same one. Kit Darling?"

"Is she doing an okay job for you guys? Why do you ask?"

Daisy feigns a big sigh. "Seems Kit has some scheduling conflict, so we have a new cleaner. I wanted to send her a thank-you note—and I—you wouldn't happen to know where she lives?"

Vanessa is silent for a moment. Daisy can hear the questioning in Vanessa's pause, and she realizes she must be coming across as really strange. Especially after their weird lunch. She needs to take it down a notch. "It's okay. Never mind. I was just hoping to send her a thank-you note."

"You could send it via her agency," Vanessa offers.

"I'll do that. Thanks."

"Hey, before you go. Do you and Jon want to come round for dinner? I'd love for you to meet Haruto properly this time. And for us both to meet your Jon. I was thinking maybe Halloween night? It might be nice to do something a little special. Before we're both surrounded by diapers and leaking breasts and sleepless nights—while we're still both vaguely autonomous human beings?"

Daisy laughs. But anxiety bites as she recalls her confession about Jon. What if Vanessa brings it up in front of Jon? She was clearly shocked. Daisy should never have mentioned it, but she was not herself that day. Her paranoia stirs again, winding tighter around her chest. She glances out the window at all the anonymous faces walking past the café. Wind gusts and bare branches bend. She senses winter coming today. It brings a dark feeling.

"Daisy? Are you there?"

"I—yes, dinner would be amazing. I'll check with Jon, but I'm sure he'll be fine with it."

"Around six p.m.? Cocktails—or mocktails—to start?"

"Sounds great." Daisy forces a laugh. "And yes to the mocktails. I'm done with my pregnancy wine experiment. After not having alcohol for so long, and mixed with hormones—I must have overdone it. I was not myself. I'm even having trouble recalling parts of our conversation. I didn't say anything terribly weird, did I? Because if I did, please just forget it."

Vanessa hesitates, but only for a nanosecond. "No problem at all. So we'll see you guys Thursday?"

Daisy agrees, then kills the call. She feels totally off center. Vanessa is probably now wondering why she pressed about the maid. Daisy hears Charley's words in her head again.

*"I—oh, wait, I get it. This is about Kit, isn't it?"*

Kit Darling was cleaning Rose Cottage when that Chucky thing appeared in their letter box. Daisy's neighbor said no one else apart from the maid had approached their house.

Could her maid—the person with a key to her home—have been the one who sent the other notes and commented on Daisy's Instagram account? The person who got inside her car? Like a bolt of lightning, Daisy is hit with an image of her and Jon's spare car keys hanging in the hall closet. The maid had access to those.

Could Kit the maid also have stolen her diamond? What else might she have gotten into?

Daisy feels ill. It's totally possible. But *why* on earth would this maid do these things?

222

The image of the Chucky with knife *stabbing stabbity stab stabbing* rises into her brain. The image is followed by those words: *I hope your baby dies. Dies. Dies.*

Anger thumps harder and harder into Daisy's blood. She grows fidgety and hot and irrational. She crunches the napkin with the word *Darling* on it into a ball in her fist, and she swears.

*If "Kit" is doing this, I will find and stab that maid myself.*

# MAL

*November 1, 2019. Friday.*

Mal shrugs out of her wet coat and hangs it on a hook in the hallway of her duplex.

"Peter?" she calls out as she sits on the bench to remove her boots.

There's no answer. It's late, but all the lights downstairs are on. Anxiety sharpens. Quickly, Mal pads through to the kitchen on socked feet.

Peter is at the kitchen table. He glances up from the newspaper he's reading and smiles. It's warm inside. He has the gas fire going in the living room.

"Hey, hon," he says as he lowers his paper. "How'd the rest of the day go? You locate the victim?"

Mal's chest squeezes. For a cruel second it seems all is back to normal. Cautious, unsure whether her husband is just having a good, lucid moment, or if it's wishful thinking on the part of her exhausted brain, she says, "Not yet. I—I've forgotten what I've told you already," she says as she opens a cupboard and takes out a wineglass. She pours herself a glass of red wine, holds the bottle out to him. "Would you like some?"

"No. Just had some tea, thanks. You said on the phone there was a violent incident at a luxury home on the North Shore. But no sign of the occupants or a victim."

She sips and briefly closes her eyes, swallowing both the wine and a surge of emotion. She sets her glass down, opens the fridge, and takes out leftover lasagna. She dishes some into a bowl. "No sign of a victim yet," she says as she carries the bowl to the microwave. "We've located the couple who were seen in an Audi at the house. But no sign of the homeowners, or their maid, who was reportedly also at the home." Mal opens the microwave door and her heart sinks. Peter's bowl of lasagna is still sitting inside—he's forgotten it. She glances at the time: 11:15 p.m.

"Did you eat, Peter?" she asks casually with her back to him.

Silence.

She turns. He appears confused.

"I was just wondering if you want some more to eat?" she says.

"I—I'm fine. I had dinner."

She nods, removes his lasagna, and sticks her own food into the microwave. As it warms, she sips more of her wine. Peter's gaze goes to the fireplace in the living room. He watches the flames, his face blank. And just like that Mal's man has slipped away from her again, stolen by this strange and baffling disease. She first started noticing little changes in Peter more than seven years ago. Then he suffered a fall, and doctors thought he might have had a small stroke. Then came the bouts of depression. He lost interest in his hobbies, like gardening, and he seemed increasingly forgetful, irritable. Gradually he lost his social filters. He got angry with her more frequently—outbursts, swearing. He experienced some shocking cases of road rage, one of which resulted in police coming round to the house. His work got sloppy. His colleagues and students began complaining. The official diagnosis, however, took a while.

Mal carries her bowl and wine to the table and sits across from Peter. "And how was your day?"

He meets her gaze and considers her question for a moment. "I read in the paper about that seventy-one-year-old senior who's gone missing, the one with Alzheimer's."

"Sylvia Kaplan?"

He nods. "She walked out of her home in East Van and never came back. Her daughter says they've been searching for almost two months now. The last sighting was at a bus shelter on Renfrew. They think she got onto a bus and got off somewhere in the night and was totally lost."

"It's heartbreaking, I know. It happens far too often."

"They were talking about how we need an official Silver Alert system in this province. Like the Amber Alert for kids."

"I agree." She forks lasagna into her mouth as she studies Peter's eyes. They're filling with tears. She sets her fork down and covers his hand. "You all right?"

He inhales and glances away.

"We've got this, Peter," she says. "You and I. In sickness and in health. Okay?"

He refuses to meet her gaze.

"Peter?"

He turns.

"I'm not going to let you wander off."

"I want to talk to those people," he says.

"Which people?"

"The Dignity in Death people. About medical assistance in dying."

Shock washes through Mal's veins. For an instant words elude her—she had not allowed her mind to go this far. Yet.

"I don't want to be a vegetable in a seniors' home," Peter says angrily. "Just lying in a bed, my skin rotting with bedsores, forgetting how to eat, how to swallow, needing diapers changed. I don't want to do that to you, Mal, to anyone."

Mal draws in a slow, deep breath of air. "Okay," she says quietly. "We'll talk about it."

He slams his hand down on the table. Her glass wobbles and she tenses, bracing for another outburst.

"Talk! Always goddamn talk, talk, talk. I want *action*!" His gaze burns into hers. Tears leak down the side of his face. His hands shake.

"I know, Peter. I understand. As soon as this case is a wrap, we'll meet with your doctor, okay? We'll ask him about medical assistance in dying. We'll discuss *all* the options."

He glowers at her for several beats. "It's not easy to access MAID with dementia. MAID legally requires you to be cognizant right to the end."

"I know. But there is some case precedent. We'll work through it." She forces a smile. "You and I. Deal?"

"I want it down in writing," he says, jabbing his finger onto the table. "I want it stated that when I no longer recognize you, Mal, or when I no longer remember the names of my family members, from that point I no longer want to live. That's when I want MAID. I do not want you struggling to change my pants and wipe my butt and the drool from my mouth."

For a moment Mal can't speak.

"Okay?" he says.

"Okay," Mal says. "We'll go step by step. But how about you sleep on it tonight and see how you feel in the morning?"

"I've been sleeping on it for bloody months. One morning I'll wake up and it'll be too late."

Mal finishes her dinner halfheartedly while Peter sits, watching the fire. She then helps her husband up to bed. He seems particularly tired tonight. She drapes a blanket over him, kisses him, and switches off the lights.

As Mal heads back downstairs to finish her wine by the fire and to mull things over, her cell rings. It's Lula.

"Hey, Lu," she says tiredly as she reaches the kitchen. "What're you still doing up?"

"Likewise, boss. This could wait until our six a.m. briefing, but I figured you'd want to know right away."

"What is it?"

"We've located Vanessa and Haruto North with assistance from Interpol. We—"

"*Interpol?*"

"The Norths are in Singapore. At their primary residence. Northview is their second home. They acquired the house just over eight months ago. I spoke with them by phone while they were in the presence of law enforcement on the Singapore end, so we can be confident their IDs are solid."

"How—when did they depart for Singapore?"

"They claim to have been in Singapore at their primary residence for the last six months plus a few days."

"*Both* of them?"

"Both of them."

Mal's brain reels. "Beulah Brown says she saw a pregnant Vanessa North next door last week."

"And here's the kicker," Lula says. "Vanessa North is not pregnant."

"*What?*" Mal says.

"Vanessa North is not pregnant. She's in her midforties and says it would be a miracle if she was."

# JON

*October 28, 2019. Monday.*
*Three days before the murder.*

Jon sits with Mia in a discreet booth. It's 9:34 p.m., and they're in a small piano lounge downtown. He's got a buzz on from the drinks he downed before he arrived, and from the cocktails he and Mia have already shared. A hot, sexual energy crackles over his skin. Daisy and the unborn baby are fast fading to a peripheral wilderness in Jon's mind. His focus is solely on the seductive woman in his presence.

This place was Mia's suggestion, and it's perfect. Tucked away. Private. Jon feels safe in this dimly lit cocoon of elegance. No tacky Halloween-season decor. Soft jazzy piano tunes. A lounge singer with a voice like smoke and whisky. Miles away from where he told Daisy he would be with prospective TerraWest investors from China.

"So how *did* you find my number?" he asks Mia, who is even more beautiful than he remembered. She wears a ruby-red velvet dress with her hair loose over her shoulders. The dress shows off the green of her eyes.

She smiles, sips her martini, and says softly, "Where there's a will, there's a way, right?"

He smiles. That this siren hunted him down is intoxicating. That she wants his body is driving him nuts.

She leans forward and his breathing quickens. "You know what that's like, don't you, Jon? Having a hunger? Relentlessly pursuing, taking what you want, what should be yours?"

"Is that how it is for you in banking?"

"It can be a mercenary business." She traces the back of his hand with her fingers, her gaze locked on his. "What is it that you want right now, Jon, right at this minute? What is it that should be yours for the taking?"

He swallows. His skin goes hotter. "I think you know."

She angles her head. The candlelight shimmers on her hair. Her green eyes bewitch him. "I mean, beyond sex. What do you feel is missing in your life right now? Because on the surface you seem to have it all, right? Attractive wife with a family fortune to her name. A baby on the way. And resort industry buzz says you're tipped for the new COO position at Claquoosh Resort when it comes on stream."

Jon feels a discordant clang in his head at the mention of Daisy, their unborn son, and the job that is no longer guaranteed him. He breaks her gaze and reaches for his drink, sips. For a moment he watches the singer near the grand piano. She's crooning lyrics about taking risks in love.

"I'm sorry," she says quietly. "I hit a nerve."

"No. No, it's fine." He meets her gaze again.

She leans closer. Jon notices her cleavage. Heat pools in his groin—a throbbing kind of heat that makes him so hard it's exquisitely painful. She feathers her fingers across the back of his hand again.

"I won't go there again. Won't mention your family. I just want to be clear about our parameters, Jon. I'm aware you're a well-married family man. Yet here you are. And I don't want to get off on the wrong foot and lead you to believe that there is something more . . . you understand what I mean?"

"I—"

But she silences him with her finger on his lips. "I, too, have a comfortable life." She hesitates, as though unsure whether to divulge more. "A relationship. I want to keep that relationship intact, yet here I am. But I am clear in my own mind on the reason I'm here. Physical connection, no strings. How about you?"

His heart thuds like a drum. It sends blood pumping through his veins with a rhythmic pulse. It throbs with the same rhythm in his groin. He's dizzy. Oddly dizzy. Like his entire world is narrowing onto just this siren named Mia in a ruby-red dress, and he can't seem to think in a bigger picture. He feels woozy.

"Shame thing," he says. "I mean, *same* thing. No shtrings." His words are slurring. How much have they both had to drink anyway? How many drinks did he have at dinner with the clients before he arrived? Still, he feels like another one, and he raises his hand to order refills.

The server replenishes their drinks, and Mia says, as she reaches for hers, "So you want both worlds? Family man and philandering man."

"Don't we all want it all?"

She laughs. He watches the pale column of her throat. He can't seem to think straight at all. He sips from his drink, spilling a little down his front.

"Is talking about your job off limits?" she asks.

Her words hover in front of his mind, then slide away. Jon struggles to pull his brain back into focus. "Talking about my job is fine. It's—" He laughs. And his laugh sounds funny to his own ears, so he laughs harder, then feels a little ill. He clears his throat and tries to explain. "I laugh becaush it was a done deal, and now . . ." He fades as he loses track of his thought. He sits in silence for a moment, trying to pull himself back into focus, trying to remember what he was saying. He sees two men in an alcove across from him and Mia. Are they watching him? From the shadows. Can't really make out their faces, but Jon feels watched.

"What was a done deal?"

"What?"

She places her hand on his thigh. Moves it higher toward his groin. Jon suddenly feels uneasy. A little trapped. As if something is going wrong, but his brain is not warning him fast enough. Her hand goes higher, covers his erection.

"Jon," she whispers, "you're safe here, with me. It's our secret. You can talk."

"It's nothing. Jusht—the company is conshidering hiring someone of color. Optics. I . . . need to show . . I best viable candidate for—for that posish—position."

She watches him. His vision is distorted. Her red lips seem larger than they were. Her big eyes more green.

"How will you show them?" She cups his erection, and Jon can barely think with the hot pleasure of her touch.

"I . . . find something—some dirt—that proves rival is bad news."

"How will you find dirt?" She rubs his erection.

Jon's vision swirls. He nods. "PI. I hired a PI."

She smiles. "And who's this rival, JonJon BergBomber?" she whispers near his ear. The wet tip of her tongue touches his lobe.

"Ah—Ahmed Waheed. Tell me about you, Mia . . . your—"

"Come upstairs with me, Jon." Her breath is hot in his ear. "I have an Airbnb upstairs. I have a nightcap waiting. We can continue up there. Come." She takes his hand. "Come with me."

Jon isn't sure if he is dreaming, or totally plastered. How many whiskies and beers did he have? He knows he definitely had several shots of tequila before he arrived. He's lost track.

They're in the elevator. Kissing. He cups her butt with his hands, pulls her pelvis against his thigh as the elevator climbs, climbs. He can't remember getting to the elevator. Or into it. Or to her suite. They are backing into her suite. She's kissing him, her tongue deep inside his mouth.

They're inside a bedroom. Low bed. Walls of glass that look out over the city lights. What part of the city is this? It looks different. He hasn't seen this aspect. There's a flashing pink neon sign. Jon squints at the pulsating pink sign. CABARET LUXE. He recognizes that sign. He's taken clients there before. Yes, he realizes where they are. Yaletown area. Trendy. They must be looking out toward False Creek. Mia is undoing his tie, his shirt. Her hands are on his bare chest, sliding his shirt off his shoulders. She's laughing, pushing him backward onto the bed.

She pulls up her dress, straddles him. Just glass, he thinks as Mia undoes his zipper, only glass windows between him and Mia and all those sparkling lights of the city and all those high-rise condo windows looking back at them. Another vague thought forms in his brain—anyone could be watching them from any one of a million windows . . . then he can think only of what she is doing to his body. Everything else spins away in a blur.

# MAL

*November 1, 2019. Friday.*

"Let me get this straight," Mal says to Lula on the phone. "Vanessa North claims she's *not* pregnant, and she and her husband have been in Singapore for the last six months?"

"Correct. The Norths are both citizens of the Republic of Singapore," Lula says. "Haruto is a banker with Singapore-Pacific International. He spends a few months each year at the bank's North American headquarters located in Vancouver, which is when he and his wife plan to reside at the Glass House. They're due back in January. They were in the house only two months before they left again for Singapore. Vanessa is originally Canadian. She works for an NGO and travels a lot throughout Africa. We've confirmed these details with our Interpol liaison. I'm forwarding you photos of the Norths and copies of their passport details. They claim to have no knowledge of what has occurred at their home. They've used Holly's Help since May 1 to maintain their property and keep a check on the gardening service and security system while they're away. The Norths do not know which specific maid services their home, and say they have not met Kit Darling."

Beulah Brown's words rise in Mal's mind.

*She's certainly showing now. I saw Vanessa last Friday. It was the first time I saw that brunette as well. The two of them had a late lunch by the pool. It was very clear they're both pregnant.*

"Yet Beulah Brown claims she saw Vanessa North last Friday, having lunch by the pool with Daisy Rittenberg, and that she definitely was pregnant," Mal says.

"Well, it couldn't have been her. I've confirmed the Norths' details," Lula says. "They have not been on Canadian soil for just over six months."

Mal thanks Lula and immediately calls Benoit.

"That could explain that cold, staged, and unlived-in feeling in that house," Benoit says.

"But it sure as hell doesn't explain anything else."

"You think Brown was just mistaken?" he asks. "Those opioids can really mess with one's sense of reality. And we do have Horton Brown on record saying his mother imagines things; plus there's a history of five false 911 calls."

"Or . . . Beulah Brown saw someone she *thought* was Vanessa," Mal says. "She did mention her prescription glasses had been failing her, and that she only had the new binoculars for two weeks. Plus if the Norths acquired the Glass House eight months ago, and were only there for two months before departing for Singapore, perhaps Brown never really got a close look at the real Vanessa when she was in town. Perhaps Brown just made an assumption it was the same person."

"Well, we can cross Vanessa North off our possible victim list. It's not looking good for Darling now."

# JON

*October 29, 2019. Tuesday.*
*Two days before the murder.*

When Jon wakes, his head is thick. The last thing he remembers is laughing. He struggles to orient himself. Nothing makes sense. He's in a bed. Naked. He can see city lights. A pulsing pink neon sign. He feels sick. So sick. Nauseous. He tries to sit up, but his world spins and his arm jerks him back—it's secured to the bed. His stomach clutches, and he throws up over the side of the bed onto the carpet. The smell makes him gag again. He wipes spittle from his mouth with the back of his free hand. He winces, turns his head. Shock slams through him.

His wrist is cuffed to the bed frame. Handcuffs—*padded* handcuffs. He yanks his hand. It's locked. Panic strikes. He can't breathe. His vision starts narrowing from the sides. He's sweaty, hot.

*Focus. Panic kills. Think. What happened? How did I get here?*

Jon tries to control his breathing. He tries to clear his mind. He remembers now. He was with Mia.

*Fuck.*

Panic whips through him again. He fights it down as he struggles to put the pieces together.

They were in the bar downstairs. He got drunk. Very drunk. They came up in the elevator. Kissing. Backed into her Airbnb.

Another wave of adrenaline slams through Jon. Someone else's condo—he's in a stranger's condo. Naked and cuffed to a bed. He has to get out of here. He flicks his gaze wildly around the interior of the room. It's dimly lit. Still dark outside. He can see the red glow of a clock on the other side of the bed. It's 1:29 a.m.

*Daisy! Daisy will be going wild with worry. She'll call the cops.*

Jon's vision swirls again. His groin is sticky. His anus burns. *Oh God.* His clothes are in a bundle on the floor. There is an empty bottle of tequila. Three shot glasses. A whisky tumbler. Jon's heart kicks.

There were others? Who in the hell was all here? What happened? Tears sear into his eyes. He's shaking. He sees a key on the bedside table.

Handcuff key?

With his free hand he gropes for it and uncuffs himself. He sits up, rubs his face, then touches his groin. He's had sex. His gaze shoots back to the glasses. But who with? What in the fuck has he done?

*She did this. She drugged me. She spiked my drink. I should have realized something was happening downstairs. She was asking too many questions.*

It strikes Jon like a mallet as he recalls Mia pressing him about his competition, asking for Ahmed Waheed's name, him telling her that he'd hired a PI for dirt. And suddenly Jon is scared. Really scared. He has no idea what's going on, what shoe will drop next. All he can think about is Daisy. Triage. He needs to think triage.

Daisy can*not* find out about this. Or Jon will be finished. He knows it with every fiber of his being.

A worse thought hits him.

What if Labden and Henry are behind this? Mia was observing him from the bar the night Henry invited him to that pub. Was it a setup? Did they know he'd fall for it?

Or what if Daisy is actually behind this? Testing him?

Jon drops his face into his hands, rocks back and forth, moans.

Think fast. If Daisy hasn't already called the police, she will soon. He has to get out of here.

Jon scrambles on hands and knees, swaying, trying to avoid his own vomit as he gathers up his socks, tie, shirt, pants, shoes, underwear.

He finds his wallet and opens it. Everything is still in there. Including $250 in cash. This was not about petty theft.

He finds his mobile. At least they left his phone. He glances at the shot and whisky and wineglasses again and feels his stomach roil.

*What did I do? What in the hell did* they *do to me? Why does my butthole burn?*

Crying, Jon pulls on his pants, then his shirt. But as he sticks his arm into his sleeve, he sees a small round plaster stuck on the inside crook of his elbow. Jon freezes. Carefully, he peels off the tiny plaster. There is a small hole in his skin. Adrenaline explodes through his blood. He's been injected with something. Panic snakes through him. This could be why he passed out, why he doesn't recall anything. Unless . . . it's something worse. Some poison, some virus that will still take effect maybe years down the road. Like AIDS.

He goes into the bathroom and stills as he sees a line of white powder next to a razor blade and a straw.

*Shit.*

Cocaine? Did he do drugs? He's got to get out of here. Fast.

Quickly, he rinses his face, and he tries to squint at his reflection in the mirror. He looks like death. He remembers something. Mia straddling him. He tries to recall who else was in the room, when they might have arrived, but he can't. He just can't. He thinks of his sticky penis, his burning anal area. He doesn't even want to begin to imagine what happened down there. Jon's eyes fill with hot tears again. With a burning shame. Humiliation. Horror. Raw fear.

He braces his hands flat on the bathroom counter and stares at his face in the mirror.

*I don't know what you did to me, Mia Reiter, but I swear, if I find you, I will kill you. I will fucking kill you.*

# THE PHOTOGRAPHER

It's 1:44 a.m. when the photographer sees Jon Rittenberg stumbling out of the Yaletown condo tower. The photographer powers down his driver's-side window, focuses his lens, shoots several frames as his subject staggers into the road.

The photographer tenses. For a moment he's confronted with the possibility Jon Rittenberg is going to step in front of a vehicle and get himself killed. This changes everything. He reaches for the door handle, but just as he begins to swing open his door, a yellow cab pulls up, and Jon weaves toward it.

The photographer's pulse steadies. He watches for a moment, then raises his camera and shoots as Jon Rittenberg climbs into the back of the cab. Rittenberg must have phoned for a ride. The photographer starts his engine and follows the cab as it heads down the city street. There's not much traffic at this hour, so the photographer is careful to stay back. He imagines the cab will be directed to the parking garage beneath the TerraWest building, where Jon Rittenberg has parked his Audi. However, the man is in no state to drive. This again causes concern. The photographer does not want to be responsible for Rittenberg driving impaired, nor does he want to be forced to engage with his subject.

Once more the photographer relaxes as the cab goes in a different direction. But it's not the route to Rose Cottage. Jon Rittenberg is not going home.

*Where in the hell is he going?*

A few blocks farther on, it dawns on the photographer.

*Oh, you sneaky boy . . .*

The cab turns into the Vancouver General Hospital complex and pulls up in front of the ER admissions area.

Jon exits the cab and stumbles toward the emergency entrance. He enters the glass doors.

The photographer pulls into a nearby parking space. He kills the engine, checks the time, then watches. From his vantage point he can see through the big windows into the well-lit ER waiting area. He sees Jon Rittenberg make his way to a plastic chair. Rittenberg takes a seat. He hunches forward, dropping his head into his hands. But no one comes to admit him. The photographer begins to wonder if Rittenberg has checked in at all.

Within twenty minutes a small white BMW wheels into the ER turnabout. The BMW stops abruptly in front of the ER entrance. A woman gets out of the driver's seat. She is heavily pregnant. She rushes in through the sliding doors.

Daisy Rittenberg.

Jon has called his wife to fetch him.

*Tricky bastard.*

The photographer watches through the windows as Daisy Rittenberg catches sight of her husband, momentarily stalls, then rushes toward him. Rittenberg comes to his feet and hugs his wife. She holds on to him for a long while, stroking his back, then his face. She seems to be sobbing. Her husband places his hand on her tummy. He asks her something. She nods and wipes her eyes. Then she hooks her arm through her husband's and helps him toward her waiting BMW.

# THE MAID'S DIARY

You won't remember exactly what happened because of the spiked alcohol. You won't be able to completely forget, either. You'll spend the next day, the day after, the following weeks, months, years, decades trying to do both. Remember and forget. You both want to know and don't. And every bit of memory you do manage to pull out of the horror of that night, you'll also doubt. Because everyone else who was there tells a different story. They say it's your fault. You're a liar. You're a drunk and a whore and you're being opportunistic and vindictive. You're unwell in the head. Because it's just not possible that what you say happened did happen—how could good boys do something like this?

*Sometimes, years later, while going about your ordinary business, thinking you're okay and that you've left it all behind, a random scent, a snatch of music, a certain color, will slash a broken shard of memory through your brain. You'll stop dead in your tracks, feel confused as all your neural circuits waken fight-or-flight hormones into your body—the same neuro-chemicals that were associated with that night, because as neuroscience will tell you, what fires together, wires together. So while your mind won't hold the whole picture, you real-ize your body does. Your body knows. But your body is not communicating properly with your brain in a way that will give you a narrative around that trauma, something you can understand. And you need that narrative in order to become whole again. In desperation you reach for a bottle of wine, or pills, or you doggedly escape into some other addictive behavior, whether it's long-distance running, or kickboxing, or dieting, or excelling at work, or dangerous snooping, or hiding behind masks and makeup and theatrical roles, becoming an Anonymous Girl. All of it helps you hide from the Monster inside. And when that takes its toll, you try something else. But always, you are running from that faceless Monster. That dark place. And you know what? You can't run. Because it's inside of you. The Monster is you.*

*Then one day you find yourself inside his house.*

*You see a painting.*

*You finally find that proof you are not the liar. Everyone else is.*

*And buried inside that proof is evidence of an even bigger betrayal that slices far too close to your bone. It undercuts everything you thought you knew in your life.*

*You discover your best friend does not have your back. He's a liar, too.*

*And you discover your mother, whose ashes you couldn't let go, coerced you into getting rid of your baby in exchange for money. Money she might have believed would help you go to college. Money she might have thought would help you put the assault behind you and help you achieve all your childhood dreams. But it didn't. Her apparent lack of support at the time, her trying to sweep it under the rug, her trying to shield your father from the ugliness of it all—it just did more damage. You almost took your own life and ended up dropping out of school and leaving town instead.*

*And you know what that feels like, Dear Diary? To see those paintings, to discover you're inside his house, where he is having a baby that you never can, to find your mother's signature at the bottom of a gag order in a safe alongside the signature of a woman named Annabelle Wentworth? It feels like a trigger has been pulled and the bullet hits directly in your head. Everything in your brain explodes. That carapace the decades have hardened around you—it's obliterated in an instant, and all the darkness comes rushing in through the cracks and fills you up so hard and fast you think you are going to burst out of the confines of your own delicate human skin.*

*You realize you are on your own. You have always been on your own.*

*How does one deal with this?*

*I churned it over and over in my mind, then asked myself on these pages—like my therapist suggested—why? Why did my mother do it? Why did Annabelle Wentworth, Daisy's mother, protect her daughter's predator boyfriend? Why do women betray other women like this? Are we so co-opted and dependent on some ingrained adherence to a patriarchy? Are we so afraid of "trouble"?*

*Why did my best "friend" deceive me like this? Why did Boon even approach me in the coffee shop that day long ago? Because I am certain now that it was not fate. He sought me out for a purpose. Was it to save his own soul? Salve his own guilt? Was it all about him?*

*Whatever the answers, I am now pushed up against the Monster I've been trying to hide from. And suddenly I face two paths. Just two choices: Either accept this and allow myself to be violated all over again—remain the Anonymous Girl and hide even deeper behind my masks and coping mechanisms.*

*Or this time stand tall. Fight back. Be seen. No longer the ghost.*

*If the police and justice are never going to be there for me, I need to find justice myself. And now I have the tools to do this.*

*So, Dear Diary, what does justice even look like? Does it mean getting even? Spreading the hurt around? Forcing reparation? Demanding a confession, an apology? I'm not even sure. None of those things will take away the damage done. I am then struck by something: If Boon and others had been brave enough to speak up all those years ago, if my mom had told Annabelle to fuck off with her money, if my mom had fought to keep the cops digging, then Jon would have been stopped. Those other guys would have been stopped. Charley would never have been attacked. Maybe there are more now. Maybe there will still be more. This gives me purpose. This empowers and fires me. I don't need justice. I need to stop him.*

*And her.*

*And others like her.*

*Women like me—we need to show men they will not get away if they try something like this.*

*"What's wrong?" Boon asks me as we sit on a log at Jericho Beach, eating sandwiches in the sun and watching a group of swimmers in wet suits dragging bright-pink buoys behind them. The swimmers rise and fall with the swells. It's a clear day, hardly a breath of wind in the air. Neither warm nor cold. The snowcapped mountains across the water seem bigger, closer. Monstrous, really, due to some trick of atmosphere bending the light. That mountain range stretches north, all the way to my old home, the little world-class ski resort where my mother cleaned rooms and my father processed the shit that forty thousand visitors left behind in the resort each weekend.*

*We used to be able to tell from the stink of the treatment plant whether it had been a good weekend for business.*

"What do you mean, 'What's wrong?'" I bite into my avocado sandwich. Boon has come to meet me at the beach during my lunch break before I go to another job. He's worried after my call.

"Kit, you phoned and said you had to see me. I'm sorry I couldn't come right away. But I'm here now. What in the hell is going on?"

I take another bite of my sandwich and chew slowly. From our log I can see across the water to where the Glass House is. I imagine Beulah Brown next door, training her binoculars toward me and Boon on our silvered log.

"I feel bad for Beulah," I say. "Her son is a freak, too. Beulah spying on her neighbors is one thing. But Horton—he's creepy. I don't trust him."

"You're changing the subject now."

I glance at him. He holds my gaze. I don't smile. This is it. I'm going to cross this line. Our friendship will never be the same. Which is laughable that I even consider this—our friendship never was what I thought it was.

"You remember how we met, Boon? In that coffee shop?"

He frowns. He looks nervous. "Yes, why?"

"You were this random guy who asked if he could sit at my table. I said, sure, and I wondered at the time if I knew you from somewhere because you looked vaguely familiar. And then you said, 'You're Katarina, right?' Do you remember that?"

"Kit, where is this go—"

"I must've looked like a deer in headlights," I say. "Because at that instant I'd just realized where I'd seen you before. My school days. And I wanted nothing to do with people from *my old school or hometown. And I was suddenly mentally mapping all my possible escape routes from the mall. That's when you said, 'You're from Whistler, right? You were a couple of grades behind me.' And you sipped your hot chocolate, watching me over the rim of your cup, and you got this huge blob of whipped cream on the tip of your nose, which made me smile in spite of myself. You remember all that?"*

*"Dammit, Kit, just spit it out. Where are you going with this?"*

*"You said I'd changed. That I looked amazing. You liked the new blonde hair. You were smart enough not to say you liked my new skinny figure. You told me your name was Boonmee but that everyone calls you Boon. We walked to the bus together, and I said, given that we both lived in such a tiny town, you must've been aware of what happened to me."*

*"It's why I went over to your table, Kit. I'd seen you coming into the coffee shop a few times. I always felt bad for you because of what happened. A lot of us in town did. I believed your story. I always did. I one hundred percent believe your story about Jon Rittenberg and the ski team."*

*I lower my sandwich and stare at him. My heart begins to pound.*

*He says, "And I told you that day that I was bullied at school, too. I told you I knew guys like Jon Rittenberg. They would single me out after school because I was gay and they could smell it even though I hadn't come out yet, or even fully admitted it to myself. In a small town like that, with only one school, where the same class cohort goes all the way from kindergarten to grade twelve, always the same faces in that one class, year after year as you all go up a grade, you can't escape. There's nowhere to hide, nowhere to run. You get branded the target from kindergarten and stay the target your entire school career. Bullied. Humiliated. Disliked. You start to wear that label. You start to believe them. And when I saw you in that coffee shop, after all that time, I needed to tell you that I felt bad, that I believed in you. I-I guess I wanted to say sorry. I'm sorry for what happened to you."*

*"But are you? Are you really sorry, Boon?"*

*He looks shocked.*

*I inhale deeply and turn my face up toward the weak sun. I close my eyes, just feeling the gentle rays on my skin. "You know how I told you the other day that I got new clients?"*

*"Yeah," he says.*

*I turn to Boon. "He's back in town. I got his house."*

*"What?"*

*"My new client is Jon Rittenberg. I'm cleaning his house."*

*Blood drains from his face.*

*"You know what else? I did a bit of snooping. Okay, a lot of snooping. And I found a recording. From that night."*

*"What are you talking about?"*

*I hold his gaze for a long time. I see the moment it begins to dawn on him. His face goes slack and totally bloodless. He tries to swallow. His eyes water. "You mean . . . that night at the ski team lodge?"*

*"You know exactly what I mean." My voice is soft, quiet. "Someone recorded the drugging and assault on a phone. They recorded who was there that night. Sound and everything. All those kids who said it never happened—they're all there. On that recording. Daisy Rittenberg was also at the party. She saved it. She has kept it locked in a safe all these years, and now I have a copy on my phone."*

*His mouth opens. No words come.*

*"I don't know what I am to you, Boon—"*

*"You're my friend, Kit. I'm your friend. Best friend."*

*"I don't know what truly drove you to seek me out in the coffee shop that day, or why you have tried so desperately to be my friend. Or why you work so hard to be so nice. So kind. Maybe I can guess. Shame. Guilt. Maybe you were afraid that if you were the only one who spoke up and told the police what you witnessed, you would be bullied to death and not survive the year you still had left at school. Maybe you were afraid those guys would tell the world and your parents you were gay. So you hid. You kept quiet. You kept your head down. You helped perpetuate evil. But all this time, you knew. You could have saved me. Maybe even saved my baby."*

*"Kit, please. I can explain. I can—"*

*"All I know, Boon, is you owe me. You owe me big. Not just for staying silent, but for deceiving me all this time."*

*I reach into my bag for my phone, and I make him watch the recording.*

# MAL

Mal reaches for her coffee and takes another sip. It's 5:55 a.m., and she and her team are assembled in the incident room. She didn't sleep last night and is running on pure adrenaline boosted by caffeine.

"Now that we've located the Norths and identified the Rittenbergs, we're working on the assumption Kit Darling is our assault victim," Mal says as she sets her coffee down. "We've sent personal items from Darling's apartment to a private lab along with blood samples from the crime scene so a DNA comparison can be expedited. We should have preliminary results before nightfall today."

Benoit says, "Vanessa and Haruto North so far appear to have no direct involvement, since they are out of the country, but it is their house, and Darling is their maid. What we do have is a direct link between the Rittenbergs, the crime scene at the Glass House, and Kit Darling. What we need is motive. Opportunity. Means. We need that rug. We need that Subaru Crosstrek. We need DNA from both Rittenbergs to definitively place them inside the house. And we need to search Rose Cottage and impound and search that Audi. Our goal is to find additional evidence that will secure us those warrants."

"What about the mystery pregnant woman that Beulah Brown thought was Vanessa North? And the woman who visits the Pi Bistro with Daisy Rittenberg who Binty believes is Vanessa North?" asks Jack. "And the woman Daisy Rittenberg says invited them for dinner at the Glass House?"

"We'll show Ty Binty Vanessa North's photo today," Mal says. "And see what he says. We'll also take her photo to the yoga studio, and we'll bring both Daisy and Jon Rittenberg in for further questioning."

"His Audi is full of mud," says Arnav. "The mud could come from a dump site. It was raining heavily that night."

"Right," Mal says. "We'll keep scouring cam footage to see if we can pick it up along Marine. And we'll also need to secure warrants to access Darling's phone and financial records. Her recent financial transactions, who she called or texted, who contacted her—it will all give a clearer picture of her movements leading up to the violent event. We also need to keep eyes on socials."

Mal checks tasks and questions off on her fingers. "Do the Rittenbergs have social media profiles? We know Darling runs an Instagram account using the handle @foxandcrow. What has she posted there? Does she have any other accounts in her own name? We need history going back to her ski resort days. Her friend, Boon-mee Saelim, spoke of a traumatic event in her past that caused Darling to drop out of school and leave town. What was that event? We need to locate her diary. We also need to delve into the Rittenbergs' backgrounds. Jon Rittenberg was on the national ski team. The ski team has a lodge and trained in the town where Darling grew up. There's potential for crossover there."

As Mal assigns tasks, there is a sharp knock on the door. They all look up as a uniformed officer enters. His eyes are bright.

"We've got 'em!" he says. "We found the two vehicles on CCTV footage. The Subaru and the Audi."

Tension ripples through the room.

"Can you bring it up on this monitor?" asks Benoit.

Within minutes they are gathered around the table, leaning forward in silence as they study the grainy CCTV footage.

"See here." The officer points. "A Subaru Crosstrek and an Audi S6 sedan are captured exiting Marine Drive. And on this cam, where they're heading into the North Vancouver industrial area. And over here we pick them up again outside the ADMAC construction site on the water. The area is fenced off for the redevelopment of the abandoned grain silos and old dockyard. We approached ADMAC, and they have security cameras on site. They gave us access." He hits a key.

They watch the Audi S6 sedan and Subaru Crosstrek traversing the area in front of the grain silos.

"Another ADMAC cam picks them up again there." He points. "Crossing the railway tracks heading toward the water." They watch as the two vehicles, one behind the other, cross the tracks and move away from the camera. The vehicles bump along what appears to be a potholed and muddy track parallel to the shore. They disappear from camera range. The weather is foggy. Wet. It's dark.

"Unfortunately the cam trained on the dock is out of order. But seventeen minutes later, here the Audi is, returning. It crosses in front of the silos here"—the officer points—"then exits the ADMAC site there, and heads back up to Marine. We pick it up again crossing the Lions Gate Bridge."

"Possibly going home to Point Grey," Benoit says.

"What about the Subaru—any footage of the Subaru exiting the site?" Lula asks.

"Negative. The Subaru never came out. We sent officers to the site. We just got a call from them. There are three fairly fresh sets of tire tracks. Tracks matching standard-issue Subaru tires go straight to the dock. There are signs the vehicle went right over into the water. Two sets of footprints around the area. Also drag marks through mud. As though something heavy was pulled to the edge of the dock."

"I think we found our dump site," Mal says quietly.

The mood in the room shifts.

Benoit says, "The Audi is the same S6 model as the sedan parked outside Rose Cottage."

Mal clicks the back of her pen, in out, in out. "We need samples of the mud on Rittenberg's tires. Can you zoom in on the Subaru and Audi registrations as they enter the ADMAC site?"

"We managed to enhance the Subaru plates. It's registered to Katarina Darling. But mud obscures the Audi plates."

"You said three sets of tire tracks," Mal says.

He smiles and pulls up different footage. "This is shot from the cam up on the bridge—the so-called jumpers cam. It captures some of the area below the bridge. Watch this—it occurs eleven minutes before we see the Audi and Subaru arrive at the ADMAC site." He hits PLAY.

They watch in silence as a large luxury sedan drives along the water, approaching the bridge, then disappears under it.

A sly smile curves the officer's mouth. "That, my friends, is another vehicle. The third one. A Mercedes-Maybach. And while the Subaru disappeared over the edge of the dock, that Mercedes Maybach was still parked in the shadows under the bridge. There is no way out other than the way it drove in." He hits PLAY. "And there it goes again. Leaving."

They watch the Mercedes-Maybach exiting from under the bridge. It drives through the fog and rain back along the track that parallels the water. It disappears out of camera range before it reaches the dock.

"After we picked up the Mercedes," the officer says, "we searched farther back in the ADMAC cam footage. The Mercedes enters the ADMAC site eleven minutes before the Audi and Subaru arrive." He points to the footage. "You can see there—looks like two people inside the Mercedes. One in the driver seat, one in the passenger seat. The driver looks to be female because of the long hair. The Mercedes then exits the ADMAC site seven minutes after the Audi leaves the area. Still two people inside."

"Did you get the registration on that Maybach?" Benoit asks. "Because whatever went down off camera at those old docks, the occupants of the Mercedes-Maybach had to have witnessed it."

The officer pulls up an enhanced close-up of the Mercedes plate. He meets each of their gazes in turn and grins. "You're never going to guess who the sedan is registered to."

"Oh, go on, spill," says Lula in a mocking voice.

"Tamara Adler. Of Kane, Adler, Singh, and Salinger. The top city law firm handling that big case that's been in the news involving a member of the Legislative Assembly for Vancouver–Point Grey, the Honorable Frank Horvath?"

"*Adler* is our witness?" Gavin asks.

"Whoever those two people are inside Adler's car—they are our potential witnesses," Mal says quietly. "And whoever they are, if they did see what went down, they did not call this in, and they did not come forward. I want to talk to Tamara Adler." She surges to her feet. "Lula, loop the North Van RCMP in on this. Have them cordon off that entire ADMAC construction site. Jack, contact ADMAC—all work on their site stops right now. Gavin, get the paperwork rolling on the warrant for Rittenberg's Audi and a search of Rose Cottage. I want Jon Rittenberg brought in. I want a DNA sample from him, scrapings from his nails, photographs documenting his injuries, the works. I want DNA samples from Daisy Rittenberg, too. And we need a dive team and support craft out to that dockyard stat."

# DAISY

*October 29, 2019. Tuesday.*
*Two days before the murder.*

Daisy helps her husband into bed after picking him up at the VGH ER. Her emotions are a churning quagmire of relief and anxiety. She'd been so worried when Jon was not home by 1:00 a.m. that she phoned one of the colleagues Jon was supposed to have been out with, entertaining the Chinese clients. But the colleague said they all left the supper club around 10:00 p.m. He thought Jon was headed straight home.

Daisy was about to call the police when her phone rang. It was Jon. He was at VGH. He'd experienced a blackout on his way back to his car after dinner. Someone found him passed out on the sidewalk and called for an ambulance. Jon said the ER doctor believed he'd experienced a minor stroke. He was okay, but he needed to return for a follow-up, and he should make an appointment to see a specialist.

"Thank God for the Good Samaritan who found you," Daisy whispers as she seats herself on the side of the bed, holding his hand. "This could have ended up so differently."

He closes his eyes, nods. She strokes his hair. He looks awful. Pale as a ghost. His eyes are dark hollows. He smells of vomit.

"We can clean you up in the morning," she whispers and kisses his cheek. "I am so thankful to have you home."

He nods again with his eyes closed and squeezes her hand.

Daisy turns the lights way down, but not off completely. And she goes downstairs to make some tea.

As she puts the kettle on, she says a silent thank-you to whoever runs the universe. When it comes right down to the wire, as with this close call tonight, Daisy realizes she doesn't want to be a single mother. Ever. She wants her husband at her side when their son is born. She *needs* Jon. She needs him to be a good and faithful man in sickness and in health until death do them part. Tears fill her eyes. She's always needed that. From the day she met him at school. It's why she was so damaged when he made stupid mistakes. It's why she tried desperately to clean up after him. Daisy *needs* to believe she married the right man. She needs to believe he is good. And that he will be a wonderful father. And that he loves her. Because what is the alternative?

Daisy refuses to accept the alternative.

People might call it cognitive dissonance. Psychologists might point out to her that humans are perfectly capable of believing two opposing ideas at the same time, or engaging in behaviors that contradict their core beliefs. They might tell her that humans are highly adept at inventing thoughts and narratives to support the dissonance within. Daisy knows this is true. She's able to bury dark things deep in her subconscious and to look the other way. It's a survival tool. All she wants is to survive.

Daisy wipes her tears. She hopes her son will grow up good. There's so much pressure on guys to "man up," to "be a man," to "take it like a man." Jon had that pressure but no male mentor to help him navigate this world. His own father abandoned him. He was raised by a single mom. He was a lost boy who constantly sought to prove himself. Perhaps it was always about winning the attention of his absent dad. Perhaps little Jon was permanently struggling to make his missing father proud, to make him come home. Perhaps Jon blamed his little self for his dad's leaving. And then teenage Jon got lost.

Daisy swipes away more tears. Her hands shake. She refuses to think about the stink of alcohol on her husband. The smell of vomit unexplained. The fact she never saw the ER doc with her own eyes. She tells herself this minor stroke—or whatever Jon says the doctor called it—is a blessing in disguise, because she doesn't doubt the fear she saw in his eyes. Jon is scared by what happened.

Perhaps she and Jon can both be more thankful now. More fierce in protecting each other and in safeguarding what it means to be starting a little family.

# MAL

Tamara Adler shows Mal into her sumptuous office. The woman is a partner in the exclusive law firm Kane, Adler, Singh, and Salinger.

"Please take a seat," she says to Mal. The view from Adler's office must be breathtaking, Mal thinks, but right now it's bleak and smothered with low clouds. Rain streaks the windows. Mal sits on a sofa near the window. Benoit is at the ADMAC construction site, awaiting the arrival of the police dive team and ident units.

"What can I do for you, Sergeant?" Adler is poised and impeccably attired in a cream suit. Her perfectly coiffed red hair swings neatly at her jawline. Her nails are manicured. *Expensive* is the word that comes to Mal's mind. And *controlled*. Tamara Adler certainly does not exhibit the signs of a woman who witnessed an atrocity from her car parked under a bridge at a construction site in the very dark hours of the morning. But Mal knows that people are seldom what they seem.

She cuts straight to the chase. After opening a file, Mal extracts several images printed from the CCTV footage. She spreads them out over the coffee table in front of Adler.

"These images were captured by security cameras on the ADMAC construction site near the old silos and dockyard in North Vancouver. As you can see from the time and date stamps, they were taken in the very early hours of Friday, November 1. The Mercedes-Maybach in these images is registered to you, Mrs. Adler." Mal meets the lawyer's gaze. "Can you tell me who was driving your car in these photos? If you look closely at this enhanced image here"—she points—"the person in the driver's seat appears to be you."

Tamara Adler regards the photos. Not a muscle moves in her body, but Mal can feel her tension. The wheels in this woman's head are turning, seeking explanation, escape. Mal notices the exact moment the lawyer decides to face this head-on. Adler looks up. Her eyes lock onto Mal's.

"Can we keep this out of the press?"

"I can't promise anything. But the more cooperation we have right out of the gate, the easier it might be for you and whoever else was in your car to remain beneath media radar."

Adler inhales deeply and returns her attention to the photos. She studies them, as if calculating her odds on whether law enforcement will figure out for themselves who the person in the passenger seat is.

"Who is he, Mrs. Adler? And it does appear to be a male. We'll eventually identify him without your assistance. Especially if we post these images and put out a call for information via social media. We get a lot of tips crowdsourcing this way."

Adler moistens her lips, reaches for the water jug on the table, and pours herself a glass. She holds the jug out to Mal.

"I'm fine," Mal says.

The lawyer takes a delicate sip. A faint sheen has developed on her brow. Tamara Adler is finding this distressing.

"I was with Frank Horvath," she says finally. "And I cannot stress enough how damaging this will be to his—our—reputations if this gets out. It will scuttle a court case that—"

"What did you and the Honorable Mr. Horvath witness at the ADMAC site that morning, Mrs. Adler? Judging by the location of your vehicle, you must have seen something."

The lawyer glances out the windows.

"Was there anyone else present? Any other vehicles?"

Adler does not meet Mal's gaze. She continues to stare out the window.

"A young woman is missing. We have reason to believe you and the passenger in your car can help us figure out what happened to her." Mal taps her finger firmly on an image secured from the jumpers cam. Adler turns to look. "See how your vehicle arrives here, then exits facing east? Your vehicle at one point was directly pointed toward the old dock."

Adler inhales. "You don't know that we saw anything."

"Like I said"—Mal's tone is cool, crisp—"cooperation is going to make things a lot less difficult for you and MLA Frank Horvath. And for both of your families."

Adler surges to her feet. She walks on her expensive pumps to the floor-to-ceiling windows. She folds her arms across her stomach and stares out into the mist and low clouds.

"We saw the two cars," she says quietly with her back to Mal. "A larger sedan and a smaller hatchback. The sedan was dark in color. The hatchback light. I believe it was a Subaru Crosstrek. We gave one to our son for his birthday, so I am very familiar with the model." She pauses, then turns to face Mal. "Two people in rain gear got out and took a rolled-up rug or something similar out of the back seat of the sedan. They dragged it to the edge of the dock and rolled it into the water. Then we witnessed them sending the hatchback off the edge of the dock." She regards Mal for a long beat. "It appeared as though they jammed down the Subaru accelerator. Frank and I—we were having an affair. It's over now. We were both afraid that if we came forward, our liaison would be exposed. The consequences will be catastrophic to both of us, and our spouses, children, my clients, and his constituents."

"What is it that you thought they had in the rolled-up rug?" Mal asks.

"I don't know what was in the rug."

"You didn't think that two people sending a Subaru Crosstrek into the Burrard Inlet in the dark of night might be doing some serious crime, trying to cover up something, hide evidence?"

Her jaw tightens. Her arms press more firmly across her stomach. Her eyes water. "It could have been anything," she says quietly. "Illegal dumping. Anything."

"Right. And what did you and the Honorable Horvath do next?"

"We left. I dropped Frank off at his vehicle parked in the city. We went to our respective homes." She takes a seat opposite Mal, leans forward. Her gaze is intense. "I—we—will come in and make official witness statements. But that is all we saw, all we know."

"Would you be able to identify the two drivers?"

"No. They were a distance away. It was dark, rainy, very foggy, and they were fully covered in dark rain gear. One seemed to have a hood over his head, and—"

"*His* head?"

"I . . . assumed he was male. He was the taller one. The other seemed rounder, shorter."

"Could the shorter one have been a female?"

"Possibly."

"Could she have been pregnant?"

"What?"

"Could the shorter person have been pregnant?"

"I-I never thought. I . . . suppose it's possible."

"Can you come in and make a formal statement today?"

"Yes. I will bring Frank. It would be better if you did not go to his office."

In silence, Mal gathers up the photos and inserts them into the file folder.

"Frank's kids are younger than mine," Adler says. "It would be very hard on them if his marriage collapsed. And as a member of the Legislative Assembly—what he does for the homeless, the opioid crisis, social housing—if this is exposed, all that good work will be for nothing. His opponents will crucify him. We never dreamed anyone would see us having a fling in my car, or that anything like this could happen. We are careful. It's why we go to places like that."

Mal looks up and meets the lawyer's gaze. "Our missing victim also has people who care about her, Mrs. Adler. She never dreamed she might be attacked and rolled into a rug and dumped into the sea. If that is what happened." Mal comes to her feet. "For your and Frank Horvath's sakes, I hope your decision to not call 911 did not result in a delay that cost her life."

# JON

*October 31, 2019. Thursday.*
*The day of the murder.*

Jon winces as morning light slices in through the shades and points an accusing finger at his face. He squints, taking a moment to adjust. As he comes more fully awake, fear and anxiety crawl back into his consciousness. He's in his bed. He's safe. But the nightmare with Mia Reiter still roils through his mind and body.

He sits up and gingerly hangs his feet over the side of the bed. He stayed home from work both Tuesday and Wednesday. He slept most of the time but still feels spaccy. He still cannot recall exactly what transpired. He believes Mia drugged him. He doesn't know why. Yet. He has absolutely no memory of who else was in the room. Perhaps that's the most terrifying thing of all. And that he was tied up. Most likely sexually assaulted, given the pain around his anus.

He hears Daisy downstairs in the kitchen. She has music playing. He can smell bacon, coffee. His stomach recoils. How can she play music at a time like this? But she doesn't know what happened. The fear that she will soon find out is raw. It's a ticking time bomb in his brain. Just tick tick tick ticking away, waiting for the other shoe to drop. Will he be blackmailed? Is this extortion? What did Mia Reiter want from him? Why does he have a needle mark in the crook of his arm?

The music downstairs increases in volume as Daisy turns the stove hood fan on. He catches snippets of lyrics about a betrayed heart and a love gone sour. His mood worsens.

He reaches for his phone. No messages. No missed calls. Jon hesitates, gets up, and closes the bedroom door. He calls Mia's number.

Instantly he gets a recorded message.

*The number you are calling is no longer in service.*

His pulse rate spikes.

He tries again.

*The number you are calling is no longer in service.*

He sits for a moment in the weak autumn-morning sun pouring through his window, paralyzed by the idea that this is far from over. He's been terrorized, gaslighted. He's been forced to wait in trepidation for a bomb to drop, and he has no idea when it will come whistling through the air above him. Or what it will look like.

He called in sick to work yesterday and the day before. He *was* sick. Felt like crap. Still does. He lied to Daisy about the doctor needing a follow-up, so he had to follow through with a fake appointment yesterday. Daisy insisted on coming with, which made things complicated. She drove him and waited in the car while Jon walked in through the main hospital doors. Once inside the massive complex, he went to find the chapel. He sat there in the quiet in front of candles and waited his alleged appointment out. When Jon returned to the car, he told Daisy his doc said the blackout was likely stress induced. It happens sometimes. But to be safe he was being recommended to a specialist. The specialist would call to set an appointment. In the meanwhile, Jon was supposed to take things easy. Rest. Eat well. Hydrate. Get exercise. Keep stress low. Jon told Daisy he'd let all these things slide. Daisy held his hand and said she'd do what it took to help him. She reminded him they were a team. Jon felt the old love he'd once had for his wife. In that instant he believed it could still all come right. But now, in this bleak light of dawn, he feels the pressure of the unknown hanging above his head, and he regrets he might already have blown it all.

He checks the time. He has a big meeting at work today. He needs to pull himself together. Jon showers, dresses, and goes downstairs.

He sees Daisy from the rear. He notices the weight she's gained on her bum. She's holding a large knife. It glints in the sunlight as she slices open a grapefruit. The two halves of the fruit split open, revealing glistening ruby flesh. Jon stares at the blade. So much sharpness. So much whiteness and glass and brightness. The red flesh. His head hurts.

She turns. Smiles.

He sees her teeth. The flush in her cheeks. Her belly. She wears a weird Halloween apron with a pumpkin on it.

He feels ill. It's the lingering effect of drugs from the other night, he thinks. Combined with fear. And the cortisol pounding through his body like poison. His gaze locks on her belly. She's due so soon. Their progeny growing, turning, kicking, sucking his thumb inside her. A baby boy. Kicking, kicking. A future little ski racer perhaps. Jon feels a bolt of sadness as he thinks of his own dad—that shitty example of paternal guidance and love. He makes a bargain with the devil. Or God. He's not sure which. But he vows that if he's spared the fallout from his terrible misguided mistake with Mia, he will be the best dad he can. For the rest of his son's life. He will be there for him. He will be present. And he will love his boy.

Daisy's smile fades to a look of worry. "Did you sleep okay? Are you sure you're well enough to go in today?"

"Yeah. Got that big meeting." He pours himself a coffee.

"I phoned a dietitian," Daisy says. "And a personal trainer for an assessment. I told them your history, and—"

"Daisy, not now."

She dials it back. She looks overly flushed. "What time will you be home?"

"Regular dinnertime."

"Oh, you've forgotten?"

"Forgotten what?"

"Halloween dinner—Vanessa and Haruto's thing tonight."

"What? Christ, not tonight. I—"

"Please, Jon. For me. It might be good for both of us to do something different."

He regards her in silence. He feels bad. For everything. He's afraid he's going to lose her. "Sure. Fine. My time is all yours."

"Thank you. They said we should come around six p.m. for cocktails. I thought we'd pick up some flowers and some pie for dessert on the way over. Okay?"

"Sure. Yes."

By the time Jon parks his Audi S6 sedan in the underground garage at work, his head is a little clearer. From his car he calls Jake Preston. He's paranoid that the thing with Mia was orchestrated by Labden, or Henry, or perhaps even Ahmed Waheed. Threads of Mia's sultry voice snake through his brain.

*And who's this rival, JonJon BergBomber? . . . How will you find dirt?*

Jake picks up on the second ring. "Jake Preston."

"It's Jon Rittenberg. Have you got anything yet?"

"Might need a while longer. Your guy is squeaky damn clean, Jon. So clean it's enough to think he's gotta be hiding something. But we've found no criminal record. He doesn't party. He runs miles every day. Lifts weights. Does yoga—"

"Yoga? For Pete's sake."

"Yeah. Yoga. He's into the holistic health shit. Shops for fresh produce at the market. Likes to buy local, spends weekends visiting galleries. Passionate about sports. Snowboarder in winter. Kite boards in summer. He's got a steady girlfriend. She moved to Vancouver with him. She works in finance."

"Finance?" Jon's pulse blips. "Like what kind of finance—banking?"

"Yeah, you got it. She's with a firm based out of the UK. Works long distance, but also travels a lot for her work."

Jon's hand tenses around his phone. He peers into the shadows of the parking garage. "What's her name?"

"Listen, buddy, I thought you didn't want to do this on the phone. Thought you preferred in person."

"Just give me her damn name."

"Mila Gill."

*"Mia?"*

"No, Mila. *M-I-L-A.*"

"Where's she from? What nationality?"

"British."

"You said you'd find dirt, Jake. I *need* something, dammit. What you've told me—I could've scored all that myself. It's worthless. I need something I can use. Now." *Before something comes down on me.* "You promised you'd find it."

"I said I'd find it if it was there to be found. Manufacturing kompromat, Jon, is a whole other kettle of fish. I told you at the outset I needed to know where we were to draw the lines. Planting kompromat comes with a whole other price tag, too."

Jon drags his hand through his hair. *Mia. Mila. Banker. Finance. Foreign. Travels a lot . . .* He has a horrible feeling. "Plant the dirt," he says. "I don't care what it costs. Just do it."

Jon kills the call, exits and locks his car, and goes up in the elevator. With each floor that the elevator goes higher, the heavier the sense of trepidation pushing down on his head.

He exits the elevator and walks into the office. Anna the receptionist is dressed like Morticia, and Jon is instantly reminded it's Halloween today.

"Morning, Anna," he says.

She stares at him from under her black wig as he approaches. Her face is powder white and her black-lined lips are unsmiling. There's a weird atmosphere in the air. Jon notices Ahmed in his glass cubicle. His rival meets his gaze. Ahmed doesn't smile, either. His mouth is set in a grim line. Ahmed watches Jon steadily with dark, unreadable eyes behind his round glasses, and a warning bell begins to clang in Jon's head. He tells himself they're just pissed because he forgot to dress up. They think he's not being a sport, spoiling their fun.

"Jon," Anna says, clearing her throat before she speaks again. He notices fake blood dripping out of the corners of her mouth. "Darrian wants to see you in his office."

*The big boss.*

Jon stills. "Why? What's up?"

Anna won't meet his eyes. "He just said to go through as soon as you come in."

"Right." Jon starts toward his own office.

Anna lurches up from her chair and hurries after him. "Jon! Darrian said straight through, Jon—"

"I'm just putting my damn briefcase down first, okay?"

She swallows and looks freaky with her bloody mouth. "I'm sorry, Jon. It's just that he insisted you go directly to his office."

Jon holds her gaze. In his peripheral vision he can see others in their glass cubicles, looking up, watching him. All still. Silent. And he knows. He just knows.

The other shoe has already dropped.

# MAL

"Vanessa North's first class with us was on Wednesday, August 7," the yoga instructor tells Mal as she scans her computer database.

"Did she attend often?" Mal asks. She came to the yoga studio directly after her meeting with Tamara Adler. On her drive over she called Benoit and updated him with the information from Adler. Benoit told her the divers were commencing the underwater search.

"Yes. It seems Vanessa came pretty regularly after that first session, both for the Monday and the Wednesday classes." The instructor glances up. She's an earnest-looking woman in her early fifties with an open face, no makeup, and long, wavy gray hair. "What's this about? I only ask because Vanessa hasn't attended the last few classes, and I was wondering how things were going with her baby."

Mal sidesteps the yoga instructor's question. "Do you have Vanessa North's credit card details in your system?"

The woman checks, frowns, then says, "Oh, it looks like Vanessa always paid cash."

"What about her contact details? Did she fill out any fitness or health forms?"

The woman checks her system again. "Yes, she completed the required forms. And we do have an address on file. But I really can't give you anything, Sergeant. I'm so sorry. Not without a warrant."

"I can return with a warrant, ma'am, but this is highly time sensitive. A woman's life might be in jeopardy. How about you either confirm or deny that the address you have on file is 5244 Sea Lane, West Vancouver?"

The instructor looks nervous now. "Yes. I can confirm that. I-I suppose there is no harm in giving you her mobile number." The yoga teacher reads the number out for Mal.

Mal enters it into her phone.

"One more question," Mal says as she pulls up the image of Vanessa North provided by Singapore law enforcement. She shows it to the instructor. "Is this the woman who attended your yoga classes?"

"No. Vanessa has longer hair. More auburn highlights. Big hazel eyes. Different nose and cheekbones. And she's a bit younger." The yoga instructor's brow furrows. "Who is this?"

"This is Vanessa North."

"Then . . . who's the woman who comes to yoga?"

"That's a good question. Thank you for your time." Mal slides her card across the counter. "If you think of anything else, or if your client shows up again, please call me directly."

As Mal walks back to her unmarked vehicle, she calls the number the yoga instructor gave her. It goes straight to a recorded message.

*The number you are calling is no longer in service.*

◆  ◆  ◆

As Mal drives to the Pi Bistro to talk to Ty Binty, Benoit calls.

"Hey," Mal says. "They find anything?"

She can hear the noise of a truck in the background, beeping. Benoit answers someone else's question, then comes back on the line.

"Divers have located the Subaru. It's where we anticipated, right off the side of the dock. It's deep down there. Went straight down. Crews are strategizing how best to bring it up. We've called for a tow truck with a crane and a flatbed so we can transport the vehicle to the ident lab," Benoit says.

Mal inhales slowly, trying to tamp down her rush of adrenaline. Her mind goes to the pretty maid with her messy space buns and her tiny apartment with its boho decor and postcards and travel dreams and Morbid the crow, and Mal feels a sudden and profound sadness. Her eyes prick a little, and then she clears it all away.

"Any sign of the rug?" she asks.

"Not yet. There's a strong tidal current that moves both ways, so it could have flowed a distance. A lot of urban debris down there, too. Very poor visibility. It's slow going. Dangerous work."

"Okay, thanks. I'll head over as soon as I'm done talking to Ty Binty. Warrants?"

"In hand. Lula's got the guys combing through Darling's financials and phone records. And our surveillance detail outside Rose Cottage reports that Jon Rittenberg has not left his residence since we paid him a visit. They're on standby to bring him in—just waiting for the tow truck to arrive so they can impound his Audi and transport it to the lab. We're working with West Van police to bring Daisy Wentworth in for fingerprinting, a DNA sample, and additional questioning."

"I want the Rittenberg samples and digital prints sent to the private lab for expediting as well," Mal says. "If we can link the Rittenbergs directly to the crime scene, we can bring them in front of a judge and charge and hold them."

Mal signs off, exits her car, and enters the bistro doors. The scent of freshly baked bread triggers her hunger instantly. She eyes the pastries while she waits for Ty Binty to come out of his office at the rear of the bakery.

"Hey, Sergeant. Good to see you again. What can I get for you?"

Mal smiles. "This is business. But I'm not going to say no to one of those danishes and a large cappuccino, dry, with an extra shot."

He grins broadly. "Better than doughnuts, eh?"

"Infinitely."

While he puts her order through, Mal brings up her photo of Vanessa North. She shows Binty.

"Do you know this woman?" she asks. "Has she been in here?"

Ty Binty leans forward and carefully studies the photo. He purses his lips. "No. I can't say that I do. She might well have been in here, but she's not someone I immediately recognize."

"But you would recognize Daisy Rittenberg's friend, Vanessa North?"

"Oh yeah. For sure. Attractive woman. Big hazel eyes."

"Did Vanessa North pay for her meals here? Or did her friend Daisy Rittenberg usually pay?"

"Vanessa paid often. They seemed to switch it up on a regular basis."

"Credit card?"

"Cash. Vanessa always paid cash. She seemed to like to pay with cash."

# JON

Briefcase in hand, Jon strides past his colleagues watching him from behind their desks in their glass cubicles. Darrian Walton's door at the end of the corridor is slightly ajar. Jon knocks once and enters the big boss's expansive corner office.

Darrian, tall and tanned with a gray buzz cut, stands stony faced behind his monstrous black desk. Jon's pulse kicks up another notch when he sees a manila envelope on the desk in front of Darrian. As Jon stares at the envelope, he becomes aware of a presence in his peripheral vision. He turns to see Henry sitting like a silent toad in a wingback near a bookshelf.

"Darrian," Jon says. "You wanted to see me."

Jon expects to be asked to take a seat. But he is not. Darrian remains standing. He tents the fingertips of his right hand atop the manila envelope on the desk.

"This was hand-delivered to the office today," Darrian says in a monotone. His ice-blue eyes laser Jon's.

Jon moistens his lips.

"Do you know what's in here, Jon?"

Broken shards of memory cut through his brain. Mia's red mouth. Handcuffs. Several shot glasses. The burn around his asshole. The puncture mark in the crook of his arm. His sticky penis. Dread rises from the pit of his stomach.

"No," he says.

Darrian lifts the envelope and spills the contents onto the desk. Glossy photos slide over the surface.

Shock rams through Jon. His breath snares in his throat. He steps forward involuntarily. The images show Mia kissing him outside the Hunter and Hound on the first night he met her. They show him and Mia in the booth after Henry left. Him with his hands in his pockets as he watches Mia walk down the street. Him and Mia kissing as they back into her Airbnb suite. Him and Mia touching hands in the piano lounge downstairs. Him stumbling out of the condo tower into the dark street, right before the cab arrived to take him to VGH.

Darrian spreads the photos out, exposing others that lie beneath. Horror swamps Jon as he sees himself naked on the bed. Mia, half-dressed, straddling him. The other photos show two different men. On top of him. Next to him. Their naked bodies entwined with his. Bile rises in Jon's throat. He can't breathe. He's going into anaphylactic shock. Henry remains dead silent in his corner. Air seems to suck right out of the room.

Darrian moves the photos again, and Jon sees yet more—his Audi parked at the Jericho Beach lot with the passenger door open, Jake Preston climbing out with an envelope in his hand. Another image shows a plaque next to a door that says PRESTON PRIVATE INVESTIGATIONS.

"I feel sorry for Daisy, Jon," Darrian says. "I feel bad for Labden and Annabelle. But while your sex life is one thing, this"—he lifts a document—"*this* is unacceptable. Do you know what this is, Jon?"

Cold drops like a stone through his bowels. He says nothing.

"This, Jon, is a contract with a notorious private investigator hired by you to dig up dirt on a TerraWest colleague. Using race and religious affiliation. Dirt on a competitor for a TerraWest job. And this"—he picks up a copy of another printed document—"is a list of personal details stolen from confidential TerraWest HR files and given to this PI."

Rage burns into Jon's eyes. He shoots his gaze to Henry, who meets Jon's eyes but does not move a muscle.

"Did you do this, Henry?" Jon points to the photos and documents. "Did you set me up?"

"Get out of here, Jon," Darrian says calmly, coolly. "Get out of my office. Get out of this building. And don't ever come back."

"Who delivered that to you?" Jon demands. "Who brought it into this office?"

"I said, get out."

"I-I can explain. I was set up. I—Ahmed Waheed—*he* did this. With Henry. They set me up."

"Get the hell out. I don't want to see your face again. Ever."

Jon goes numb. He stares at Darrian. Then he looks in desperation at Henry.

"Don't make me call security," Darrian says.

Jon turns and walks slowly, woodenly, to the door with his briefcase in his hand. Everything feels surreal. Time has turned elastic. Sound stretches and distorts. It's as though he's hearing and seeing everything through a very long tunnel.

He reaches the door.

Darrian says, "Henry, follow him. Make sure he goes directly to the elevator."

Jon turns. "I have things in my office. I—"

"Security will box up your personal effects and deliver them to the front door of the building. Your vehicle will be brought around. You can wait on the sidewalk outside."

As Jon exits the office, Henry pushes himself to his feet and comes after him. In the corridor outside Darrian's office, Jon spins abruptly and turns on Henry.

"This was you. It all adds up now. You invited me to the pub, and she was waiting there. She moved in after you plied me with whisky, after you gave me the card for the PI. And then my drink was spiked. You fucking set me up. Ahmed Waheed was probably never in line for the COO position. You just wanted to make certain you sank me so he could have a crack at it. Is that what this is about?"

Henry lowers his voice to a gravelly whisper. "Be careful, Jon. Be very careful. I tried to help you. I threw you a lifeline. I can't help it if you used the line to hang yourself. You should be ashamed. You've humiliated your wife, your father-in-law, your mother-in-law. You could have had it all. You'll be lucky if you ever work in this business again."

As Jon tries to argue with Henry, two burly security guys approach down the corridor.

"Mr. Rittenberg," one guard says loudly, "we need your key card and your parking card. Please come with us."

"No. No fucking way. I'm going to get my things out of my office."

The men flank Jon. They grasp his arms and start marching him toward the bank of elevators.

"Get your hands off me. Get the hell away from me!"

He sees everyone watching, sitting there in their stupid Halloween costumes, gleams in their eyes. The kind of bloodthirsty gleam that comes when you see someone you don't like being taken down. Maybe they always all hated him. Maybe he was a bully. Maybe he was just an arrogant ass, and what he sees in their eyes now is the gleam of schadenfreude. He falls silent and walks in submission with the security guards to the elevator doors.

Once downstairs, they usher him out the front entrance of the TerraWest building.

He steps onto the sidewalk. The doors to TerraWest swing shut behind him. It's begun to rain, and the wind has turned bitter. Dead leaves plaster the paving. Pedestrians bend their heads as they hunker behind umbrellas.

Jon stands without his jacket. Rain wets his face and hair and shirt. His body vibrates with shame and humiliation.

And rage.

He will fucking kill Mia Reiter and the people behind this. He will rip their throats out with his own bare hands.

# MAL

*November 2, 2019. Saturday.*

Mal and Benoit stand in the rain, watching as the tenders on the dive boat feed crane cables to the divers in the water. The divers will go down and hook the cables to the Subaru. A flatbed awaits at the dock edge to receive the submerged vehicle. Ident vans are parked nearby, ready to receive evidence. A tent has been set up as a command center.

A second dive team continues searching beneath the bridge area for the rug and a body. Rigid hull inflatables with tenders guide the divers below, using lines. It's dangerous work. Poor visibility, a strong tidal current, and underwater urban detritus hampers progress. The entire construction site is cordoned off, but pedestrian onlookers have begun to gather on the bridge high above, watching the scene unfolding below. A helicopter thuds overhead in the low clouds.

Benoit glances up at the chopper. "News chopper. The story is breaking."

"Just wait until they catch wind an ex-Olympic skier is involved, never mind the married MLA humping a hotshot city lawyer in her Mercedes on Halloween night near the abandoned silos," Mal says.

Her phone rings just as the dive boat operator signals to the crane operator to start winching the submerged vehicle up.

"Sergeant Van Alst," she says as she answers.

"It's me, Lula. I'm using someone else's phone. Jon Rittenberg has been brought in. His Audi has been impounded and is en route to the crime lab. We've got a team searching Rose Cottage as we speak. We've taken Rittenberg's fingerprints, DNA, and scrapings. We've taken his clothing into evidence as well, and we've documented his injuries. The samples and prints have been sent to the private lab as requested. We'll hold him until you're ready. But just so you know, he's lawyered up with a big gun."

"And what's the status with Daisy Rittenberg?" Mal asks.

"West Van PD is en route to pick her up."

The winch starts.

"Thanks, Lu. I'm on my way."

She kills the call. In silence she and Benoit watch as the cables move. The yellow car breaks the surface. Seawater gushes out of an open window and pours out from beneath the doors as the Subaru is swung out over the waiting flatbed. Slowly, it's lowered down. The Holly's Help logo looks heartbreakingly innocent. The flatbed dips slightly under the weight of its new burden as the tires settle onto the bed.

Two crime scene techs in white boiler suits climb up onto the flatbed and begin photographing and checking the car before it's prepped for transport to the lab.

"Sergeant, Corporal." One of the techs on the flatbed calls Mal and Benoit over. With a gloved hand he holds up a ziplock bag. Water drips from the bag. Inside, awash in seawater, is a fuchsia-pink book with purple polka dots. "Found it in the glove compartment," says the tech. "Glove compartment was open. Also got a woman's purse on the passenger seat. The contents have spilled out on the passenger side. So far we can see a Subaru key fob, wallet, mobile phone."

Mal's heart tightens.

"Her diary," Benoit says softly. "We've got her diary."

The tech says, "The ziplock is sealed, but the plastic has been punctured. We'll need to separate the pages and dry them out carefully."

The tech with the camera leans into the open Subaru window and shoots.

"It appears the gas pedal was wedged down with a block of wood," he calls to Mal.

Mal's phone rings again. She checks caller ID.

"It's the lab," she tells Benoit. Mal steps away from the noise to answer. "Van Alst."

"Hi, Mal, this is Emma Chang, from the lab. We have some prelim results. DNA samples from Kit Darling's hair and toothbrushes are a match to blood DNA from the crime scene."

Mal sucks in a slow, deep breath. As thrilling as it is when the pieces start slotting together, it still guts her that a young woman's body is likely to be the next thing the divers will pull out of that dark, cold inlet.

"Thanks, Emma."

"There's other DNA in the crime scene blood samples, though," Emma says.

"Run it against the fresh DNA samples coming your way."

Mal signs off and goes up to Benoit. "It's Darling's blood in the Glass House. But not hers alone. Someone else did some bleeding."

"Rittenberg? His injuries?"

She nods slowly, biting her lip, thinking as they watch the techs in their boiler suits moving around the yellow vehicle on the big flatbed trailer. Fog has started to blow in. "Can you hold the fort here? I want to have a go at Rittenberg before his legal team gets up to speed."

# DAISY

Daisy sits in her parents' living room, watching the television news with her feet propped on a pillow. Her legs are really swelling up. She's retaining water in her face, too. She feels ill. Exhausted. Her hands rest on her belly, where she can feel her unborn son moving. Emotion fills her eyes. She's waiting for her mom to get ready. Her mother will drive her to the doctor. Her parents fear for her health, given all the recent stress.

A breaking-news chyron flares across the TV screen.

Police divers find car of missing maid

Daisy sucks in a sharp breath. Her body goes still. She watches footage coming in from a construction site at the water in North Vancouver. Where the old silos stand—the place being developed for luxury condos. It's all taped off with yellow police tape. Police cars with flashing lights and barricades block the streets to the site. Aerial footage from a helicopter shows people gathering along the bridge to watch. The chopper footage pans across police cars near the water. Vans. A truck with a crane. A flatbed truck with a yellow car on top. There are police boats in the water.

A reporter with a mic stands in front of one of the road barricades near the construction site. It's raining. Someone holds an umbrella over his head.

"We have breaking news coming to you live from the ADMAC construction site in North Vancouver, where police divers have located the yellow Subaru Crosstrek owned by Kit Darling, a missing maid who works for Holly's Help cleaning services. The vehicle has been brought to the surface and will be transported to a crime lab. Divers continue to search for more evidence underwater. This case is said to be linked to a crime scene at a luxury waterfront home in West Vancouver, where Kit Darling and her car were apparently last seen on Halloween night."

A photo of Kit Darling appears on-screen.

The news feed then segues to a female reporter outside the Glass House. "The home behind me is where neighbors reported seeing the Holly's Help Subaru along with a dark-gray Audi parked on Halloween night. It is now the scene of a violent crime. So far police are saying little."

Daisy thinks she's going to throw up. But she also can't move. She's riveted by the reporter's words and the unfolding scene.

"Kit Darling has been cleaning this house—owned by a Vanessa and Haruto North—for the last six months or so, according to another cleaner from Holly's Help. A neighbor reports seeing Darling herself at the house that night, as well as another mystery couple who arrived in the Audi. The as-yet-to-be-identified woman is described as a heavily pregnant brunette. The man is tall, well built, with sandy-brown hair. One witness claims to have seen upturned furniture and copious amounts of blood through the living room windows."

The camera flashes to a pale-faced male with thinning brown hair.

"Next door neighbor Horton Brown says it was his elderly mother who placed the initial 911 call."

The camera zooms in on Horton. He stands in the street outside the Glass House. Crime scene tape flaps behind him. Rain falls steadily.

"Did you see the mystery couple who arrived in the Audi?" the reporter asks Horton before sticking the mike in front of his mouth.

"My mother saw them both. My mom is confined to her upstairs bedroom. She's in palliative care. But she got a good look from her window up there." He points. The camera pans to the brick house, then back to Horton. "She says the pregnant woman is the same woman who also visited the Glass House a week ago. The woman had lunch with Vanessa North by the pool."

"But we understand Vanessa North is presently in Singapore and has been for several months," the reporter says.

"Well, I only saw the back of her, and it looked like Vanessa. The other woman was sitting facing our house, so my mother got a good look at her. She arrived in a small white BMW that day."

Daisy's hand covers her mouth. She can't seem to blink.

"Where is Jon?"

Daisy jumps, whips her head around. Her mother is standing there. She saw the whole thing?

"Where's Jon—did Jon do this?" Her mother looks weird. Intense.

Daisy can't seem to speak. Fear has claws in her throat.

Her mother enters the living room, pulls up a chair. She sits, leans forward, takes Daisy's hands in hers.

"Daisy, honey, you need to talk. You need to tell me what happened. Was that man talking about you and Jon? That's the house of your friend, isn't it? You told me she lived in the Glass House. Is that where you went for dinner? What happened?"

Tears fill Daisy's eyes. "I didn't do anything. We didn't do—" Her voice stalls as a notion strikes her. She gathers herself quickly. "Jon and I arrived at the house. I got cramps at the door. We left right away."

"Was the missing maid there? Did you see the maid? What happened to her?"

"I didn't see her."

"And what do they mean about your friend, Vanessa, being out of the country? If she invited you for dinner—"

"Daisy!" Her father storms in through the french doors. "There are police cars coming up our drive."

As he speaks, red and blue lights pulse into the living room. Daisy pushes herself clumsily up from the chair and hurries to the window.

Three black-and-white West Vancouver PD vehicles with flashing bar lights come up the curved Wentworth driveway. Two pull in beside her BMW. One parks at a sharp angle behind Daisy's car, blocking her exit.

Her mind shoots back to that night at the Glass House.

"I need a lawyer," she says quietly to her mom. "I need a really good lawyer. Will you find me one?"

# DAISY

Daisy is dressed and made up for dinner when Jon carries his briefcase in through the door.

Waddling up to him, she smiles, goes up on her toes, and kisses him. "I put some clothes out on the bed for you." She wants him to look his best. Daisy has pride—she needs to impress Vanessa and Haruto.

"I don't know that I'm up for this, Daize."

She takes a good look at her husband and realizes he looks terrible. "Oh, Jon, you look ill. What happened? Do you want me to take you back to the hospital?"

"No, I'm fine. Just beat." He rakes his fingers through his hair. It sticks up, wet from the rain.

She becomes aware that his shirt is damp, too, and he smells of alcohol. Worry worms into Daisy. "What's going on?"

"Just a . . . rough day. Those investors pulled out."

"Was that what your big meeting was about this morning?"

"Yeah." He turns away from her, opens the hall closet. He shrugs out of his damp jacket, drapes it over a coat hanger.

"You get caught in the rain?"

"Obviously."

"Jon?"

He faces her.

She regards him. "Did you hear something bad about the new job? Is this to do with that Ahmed Waheed guy?"

"No, Daisy. I said it was just a rough day."

She stares at her husband's back as he turns away from her. Something awful has happened. He's lying to her.

"Are you sure going out to dinner is—"

"It's fine," he snaps. "I said I'll be fine."

He goes up the stairs to change. And Daisy knows—she just knows. Nothing is fine.

When Jon comes back downstairs, he's showered and dressed, and looks presentable. She forces a smile, kisses him on the cheek, and tells him he looks handsome.

"I called ahead to order a pie and flowers to take to the Norths," she says. "We can pick them up along the way. Is that okay?"

He nods and finds his car keys.

Rain falls steadily as they leave Rose Cottage. Their neighborhood streets are cluttered with little ghosts and goblins carrying jack-o'-lanterns, treat bags, and flashlights. Carved pumpkins flicker and glow in windows. As Jon drives, Daisy keeps glancing at him. He's distant, definitely preoccupied.

"I'm sorry about the clients," she says.

He nods. A muscle twitches at the base of his jaw.

"There will be others," she offers. "Other investors. The new resort is such an—"

"It's okay, Daize. Don't worry about it."

She bites her tongue and stares out the window. She wants to ask him more about how things are progressing with the decision on a new COO, but she doesn't dare. Not tonight. She wants things to go perfectly tonight in front of her friends.

When they enter the seaside lane on the North Shore and turn into the Glass House driveway, Daisy sees a car parked there already. It's yellow. A Subaru Crosstrek. On the side door is the logo for Holly's Help. Her heart flips and starts to hammer. Vanessa has the maid here? Her mind spins back to the conversation she had with Vanessa.

*I was just wondering if we might have the same maid.*

*You mean Kit?*

*Yes—yes, I think that must be the same one. Kit Darling?*

Daisy thinks of Charley Waters and the Chucky doll.

*This is about Kit, isn't it?*

Her mouth turns dry. Anxiety rushes into her veins. She glances at her husband.

Jon is peering at the Subaru, then his gaze goes to the large, modern mansion of glass and steel and concrete. It's all lit up inside. A glowing glass box in the bleak Halloween darkness.

"Nice place," he says quietly.

"I know, right?" Daisy says. But her mind is on the Subaru and the maid. Her pulse is galloping. Maybe it's another maid from Holly's Help.

"What is it?" Jon asks. "You look like you've seen a ghost."

"I—it's nothing. I'm just thinking that Vanessa and I—we probably have the same maid."

They exit the car. Daisy carries the pie and the bouquet because Jon is checking something on his phone.

Daisy steps up onto the paved entryway. She can see straight through the glass door and side panel into the home. Candles have been placed everywhere. Jon lingers just behind her, still busy with his phone.

"Jon, can you ring the bell, please? My hands are full."

He puts his phone away and steps forward to ring the bell.

It clangs inside.

Daisy watches the candles flicker.

Jon rings again.

Vanessa hurries into Daisy's view. She wears glittery red devil's horns on her head, and she's carrying a trident. Daisy begins to smile. Her friend is dressed for Halloween—tiny black skirt, a devil's tail with an arrow at the end, striped witchy stockings, black shoes with high, square heels. Frilly little white maid's apron. A velvet choker around her neck. Daisy's smile suddenly begins to fade as Vanessa nears. It strikes her in slow motion. Vanessa-the-devil is wearing a cropped black T-shirt imprinted with a Chucky doll holding a knife.

*Die die die die Baby Bean die . . .*

Daisy's brain folds in on herself.

Her friend has no baby bump.

Her heart begins to thump.

*Ticktock goes the clock . . .*

Vanessa swings open the door. She smiles broadly, revealing sharp vampire teeth.

"Well, hello, Daisy," Vanessa says. "And you must be Jon? Come in—come on in."

*Well, hello, Daisy.*

*Welcome home, Daisy.*

*It's been a while, Daisy.*

*Chucky knows who Bad Mommy iz. Chucky knows what Bad Mommy didz.*

Daisy blinks. Her world narrows.

It's Vanessa. It's her friend. But she has no baby tummy.

"What—what happened to—" The question tumbles from Daisy's mouth as her brain struggles to interpret her visual stimuli and catch up.

"Oh, you mean this?" Vanessa reaches up, removes her horns, and takes off her hair. She replaces the devil horns, smiles her vampire smile again.

Daisy's gaze drops to her hands. The devil is holding Vanessa's hair. Daisy's eyes shoot up. Her gaze locks on the devil-woman's. Her eyes are not Vanessa's eyes. They are bright blue.

Daisy feels dizzy. Her hands go limp, and the pie and flowers clatter to her feet. The pie smashes open, the box breaks, and dark-purple blackberry filling oozes out. In slow, thick motion, Daisy turns to her husband.

His face is sheet white. He's frozen. As though he's seen the devil . . . and it's real.

# THE MAID'S DIARY

So what if people pretend they are something they aren't? Is it a lie? A crime?

*Is it just perception? A sleight-of-hand narrative?*

*We all project something. Be it in the way we choose to dress—boho, smart casual, sporty, artsy, goth, sophisticated, wealthy socialite, sex kitten, tomboy, biker chick, dancer chic—we put it out there in one shape or another.*

*How different is wearing a wig and makeup and colored contacts and talking in a different accent, walking in a different way, from posting an Instagram selfie in blurred portrait mode, or with an applied filter, or cutting out background that doesn't mesh with the brand we want to project to the world? How different is dressing up from posing in front of a five-star hotel that we could never afford, but not saying that we never actually stayed there, just allowing people to draw their own conclusions by juxtaposition? (Like posing in front of the blue Tesla, or the baby's crib in another woman's house, or in Vanessa North's designer outfits from her closet.)*

*We're all tricksters. Each and every one of us. No one is a totally reliable narrator. Life is all Story. Every bit of it. We see things through the filter of our own unique worldviews, through our own longings and fears and loves, through our own traumas. Not one single person on this earth is able to interpret a thing in exactly the same way. The world is dynamic in that respect.*

*When I mention to my shrink that I play roles in public—acting wild-style—she smiles and I ask her what's funny.*

*"You're a trickster, Kit," she says. "That's not a bad thing. Tricksters have a key function in life and art. I maintain that if a trickster pranks her way into your life, it's time to pay attention. They are the definition of duality. Both heroic and villainous, foolish and wise, benign and malicious. Both lovable and hateful. Friendly and fearsome. Both light and dark. If you find yourself drawn to or repulsed by a mischievous trickster or a clown, a rule breaker or magician, it's a clear sign you need to explore the hidden—the buried—parts of your own nature, because the trickster is trying to poke a stick at your pretensions, your worldviews, your illusions, your false beliefs, your rigid 'rules.' In the trickster's playful provocation, there always lies a hidden message."*

*I think of my @foxandcrow account. I think of the things I post there—the mirror I playfully hold up to the world of poseurs and facades. And I believe my therapist.*

*"If we fail to embrace the lessons of the trickster, Kit," she says, "we deny ourselves the capacity to witness our own shadow."*

*So, Dear Diary, you see? Right from the mouth of my shrink: I play an important role. Mine is a game with purpose.*

*But sometimes a game turns dangerous.*

*Not everyone likes being tricked . . .*

# DAISY

*October 31, 2019. Thursday.*
*Five hours and five minutes before the murder.*

Daisy's gaze shoots from her stricken husband back to the woman in the devil horns. Her gaze locks with the devil's big blue eyes. Not Vanessa's kind, warm eyes. Not her friend. Not pregnant. And because Daisy's brain is a churning soup of cognitive dissonance and not working at all properly, she says, "What—where's the baby?"

"You mean my bump?" She grins broadly, and the vampire teeth catch the light. "Silicone. Do you know how many different kinds of these pregnancy prostheses you can buy online? You should google it. Does make one wonder what people use them for. Fake photo shoots? Just to walk around in? Test-drive pregnancy? Did you know that you can even buy very realistic fake little babies online? I borrowed the silicone belly from my theater company. Two different sizes to show pregnancy progression. Borrowed the wig, too. I used it all for a production—*The Three Lives of Mary*. That's what first gave me the idea." The devil's red lips part into a grin again, and Daisy can't take her eyes off her vampire teeth.

The devil turns her smile on Jon.

"And how are you doing, BergBomber?"

"Mia," he says quietly, darkly.

"Who—who's Mia?" Daisy asks, afraid to know.

"Aren't you guys coming in, then?" The devil smiles sweetly.

Jon seems rooted to the concrete. A funny little clang begins in Daisy's brain. There's something dangerous about the way devil-woman and Jon look at each other. Some micro-level vibe. And it's telling Daisy this is not the first time her husband and this blonde have met. There's a much deeper current here.

"Actually, it's Kit," says the woman. "I'm your Rose Cottage maid." Her smile fades, and her face turns serious as she meets each of their gazes in turn. Light glints off the sparkles on her red horns. "Or perhaps you will both remember me better as Katarina." She pauses. "Katarina Popovich. But then maybe you don't. I was only sixteen at the time. I looked different, too. Life can change people profoundly, no? Either by design or accident." She steps back and holds the glass door open wider. "Come in."

"Daisy, we're leaving. Now." Jon grabs her arm.

"Things could go very, very badly for you if you don't come in." The woman angles her blonde head. "A bit like they did today, Jon. Now wasn't that awful? It must've been such a terrible blow. To be fired like that? Thrown out by your ear and kicked to the curb in the rain. Security muscle dumping your belongings onto the sidewalk in a cardboard box. And you weren't even allowed to drive your own car out of the garage." She makes a *tsking* noise.

"Jon?" Daisy's voice comes out in a hoarse croak. "What—what is she talking about? What does she mean about your job?"

Jon spins to face Daisy. His features twist in anger. His eyes are thunderous. "Are you a fucking idiot, Daisy?" He points at the woman. "This is your friend? Your 'perfect' Vanessa? You bloody little idiot woman. How could you be duped like this? For fuck's sake. You've been seeing this woman in a fake belly since July, and all the while it's Katarina? The bitch who tried to take me down all those years ago? And you let her into our lives like this? What in the hell is wrong with you?"

293

Daisy begins to shake. She recalls the day "Vanessa" rolled out her yoga mat on the grass beside her. How the new woman smiled at her. How it was Daisy herself who approached the new, friendly, pregnant mom-to-be. How *she* invited Vanessa for a coffee at the bistro after. How easy Vanessa was to talk to. How badly Daisy needed a friend. How quickly she latched on to Vanessa, thinking how amazing it was that their babies were due so close. And all the while "Vanessa" was also cleaning Daisy's house? Poking in her things? But how . . . and Daisy realizes—although yoga was on "maid day," and although she had lunch with Vanessa on maid days, it was always after noon. Vanessa could never make an early lunch. She always had some meeting or another "arrangement" before noon. Daisy feels faint as she thinks about what she confessed to Vanessa by the pool.

"What happened today, Jon?" Daisy demands. "What is she talking about?"

"He was fired," says the devil maid. "Jon, you didn't even tell your wife you were sacked today? You didn't tell her you went to sit and drink in the park with the homeless people until it was home time?"

Daisy's jaw drops. She stares at her husband. Her entire body thrums. "Is that true, Jon?"

Vanessa-Kit says, "I suppose he didn't tell you either about his affair with Mia, and those men he slept with in a threesome."

"*What?*"

The woman smiles. "And, Jon, I'm betting Daisy has not told you about the 'insurance' she keeps?"

"What insurance?" Jon says.

"See? We have so much to discuss. And, please, before you come in, do take note—very careful note." She points her trident up toward the security camera outside the front door, then points it back to a corner inside the house. "Cameras," she says. "This house is fully rigged with CCTV. The cams are all feeding live to a monitor being watched from another room inside this house. The feed is also being watched at an off-site location. And the footage is being recorded." She pauses, letting it sink in. "If anything happens to me, if you try to hurt me, there are others inside this house who will respond. And if I disappear, police will automatically be forwarded copies of this recording along with copies of Daisy's 'insurance.' Got it?"

Daisy glances up at the camera outside, and a chill trickles down her spine. She and Jon are lab rats in a petri dish of a glass and marble house.

"You're lying," Jon says.

"Try me," the devil answers. "Oh, and if you two choose to walk away instead, Daisy's insurance goes directly to the police and to a prearranged list of top media outlets." She pauses, eyeing Jon. "It will send you to prison, JonJon. Mark my words. There is no statute of limitations for what is contained in that 'insurance.' It will destroy you. The Wentworths, too."

Daisy says quietly, "Jon, let's go inside. We need to go inside."

# MAL

*November 2, 2019. Saturday.*

Mal returns to the station to question Jon Rittenberg. Things are coming to a head. Media is closing in fast.

As she walks into the major crimes bullpen and shrugs out of her wet coat, Lu summons Mal over to her desk. An urgency tightens Lula's features.

"We've got Jon Rittenberg in interview room twelve, and Daisy Rittenberg in six," she says. "Daisy is claiming medical discomfort, and her counsel is with her, so you might want to do her first. She's apparently thirty-six weeks pregnant now. But before you go, you need to see something." Lu pulls up on her screen a series of newspaper articles. "We were searching online for background on the Rittenbergs and Darling, plus the ski town Darling grew up in. Take a look at this."

Black font blares across the top of a digitized newspaper page:

"It Never Happened"

World-class skier "JonJon" Rittenberg says claims of
sexual assault are "all lies" and "it never happened."

Slowly, Mal draws up a chair and seats herself in front of Lula's monitor as she reads:

> A young woman who has not been identified by Whistler law enforcement alleges she was drugged and sexually assaulted by Olympic hopeful Jon Rittenberg and fellow members of his ski team at a wild ski lodge party last Saturday night.

Mal's pulse quickens. She leans closer, reads further.

> Police brought Rittenberg and others in for questioning, but so far no charges have been laid . . .

Mal reaches for the mouse and clicks open the next link. Another news article fills the screen, this one from a tabloid with a salacious reputation.

**Sex Assault Allegations Dropped**

**Rittenberg Free to Ski**

Mal scans the text.

> . . . the unidentified young woman has dropped all allegations against Jon Rittenberg and other unnamed ski team members. She retracted her claims after no witnesses at the well-attended lodge party came forward to corroborate her version of events. Party attendees say the "girl" was lying and that if she did in fact engage in sexual relations with the Olympic

hopeful, it was consensual. They added she was very drunk and infatuated with the famous young racer.

Mal scrolls down, then clicks open another article.

Whistler police say they are not at this time pursuing the issue. The accuser has completely withdrawn her charges.

"It was all lies," says Max Dugoyne, a downhill skier who was at the party. "I know who the accuser is. She basically threw herself at Jon. She has a poster of him inside her locker. She arrived drunk and crashed the party expressly trying to meet him. If anything happened between her and JonJon, this is her way of retaliating—her feelings were probably hurt when she learned it was nothing but a one-night stand for him."

Another partygoer, Allesandra Harrison, says she also knows the accuser. She claims the young woman learned she was pregnant and was trying to pin it on Rittenberg. "Either that or she was crying 'rape' so her parents wouldn't think she was promiscuous or something."

"Wow," Mal says softly after scanning several more news stories in this vein. She glances at Lu. "If she had a locker with 'JonJon's' poster, she was likely a high school student. How old was Rittenberg at this time?"

"Nineteen," says Lula. "I've located the initial investigating officer mentioned in the articles—Corporal Anna Bamfield. I just got off the phone with her. She's still with the RCMP but is now a staff sergeant stationed up at Williams Lake. Bamfield said she remembers the case well. She told me that she believed the victim's version of events. The complainant was only sixteen years old. She was medically examined, and there was evidence of aggressive sex—vaginal tears, multiple semen samples. But not one person from that party would come forward and talk. And no one claimed to know when the victim left the lodge party or how she got home. The kids Bamfield interviewed either said it was a lie, nothing happened, or they said there was a consensual interaction between the girl and Rittenberg. Some claimed she was a 'whore' and slept around. Bamfield said there were rumors that someone with a phone might have recorded the events, but she was not able to verify this. The victim then suddenly withdrew charges and went away."

"Went away?" Mal asks.

"Left town. Left school. Dropped out. Parents declined to pursue anything."

Mal regards Lula. "Her name?"

"Katarina Popovich."

Quietly, Mal says, "I think we just found our motive."

# JON

Jon grabs his wife's arm as she tries to enter the Glass House.

"Don't. She—"

"We *must.*" Daisy jerks free and steps over the threshold. Jon's body is electric. With shock. With outrage. With fear. This woman who posed as Mia Reiter—who seduced and set him up to be sexually abused—is Katarina Popovich? It's a name he hoped never to hear again in his life. He thought she was gone. He never dreamed she would rise from the past and cross his path again.

Not like this.

Not in a wig and red lips, all slender and seductive and sultry with beautiful false green eyes and an accent and walk that made him weak at the knees. The sixteen-year-old Katarina who reported him to the Whistler police, who accused him and his friends of gang rape, was a fat-ass, pimply-faced, desperate little slut of a schoolgirl. A fangirl who, according to other students at her school, had a poster of him on the inside of her locker.

She *wanted* to spread her legs for him. And for half the ski team.

Jon's cauldron of emotions sharpens to a white-hot rage. *She* did this. She spiked his drink, lured him up into that high-rise apartment, cuffed him, brought other men into the apartment, took compromising photos that she delivered to TerraWest.

How did she know about the PI?

*I told her. When she was Mia. In the piano lounge—I told her I'd hired a PI to find dirt on a colleague named Ahmed Waheed.*

Where had she gotten the contract he signed with Jake Preston?

*I am your maid.* And it strikes Jon hard—he has a copy of the contract in his home computer. Did Katarina get into that? She's been inside their house for months. Snooping around. What else has she gotten into? She's been Daisy's fake friend since July. What secrets has Daisy let slip?

*I'm betting Daisy has not told you about the "insurance" she keeps.*

*It will send you to prison, JonJon. Mark my words. There is no statute of limitations for what is contained in that "insurance." It will destroy you. The Wentworths, too.*

Jon steps over the threshold and follows his wife and his devil nemesis into the house of glass and flickering candles.

Katarina leads him and Daisy into a white living room. Beyond the glass sliding doors, he sees the greenish glow of a lit infinity pool. The surface ripples with rain and wind. A few dead leaves float on top. Fog hides the ocean that lies beyond the pool, and Jon hears the mournful moan of a foghorn coming from a hidden tanker.

He feels spacey. Disoriented. Still sick with a hangover from being drugged three nights earlier. He's struggling to assimilate what Katarina has done to them. She must have followed him—or had him followed—from work this morning to the park. He was not able to go home and tell Daisy he'd been fired. Instead, he drove to a liquor store and bought a fifth of whisky. He walked with his drink to a bench under a large chestnut tree in the park near the beach, and he sat there, his briefcase on the bench beside him, sipping from the bottle hidden inside a brown paper bag.

A homeless drunk seated himself beside Jon with a brown bag of his own. The reeking loser actually offered Jon a sip, like they were two of a kind. Disgusted, Jon got up and moved to another bench. He sat there alone, drinking, watching the rain and the mist over the sea until it was time to go home to Rose Cottage.

When he arrived home he was unable to confess to Daisy what had happened at work. It still doesn't feel real. Everything is twisted and upside down, he thinks as he watches Satan in her tiny top and short skirt with her red tail and horns. How could this blonde maid even look like Mia? Or sound like her? Or walk like her. At the same time he can also see it is her. But he can't seem to discern the old, plump, teenage Katarina buried in this woman.

"Sit," the maid says, holding her hand out to the white sofa.

Neither Jon nor Daisy sits.

"I'd listen if I were you." Her voice turns crisp, cool, all business.

Slowly, they both take a seat, staying at the edge of the cushions. Jon can feel Daisy glancing at him. He can feel Daisy's questions about "Mia," about a threesome including males. He recalls the burn around his butthole. The tiny puncture mark in the crook of his arm. He's going to throw up.

"You can call me Kat," the devil maid says as she pours drinks into glasses in front of them. "A chilled sparkling rosé for the lady," she says as she fills the wineglass in front of Daisy. "I know how much you need it. And for you, Jon, a Balvenie Caribbean cask fourteen-year-old." She reaches for the whisky bottle and pours. She hands the glass to Jon with a dark smile. "I know how much you like the Balvenie, Jon." Her smile deepens. It makes her vampire eyeteeth seem to grow.

"Kat" seats herself in a chair across from them. She sips her own drink. It appears to be a vodka martini with olives.

"Full disclosure," she says as she sets her glass carefully on a small table at her side. "I only became Mia after I saw what Daisy had locked in her safe. It really was a point of no return, seeing that recorded footage—that *proof*—of what happened that night at the ski lodge party. Along with two nondisclosure documents, one of which will scuttle the Wentworth reputation." She shrugs. "Maybe it'll even drag Annabelle Wentworth into court, because to my mind, it adds up to obstruction of justice."

"*What* proof?" Jon snaps. He turns to his wife. "What is she talking about, Daisy?"

"Who's Mia, Jon?" Daisy's voice is low and eerily calm. It scares him. Her complexion is going redder—two violent hot spots forming high on her cheekbones. Her blood pressure is rising, and Jon is peripherally concerned for the baby but a hell of a lot more worried by what's coming down the pike from this Kat woman.

Daisy turns to Kat. "What do you mean, this will drag my mother into court?"

Kat crosses her stockinged legs and leans back in her chair. She reaches for her martini glass, takes another slow sip of her drink. "It seems as though you two need to process a few things. Daisy, your husband was fired this morning. He was caught stealing personnel information from TerraWest's HR database and hiring a PI to dig up dirt on a colleague named Ahmed Waheed. The information Jon provided the PI stipulated that the PI dig for leverage around Ahmed Waheed's race and religious affiliation. Your husband was also photographed naked with a woman named Mia and two unidentified males." She sips again, leans forward, and puts her martini glass down.

"Jon, your wife has a phone recording of what happened in the ski lodge in Whistler when you were nineteen. It shows you spiking a sixteen-year-old girl's drink and laughing about it with fellow team members. It shows you giving the drink to the girl, who was so excited just to meet you that night. It shows her passing out, and you and a group of guys helping this drugged girl stumble upstairs and into a bedroom. It shows you taking off her jeans, spreading her legs, and raping her while others cheered you on." Kat pauses. Her gaze lasers into Jon's. "I guess that's why you and your friends call the drug the 'leg spreader.'"

He swallows. He's going so hot, so dizzy, he thinks he will faint. Jon's gaze shoots to Daisy. "Where'd you get a recording like that? Why in the hell would you keep something like that?"

Daisy refuses to look at him. Her gaze remains riveted on the maid.

"And, Daisy," Kat says, "I don't suppose you told your husband how you tried to threaten and gaslight Charley Waters into getting rid of Jon's baby? And how, when that didn't work, you paid her a huge sum of money to kill the baby? What was it again, five hundred thousand dollars? All hers as long as she went through with the abortion, signed a gag order, and retracted her allegations of sexual assault against Jon. You in turn would ensure all stalking charges against her were dropped."

Daisy still refuses to look at Jon. Her hands press down hard on her thighs.

Kat says, "Did you tell Jon where you got that idea? Did you tell him what inspired you?"

Kat turns her attention to Jon. "She didn't tell you, did she? Daughters learn from their mothers. Annabelle Wentworth paid a small fortune to the poor immigrant parents of the sixteen-year-old schoolgirl who learned she was pregnant after the rape. On condition that her mother persuaded her to get rid of the baby. On condition that the parents would not pursue charges on behalf of their daughter."

"It wasn't my baby," Jon snaps. "It could have been any one of those guys' sperm."

Kat falls silent. A hard and frightening look enters her eyes. "Oh," she says softly. "Are you admitting, then, what happened?"

Jon glances at the walls, the ceiling, looking for the CCTV cameras. "Who's watching this?" he demands.

Kat leans forward. "I guess Annabelle thought it wasn't worth the risk of the girl having the baby, because if a paternity test did prove it was yours, you would be irreversibly tied to me via our child for the rest of our child's life. And that's not what Annabelle wanted for her Daisy, was it? Better to make the problem with a poor schoolgirl go away. Easy enough since money was no big deal for Annabelle, but it was a very big deal to my parents."

Kat rises to her feet. She crosses the room on her high, square heels. She spins, faces them both as they sit on the edge of the sofa. "The contents of that NDA make it pretty clear Annabelle Wentworth knew the truth of what happened that night. Probably because Daisy knew the truth of what happened that night. And so did the other rich boys and girls. And you know what hurts me most? That my mother never told me what she signed. I was devastated when she suggested we just make it all go away because we could never win against people like you. She coached me into keeping quiet. She said if I made a fuss, you might sue us for defamation or something—I imagine this was Annabelle's threat to my mom. And my mother probably never told my father, either. He was old school. Old morals. My pregnancy, my accusations of assault, the fact I was drinking—I became a disgrace to him. My father disrespected me. He was disgusted by me. He heard everyone say I was a liar, a drunk little whore who threw myself at 'JonJon' Rittenberg and the other boys, and who got pregnant and tried to defend my promiscuity by crying rape." Kat reaches for what looks like a television remote on the bar counter.

"And when I did get rid of the baby, my uterus was ruptured. I got an infection. And I could never have kids again."

She presses a button on the remote. A huge television screen rises slowly like a phoenix from a white block of concrete. She hits PLAY.

Jumpy, grainy footage from the night at the ski lodge party fills the screen. The sound of laughter, jeering, music fills the house. Kat turns the volume up.

Jon's jaw drops. He feels bile surge to his throat.

"Turn it off!" Daisy lurches to her feet. "Just stop it. Now."

Kat hits PAUSE.

"What do you want?" Daisy's words come fast. "Just tell us what you want."

"Remember the newspaper headlines, Jon?" Kat asks. "They read, 'It Never Happened.' Tell me it did happen. Admit it. To my face. You raped me. You and your friends drugged and gang-raped me. I want to hear you say it."

Jon's gaze shoots in desperation to Daisy. He thinks of all the things Kat has already done to him. He's terrified what she will do next. She's crazy. Insane. He needs to buy time. They must placate her, get out of this house, and then figure out how to stop this, how to make her go away.

"Fine," Jon says slowly. "It happened. You can see it happened by that footage. It was in the heat of the moment. We were all drunk, high from the day's race events, our wins, our own sense of glory and power. Things went sideways. They went wrong. I'm sorry. Just tell us what you want."

"Nine hundred thousand dollars."

"What?" Jon blinks.

"She said she wants nine hundred thousand dollars, Jon." Daisy's voice is strangely calm. Her neck is wire tight, her mouth a thin line.

"That's impossible," Jon says.

Kat says, "I'd like it transferred directly from your CityIntraBank account to my CityIntraBank account. It's an intrabank transfer. It can be done via this tablet here." Katarina picks an iPad up from the bar counter, and she comes over to Jon. She holds the tablet out to him. "I've pulled up the bank website. And I've already alerted my account manager that I will be receiving a gift from the father of my child. It's been cleared. All you have to do is open up your account page and make the transfer."

"That's absurd. My child? That's a lie—"

"Is it, though?"

Jon moistens his lips. "I don't have that kind of money. Not immediately accessible. Not—"

"Pay it, Jon," Daisy says quietly.

He spins to Daisy. Her eyes are ice cold. Her face is all tight and ugly in its puffy thickness.

"Pay it," she whispers.

"We don't have the assets. We—"

"Pay it from our joint US dollar account. Pay it now. Do as she says."

"Daisy—this is—"

"I believe her. She'll send this footage to the media. It'll go to the police. You saw what's on there. And all those other guys who were present—you can see their faces. They can be identified. They'll be named, too, after all these years. They also have jobs and kids and wives and lives, and mark my words, they will fight their damnedest to protect those things. They will smell blood in the water, and they'll turn on you. They'll do deals and testify against you. Pay that nine hundred K and you might save yourself from prison. You might get to see the birth of our son."

"What the *fuck* did you keep that footage for, Daisy? This is your damn fault. Without it we would not be sitting here at this bitch's mercy. Where did you get it anyway?"

"From one of your friends. I saw him recording at the party. I demanded his phone. I copied his recording to mine and made him delete his."

"You copied it?"

She swallows.

"Why?"

Kat says, "Like mother, like daughter. She likes to keep insurance on her questionable man. With insurance she has leverage. She can make things go her way. I guess you never realized, Jon, how she controls you. She is in charge of everything in your relationship. She and her family and their money."

"If we pay you now," he snaps, "how can we be sure you won't come back?"

"You can't be."

Every fiber of Jon's being screams to attack this woman. Just shred and obliterate her, make her go away. Forever. So she can never rise again in his future.

"I want that video," he says.

"Don't be stupid, Jon," Daisy snaps. "There could be any number of copies out there now. Buy her silence. It's worked before."

"Yet here she is, back again for more." He spins to face Katarina. "I will kill you," he says. "I will fucking kill you if you even think of coming back. I—"

"Remember, everything you're saying now is being recorded, Jon," Kat says. She nods at the tablet. "Transfer the money."

Jon takes the tablet. Sweating, he punches in the password for his online account. He tells himself that the instant he leaves this house, he'll go back online and attempt to reverse the transfer. His mobile pings. He checks his phone, then copies the code he was sent by the bank. He smells fear on himself. Acrid. Mixed with old alcohol from the day's drinking at the park. He glances at Daisy.

Her eyes are flint. "Do it," she says.

He inhales and asks Kat for her account details. She gives them. He enters the information, punches in the amount. He hesitates, then hits "Transfer."

"Thank you, Jon." Kat reaches for the laptop. She seats herself and taps away on the iPad.

"What are you doing?" Jon asks.

"Just transferring it to my offshore account. Don't worry. Like I said, I did go into the bank ahead of time and clear all the details with my account manager. The bank is anticipating the transfer. Just imagine how much you might have had to pay in child support, education, medical costs. Not only for my baby if it was proved to be yours, but for Charley's, too." She hits a final button, glances up. "Or if I sued you in civil court, as I still can do, especially with this evidence now, I reckon that given what you did to me, how you destroyed my physical health, threatened my parents, the ensuing mental trauma, the stress, the loss of my own education and a chance for me to earn a more lucrative living, I'd get more than nine hundred K. Plus you'd incur legal costs. And there would be the press. So much press. Imagine the headlines: 'Gold medalist, national ski hero, ex-Olympian, admits to gang-raping Whistler schoolgirl with members of ski team.' Then he and his girlfriend's family—TerraWest founder Labden Wentworth and top Realtor Annabelle Wentworth—tried to thwart justice? Consider this a simple solution." She holds his gaze. "Consider this the justice that the system denied me."

She checks her tablet. "There, it's gone through. How about we drink to that?" She reaches for her glass and holds it up. "Cheers."

"Will that be all?" Daisy asks.

Kat angles her head. "That's all."

"Can we go?" Daisy asks.

Kat holds her hand toward the door. "Be my guest."

"I swear, we're not done here," Jon says.

"Maybe you aren't," Kat says quietly. "But I am."

# DAISY

*October 31, 2019. Thursday.*
*Three hours and forty-one minutes before the murder.*

Daisy sits like a stone as Jon drives. The wipers clack across the windshield. Fog is thick as they near the bridge.

"What did she mean, 'Maybe you aren't done, but I am'?" Jon says.

Daisy clenches her teeth and fists her hands in her lap. Her pulse is high. Too high. She's not going to do this now. Because she is done. She should've been done with Jon when Charley happened. She was stupid. Cognitive dissonance—that's what it was. She wanted to believe something different, but men like Jon don't change their spots.

*They just learn. They evolve. Adapt. They figure out how to be more careful, how not to get caught.*

"We'll get it back," Jon says for the tenth time. "We'll get our money. All of it. Talk to me, Daisy. Please, dammit, just say something."

"You said you were with clients, Jon. *Mia? You* have got to be kidding me. And you call *me* a fool for falling for her yoga-mom ruse? Meanwhile some female in lipstick and a tight dress just has to look at you a certain way and you can't keep your dick in your pants. And what did she mean about those other men?"

"I was set up. I was drugged and set up."

"Because you're an asshole! Because you can't think beyond your dick. You are a weak, vulnerable target. You and your fragile male ego. I—" She swipes tears from her face. "I knew you were lying. Deep down, I knew. But I so badly wanted to believe you. I thought with our son coming soon that things really could change. And this business with a private investigator? Looking for dirt on a colleague? That Waheed guy probably deserves your promotion one thousand times over. He deserves every goddamn ounce of that new COO job. And you deserve exactly what you got."

Jon swerves as a car cuts in front of him. He almost clips a motorbike in the next lane. He curses violently.

"She sexually assaulted me—her and those men. They drugged me and handcuffed me to a bed."

Daisy stares at her husband. It's like she doesn't know this man at all.

"And I suppose you didn't go up to her room willingly? You didn't *want* it?"

"Not like that, I—" His voice catches. Daisy sees tears on his face. "I don't even know what happened, Daize. I don't know if I had sex with those guys. I don't even recall their faces."

"Do you see what just transpired here? Do you honestly not see? She just gave you a small taste of your own medicine."

He slams on the brakes, almost hitting the car in front of him.

"Just focus on driving before you kill your unborn child," she snaps.

"This is bigger than what she did to me. This is more than just the money she took."

"You mean the money you willingly gave her when she asked."

"It's blackmail. Extortion."

"Why? Because you could be charged and tried and go to prison if this gets out?"

"Goddamn it, that's exactly what I mean, Daisy. She's not going to go away. For all I know, she's going straight to the cops tomorrow to hand over that footage. That's all she ever wanted when she was sixteen, to see my ass in prison."

Daisy leans her head back and closes her eyes. A hardness coalesces around her heart. "Might be better that way."

"What are you saying?"

"You don't even have a job. You've lost it all. Everything. Everything we tried to build all these years—"

"You're not hearing me. She's going to come back at us, Daisy. That woman is going to come asking for more. She has this power over us now, and she's not done. She's taken her pound of flesh, but she can *still* turn me in. As long as she exists, she has power over us. You heard her—there's no statute of limitations for sexual assault in this province. We need to fix it. Fucking bitch. I swear I will—I'll kill her. She has power over us as long as she is out there."

"Jon."

He goes quiet at her tone. He turns the Audi down their street. Such a pretty street, thinks Daisy. Such an attractive house they live in. But now it looms like a prison as they pull into the driveway.

"What?" Jon asks.

"Are there others?"

"What do you mean?"

"Will others come out of the woodwork if this gets out? Have you crossed lines with other women? On work trips, with employees, with other exotic dancers, sex workers? If Katarina goes public, will they suddenly all have courage to come after you, too?"

He stops the car in the driveway and turns to face out the side window.

His silence is her answer.

Daisy opens the passenger door and pushes up out of the seat. She holds her coat over her head against the rain as she makes for the door of Rose Cottage. There is only one mission on Daisy's mind. Pack a bag, get her car keys. Leave this house. Leave him.

Daisy goes straight upstairs, finds a suitcase, throws in some cosmetics, underwear, pajamas, a change of clothing. She fishes her document safe out of her underwear drawer and places it in her suitcase on top of her clothing.

Jon appears in the bedroom doorway. "Daisy, listen to me—I mean it. She has power over us."

"No. Not *us*. She has power over *you*, Jon."

"We're a team. This is our reputation. We—"

"We were never a team. I see that now." She shuts her suitcase and hefts it to the floor. She drags it to the bedroom door.

"Your parents will be raked through the mud with this."

"I'm done. We're done. Step aside, please."

He reaches for her. "Daisy—"

"Stay away from me." She points her finger at his face. "I swear, if you come near me, I'll take this stuff to the police myself."

"Why were you so fucking stupid to keep that footage in the first place? This is *your* fault. If this footage did not exist, none of this would've happened."

Daisy pushes past her husband. She drags her case, which thumps down the stairs behind her. He comes after her, follows her past the kitchen island, and cuts her off on her way to the front door.

"And if your mother hadn't gone and paid her parents—"

"Then they would have had a paternity test done, Jon. Maybe it was your baby. Maybe it was one of the other guys' baby. But whoever made that baby might have turned on you and the other guys involved in order to share the blame. Same with Charley—she would've been tied to you forever. These girls didn't just go away. I cleaned up after you, and the NDAs are so they couldn't come back without paying huge fines they can't afford. I kept the documents for that reason. I kept the footage in case you turned out to be the total asshole you are." Daisy is so angry that she's shaking. Which makes her worried for the baby. She needs to get out of here, calm down.

He points his finger into her face, almost touching her nose, and says with a sneer, "You *know* I'm right. As long as she's alive, that woman is a danger. A monster."

"A monster of *your* making. Please get out of my way."

He refuses to move. Daisy doesn't like the thunder on his face. He's frightening her. She glowers at him, trying to show power. And she attempts to push past him.

His hand clamps onto her arm, hard, his fingers digging into her. She grabs the carving knife on the island, points it at him.

"Get the hell back. Get out of my way."

He lets go in shock and steps aside. Clutching the knife in a death grip in one hand, facing her husband, Daisy backs slowly away from him toward the front door, pushing her suitcase with her other hand.

"Where are you going?" he yells as she steps out the door.

She slams the door shut and hurries through the rain to her BMW with her case bumping behind her. She opens the passenger's-side door, throws the knife onto the floor, and hefts her bag onto the seat. She goes round to the driver's side, climbs in. She starts the engine. Shaking, she backs out of the driveway as Jon comes barreling out of the front door and starts running toward the car.

Daisy clips the mailbox with her bumper as she wheels out of the drive. She leans on the gas and overcorrects, taking out the neighbor's recycling bins with a crash. Trembling like a leaf, panting, Daisy rights her car and drives back toward the North Shore.

# JON

*October 31, 2019. Thursday.*
*Three hours and eleven minutes before the murder.*

Jon watches Daisy's car reverse at speed out of their driveway. She smashes the mailbox and then rams the trash cans on the neighbor's verge in her haste to flee from him. He curses and storms back into Rose Cottage. He paces up and down the living room. He grabs a bottle of tequila and slams back several shots in a row. He has a few more shots. He's desperate. Getting more and more angry. More irrational. He *still* doesn't know if Katarina had him sexually assaulted. Raped, even. He never asked Katarina about the needle mark in his arm because he was too scared to let Daisy know about that. What did she inject into him? Will he need blood tests? Should he be tested for sexually transmitted diseases?

He drags both hands over his hair. Daisy is right. He's lost everything. His job. His wife has walked out with his baby. Daisy has gone to her parents—he's sure of it. Which means he's toast. Done.

Labden Wentworth will come after him with everything in his arsenal. They're going to cut him loose and hang him out to dry. That way, if he does go to trial, if he goes to jail, they will have washed their hands of him.

He has more shots. Once the tequila is finished, he looks for whisky. There is none. He finds some brandy. He pours himself a fat glass and drinks it. He paces some more, tries to call Daisy. She doesn't answer her mobile. It goes to voice mail.

Jon tries the landline to the Wentworth house. No pickup. He calls Annabelle Wentworth's mobile. To his surprise, she answers.

"Annabelle, thish ish Jon." He's slurring his words. How much has he had to drink? How much time has passed since Daisy left? He catches sight of his face in the hall mirror and is shocked at what looks back at him.

"Ish Daisy there?"

"What?"

He fights to form the words properly. "Daisy. I want to speak to Daisy."

"Are you drunk, Jon?"

"Daisy—"

"She's not here."

"Where ish she?"

"I don't know. Isn't she at home? You have me worried, Jon. What's happened?"

Jon hangs up quickly. Either Annabelle is lying or Daisy has gone somewhere else. He believes Annabelle is hiding Daisy.

He's done.

And if that Katarina-devil-woman sends that footage to the cops, he's going to prison on top of it all. What will happen to a man like him in the slammer? Oh God.

That is *one* thing he can still stop.

It's the only thing still within his control.

He can stop her going to the police.

Jon grabs his jacket and hurries out to his Audi. He climbs in and takes a few deep breaths, trying to focus. If he's pulled over, he's going to get a straight-to-jail-do-not-pass-go card. He must drive carefully. He also needs to get there fast.

He starts the Audi engine and pulls out into the street. Jon squints through the rain and wipers, peering intently at the yellow and white lines as he drives toward the bridge and crosses over to the North Shore. Traffic has thinned. This miserable weather has driven the trick-or-treaters home and into their beds.

Jon turns into the seaside lane. Instantly he sees all the lights in the Glass House are still on. Hands tight on the wheel, shoulders stiff, he kills his headlights, and the Audi crawls slowly through the fog and darkness toward the house. His heart blips as he sees her yellow car is still there.

He's got her.

Tires crackling on the wet paving, he drives past the house and pulls up onto a verge diagonally across from the property. He turns off his engine and watches the house. Now that he's here, he's unsure of his plan. He reaches for the hip flask he brought with him and takes a swig, building courage. He's thinking about the cameras. He needs to be careful not to be caught on the CCTV. There's a yard gate off the side of the driveway near her Subaru. If he goes in that gate and creeps around the side of the house by the pool, maybe he can gain entry through the big glass sliders.

He tenses as another car turns onto the street. Headlights beam toward his car, momentarily blinding him. Jon sinks down into his seat, waiting for it to pass.

But it slows. The headlights turn into the driveway of the Glass House.

Jon edges up. Surprise washes through him. It's another Audi. Same model and color as his. Muddy plates.

He watches as someone in black rain gear exits the driver's seat and hurries in through the yard gate. Jon's heart begins to hammer. He sees shadows moving inside the house. Fifteen minutes later, as the clock on his dash glows 11:21 p.m., an ear-piercing scream cuts the air. A woman's scream. Jon catches his breath. He's suddenly afraid. He stays low in his seat and observes through his fogged-up window.

He sees two figures in rain gear, coming out of the garden gate. Dragging something big.

It's a rolled-up rug.

*Fuck.*

He's too drunk to think straight, to do anything. Too drunk to call the police because his brain is suddenly so thick he can't figure out what to safely say without incriminating himself. All he knows is that he doesn't want to be here.

He doesn't want anything to do with this.

The figures heft and heave and push the carpet onto the back seat of the Audi. One person gets into the driver's seat of the Audi. The other rushes to the Subaru and climbs in. The cars speed away. A light comes on in the upstairs window next door. He hears the car tires squealing as they turn the corner at the end of the lane.

Jon panics. He starts his engine. Without putting on the headlights, he drives slowly away. A little farther down the lane, he sees an off-street parking space. The branches of a large tree hang down low over it. He hesitates, then pulls in. He kills his engine and slinks down into the seat. He's afraid now. He's too drunk to drive without being caught.

# MAL

*November 2, 2019. Saturday.*

As Mal makes her way down the sterile corridor to interview Daisy Rittenberg, she replays Boon-mee Saelim's words in her mind. *I think something bad—really bad—happened when she was at school. And that's why she dropped out and left town.*

If the sexual assault allegations were all over the news, and Saelim was a kid at the only high school in town, how is it that he didn't know what the "bad" thing was? Mal had a feeling Saelim was lying, or hiding something. She is more certain now. As she reaches the room where Daisy Rittenberg is being held, she calls Lula.

"Hey, Lu. Did Saelim come in to make an official statement and give a DNA sample?"

"Negative. We're looking for him. He seems to have gone AWOL from both his residence and place of employment. Not answering his phone. Friends don't know where he is. His vehicle is not at his home."

"Let me know as soon as you find him." She ends the call and opens the door to interview room six.

She enters to find a puffy and flushed Daisy Rittenberg seated beside an impeccably attired, hawkish-faced man with a swarthy complexion and piercing black eyes. Mal recognizes him instantly. Emilio

Rossi. A top criminal defense bulldog of a lawyer who has a reputation for taking high-profile organized crime and murder cases.

"Emilio," Mal says.

The guy doesn't waste a beat. Before Mal can even take a seat, he says, "My client is in need of immediate medical attention. She's suffering from increasing edema and elevated blood pressure. We have concerns about possible preeclampsia, deep-vein thrombosis, a heart disorder, cellulitis—all these things need to be medically ruled out. She needs to see her doctor. She needs bed rest and to minimize stress."

Worry threads through Mal. She must work fast.

"Good afternoon, Mrs. Rittenberg, or is it evening? Time is flying today. Can I call you Daisy?"

The woman refuses to meet Mal's gaze. She does not respond to the question.

Mal places her notebook and file folder on the table in front of her. "I'm afraid it's not looking good for you, Daisy. We have witnesses and evidence that place you at the scene of—"

"My client doesn't deny being at the house, Sergeant," Rossi says crisply. "She doesn't deny using the same maid service. My client will admit she was invited for dinner at Northview. She arrived with her husband in their Audi around six fourteen p.m. But as they were ringing the doorbell, my client experienced painful cramps. In shock, she dropped a bouquet and dessert she had brought with her. Mrs. Rittenberg and her husband left immediately."

"Did you go seek immediate medical attention, Daisy? Is there a record of—"

"The cramps resolved on the way home," Rossi says. "The Rittenbergs decided bed rest was the solution, and at the time they intended to visit the doctor the following day. Once home, my client had an argument with her husband. She packed a bag and drove to her mother's house."

"With the severe cramps?" Mal asks.

"Cramps had resolved to a degree at that point," says Rossi. "Once my client arrived at her mother's, she took to bed rest. She has not left the Wentworth residence until now. She says her husband was very angry when she departed her home. He threatened her physically. He'd already had a fair bit to drink, and she suspects he began drinking again heavily after she left. She cannot vouch for his whereabouts or say whether he returned later to the Northview residence."

Mal sits back, crooks up her brow, and studies Daisy. "And why might you think your husband would return to the Glass House without you? To finish dinner?"

Rossi says, "My client is simply relaying the fact that she has an alibi—her parents. But she is unaware if her husband has one."

Mal moistens her lips, her gaze still locked on Daisy. "Why did you and your husband have an argument, Daisy? Why did he threaten you?"

"My client confronted her husband about an affair."

"An affair with who?"

"A woman named Mia," Rossi says. "That's all she knows."

"So now you're throwing Jon under the bus?" Mal asks.

"She's doing nothing of the sort."

Mal leans forward. "And how do you explain the carving knife that the West Van PD found in your car?"

"Like I said, her husband threatened her at Rose Cottage. My client grabbed the knife from the kitchen counter to stop him from following her."

"Did you go directly to your parents', Daisy, or did you perhaps go back to the Glass House first?"

"Look, if this is a fishing expedition—"

"Daisy, we have sent in your DNA sample and prints, and we'll have expedited results very shortly from a private lab. We will then run your DNA against DNA evidence found at the crime scene. If—"

"If you do find her DNA inside, it's because she went to lunch at Northview last Friday. She drank from glasses and handled a carving knife to cut sausage."

Mal inhales slowly. She opens her folder and slides a photo toward Daisy.

"Do you recognize this pendant?"

Daisy glances at the photo but says nothing.

"How about these images?" Mal shows Daisy several photos copied from @JustDaisyDaily's Instagram account. Selfies that all show the diamond necklace hanging at the hollow of her throat.

"This pendant," Mal says, tapping a photo, "was found between sofa cushions at the Glass House."

Rossi sighs impatiently. He checks his watch. "Like I said, my client doesn't dispute she was ever inside the house. She could have lost the pendant last Friday. Or her maid might have stolen it. The same maid worked at the Glass House. The maid could have dropped it there. None of this will hold up in court, and you know it."

Mal runs her tongue over her teeth. "Daisy, why did Kit Darling recently ask to be excused from cleaning your home?"

Rossi says, "My client inquired about the change because she felt her maid was doing a good job. She was informed by Holly's Help that it was the maid herself who requested a transfer due to a scheduling conflict. Now if you're done here, Sergeant, we need to get my client to see a doctor."

"Two more questions. Daisy, did you know that your maid, Kit Darling, was the sixteen-year-old schoolgirl who accused your husband of aggravated sexual assault eighteen years ago?"

Daisy's face goes deep red. She wipes her mouth with a trembling hand and says to her lawyer, "I'm not feeling well. I'm going to faint."

Emilio Rossi surges to his feet. He reaches for Daisy's arm to help her up from her chair. "We're done here."

"One more," Mal says firmly. "Do you recognize these people?" She slides two photos across the table and turns them to face Daisy.

She glances at them. "No."

Mal taps one photo. "This here is Vanessa North. And this here"—she taps the other—"is Haruto North. These are your friends."

The redness deepens in Daisy's face. She refuses to look up. "That's not them."

"It is them. These are the owners of the house you attended for dinner."

"I don't know what you're talking about. I think I'm going to pass out. I—I need a doctor."

As Rossi helps Daisy up and assists her to the door, he glances over his shoulder and says to Mal, "The missing maid was a sixteen-year-old schoolgirl who accused Jon Rittenberg of aggravated sexual assault? Sounds like you have motive for the husband right there, Detective. Imagine finding out your maid was the same woman who tried to sink your career and take you down all those years ago."

They exit. The door swings shut behind them.

Mal hurriedly gathers up her file and photos. Before going to interview Jon Rittenberg, she stops by the bullpen.

"Any word on Saelim?" Mal asks Lula.

"Negative," Lula says as she reaches for her phone. "He's still MIA. How'd it go with Daisy Rittenberg?"

"She's seen the writing on the wall," Mal says. "She just threw her whole husband under the bus. Now to hear what *he* has to say about that."

# MAL

*November 2, 2019. Saturday.*

Ex-Olympian, double gold medalist "JonJon" Rittenberg, once a shining example of male athletic prowess, sits slumped with his head in his hands on the table. His lawyer—a woman who puts Mal in mind of Tamara Adler—comes sharply to her feet as Mal enters the interview room. She offers a manicured hand. "I'm Sandra Ling, Jon Rittenberg's counsel."

Mal grips the lawyer's slender, soft hand and pumps it hard. "Sergeant Mallory Van Alst." She takes a seat and puts her file on the table in front of her. The room is warm and stinks of body odor and metabolized alcohol radiating out of Jon Rittenberg's pores. He's unshaven, disheveled. The bandage on his hand is filthy.

"I'm going to call you Jon, if that's okay?" Mal prefers to use first names in interrogations. It hits harder, closer. More personal.

Jon lifts his head from the table and glares at her. A bitter hatred coils in his eyes.

"No comment," he says. "You have nothing to charge me with, no right to hold me. I have done nothing wrong. Tell her, Sandra," he orders his lawyer. "Sandra will say whatever we need to say." He puts his head down with a small groan. Clearly unwell. The scratches down his face and neck appear infected.

"My client needs medical attention," Sandra Ling says. "Police officers caused him bodily injury during arrest, and—"

"I heard you attempted to flee and fell because you were intoxicated, Jon," Mal says. "And those scratches on your neck and the injury on your hand—I saw them myself prior to your arrest. How did you get those cuts?"

"He was pushed to the ground by police officers during arrest," says Ling.

"Oh, please," Mal says, turning her attention to the lawyer. "You can see yourself those scratches are not fresh. They look to me like defensive wounds incurred during a violent assault. Is that how you got them, Jon? What happened? How did you hurt yourself?"

Jon refuses to lift his head to look at her.

"How about you tell me in your own words what happened when you and your wife arrived at the Glass House at six fourteen p.m. on Halloween evening?"

He still doesn't move. His lawyer says, "He was never at the—"

Mal raises her hand, halting the lawyer. "We don't need games. Jon. We have your wife's statement. She says you both arrived in your Audi at the Glass House around six fourteen p.m. We have witness statements that corroborate this. We also have witnesses who saw your car enter the ADMAC construction site in North Vancouver later that night."

He glances up sharply. "That's bullshit. I was never there. I—"

His lawyer places her hand firmly on her client's arm and shoots him a warning look.

But he continues. "I wasn't at any ADMAC site. I did return to the Glass House, okay, I—"

"Jon," his counsel snaps. Heat flashes in her eyes.

His gaze darts to his lawyer. "I'm not having this pinned on me."

Ling leans forward and says very quietly near his ear, "I told you. You don't need to talk. We just need to hear what the police have got. They're fishing."

Mal says quickly, "So you do admit you returned to the house?"

"Look, Sergeant," Ling says, "unless you're prepared to bring my client in front of a judge and charge him so we can discuss bail terms, we have nothing further to contribute at this moment."

"When those DNA and fingerprint results come back, we—"

"If you have something to say at that point, you know where to find my client. Come, Jon. We're leaving."

Jon pushes himself to his feet.

Mal says, "When did you learn that your maid is the same person who once accused you of sexual assault?"

His body stiffens. His gaze bites into Mal's. His lawyer moves quickly toward the door, opens it wide. "Jon?"

He starts toward his lawyer and the open door.

"Who is Mia, Jon?"

His eyes flicker. His features tighten and his mouth flattens. His lawyer reaches quickly for his arm, refocusing her client on herself, and they step out into the corridor.

Mal leans back in her chair. As she watches them go, her mobile rings. It's Benoit.

She connects the call.

"They've got her, Mal. The divers have found her and the rug. She's deep down, trapped under rusted metal debris at the bottom. Lots of silt. She must have been pushed there by the current. They're strategizing how to safely bring her up now."

# AFTERSHOCKS

Mal feels flattened and tired. The divers were not able to free the body before nightfall due to tidal-current windows and visibility issues, but they did bring up the rug and a white sneaker with an orange stripe that matches the one found next to the king-size bed at the Glass House. Mal is now home for the night. She sits beside Peter on the sofa in their crowded little living room, surrounded by bookshelves, but her imagination is filled with mental images of Kit Darling's body trapped deep underwater, covered with silt, her soft blonde hair flowing about her face in the darkness. Peter stares at the TV. They have the news on. A cat curls in his lap. He also looks tired, Mal thinks. Her husband seems more vacant than usual tonight. She feels a bolt of loneliness and moves closer to him. She places her hand on his thigh. "You doing okay?"

He glances at her. For a moment he looks confused.

She smiles. "Had enough supper?"

He frowns, then nods. "I think so. How was your day?"

Peter already asked this when she arrived home, and she told him about the body finally being found. She explained how the divers would go down and try again first thing tomorrow. But now she just says, "It was fine. I'm looking forward to the early retirement, though." It's a lie. But also a necessity. Peter clearly needs someone at home. She could hire a caregiver—Mal thinks suddenly of Beulah stuck alone upstairs in her home with her carers. Peter and Mal long ago promised they would be there for each other when times got rough. In sickness and in health. And times are going to get rougher much sooner than Mal ever anticipated. Her mind dwells on Beulah. She decides she'll pay the old woman a visit once this case is wrapped up, and thank her for making that 911 call.

The newscast flashes onto a scene near the ADMAC construction site.

"Oh, here it is." She reaches for the remote and quickly bumps up the sound.

A female reporter stands under klieg lights in the darkness near the cordoned-off entrance to the site. She holds a mic.

"The search for missing maid Kit Darling appears to have come to a sad conclusion earlier this evening. A source close to the investigation says divers located a woman's body underwater near the area where Darling's yellow Subaru was pulled out of the Burrard Inlet. The body is trapped in debris at considerable depth. The team is currently devising a strategy to safely bring the remains up, hopefully tomorrow."

The camera switches to the anchor in the newsroom. "Pamela, are the police saying anything more about other aspects of the investigation?"

"At the moment, all we know is that ex-Olympic skier Jon Rittenberg and his wife have been brought in for questioning. They have since been released. Forensic evidence from the crime scene at the so-called Glass House is still being processed. I imagine results could take a while. But once the body has been retrieved, an autopsy will be performed, which should yield additional clues about what happened on that violent and fateful night at a luxury mansion on West Vancouver's waterfront."

Beulah watches reporter Pamela Dorfmann on her small television set in her room.

She feels profoundly sad to hear they've found Kit's body. As images of skier Jon Rittenberg and his wife, Daisy, flash onto the television screen, Beulah knows without a doubt that this is the same couple she saw getting out of the Audi.

Beulah is pleased she dialed 911. She didn't *really* think Horton could have hurt anyone, but she's relieved to hear other people are being questioned and not her son. She's seen Horton behind the hedge on a few occasions, watching the maid working next door. She also saw Horton spying on the ladies having lunch by the pool. She's been worried about Horton for quite a while.

She rests her head back in her chair and closes her eyes, feeling content to have had some purpose, to have played an important and exciting role. But she will miss the maid. Beulah will miss her happy wave and smile. As Beulah drifts into an opioid slumber, she tells herself it's silly to believe she'll see people again in a heavenly afterlife. But she does like to imagine she might bump into Kit the maid and get to know her properly this time.

Beulah drifts deeper. Part of her knows tonight is the night she will not wake from her slumber. Come morning she will be gone, and this house will be Horton's.

Boon enters a small and brightly lit gas station supermarket near the town of Hope. It's pitch dark outside and pummeling with rain. He's come down from a remote cabin in the mountains to purchase supplies. He fled to the cabin after those cops came to speak to him. He has zero intention of going in to give a DNA sample, or to talk to the police. He could see where their minds were going.

As he puts tins of beans into his shopping basket, he catches sight of the small television screen behind the store counter. He stills as a chyron flashes across the bottom.

POLICE DIVERS FIND BODY.

Boon drops the tin he was holding. It rolls beneath the shelves. Fixated on the television screen, he slowly walks closer to the counter.

"Can you turn that up?" he asks the cashier.

The cashier glances at the TV, reaches for a remote, and turns up the sound.

Boon stares as he listens.

"The search for missing maid Kit Darling appears to have come to a sad conclusion earlier this evening—"

"They found her body," the cashier says, jerking his thumb at the screen.

Boon swallows as tears fill his eyes. Carefully, he sets his basket on the counter and exits the store. He walks through the rain to his car.

# THE MAID'S DIARY

We're on the log at the beach, my half-eaten sandwich fallen into the sand, and Boon puts his face into his hands. He rocks and moans as though in pain. I have just forced him to watch the recording I copied to my phone.

*"I'm sorry, Kit. I am so, so sorry. God, I am sorry."*

*"I loved you, Boon. With my whole heart. You were the center of my world, you know that?"*

*He looks up. His eyes are full of tears. They run down his face. My chest hurts. Part of me died when I heard his high, whooping, nervous laugh on Daisy's recording. Another part of me is cold and dead as stone and can't feel anything at all. I will not be able to trust or let anyone in again.*

*"I hadn't come out as gay yet, Kit. I was scared. Some of the guys who were at the lodge that night, they were the same guys who beat me at school. Who called me a faggot. Who cornered me in the locker room at the rec center one day and pulled down my pants and taunted me with a bottle, saying they would push it up my butt. I was terrified that if I was the only one who stuck my neck out and told the truth of what we all saw, I'd be outed and worse. I honestly believed they might*

*beat and kill me if I came forward and ratted on them and Jon and the other team members."*

*He swipes his tears away. "I was a stupid, frightened kid with no one to turn to. My parents would've died in shame if they'd found out what I was—what I am. Kit, listen to me, you know that my mom and dad still don't know. I have come out to the whole world, but I still can't tell them. I just can't. Not after everything they've done to try and make a life for me in this country. They're just incapable of understanding. And now my mom is sick, and she probably won't get well. And I would rather let both my parents pass without ever having to know this about their son. I—I am so ashamed by how I never stood up for you. I . . . I wish I'd been brave, bold. I wish I could've been the kind of kid hero you read about in books. The kid who risks everything to stand up for the underdog. But I wasn't. I was a scared-shitless boy who didn't fully understand his own sexuality. A kid who only wanted to belong. To be accepted. Loved. Can you possibly find it in your heart to understand this?"*

*"You've been my closest friend all these years, Boon. You could have told me you were there."*

*"But then I would have lost your friendship, Kit. And I can't bear losing you. My whole life I've been trying to make it up to you."*

*"Yet you've lost me anyway."*

*"I'll do anything, Kit, if you will forgive me. Can you ever forgive me? Please."*

*I turn away and stare at the sea. On one level I do understand what kid Boon did, or rather did not do. I know fear. I know marginalization. I was badly bullied myself. All I ever wanted was to belong, too, to be loved, accepted, admired. Maybe time will help me process and accept. Maybe it won't.*

*Why should we always "understand" our abuser, the villains, the mendacity of evil, the people who let us down? Does understanding help us heal?*

*I don't think anything really heals trauma. You just find some kind of narrative to learn to cohabit with it.*

*I suppose now is the time to admit to you, Dear Diary, I never had a therapist. I always imagined that if I did she would coax me to start a journal. But the reason I really started this diary was to tell my Story. To leave something behind specifically to be found by the police.*

*To tell them about Jon and Daisy. And what happened that night in the lodge.*

*I started my diary the day I learned I was inside their house.*

*But you know what? My imaginary therapist was right. While I might have started this diary for one reason, it became something else entirely. I did ask why, why, why. And, finally, I did drop through that trapdoor.*

*You helped me see my world a different way, Dear Diary.*

*You helped me stand my ground. You helped me fight back.*

*You helped me realize I no longer wish to be Anonymous Girl. Or a ghost.*

*Now I plan to be SEEN.*

*Am I frightened that I've gone too deep and am in way over my head? Hell yes. I'm terrified I won't survive this. That it will backfire. That I might die.*

*But I'm well past the point of return. I am Thelma and Louise racing at speed for that cliff . . .*

# MAL

Mal is at the crime lab. It's early Monday morning, and Benoit is back at the ADMAC site overseeing renewed attempts to bring up the trapped body. The retrieval was called off yesterday due to a severe storm and high tide that brought powerful currents.

"We found blonde hair trace here on the back seat of the Audi where the seat joins the back support," says Otto Wojak, lab boss. Otto is walking Mal around Jon Rittenberg's impounded vehicle, pointing out where evidence has been found in the car.

"Was the hair dyed?" Mal asks.

"Yes. Dark roots. Consistent with the hair trace from the main bedroom at the Glass House. We also found blood on the back seat here. And a ripped velvet choker also with blood trace."

The photo of Kit Darling with the black choker around her neck surfaces in Mal's mind. "What about the mud on the tires and on the plates?" she asks. "Does it match the ADMAC soil samples?"

"We'll have results on soil comparison tests shortly." Otto crouches down and points at the tire treads. "However, these tread patterns are consistent with the tire tracks found at the ADMAC site. Same with the Subaru treads."

"Can I see the items taken from the Subaru?"

Otto takes Mal over to a long table near the yellow Subaru Crosstrek on the other side of the lab garage.

"Everything here has been photographed and documented. This here is the wooden block found wedging the gas pedal down." He points. "And this wallet was found in front of the car. Inside the wallet were these items." He moves his finger over the objects as he speaks. "Darling's driver's license, a Visa and MasterCard in her name, a CityIntraBank card, seventy dollars in cash, coins, a gym membership card, a drugstore points card. Grocery store card. Library card. Theater tickets. A receipt from a fast-food outlet. This is the purse found in the vehicle. These items were found inside the purse."

Mal moves along the table, studying the items. Makeup—lots of it. Lipstick in bright, bold colors. Hairbrush. Five lollipops in different flavors. They look sticky from the water, their wrappings coming off. Sticks of hot cinnamon gum. Subaru key fob. A tiny locket containing an image of a man and a woman. Mal peers more closely at the image, wondering if it could be Kit Darling's mother and father. She thinks of the cremains urn on the floor in Darling's room. In her mind she hears Boon-mee Saelim's words.

*Kit was pretty messed up by her mom's dying . . . It was on the same day, right after the scattering of her mother's cremains, that she started a new cleaning job. She's been getting progressively weird since then.*

"It's everything a woman carries with her," Mal says, staring at the contents on the table. "Her ID, driver's license, credit and bank cards." She glances up at Otto. "Where's her phone? And the diary?"

"We carefully separated the wet pages of the journal and have them drying out separately. The words on the pages were written in a purple gel ink that runs easily in water compared to standard ballpoint ink. But it should still be legible once we're done. And we're working to retrieve data from the water-damaged mobile device."

"It was sealed in a ziplock bag?"

"Yes, but the bag was punctured, presumably when the car was damaged going over the dock."

"Would you say it's unusual to carry your journal around in a sealed ziplock?"

"That's your job, Detective. I just tell you the science behind what we find. But if I had to venture a guess, I'd say whoever sealed the journal in there wanted to keep it dry."

She glances at Otto.

"We'll photograph the pages once they're dry, and digitally enhance them where necessary. We'll copy the pages to your team as soon as the process is complete. We'll attempt to access the contents of the cell phone once it's dried out, too."

"And the items from Rose Cottage that were brought in?"

Otto leads her through to his lab. Various white-coated techs glance up from their stations and nod in greeting. Otto pulls images up on a large monitor.

"These are the shoes found at the back of Jon Rittenberg's closet. Mud in the lugs appears similar in appearance to the ADMAC site mud. As I said, we're still awaiting the soil comparison tests." He points. "We also found traces of human blood in the lugs here, and on the surface of the toe there." His gaze meets Mal's. "We got results from the DNA samples you sent to the private lab early this morning."

Her heart kicks. A quiver of a grin curves Otto's mouth.

"Christ, Otto. And?"

"The blood on Rittenberg's shoes belongs to Kit Darling. It's also her blood in the back of his Audi. It's her hair, too."

"You could've told me this the second I walked in here."

He laughs a great big belly laugh and says, "And what fun would that be?"

Mal rolls her eyes, but her pulse is racing. "What else are you holding back?"

"The partial shoe prints in the blood at the crime scene show patterning consistent with the soles from the shoes from Jon Rittenberg's closet. His blood is at the scene, too. And latents and patents from items in the living room match both Daisy and Jon Rittenberg's fingerprints."

Otto pulls up images of the broken glasses that were found near the upturned coffee table. "Daisy Rittenberg's DNA is on the rim of this piece of wineglass. Jon Rittenberg's DNA is on this whisky glass piece. Kit Darling's DNA is on the broken martini glass, here." He brings up another photo. "This is the carving knife retrieved from the pool." He points. "A small amount of Darling's blood was detected deep in the grooves of the hilt here. And Daisy Rittenberg's prints are on the knife hilt."

Mal stares at the images. Emilio Rossi's words float into her consciousness.

*If you do find her DNA inside, it's because she went to lunch at Northview last Friday. She drank from glasses and handled a carving knife to cut sausage.*

She thinks of Rossi's earlier comment.

*Her husband was very angry when she departed her home. He threatened her physically. He'd already had a fair bit to drink, and she suspects he began drinking again heavily after she left. She cannot vouch for his whereabouts or say whether he returned later to the Northview residence.*

Mal purses her lips. This evidence puts the Rittenbergs inside the house despite their assertions they left after they dropped the flowers and pie. Plus they have motive. There are witnesses, a timeline. CCTV footage that tracks the Audi to the ADMAC site. More witnesses who saw the Subaru and rug being dumped. But it's not quite adding up in her mind. She's missing something.

Mal thanks Otto and returns to her vehicle. She calls Benoit as she drives back to the station.

"Still nothing on this end," he says. "The front plus a king tide has brought in silt and a big current. The team has paused the search again.

337

They hope a safer window will present within a few hours when the tide turns. I'll keep you posted."

Mal kills the call and drives the rest of the way to the station, feeling edgy and impatient for more results from the lab. She also called in a blood-spatter expert to assess the crime scene and is keen for his report, too. It all feels so close yet so far.

As Mal enters her unit's bullpen, Jack Duff comes up to her.

"Guess who just walked in of his own accord?"

Mal shakes out her coat and hangs it up. "Suspense is killing me, Jack. Who?"

"Boon-mee Saelim."

She flicks her gaze to Jack. "Last I heard he was nowhere to be found."

"He looks pretty messed up," Jack says. "Like he hasn't slept in days. He insists on talking only to you or Benoit."

# MAL

Mal finds Boon sitting on a dark-blue sofa in one of their more comfortable interview rooms. He looks like hell. His leg jiggles and his fingers fidget.

Mal takes a seat on the chair opposite Boon. She places her notebook and pen on the low table between them.

"Do you know that we've been looking for you, Boon?"

"Do I need a lawyer?"

"You're free to obtain counsel. I can also provide you with a number if you'd like to access legal aid. Let me know. Meanwhile, let's start with where you've been. And just so you know, you are on camera, and this is being recorded."

Boon's gaze darts up to the camera mounted near the ceiling. He then glances at the closed door as though he's having second thoughts.

Mal waits.

"I was at a cabin near Hope," he finally says as he rubs his thigh with his hand.

"Why did you run?"

"I didn't run. I needed to grieve. I lost a friend. My best friend."

Tension quickens in Mal. "So you *knew* Kit was dead?"

"No. I was grieving because I lost her as a friend through something I did a long time ago, and she found out."

"So why've you come in now, Boon? What brings you back from the cabin?"

"I was at a gas station and saw on the news that divers had found her body. I—" His voice cracks and his eyes pool with tears. "It wasn't supposed to go like this. She wasn't supposed to die." He sniffs and swipes tears away.

"Tell me what you mean. Take your time. Start at the beginning."

He wipes his nose, and Mal pushes a box of tissues toward him. He takes one, blows his nose.

"Kit and I—our whole group—we would often dress up for role-play on the fly, you know? Like pop-up improv. We'd go into a Walmart, or to a supermarket, or an outdoor park, and interact with people, messing with them. It was our private game. A joke."

"Like Kit's Instagram was also a joke? We did check her @fox-andcrow profile that you told us about. A good percentage of those Instagram photos are posed with you, Boon."

"Like I told you. We played these games. It wasn't unusual." He rubs his face. "At the end of September, she asked me to participate in another 'game.' She wanted me to pretend to be a character named Haruto North. She asked me to come to this bistro and fetch her. She was going to play Haruto's wife, a woman called Vanessa. I arrived at the bistro to find Kit in the wig and the fake pregnancy belly she wore for her character, Mary, in this play we put on—*The Three Lives of Mary.* She was lunching with a woman I later learned was Daisy Rittenberg. I played along, improvised. I acted controlling, a little aggressive. Like a domineering husband."

"And why did Kit ask you to do this?"

He inhales deeply, and for a moment Boon-mee looks like he's deciding whether to jump off a cliff and end his life. "I—I wasn't totally up front the first time we spoke, Detective. I did know what happened to Kit in Whistler at that ski lodge. I was there."

"You were at that party? You witnessed the alleged sexual assault?"

He looks down at his hands in his lap. "I did. And I never came forward. I could have saved her and stopped Jon and the others ever doing that again, and I didn't. I was an enabler, and the guilt became a monster inside me. Kit discovered recently that I was there. I said I'd do anything to make it up to her, anything that would help her find it in her heart to forgive me for lying to her by default all these years. She then asked me to do some things, including playing Haruto." Boon looks up and meets Mal's eyes.

"I did owe her, Sergeant. If I had spoken up eighteen years ago, maybe Katarina would have had her baby. Maybe her father wouldn't have been disgusted by her and wanted to kick her out. Maybe her father would not have been so stressed that he had a heart attack and died. Kit was so smart, her grades so good—she would have gone to university. She'd have had her self-esteem. Her life would have been different. The cops would have charged Jon and the others. But I didn't speak."

Adrenaline zings through Mal's blood. "You do realize there's no statute of limitations for sexual assault in this province, Boon, and that anything you say right now might be used as evidence."

He nods.

"At the time, why did you not come forward?"

"I was gay and had not come out at that time. I was horrifically bullied at school, and I still had half a year before I graduated. I was terrified to stick my neck out and put a target on my back. So I hid. I stayed quiet. I failed Kit. So, yes, Sergeant, I owe her." He wavers and tears fill his eyes again. "There are many different kinds of love, you know? I love Kit. She is my world. My sister, my best friend, every-thing. I wanted her back. I hated myself deeply for deceiving her. So I did it. I played the parts she asked me to. Then, when I fully realized what she was doing, I warned her it was too dangerous. I told her if Jon Rittenberg or Daisy found out, they would do *anything* to stop her from exposing them. But she continued like she had nothing to lose. And maybe she didn't have anything left to lose," Boon says quietly. "Not after she found out I'd also betrayed her."

"And what was Kit doing to the Rittenbergs, exactly?"

"Gaslighting them. Messing with their heads. I only know some of it. She'd troll Daisy's Instagram account, leave threatening notes on her car, inside her car. She left threats in the mailbox at Rose Cottage. She even cost Jon Rittenberg his job. She asked me to follow him and take photos. Kit had access to Jon's computer, so she knew on occasion where he would be. She posed as some siren named Mia, and I took photographs of her and Jon together. While I was following him, I learned Jon had engaged a private investigator, and Kit found Jon's contract with the PI in his computer. She eventually had me deliver all the photographic evidence of Jon and Mia's 'affair' plus a copy of the PI contract to TerraWest, where Jon works. He was fired that morning—the same morning of the attack at the Glass House. Jon drove from work to a liquor store, bought alcohol, and sat in a park, drinking all day. I—if I'd known Kit was planning to meet Jon and Daisy Rittenberg that same night, I would've stopped her. He was enraged, drunk."

"What happened that night, Boon?"

He moistens his lips and hesitates as he seems to struggle with where to start. Or how much to tell.

"I don't know. All I do know is . . . she'd 'borrowed' blood bags and other equipment from our friend who's an EMT and who volunteers at a blood clinic. She took her own blood on three occasions over the months from July, I think. She stored it in the fridge at the Glass House because she knew the owners would be away for a period of time."

Mal's heart begins to beat hard and steady. "Kit Darling was planning a false scene?"

Boon swipes a tear from his cheek, nods. "She was setting the Rittenbergs up to be investigated for murder. Except it backfired. Jon Rittenberg returned to the house. And—" His voice breaks, and he drops his head into his hands and sobs.

Mal leaves the room to fetch Boon some water. While in the bullpen, she tells the others to watch the feed from the interview cam. She returns to the room and offers Boon a glass of water and more tissues.

Boon blows his nose, sips water, and composes himself.

"Go on, Boon," Mal says. "Take your time."

"Kit wanted it to appear as though she'd lost enough blood for police to believe she was dead. She also planted her own blood on shoes in Jon's closet, and in his car. She pulled out strands of her hair and put them in the back of his car, too. She'd already scoped out the ADMAC site and collected a bucket of soil there one evening. She made mud and put some under Jon's shoes. She later used this mud to plaster over his car registration plates. She accessed his and Daisy's vehicles with spare keys from Rose Cottage. Kit returned his shoes, placed them at the back of his closet. She bought an identical pair to make prints in blood at the Glass House. She also took Daisy's necklace from Rose Cottage to leave in the Glass House."

"She was planning this for months?"

"I was never really sure exactly what she was up to. It was like her plan kept evolving and growing in scope the deeper she got into the Rittenbergs' affairs, and the more she learned about them. And you must remember, Sergeant, we all played games. It was our thing. Our group was always up for a game, for imaginative role-playing. We are tricksters and clowns and pranksters and proud of it. And if you also find Jon's blood on scene, it's because Kit took some of Jon's blood herself, after she lured him up to an Airbnb as Mia. It's one of the places she cleans. She drugged him. And before you ask me what drug she used and where she got it, I don't know. Probably from someone she knows who deals in black-market stuff like ketamine, cocaine, and

GHB." Boon takes another long sip of water. His hands tremble as he wipes his mouth.

"A while back Kit asked me in great detail about a scene I staged for a TV show I'm working on. About a coroner. I set up aspirated blood spatter, arterial spatter. Spatter arcing the walls. I—I suspect she was inspired by this to do something similar at the Glass House."

"Boon, were you present at the Glass House on Halloween night?"

"No."

"She did this alone—met with the Rittenbergs alone?"

He swallows. "She . . . Kit asked me to do some things that night without asking questions. I did. I told you, Detective, I owe her. I owed myself. I promised her on the beach that day I would do *anything* to make it up to her, and she said nothing would be illegal, exactly."

"What did she ask you to do?"

"Kit had rented a dark-gray Audi S6 sedan. Like Jon's. She parked it near her apartment that afternoon, and she also plastered those plates with mud so the registration would not be picked up by the road cams."

"So the vehicle could be confused with Jon Rittenberg's?"

"Yes. She knew there were cameras at the ADMAC site, too. She got the idea when she saw the jumper's camera on the bridge when she was stuck in traffic. She looked down and saw how it might also capture footage of the area near the silos. She drove out to the ADMAC site one weekend, late in the evening when it was dark, to check it out, and she saw the dock."

"Where she decided to dump her own car?"

He nods. "She asked me to fetch and drive the Audi from her apartment to the Glass House at a certain time on Halloween night. She told me to dress in dark rain gear and a cap. Incognito-style. She asked that I park behind her Subaru and enter the Glass House property via the yard gate, quietly, and to come around to the glass sliding doors by the pool. When I arrived and saw inside, I was shocked. Blood everywhere, upturned furniture. Broken glasses. Kit was impatient. Edgy. She was also dressed in rain gear, oversize, with a hood. She had her silicone belly underneath."

"So she looked pregnant? Like she could be Daisy, and you could be Jon?"

"I realized in hindsight, yes. She was standing by a bloodied and rolled-up rug. It had one of her sneakers inside. She asked me to help her drag the rug along the pool deck, out to the driveway, and to help her put it into the Audi's back seat. She said I had to heft it like there was a heavy body inside. I asked her what the hell game she was playing, and all she said was, 'You promised, Boon.'" He clears his throat.

"So, just before we begin dragging the rug, she throws a bloody carving knife into the pool, and she lets out a bloodcurdling scream. We lugged the rug to the cars and loaded it into the back seat of the rented Audi. She got into the Audi, dressed as pregnant Daisy. I got into her Subaru. Then we sped away to the ADMAC site in both cars. We dumped the carpet into the Burrard in view of the ADMAC cameras. She was betting, I guess, that you guys would eventually locate the CCTV footage. Then we pushed her Subaru off the dock with her ID and wallet and phone and everything inside. Including her diary. Which she sealed in a ziplock bag so you guys—the police—would find it and read it. I don't know what's in it. I'm assuming it's something that sets Jon up. I have no idea if there is truth in there, or some totally unreliable version."

"So there was no body in the rug?" Mal's brain is racing—police divers have definitely located a female body underwater, down current from where the Subaru went in.

"No."

"Are you being truthful, Boon?"

"I am."

"What happened next?"

"She asked to be dropped off several houses down from the Glass House. She said she'd forgotten something at the house. I then returned the Audi to the rental place."

"And you left her there? Near the Glass House?"

His eyes fill with tears again. "I did. It was the biggest mistake of my life. Because as I drove off, I thought I saw another Audi parked farther down the street. I didn't think much of it at the time, because I was reeling from the fact we'd just submerged Kit's car. And now I am sure it was him. He came back. He could have followed us to the dump site."

"Jon?"

He nods.

"It doesn't make sense, Boon, that Kit would want to return to the scene. She screamed. Presumably to alert the neighbors. First responders would likely have been on their way—"

"She insisted. She said she'd left something important behind, and since we'd just drowned her credit cards and phone and ID and everything with her car, I could only presume it was a burner phone or a passport or something. From where I dropped her off, she had access to the sea walk that runs along the ocean in front of the houses. I imagined that if she saw someone like first responders inside the Glass House, she wouldn't go in. She said we were done. She said goodbye. I—I never saw her again."

"What time did you leave her there?"

"About twelve thirty a.m."

Mal sits back in her chair and regards Boon in silence for a while. She tries to read him, looking for tells that he's lying.

"Surely Kit didn't actually believe Jon and Daisy would be charged with murder, Boon? Surely she'd consider forensic tests of the blood evidence would eventually reveal that the red blood cells showed signs of degradation from being stored outside the body, in a fridge? Or that her creative spatter would show anomalies to a spatter expert?"

"I don't think Kit ever believed she'd be able to create a perfect murder that never happened. All she wanted was to definitively link Jon and Daisy to an apparently violent crime scene, and to have police arrive and open an investigation that was bound to attract media. She was theatrical that way, Detective. She wanted to be seen. She wanted it all to play out live on TV, in social media, in conversation, speculation. A false narrative. Just like her Instagram account. Designed to poke holes into our fake realities. But she made a lethal mistake—she underestimated Jon. He was too dangerous. She messed with a monster and paid the ultimate price." Boon takes something out of his pocket as he speaks. He leans forward and sets a flash drive on the table. But he keeps his hand over it. Protective.

"What's that?" Mal asks.

He sucks in a deep, shuddering breath, and says, "There are two recordings on this drive. Plus copies of two sets of legal documents. The first recording and the documents are what Kit found in a safe at Rose Cottage while cleaning. It's what tipped her over the edge. The second recording—" His voice catches. He breaks down again, blows his nose. "It's from Halloween night in the Glass House. Kit recorded her interaction with the Rittenbergs."

"She captured them *inside* the house?"

"Yes. All of it."

"The security cameras were not functioning in the house that night, Boon. We checked."

"She disarmed the system. She didn't want it feeding to the website where the Norths could check it. She always disarmed it when she went in to clean. But that night she fixed one of those small sports cameras to a pair of Halloween devil horns she wore on her head. The footage she captured—it was in my in-box when I woke the next morning, an email with links to a Google Drive folder that contained these files. It's all there. Her entire interaction with the Rittenbergs. The email had a note saying she'd sent me the links the minute the Rittenbergs left the

Glass House. As insurance in case something happened to her. I . . . I should've called you guys right away."

"You said two recordings. What's on the first recording you said she found in the safe?"

"Footage shot with a phone on the night of the sexual assault—the gang rape when she was sixteen. The documents are nondisclosure agreements. One is signed by both Daisy's mother and Kit's mother, promising Kit would get rid of the baby and drop charges in exchange for a five-hundred-thousand-dollar payment to Mrs. Popovich. The second NDA is signed by Daisy and Charlotte Waters. Charlotte, or Charley, was another of Jon's victims. Same deal—Charley would drop all her allegations against Jon for an alleged assault in Silver Aspens, Colorado, a year ago."

"Okay," Mal says slowly as her brain races to assimilate this shocking news. "We're going to need to take a look at everything on that drive, Boon." And they would need to look at additional CCTV footage to see if Jon Rittenberg was captured returning later to the ADMAC site, possibly with the maid's body for real this time.

Boon removes his hand from the flash drive, allowing Mal to take it. Quietly, he says, "You'll see on the recording why Jon had no choice but to return to the Glass House and finish things off." He pauses. His eyes turn dark and haunted and seem to sink into their sockets. "You can see Kit bit off way more than she could chew. Self-destructive—that was Kit. And I did nothing to stop her. I thought I was helping. But it backfired. When I heard on the news that a body had been found, I realized Jon must have gotten her when she returned to the house, and then dumped her in the water at the ADMAC site."

# MAL

Before sitting down with her team to watch the recordings Boon has delivered, Mal checks in with Benoit.

"The divers are going back down now," Benoit says as he picks up her call. "They should have a decent window between now and nightfall. I'll call as soon as I have more."

She signs off, then joins her investigators in front of a large monitor. Silence falls over them and tension is thick as she hits PLAY.

They see Daisy and Jon waiting behind the glass front door, Daisy holding the bouquet of white flowers and the pie. Jon is busy on his phone. They see the Rittenbergs look up as the camera nears. They see raw shock on Daisy's face as her jaw drops. The door swings open. They hear what must be Kit Darling's voice.

"Well, hello, Daisy. And you must be Jon? Come in—come on in."

Daisy appears confused. She says, "What—what happened to—"

"Oh, you mean this?" Darling's voice.

Mal leans forward as Daisy drops the flowers and pie.

"What—where's the baby?" Daisy asks.

"You mean my bump?" Darling's voice again. "Silicone. Do you know how many different kinds of these pregnancy prostheses you can buy online? You should google it. Does make one wonder what people use them for. Fake photo shoots? Just to walk around in? Test-drive pregnancy? Did you know that you can even buy very realistic fake little babies online?"

The investigators watch as Jon and Daisy Rittenberg are led into the living room. They remain riveted as Darling pours the Rittenbergs drinks, then starts to show them footage from the night in the ski lodge. They watch as Jon transfers money, anger black on his face, his body wire tense.

"He looks murderous," whispers Lula.

They watch Daisy and Jon Rittenberg leave the house. The footage ends.

Suddenly Kit Darling appears on screen. She has turned the camera on herself. She smiles. Up close. Mal feels an involuntary shock of tension as vampire teeth in red lips fill the screen. Kit is heavily made up. She points to the red horns on her head. "The mini sports camera was tucked up here," she says.

It feels as though their victim is speaking directly to them all, sitting here in the room, talking to them from beyond her watery grave. It's an eerie sensation. The others feel it, too. Mal can see it in their faces.

"It's Halloween," Kit says. "Appropriate, no? The devil gets her pound of flesh."

The footage ends.

Quickly, Mal pulls up the recording from the sexual assault. She hits PLAY.

The investigators study the old, grainy footage. When it cuts out, they all sit in heavy, shimmering silence.

Mal clears her throat. "We have Rittenberg and some of his teammates on the sexual assault." She points at the monitor. "Everything we need to bring those charges is right there on that footage alone. Let's bring him in. Get him in front of a judge. Charge him. We can work on the rest while we hold him."

Jack says, "I don't buy that Saelim would have dropped Darling back at the scene. Especially after she screamed like that. Doesn't add up."

Lula says, "It's weird, but bear in mind, I checked, and it took more than ninety minutes for first responders to even arrive at the Glass House. Beulah Brown was known to make false calls. The West Van PD and dispatch are all too familiar with going out there only to find raccoons in her garbage or shadows in the wind. Brown's call was placed at a lower priority when another emergency came in right after hers. There was a significant delay in response to the scene, so it's possible Darling returned, and that Rittenberg had time to abduct or kill her, or both. It's possible Saelim is telling the truth."

"Saelim says he can identify the other participants on that ski lodge footage," Mal says. "Let's get him started. We—" Her cell rings. It's Benoit.

Mal holds up her hand, connects the call. "Go ahead, Benoit. You're on speaker."

"They've almost got her body free. They're about to bring her up now."

Mal surges to her feet and reaches for her jacket. "I'm on my way. Lu, get Saelim identifying those participants. Get a written statement from him detailing his involvement. Arnav, assemble a team—arrest Jon Rittenberg. Gavin, loop Crown prosecution in. Get things rolling on the charges. Jack, work with our media liaison, and let's get ahead of the press on this one."

Mal shrugs into her jacket and hurries for the station exit. As she climbs into her car, the irony hits hard. Kit Darling is getting exactly what she wanted. Theater. With Jon and Daisy in the spotlight.

Darling is finally exacting her revenge. She has won.

At a price—her life.

# MAL

Clouds press down low and dark, and rain whips sideways, driven by gusts of wind.

Mal stands next to Benoit at the water's edge, where giant riprap boulders shore up the bank. The ground underfoot is muddy. They're near the bridge, close to where Tamara Adler stated that she and MLA Frank Horvath parked to have sex in her Mercedes-Maybach. Traffic roars overhead and the bridge clunks.

Mal huddles deeper into her coat as the rigid hull inflatable with tenders on board guides the divers underwater. In her mind Mal sees the photo of Kit Darling. She hears Beulah Brown's words.

*She's pretty. I've seen her face through my binoculars. She always waves when she sees me. Sweet girl . . . She wears her hair up in two little buns, like cat's ears.*

Emotion tightens Mal's throat. Perhaps she's finally been exhausted by the depravity and darkness after year upon year of this job. Perhaps retirement will feel okay. She glances up at Benoit. He offers a comforting but sad smile. He feels something, too. Benoit has empathy, and while empathy can be an asset to an investigator, especially when it comes to interrogation and getting into a victim's or villain's head, the trait has a downside for a homicide cop. Those who can shut out feelings last longer, because this job takes its toll, and after thirty years, she's feeling it.

"You okay?" Benoit asks.

"Yeah. Just thinking about the irony of Rittenberg bringing her back out here."

"You think Saelim is telling the truth?"

"We'll find out. I've got the team going through additional CCTV footage."

"I'm just glad we found her."

"Helluva case to go out on."

"Some curtain call for sure." He breaks his gaze and turns away. "Gonna miss you, Mal."

"I'll be around. Any time you want coffee or to troubleshoot a case. God knows, I miss doing that with Peter."

"At least Sam Berkowitz will feed her crow," he says as four divers break the surface, wet-suited heads rising like seals coming up to play in the stormy water. Light glints off their dive masks. Mal tenses as the tender gives a shout. Slowly, the divers surface the body. She lies face-down. Mal sees her blonde hair floating like a gentle fan about her head. The divers begin to swim her to the shore. She's wearing a lilac jacket.

As the divers and the body draw closer, Mal and Benoit scramble down the bank of wet concrete boulders. A chopper thuds overhead, hidden by the clouds. Crowds are once more gathering along the pedestrian section of the bridge. By tonight the Kit Darling theater will be on everyone's TV screen and all over social media. The media will have gotten word of Jon Rittenberg's arrest for the sexual assault that occurred eighteen years ago. The other guys involved in the assault will be scrambling, worrying about what's coming down for them. Daisy Rittenberg will be awaiting the birth of her child, unsure of what this will mean for her marriage, her baby. And for her. Annabelle and Labden will watch the news and call lawyers about their own exposure.

The divers reach the boulders. The arms of the decedent bob softly at her sides—she floats in the shape of a cross. Mal sees bracelets on one wrist. A watch on the other. Jeans. Boots.

The coroner's guys make their way over to the rocks with a body bag.

Slowly, the divers roll her over. Mal recoils as a swarm of sea lice explodes in a cloud, exposing the face. Her nose is gone. Her eyes are gaping sockets. Her lips have been eaten. Her cheeks are fleshy holes that expose the teeth in a macabre grimace.

"Shit," Benoit says quietly. "I know sea lice, crabs, starfish, other underwater critters can strip a body to bone in days, but . . ." His voice fades. He clears his throat.

Mal's brain is wheeling. "Boots," she whispers. "And the hair—it's not blonde. It's silvery-white." Her gaze shoots to Benoit as adrenaline dumps into her blood.

"It's not her," she says quietly. "It's not Kit Darling."

# THE MAID'S DIARY

Kat reaches for the umbrella drink at her side and sips. The taste is coconut and lychee. The air is warm and feels rounded and soft against her bare arms. The breeze smells like the ocean. She wears a bikini, a sarong, sandals, and a big straw hat. She's on the patio of a thatched beachside bar in Bali, ironically named Karma Beach Bar. She's always wanted to visit Bali. She flew in from Laos via Jakarta this morning. Kat opens a teal-color spiral notebook. She's starting a new diary. A fresh page. She even managed to find purple gel pens at a Jakarta airport store. She takes another sip of her drink, sets it down, picks up her pen. She writes:

> *Sometimes when you start a journey—or a journal— you have a destination in mind. You aim for it. You make a plan, devise an itinerary to get there. But the road is never straight. You hit storms, are blocked by rockslides, avalanches, construction detours, accidents. Perhaps you might notice a fellow traveler hitching a ride, so you pick them up . . . and your journey, your plot, your destination changes.*
>
> *Was my diary supposed to be part of a plot to implicate Jon Rittenberg? To set him up to be investigated for murder? To expose what he and his wife did to me all those years ago? In a way, yes. I started trying to write down my thoughts the day I learned I was in his house. I had to do something. I*

*couldn't just sit with the knowledge he was back, and I was inside his private cocoon. With the fact he was finally having a baby where I could have none, because of his act.*

*I intended my diary to be a confessional for the police to find. It's why I left it sealed in my car. I wanted investigators to be able to read my words despite the car going into the water. Does this make my words misdirection? I don't think so. Not really. Because while I might've started it that way, my diary became something else. It became therapy. A way for me to heal. My imaginary therapist was right. "Just put it down, Kit. Spill it out. Ask: Why why why"—and suddenly I did fall through the trapdoor. I met the hidden Kat on the underside of my consciousness. She spoke to me from the distorted fun house mirrors in the Jungian tunnels of my soul. Kat wanted to be seen. She wanted to marry herself to the Kit I eventually became after the attack. And I suddenly saw a whole different image of myself. And of the world. I saw what I was running from. I was running from Me. Myself. I saw how my addictions and quirks helped me hide from the hurtful things. My unconscious really did start to talk to me. The real Kat found her voice in the strokes of purple pen in a book with polka dots—*

Kat glances up as an American tourist at the bar loudly asks the bartender to turn up the TV behind the counter. Kat goes still as she realizes what's on the screen. It's the *Good Morning Global* show. The anchors, Ben Woo and Judy Salinger, have invited a retired homicide cop and a criminal lawyer to comment on "The Mysterious Case of the Missing Maid and the Wrong Body."

Quickly, Kat gathers her pen and diary, slides them into her straw bag, picks up her drink, and goes to sit at the bar counter. She watches intently.

Host Judy says, "A Vancouver family finally found closure when police divers searching for maid Kit Darling brought up the body of a missing senior with dementia instead. Sylvia Kaplan, seventy-one, was last seen on a street near her home in East Vancouver nearly two months ago. Extensive searches in the area for Kaplan yielded nothing. Until Monday, November 4, when divers found her body trapped below water. Investigators have since learned Kaplan boarded a transit bus that crossed to the North Shore. She disembarked near a park east of the site. Investigators believe she must have been confused, disoriented, and she wandered near the water, where she could have slipped and fallen in. The strong tidal currents likely washed her down toward the bridge, where her body became lodged in underwater debris."

Ben says, "So where does that leave our missing maid, who staged a false murder scene in order to trip up the Olympic skier who sexually assaulted her eighteen years ago? Retired RCMP investigator Sergeant Leon Tosi and retired criminal defense lawyer Renata Rollins are here to help us solve this mystery that has riveted viewers across North America and even hit media in the UK and Australia."

Leon leans forward and says, "Ben, a word of caution—while Jon Rittenberg has in fact been charged, he has yet to stand trial, so for now we'll still refer to it as the 'alleged' sexual assault. As to where Kit is, all we know so far is that records show she used her passport to board a flight from YVR to Wattay International Airport in Laos the morning after the staged murder. And financial records obtained by the police show that Jon and Daisy Rittenberg transferred nine hundred thousand dollars US into Kit's account, which Kit promptly moved into an off-shore account in the Caymans."

"So she tried to fake her own death and fled with the money," Judy says provocatively and with a smile.

Renata says, "It's unclear to me whether Kit thought she'd actually get away with it, or if her purpose was to dramatically toss the Rittenbergs into a media and legal hot seat."

Judy says, "Will police chase her down to Laos? Will she be charged? That's the question everyone is asking on Twitter, Facebook, Instagram, TikTok, YouTube. Kit Darling has become a celebrity. An underdog's hero. Everyone is rooting for her."

"Charge her with what?" asks Ben. "Fraud? Extortion? Obstruction of justice? Staging a false scene—isn't that a criminal offense?"

Renata says, "Usually a false scene relates to falsifying evidence in order to obscure or obfuscate a *real* homicide investigation. The scene Kit staged—she never claimed it was murder. No one was actually physically hurt."

"I see her as the victim here," Judy interjects. "The system let her down. Her community let her down. Her parents let her down. Her friends, too. She was denied justice all those years ago."

"What about extortion?" asks Ben. "She took the Rittenbergs' money."

Leon says, "Daisy Rittenberg has stated on the record that the money was gifted to Kit. Jon Rittenberg is not denying this, either. Daisy claims that when she learned who Kit was, she felt terrible, and wanted to offer compensation."

"It's probably less than the Rittenbergs would have to fork out in legal costs if Kit filed a civil suit and won," says Renata. "And Jon Rittenberg is mum on everything else. He's facing a big trial. If convicted, it could put him away for a while. The others accused from that night also face serious charges. They'll try to strike deals. Some might testify against Jon."

"Plus there are the new claims of assault that more women have come forward with," says Leon.

"Rittenberg is in grave legal jeopardy," agrees Renata. "As for the police hunting Kit down across the globe, she's smart. She chose Laos, and Laos has no extradition treaty with Canada."

"But the government can still request extradition," Ben says.

"Well, this kind of diplomatic effort would be weighed against costs, the severity of the criminal offense—a murder, for example—and the likelihood of conviction. My wager is on nothing happening. Kit is going free. Jon is going to prison. And his wife is facing obstruction of justice charges, too."

"What about Kit's friend who helped her?"

Leon says, "My understanding from a source close to the investigation is that Boon-mee Saelim has been offered a deal in exchange for his full cooperation and the identification of all the other participants in the drugging and sexual assault of Kit, or Katarina Popovich, as she was known then."

"He'll also testify at Jon Rittenberg's trial," Renata says. The retired lawyer smiles and shrugs. "As for the 'murder'—it never happened. Just like the old newspaper headlines."

An image of the old newspaper flashes across the screen. The black headline blares:

"It Never Happened"

World-class skier "JonJon" Rittenberg says claims of sexual assault are "all lies" and "it never happened."

The camera pans back to Ben. "I'd call *that* ironic justice."

"Or karma," Judy says with a smile.

Kat's mind wheels back to the night she posed as Mia and lured Jon up to the Airbnb she cleaned. She'd kissed him and been repulsed by it. But anger kept her going. After Jon passed out, Boon—using gloves—coated Jon's penis with a sticky substance he had brought with him, and he rubbed Icy Hot medicated muscle pain-relief cream around Jon's anal area. That stuff burns like all hell when it touches private parts. Kat wanted the psychological—gaslighting—effects. She wanted to sow doubt in Jon's head. She wanted him to fret about what really happened on a deeply personal and sexual level. She wanted Jon to feel violated, to know firsthand what the women he abused might experience.

Boon also brought a friend of his, and they did their theatrical thing, posing with Jon while he lay drugged and naked on the bed. Kat took photos. They all left. Boon went to wait in his car across the street until Jon woke and came stumbling out of the building.

Kat doesn't feel good about that night. But Jon and other men like him do this sort of thing to women on a daily basis. Always have and probably always will. And they brush it off with *She Wanted It. She's Lying. She Was Drunk.*

*It Never Happened.*

And the world moves on.

*Unless we take a stand. Unless we show them how a victim feels.*

"Hey," says a guy with an Australian accent.

Kat spins around.

"You look just like her—that maid in the news."

She smiles. "I get that a lot."

Kat slides off the bamboo barstool and gathers up her straw bag. She steps out into the sunshine and walks a little way down the beach. Orchids scent the air. The ocean, a deep aqua, stretches to the hazy horizon. Behind her, inland, mist circles brooding volcanoes in the distance. She stops, takes a selfie.

Kat checks it, then loads it to her @foxandcrow profile. She types:

> #karmaissublime      #waterswarm      #comeonin
> #nextstoppopsvillage

She hits "Share."

Kat grins as she slips her phone back into her bag. Boon will see it. He'll know what she means.

The words from the TV show echo in her heart as she walks down the beach.

*I'd call* that *ironic justice.*

*Or karma.*

*It never happened.*

And it also did happen. Kit murdered her Monster that night. The Trauma Monster that made her hide. That made her become invisible. A ghost.

Now she is seen.

And so are Jon and Daisy.

Karma really is sublime, baby, she thinks as she peels open a red lollipop. She sucks it as she wanders into the low-angled rays of the setting Indonesian sun.

# MAL

Mal sips a coffee as she reads the final scanned pages from Kit Darling's diary. Benoit is across the bullpen, also reading. It's late afternoon, quiet, and snowing softly outside.

*When I first tried to write the HOW IT ENDS part, I had only snatches of a memory. Strands that would come to me in nightmares, wake me in a sweat. They seemed to come from afar, from some hidden interior place that was not really part of me. Almost as though the memories belonged to another person. I wondered if the act of writing it down might coax out the missing parts, the context.*

*So I started in third person. From a distance. I jotted down snippets. But the more I dug into Daisy and Jon's life, the deeper I went, and after I found that footage and heard the voices and music and saw again the faces from that night—all the pieces slammed together. I saw the whole picture. It became fleshed. It surfaced in full color.*

*So now I am going back to the beginning again. It's not HOW IT ENDS. It's HOW IT BEGAN. I'm redrafting it and putting it into first person. Me. Immediate.*

*Personal. Mine. Real. Seen. Not a dream. Not hiding. Not "she." But "I."*

# HOW IT STARTS

*Slowly, I slide in and out of sleep and consciousness. A sharp shard of cognition slices through me—not sleep. Not in my bed. Not safe. Panic stirs. Where am I? I try to swallow. But my mouth is dry. There's an unfamiliar taste at the back of my throat. A sharper jolt of awareness cracks through my mind. Blood—it's the taste of blood. My breathing quickens. I try to move my head, but can't. There's a rough, wet fabric covering my face. I'm trapped, arms strapped to my sides. Something covers my head. I become aware of pain. Overwhelming pain. In my shoulders. Ribs. Belly. Between my thighs. The pain pounds inside my skull. Adrenaline surges into my veins, and my eyes flare open. But I can't see. Panic licks through my brain. I open my mouth to scream, but it comes out muffled. What is this? Where am I?*

*Focus, focus. Panic kills. You have to think. You must try to remember.*

*But my brain is foggy. I strain for a thread of clarity, try to focus on sensations. Cold—my feet are very cold. I wiggle my toes. I feel air. Bare feet? No, just the one foot. I've got a shoe on the other one. I'm injured. Badly wounded, I think. A thick memory stirs into my sluggish brain—fighting people off, being held down. I've been violently attacked—I have a sense of that, of being hurt, overwhelmed, rendered powerless. Now I'm wrapped in something, and I'm in motion. Bumping. I can feel vibrations. Is that the noise of an engine? A car? Yes, I'm in a vehicle of some sort. I become aware of voices. In the front seat. I'm lying on the back seat. The voices . . . they sound urgent—arguing. Underlying the voices is soft music. A car radio. I'm definitely in a car . . . They're taking me somewhere.*

*I hear words.* "Dump . . . her fault . . . asked for it. Can't blame—"

*I slide toward the blackness again. I listen to the voices, and it strikes me. Daisy. It's Daisy Wentworth and her friend, whose name I don't know. The friend is arguing with Daisy. I think it's Daisy who is driving.*

*"You can't just dump her, Daisy. It's below freezing. It's going to snow tonight. She could die."*

*"It's her fault. She asked for it."*

*"She was drugged. You saw him—"*

*"Shut it. Just shut it, okay? We'll leave her at the door of her house. Her parents will find her. She won't remember anything, and if she does, it's all lies. Got it?"*

*Silence. Just soft music from the car radio. Tires squeaking on snow and ice as the car turns. I know where we are now. Near my house.*

*"You do understand Jon and all those guys, they will be kicked off the team. The coaches will get in trouble for not chaperoning the lodge party. They could go to prison. No more ski racing. No more chance at gold. This bitch will destroy them. Do you want that?"*

*"What they did—"*

*"Guys do things when in packs. Things they would never do on their own. They were high. Full of themselves. Drunk. It's not who they are. This will never happen again. He asked for my help to get her out of the lodge."*

*"He's using you, Daisy."*

*"He loves me. I won't let her do this to me—ruin my chances . . . He's going to marry me. Both our families know it. We have our future cut out, and I won't let this stupid fat foreigner kid destroy what the two of us can become. We worked for it."*

*I am fading out of consciousness. I feel them dragging me out of the car and down the few steps to our basement suite. I'm wrapped in an old blanket. It smells like dogs.*

*"She's too heavy," says a female voice.*

*"Just drag her."*

*I feel a thump, thump, thump. Pain explodes in my body. I open my mouth to scream but still no sound comes.*

*I feel a jolt as I thud against our front door.*

*"Come," whispers Daisy. "Quick."*

*"We can't just leave her here. She could die."*

*"Look, a light's gone on inside. They've heard us. Come. Run."*

*I must have passed out fully then. The next I knew it was almost twelve hours later, and I was in my bed with my mother sitting on the side, holding my hand.*

*So you see, Dear Diary, Daisy has a due to pay, too.*

Mal sits back. She runs her hands over her hair. "The prosecutor needs to see this," she says to Benoit, sitting at his desk across the room. "This throws a whole new light on Daisy Rittenberg and her mother's involvement in trying to shut that old investigation down. If this is true, Daisy played an active role in that assault, and someone who was there—Saelim, one of the others—must know who was with Daisy in that car. We need to find that other female."

"And if she talks, Daisy is going down. But will she talk? Will the others give her up?"

"We'll find her, and she'll talk if she thinks it will save her own skin." Mal is about to say something more to Benoit when Lula swings open the bullpen door, and Arnav enters behind her, carrying a large cake and burning candles. Arnav is followed by Gavin with sparkling wine and flutes, and by Jack with balloons.

"Don't be mad," Benoit says with a laugh at the shock on Mal's face. "I couldn't stop them."

"Happy retirement, boss," Lula calls out loudly. She sets the decadent cake on the desk in front of Mal. "Seeing as we couldn't get you to come and get drunk with us tonight, we brought the party to you." She hesitates. "Plus you can take cake home to Peter."

Emotion fills Mal's eyes. "Damn you people." She meets each one's gaze. "God, I'm going to miss you guys."

Lula says, "Little bird tells me you're going to be doing some consulting with that new independent cold case unit being started by the associate director of Lougheed University's school of criminology, funded with a major grant. We haven't heard the last of you yet, boss. That's my bet."

"Who told you this?" Mal says. "The request came in only this morning—I haven't even fully decided. Can no one keep a secret in this place?"

"Our job is exposing them," Benoit says. "Now blow out those candles before we all have to eat wax!"

Mal sucks in a deep breath and puffs. The candles go out, apart from one that keeps sputtering. She pauses, thinking that some flames really do not just go out. Lu is right. She'll be back on select cases. Cold and old ones. But on her schedule, on Peter's time. She blows out the final candle.

◆　◆　◆

Boon sees the new post on Instagram.

His friend. Smiling. Tanned. So pretty and healthy-looking. At peace. Traveling. Not dead. But living her best life. He thinks of how he told Sergeant Mallory Van Alst that he dropped Kit near the Glass House and saw another Audi. That part wasn't exactly true. Kit had forgotten to switch back the framed photo near the bar. She wanted to replace the one of her and him in Nicaragua with the Norths' original photo. She switched it to fool Daisy when Daisy came for lunch at the Glass House—that's how he saw the other Audi he told the cop about.

After Kit changed the photo, Boon drove her to the station, where she'd stashed her bags in a locker. She had her passport and a burner phone with her. She caught the SkyTrain straight to YVR while he drove the Audi back to the rental place.

His heart crunches.

Kit knows he will see this Insta post. She knows he will have been looking daily. She knows he will realize immediately where she is. Karma Beach. One of the places on her bucket list. Kinda like justice was always on Kit's bucket list, thinks Boon.

And the hashtag has revealed what her next destination is: #pops-village. It's code for him. Boon told Kit how much he'd like to visit the small village in Thailand where his "pop" was born, where his parents met and married. Where he, too, was born.

"Come on in. Water is warm."

Emotion fills Boon's eyes as he smiles. His friend has forgiven him. She's told him where she will be. And she's opened the door for him to join her. If he so chooses.

And he will.

# ABOUT THE AUTHOR

 Loreth Anne White is an Amazon Charts, *Washington Post*, and *Bild* bestselling author of thrillers, mysteries, and suspense, including *The Patient's Secret, Beneath Devil's Bridge, In the Dark, The Dark Bones,* and *A Dark Lure*. With more than three million books sold around the world, she is a three-time RITA finalist, an overall Daphne du Maurier Award winner, an Arthur Ellis Award finalist, and a winner of multiple industry awards. A recovering journalist who has worked in both South Africa and Canada, she now calls Canada home. She resides in the Pacific Northwest, dividing her time among Victoria on Vancouver Island, a ski resort in the Coast Mountains, and a rustic lakeside cabin in the Cariboo. When she's not writing or dreaming up plots, you'll find her on the lakes, in the ocean, or on the trails with her dog, where she tries—unsuccessfully—to avoid bears. For more information on her books, please visit her website at www.lorethannewhite.com.